By Eloisa James

ELOISA JAMES

Kiss Me, Annabel

AVON BOOKS

An Imprint of HarperCollinsPublishers

This is a work of fiction. Names, characters, places, and incidents are products of the author's imagination or are used fictitiously and are not to be construed as real. Any resemblance to actual events, locales, organizations, or persons, living or dead, is entirely coincidental.

AVON BOOKS
An Imprint of HarperCollins*Publishers*
10 East 53rd Street
New York, New York 10022-5299

Copyright © 2005 by Eloisa James
ISBN 0-7394-5996-1

Printed in the U.S.A.

This book is for Pam Spengler-Jaffee,
my terrific PR person at HarperCollins.
Thank you for giving eloisajames.com
a million hits . . .

This Kiss *is for you!*

Acknowledgments

My thanks to Biff Vernon of Tithe Farm Bed and Breakfast in Louth, Lincolnshire, both for his fabulous website about the Great North Road, *www.biffvernon.freeserve.co.uk/contents.htm,* and for his patience and knowledge when confronted with endless questions and persistent wrong-headedness.

Mr. Gordon Riddle and Mr. Kevin Waite very kindly answered questions about Scottish castles. And the Historical Maritime Society, a group of naval reenactors that specializes in the Napoleonic Era, graciously welcomed any question, however arcane or idiotic.

And finally, heartfelt thanks to my research assistant, Franzeca Drouin; my critique partner, Jessica Benson; and a three-day plotting group in the north woods of Minnesota, all of whom gave their time and imagination to this book.

One

London
April, 1817

The day the Scotsman came to Lady Feddrington's ball, Annabel's sister decided to give him her virtue, and Annabel decided *not* to give him her hand in marriage.

In neither case had the Scotsman indicated a particular interest in undertaking such intimate activities with an Essex sister, but his participation was taken for granted. And, naturally, both of these decisions took place in the ladies' retiring room, which is where everything of importance takes place at a ball.

It was in those middle hours, when the initial excitement has worn away and women have an uneasy feeling that their noses are shiny and their lips pale. Annabel peeked into the retiring room and found it empty. So she sat down before the large mirrored dressing table, and started trying to pin her unruly curls so they would stay above her shoulders for the rest of the evening. Her sister Imogen, Lady Maitland, plumped down beside her.

"This ball is nothing more than a breeding ground for parasites," Imogen said, scowling at her reflection. "Lord Beekman has twice asked me to dance with him. As if I would even contemplate dancing with that plump toadlet. He should look lower . . . perhaps in the scullery."

She looked magnificent, a few gleaming black curls falling to her shoulders, and the rest piled high on her head. Her eyes sparkled with the displeasure of receiving too much attention. In all, she had the magnificent rage of a young Helen of Troy, stolen by the Greeks and taken from her homeland.

It must be rather annoying, Annabel thought, to have nowhere to direct all that emotion except toward unwary gentlemen who do nothing more despicable than ask for a dance. "There is always the chance that no one has told the poor toadlet that Lady Maitland is such a very grand person." She said it lightly, since mourning had turned Imogen into a person whom none of them knew very well.

Imogen flashed her an impatient look, twitching one of her curls over her shoulder so that it nestled seductively on her bosom. "Don't be a widgeon, Annabel. Beekman is interested in my fortune and nothing more."

Annabel raised an eyebrow in the direction of Imogen's virtually nonexistent bodice. "*Nothing* more?"

A sketch of a smile touched Imogen's lips, one of the few Annabel had seen in recent months. Imogen had lost her husband the previous fall, and after her first six months of mourning she had joined Annabel in London for the season. Currently she was amusing herself by shocking respectable matrons of the *ton* by flaunting a wardrobe full of mourning clothing cut in daring styles that left little of her figure to the imagination.

"You have to expect attention," Annabel pointed out.

"After all, you dressed for it." She let a little sarcasm creep into her tone.

"Do you think that I should buy another of these gowns?" Imogen asked, staring into the mirror. She gave a seductive roll of her shoulders and the bodice settled even lower on her chest. She was dressed in black faille, a perfectly respectable fabric for a widow. But the modiste had saved on fabric, for the bodice was nothing more than a few scraps of cloth, falling to a narrow silhouette that clung to every curve. The *pièce de résistance* was a trim of tiny white feathers around the bodice. The feathers nestled against Imogen's breasts and made every man who glimpsed them throw caution to the wind.

"No one has a need for more than one dress of that pattern," Annabel pointed out.

"Madame Badeau has threatened to make another. She complains that she must sell two in order to justify her design. And I should not like to see another woman in this particular gown."

"That's absurd," Annabel said. "Many women have gowns of the same design. No one will notice."

"Everyone notices what I wear," Imogen said, and one had to admit it was a perfect truth.

" 'Tis an indulgence to order another gown merely to allow it to languish in your wardrobe."

Imogen shrugged. Her husband had died relatively penniless, but then his mother had fallen into a decline and died within a month of her son. Lady Clarice had left her private estate to her daughter-in-law, making Imogen one of the wealthiest widows in all England. "I'll have the gown made up for you, then. You must promise to wear it only in the country, where no one of importance can see you."

"That gown will fall to my navel if I bend over, which hardly suits a debutante."

"You're no ordinary debutante," Imogen jibed. "You're older than me, and all of twenty-two, if you remember."

Annabel counted to ten. Imogen was grieving. One simply had to wish that grieving didn't make her so—so bloody-minded. "Shall we return to Lady Griselda?" she said, rising and looking one last time at the glass.

Suddenly Imogen was at her shoulder, smiling penitently. "I'm sorry to be so tiresome. You're the most beautiful woman at the ball, Annabel. Look at the two of us together! You're glowing and I look like an old crow."

Annabel grinned at that. "A crow you're not." There was a similarity to their features: they both had slanting eyes and high cheekbones. But where Imogen's hair was raven black, Annabel's was the color of honey. And where Imogen's eyes flashed, Annabel knew quite well that her greatest strength was a melting invitation that men seemed unable to resist.

Imogen pulled another curl onto the curve of her breast. It looked rather odd, but Imogen's temper was not something to risk lightly, and so Annabel held her tongue.

"I've made up my mind to take a cicisbeo," Imogen said suddenly. "To hold off Beekman, if nothing else."

"What?" Annabel said. "A what?"

"A gallant," Imogen said impatiently. "A man to take me about."

"You're thinking about marrying again?" Annabel was truly surprised. To the best of her knowledge, Imogen was still dissolving into tears every night over her husband's death.

"Never," Imogen said. "You know that. But I don't intend to let fools like Beekman spoil my enjoyment either." Their eyes met in the mirror. "I'm going to take Mayne. And I'm not talking about marriage."

"*Mayne!*" Annabel gasped. "You can't!"

"Of course I can," Imogen said, looking amused.

"There's nothing to stop me from doing anything I wish. And I believe that I would like the Earl of Mayne."

"How can you even consider such an idea? He jilted our own sister, practically at the altar!"

"Are you implying that Tess would be better off with Mayne than with Felton? She adores her husband," Imogen pointed out.

"Of course not. But that doesn't change the fact that Mayne deserted her!"

"I have not forgotten that point."

"But for goodness' sakes, *why*?"

Imogen cast her a scornful glance. "You have to ask?"

"Punishment," Annabel guessed. "Don't do it, Imogen."

"Why not?" Imogen turned to the side and regarded her figure. It was exquisite in every curve. And every curve was visible. "I'm bored."

Annabel saw a glint of cruelty in her sister's eyes and caught her arm. "Don't do it. I've no doubt you can make Mayne fall in love with you."

Imogen's teeth shone white when she smiled. "Neither do I."

"But you might fall in love with him as well."

"Inconceivable."

Annabel didn't really believe Imogen would love again either. She had encased herself in ice after her husband died, and it would take time to melt away.

"Please," she said. "Please don't do it, Imogen. I don't care about Mayne, but it wouldn't be good for you."

"Since you are nothing more than a *maiden*," Imogen said with her new, bitter smile, "you have no idea what would be good for me, at least as pertains to men. We can have this discussion once you have some experience of what it means to be a woman."

Imogen was clearly longing for a pitched battle of the

kind they used to have when they were children. But as Annabel opened her mouth to deliver a scathing retort, the door opened and their chaperone, Lady Griselda Willoughby, waltzed in. "Darlings!" she trilled. "I have been looking *everywhere* for the two of you! The Duke of Clarence has arrived, and—"

Her words died as her eyes moved from Annabel's furious face to Imogen's rigid one. "Ah," she said, sitting down and adjusting her exquisite silk shawl around her shoulders, "you're squabbling again. How very glad I am that I have only a brother to plague me."

"*Your* brother," Imogen snapped, "is hardly anyone to desire as a family member. In fact, we were just talking of his manifold virtues. Or rather, the lack thereof."

"I have no doubt but that your assessment was correct," Griselda said serenely, "but it was a patently unpleasant comment, my dear. I notice that when you are angry your nose becomes quite thin . . . You might wish to think about that."

Imogen's nose flared magnificently. "Since I have no doubt but that you will wish to rebuke me as well, I might as well tell you that I have decided to take a cicisbeo!"

"An excellent decision, my dear." Griselda opened a small fan and waved it lazily before her face. "I find men so useful. In a gown as narrow as the one you wear tonight, for example, one can hardly walk with ease. Perhaps you could choose a particularly *strong* man who can carry you about London."

Annabel bit back a smile.

"You may fun all you like," Imogen said through clenched teeth, "but let me be very clear about my decision. I have decided to take a lover, not a jumped-up version of a footman. And your brother Mayne is my primary candidate."

"Ah," Griselda said. "Well, likely it is wise to start

with someone so very experienced in these situations. Mayne does tend toward married women rather than widows; my brother has a genius for avoiding any woman who might prove eligible for matrimony. But mayhap you can persuade him otherwise."

"I believe that I can," Imogen stated.

Griselda waved her fan meditatively. "An interesting choice lies ahead of you. Were I to take a lover, for example, I should wish to continue the affair beyond two weeks. My dear brother certainly has had many ladies on whom to practice, and yet he invariably drifts to another woman within the fortnight. Moreover, I myself would find the notion of being compared to the many beautiful women who had come before me unnerving, but I expect I am simply squeamish."

Annabel grinned. Griselda looked a perfectly docile, perfectly feminine lady. And yet . . .

Imogen looked as if she were thinking. "Fine!" she said finally. "I'll take the Earl of Ardmore, then. Since he's only been in London for a week or so, he can't possibly compare me to anyone else."

Annabel blinked. "The Scottish earl?"

"The very one." Imogen gathered up her reticule and shawl. "He's not worth a penny, but his face can be his fortune, in this case." She caught her sister's frown. "Oh, don't be such a pinched ninny, Annabel. Believe me, the earl won't get hurt."

"I agree," Griselda put in. "The man has a palpable air of danger about him. He won't get hurt, Imogen. You will."

"Nonsense," Imogen said. "You're simply trying to talk me out of a decision I've already made. I'm not willing to sit around in the corners, gossiping with dowagers for the next ten years." That was a direct insult to Griselda, who had lost her husband years ago and had (to Annabel's knowledge) never entertained a thought either of a lover or a husband.

Griselda smiled sweetly and said, "No, I can see that you're an entirely different kind of woman, my dear."

Annabel winced, but Imogen didn't notice. "Now I think on it, Ardmore is an altogether better choice than Mayne. We are countrymen, you know."

"Actually, that's a reason not to distract him," Annabel had to point out. "We know how hard it is to live in an old rambling house in the north country without a penny to support it. The man has come to London to find a rich bride, not to have an affair with you."

"You're a sentimentalist," Imogen said. "Ardmore can take care of himself. I certainly shan't stop him from courting some silly miss, if he wishes. But if I have a *cavalier servente*, the fortune hunters will leave me alone. I shall just borrow him for a while. You're not planning to marry him, are you?"

"The thought never crossed my mind," Annabel said with something less than perfect truth. The Scotsman was absurdly handsome; a woman would have to be in her grave not to consider him as a consort. But Annabel meant to marry a rich man. And she meant to stay in England. "Are you considering him as a possible spouse?"

"Certainly not. He's a lummox without a fortune. But he's pretty, and he dresses so somberly that he matches my clothing. Who could want more in a man?"

"He doesn't appear to be a man to fool," Griselda said, serious now.

"If he needs to find a rich wife, you ought to be straightforward," Annabel added. "He may well think that you would consider matrimony."

"Pish," Imogen said. "The role of a hidebound moralist doesn't suit either of you. Don't be tedious." And she swept out of the room, closing the door behind her with a little more force than necessary.

"Though it pains me to admit it," Griselda said meditatively, "I may have mishandled that situation. If your sister is determined to make a scandal, she would have done better to direct herself toward Mayne. At this point, it is almost a rite of a passage for young women to have a brief *affaire* with my brother, and so the ensuing scandal doesn't really take fire."

"There's something about Ardmore that makes me wonder if she can control him as easily as she thinks she can," Annabel said with a frown.

"I would agree," Griselda said. "I haven't exchanged a word with him, but he has little in common with the average English lord."

Ardmore was a red-haired Scot, with a square jaw and broad shoulders. To Annabel's mind, he was a world away from Griselda's sleek brother.

"No one seems to know much about the man," Griselda said. "Lady Ogilby told me that she had it from Mrs. Mufford that he's poor as a church mouse and came to London specifically to find a dowried bride."

"But didn't Mrs. Mufford spread that rumor about Clementina Lyffe running off with a footman?"

"True," Griselda said. "And yet Clementina is happily married to her viscount and shows no propensity whatsoever to court the household staff. Lady Blechschmidt generally can scent a fortune hunter at fifty yards, and there was no sign of Ardmore at her soirée last night, which suggests he was not invited. I must ask her if she has any pertinent information."

"His absence from that particular event may simply indicate a intolerance for boredom," Annabel remarked.

"Tush!" Griselda said, laughing. "You know Lady Blechschmidt is a great acquaintance of mine. I must say, it is unusual for there to be such mystery about a man; if he were English we would know everything from his birth weight to his yearly income. Did you ever meet him when you lived in Scotland?"

"Never. But Mrs. Mufford's speculation about his reasons for coming to London is likely true." Many a Scottish nobleman hung around her father's stables, and they were all as empty in the pocket as her own viscount of a father. In fact, it was practically a requirement of nationality. One either remained poor or married a rich Englishman—as Imogen had done, as Tess had done and as she herself meant to do.

"Ardmore doesn't look the sort to be fooled by your sister," Griselda said.

Annabel hoped she was right. There was a brittleness behind Imogen's artful exposure of her bosom that had little to do with desire.

Griselda rose. "Imogen must find her own way through her grief," she said. "There are women who have a hard time of it, and I'm afraid she's one of them."

Their eldest sister, Tess, kept saying that Imogen had to live her own life. And so had Annabel.

For a moment a smile touched Annabel's lips. The only dowry she had was a horse, so she and the Scotsman were really two of a kind.

Scottish pennies, as it were.

Two

Lady Feddrington was in the grip of a passion for all things Egyptian, and since she had the means to indulge every whim, her ballroom resembled nothing so much as a storage house kept by tomb raiders. Flanking the large doors at one end were twenty-foot-high statues of some sort of dog-human. Apparently they originally stood at the doors of an Egyptian temple.

"At first I wasn't certain that I quite liked them. Their expressions are not . . . *nice,*" Lady Feddrington had told Annabel. "But now I've named them Humpty and Dumpty. I think of them rather like superior servants: so silent, and you can tell in a glance that they won't drink to excess." She had giggled; Lady Feddrington was a rather silly woman.

But Annabel had to admit that from the vantage point of the other side of the room, Humpty and Dumpty looked magnificent. They gazed down on the dancers milling around their ankles with expressions that made the idea that they were servants laughable.

She pulled a gauzy piece of nothingness around her shoulders. It was pale gold, to match her dress, and embroidered with a curling series of ferns. Gold on gold and worth every penny. She threw a glance at those imposing Egyptian statues again. Surely they should be in a museum? They made the fluttering crowds around them look dissolute.

"Anubis, god of the dead," a deep voice said. "Not the most propitious guardian for an occasion such as this."

Even after having met him for only a moment, she knew Ardmore's voice. Well, why shouldn't she? She had grown up surrounded by that soft Scottish burr, though their father threatened to disown herself and her sisters if they used it. "They look like gods," she said. "Have you traveled to Egypt, my lord?"

"Alas, no."

She shouldn't have even asked. She, if anyone, knew the life of an impoverished Scottish nobleman all too well. It involved hours spent trying to eke a living from tenants battered by cold and hunger, not pleasure trips up the Nile River.

He slipped a hand under her arm. "May I ask you to dance, or should I request the pleasure from your chaperone?"

She smiled up at him, one of her rarer smiles that didn't bother to seduce, but just expressed companionship. "Neither is necessary," she said cheerfully. "I'm sure you can find someone more appropriate to dance with."

He blinked at her, looking more like a burly laborer than an earl. She'd come to know quite a lot about earls—aye, and dukes and other lords too. Their chaperone, Lady Griselda, considered it her duty to point out every man within eyesight who carried a title. Mayne, Griselda's brother, was a typical English lord: sleek and faintly dangerous, with slender fingers and exquisite manners. His hair fell in ordered waves that shone in the light, and he smelled as good as she herself did.

But this Scottish earl was another story. The earl's red-brown hair fell in thick rumpled curls down his neck. His eyes were a clear green, lined with long lashes, and the out-of-doors sense he had about him translated into a kind of raw sensuality. While Mayne wore velvet and silk, Ardmore was plainly dressed in a costume of black. Black with a touch of white at the throat. No wonder Imogen thought he would complement her mourning attire.

"Why do you refuse me?" he asked, sounding surprised.

"Because I grew up with lads like yourself," she said, letting a trace of a Scottish accent slip into her voice. *Lad* wasn't the right word, not for this huge northerner who was so clearly a man, but that was the sense she meant. He could be a friend, but never a suitor. Although she could hardly explain to him that she meant to marry someone rich.

"So you've taken a vow not to dance with anyone from your own homeland?" he asked.

"Something like that," she said. "But I could introduce you to a proper young lady, if you wish." She knew quite a few debutantes endowed with more-than-respectable dowries.

"Does that mean that you would decline to marry me as well?" he asked, a curious little smile playing around his mouth. "I would be happy to ask for your hand, if that would mean we could dance together."

She grinned at his foolishness. "You'll never find a bride if you go about behaving in such a way," she told him. "You must take your pursuit more seriously."

"I do take it seriously." He leaned against the wall and looked down at her so intently that her skin prickled. "Would you marry me, even if you won't dance with me?"

You couldn't help but like him. His eyes were as green as the ocean. "I certainly will not marry you," she said.

"Ah," he said, sounding not terribly disappointed.

"You cannot ask women to marry you whom you barely know," she added.

He didn't seem to realize that it wasn't entirely polite to lean against the wall in a lady's presence, nor to watch her with lazy appreciation. Annabel felt a flash of sympathy. He would never be able to catch a rich bride at this rate! She should help him, if only because he was her countryman.

"Why not?" he asked. "Compatibility is not something one discovers after five encounters rather than one. One must make an educated guess."

"That's just it: you know nothing of me!"

"Not so," he said promptly. "Number one, you're Scottish. Number two, you're Scottish. And number three—"

"I can guess," she said.

"You're beautiful," he finished, a fleeting smile crossing his face.

He had his arms crossed over his chest now and was smiling down at her like a great giant.

"While I thank you for the compliment, I have to wonder why on earth you came to London to find a bride, given your first two requirements," Annabel said.

"I came because I was told to do so," he replied.

Annabel didn't need any further information. Everyone knew that rich brides were to be found in London, and poor ones in Scotland. The man was hoping that her finery meant she had a dowry to match.

"You're judging on appearances," she told him. "My only dowry is a horse, although, as I said, I'd be happy to introduce you to some appropriate young ladies."

He opened his mouth, but at that moment Imogen appeared at her shoulder. "Darling," she said to Annabel, "I've been looking everywhere for you!" Without pausing, she turned to the earl. "Lord Ardmore," she purred, "I am Lady Maitland. What a pleasure to meet you."

Annabel watched as the earl bent over her sister's hand. Imogen was looking as beautiful as any avenging goddess. She gave Ardmore a look that no man, especially a man in search of a dowry faced with a wealthy young widow, would consider resisting. In fact, it looked very much like one of Annabel's own come-hither glances.

"I have an unendurable longing to dance," Imogen said. "Will you please me, Lord Ardmore?"

Unendurable? But Ardmore wasn't laughing; he was kissing Imogen's hand again. Annabel gave up. The man would have to find his own way out of Imogen's net. Imogen had always been thus: once she made up her mind, there was no stopping her. "I shall return to my chaperone," Annabel said, curtsying. "Lord Ardmore, it has been a pleasure."

Lady Griselda was holding court in a corner of the room, their guardian sprawled beside her with a drink in his hand. Not that there was anything unusual in that; the Duke of Holbrook always had a drink. He came to meet Annabel when he saw her winding her way through the crowd.

Now that she had come to know a number of English nobility, she was more and more surprised by how unducal Rafe was. For one thing, he refused to go by his title. For another, he was as far from scented and curled and sartorially splendid as could be imagined. At least his valet managed to get him into a decent coat of blue superfine for the evening, but when he was at home he tended toward comfortable pantaloons and a thread worn white shirt.

"Griselda's driving me mad," he said without formality. "And if she doesn't succeed, Imogen will finish me off. What the devil is she doing, dancing attendance on that Scottish fellow? I don't even know the man."

"She's decided that she wants a cicisbeo," Annabel told him.

"Stuff and nonsense," Rafe muttered, running a hand through hair that was already wildly disarranged. "I can escort her wherever she needs to go."

"She's being plagued by fortune hunters."

"For God's sake, why'd she choose a penniless Scot to dance about with, then?" Rafe bellowed, only belatedly glancing about him.

"Perhaps she won't care for him on further acquaintance," Annabel said, trying to see whether she could glimpse Lord Rosseter anywhere. At the moment Rosseter was her first choice for spouse.

"She's making an ass of herself," Rafe said.

For some reason, Imogen's antics always drove Rafe to distraction, especially since she'd returned to London and begun to order gowns that fit her like a second skin. But no matter how much he bellowed and raged, she merely smirked at him and said that widows could dress precisely as they wished.

"Surely it's not as bad as that," Annabel said absently, still searching the crowd for Rosseter.

She caught Lady Griselda's eyes, who called: "Annabel! Do come here for a moment."

Their chaperone was nothing like the dour old ladies who generally earned that label; she was as good-looking as the infamous, altar-deserting Earl of Mayne. It went

without saying that none of them held her brother's behavior against Griselda; she had been devastated when
Mayne galloped away from Rafe's house approximately
five minutes before he was due to marry Tess.

"What on earth is Rafe bellowing about?" Griselda
inquired, without much real concern in her voice. "He's
turned all plum-colored."

"Rafe is worried that Imogen is making an exhibition
of herself," Annabel told her.

"Already? She *is* a woman of her word."

Annabel nodded over to the right. A waltz was playing, and the Earl of Ardmore was holding Imogen far
too tightly. Or perhaps, Annabel thought fairly, Imogen
was doing the holding. Whatever the impetus, Imogen
swayed in his arms as if they were in the grip of a reckless passion.

"Goodness me," Griselda said, fanning herself.
"They're quite a couple, aren't they? All that black on
black . . . Imogen certainly was correct about the aes-
thetics of choosing Ardmore as a partner."

"Nothing will come of it," Annabel assured her.
"Imogen was just blustering. I'm sure of it." But the
words died in her mouth as Imogen threw an arm
around the earl's neck and began caressing his hair in an
outrageously intimate fashion.

"She wants a scandal," Griselda said matter-of-factly.
"The poor dear. Some widows do suffer through this
sort of thing."

She made it sound as if Imogen were coming down
with a nasty cold.

"Did you?" Annabel asked.

"Thankfully not," Griselda said with a little shiver.
"But I do believe that Imogen's feelings for Lord Maitland were far deeper than mine for dear Willoughby. Al-

though," she added, "naturally I had all proper emotion for my husband."

Imogen was smiling up at Ardmore, her eyes half closed as if— Well. Annabel looked away.

What Imogen wanted, Imogen took. She had loved Draven Maitland for years, and never mind the fact that he was betrothed to another woman. The moment Imogen had a chance, she somehow sprained her ankle in such a way that she had to convalesce in the Maitland household. That ankle injury was remarkably fortuitous. The next thing Annabel knew, her sister had eloped with Draven Maitland. In fact, given Imogen's strength of will, Annabel rather thought that Ardmore might have to find and woo his bride in the next season.

"Have you seen Lord Rosseter?" she asked Griselda.

But Griselda was mesmerized—as doubtless were most of the respectable women in the room—by Imogen's behavior on the dance floor. "Imogen is not my duty," she said to herself, fanning her face madly.

Annabel looked back at her sister. Imogen could not have made her intentions to engage in a scandalous affair more clear. She was clinging to Ardmore as if she'd turned into an ivy plant.

"Oh, Lord," Griselda moaned. Now Imogen was caressing Ardmore's neck, for all the world as if she meant to pull his head down to hers.

Annabel's elder sister Tess dropped into a chair beside them. "Can someone please explain to me why Imogen is behaving like such a wanton?"

"Where have you been all evening?" Annabel asked. "I thought I caught a glimpse of you and Felton earlier, but then I couldn't find you."

Tess ignored her question. "She may ruin herself with this behavior! People will draw the conclusion that she is Ardmore's mistress."

"And they'll be correct," Griselda put in calmly. "How are you, my dear? You look blooming."

But Tess just stared at Griselda. "Imogen has taken a lover? I knew she was distraught, but—"

"She calls it taking a cicisbeo," Annabel put in.

On the dance floor Imogen was dancing thigh to thigh with the Scotsman, head thrown back in an attitude of sensual abandon.

"We have to do something," Tess said grimly. "It's one thing to take a cicisbeo, if that's what she wants. But at this rate she'll create such a frightful scandal that she won't be invited to parties."

"Oh, she's already beyond the pale on that front," Griselda said, a little too cheerfully for Annabel's comfort. "Remember, she eloped with her first husband. And after this exhibition . . . Well, she'll still be invited to the largest balls, of course."

But Tess had raised her three younger sisters from the time their mother died, and she wasn't going to resign herself to Imogen's disgrace so easily. "That will not do," she stated. "I'll just put it to her that—"

Annabel shook her head. "*You* are not the one to give advice. The two of you only reconciled a matter of weeks ago." Tess looked rebellious, so Annabel added firmly, "Not unless you wish to engage in another squabble with Imogen."

"It's all so absurd," Tess muttered. "We never really quarreled." Just then Lucius Felton came up, dropped a kiss on his wife's hair, and winked at Annabel.

"Give me a chance and I'll scare up a reason to stop speaking to you myself," Annabel said, smiling at him. "All this marital affection is hard to stomach."

"Imogen apologized very prettily," Tess said. "But I still think her behavior was remarkably unjustified."

"Your husband—" Annabel began.

"Is alive," Tess said, accepting the point. "But does that mean I have to allow my sister to ruin herself without saying a word?"

But Annabel had a twinge of sympathy with Imogen, seeing the way Lucius brought Tess's hand to his lips before he left to bring her a glass of champagne.

"Do you think that Ardmore is aware that Imogen has only just been widowed?" Tess asked. "Perhaps you could appeal to his better self. Weren't you just speaking to him?"

"He has no idea that Imogen is my sister," Annabel said doubtfully. "I could—"

"It wouldn't make any difference," Griselda put in. "Imogen made it quite clear earlier in the evening that she fully intends to create a scandal, if not with this gentleman, then with my own dear brother. And frankly, if this is the way she intends to go about it, I'm grateful she didn't choose Mayne. I still have fond hopes for a nephew at some point and my brother may have slept with most of the available women in the *ton*, but he's never put on a public exhibition."

Tess's eyes narrowed. "She was considering Mayne?"

"Yes, Mayne," Annabel confirmed. "I believe she had some quixotic idea of punishing him for leaving you at the altar."

"That's foolish," Tess said. "Mayne punishes himself quite enough." She turned to Griselda. "Did he come tonight?"

"Of course," Griselda said, startled. "He was just inside the gaming room, last time I looked. But—"

Tess was already gone, heading like an arrow to the room where the men sat around their cards, hoping their wives wouldn't drag them onto the ballroom floor.

"I was going to say," Griselda added, "that I believe he intended to leave for his club. I barely have a chance to see my own brother now that he has given up philandering. He won't stay at a ball over a half hour."

Annabel looked back at Imogen. Would this waltz never end?

But at that moment Rafe shouldered his way onto the floor. Before Annabel could take a breath, the redhaired Scotsman was bowing, and Rafe had swept Imogen away.

Imogen was as surprised as her sister. One moment she was gliding around the ballroom with Ardmore, thoroughly enjoying every scandalized glance directed at her, and the next she was jerked from his arms by her ex-guardian. "And just what do you think you're doing?" she demanded, holding her body as far from Rafe's as was possible.

"Saving your miserable little ass," he snapped back. "Do you have any idea what a disgrace you're making of yourself?" Rafe's hair was standing up on end and his normally brown eyes were black with rage.

Imogen raised an eyebrow. "Just remind me again where your authority over me lies?"

"What do you mean?" He swung her into a brisk turn and began back up the ballroom floor.

"What right have you to interrogate even the smallest aspect of my behavior? I ceased to be your responsibility the moment I married Draven."

"I only wish that were the case. As I told you when you broached that ludicrous idea of renting a house, I consider myself still your guardian, and you'll live with me until you marry again. Or grow old enough to govern yourself, whichever comes first."

She smiled at him, a movement of her lips belied by her angry gaze. "This may surprise you, but I don't agree with your assessment of my situation. I'm planning to set up my own establishment in the very near future."

"Over my dead body!" Rafe snapped.

Imogen glared at him.

"I don't know what you're playing at with Ardmore," Rafe said, "but you're ruining yourself for nothing. The man is looking for a bride, not a flirtation with a silly widow with no plans to marry."

Suddenly he looked sorry for her, as if his anger were draining away. The last thing Imogen wanted was sympathy from her drunken oaf of a guardian. "For nothing?" she said, taunting him. "You must be blind. Ardmore's shoulders, his eyes, his *mouth* . . ." She gave a little shiver of supposed delight.

Which turned into something quite different, although it took her a moment to realize it. He was shaking her! Rafe had dropped her hand and given her a hard shake, as if she were a child in the midst of a tantrum. "How dare you!" she gasped, feeling pins slide from her hair.

"You're lucky I don't drag you out of here and lock you in your chambers," he snapped. "You deserve it."

"Because I find a man attractive?"

"No! Because you're a liar. You said you loved Maitland."

She flinched. "Don't you *dare* say that I didn't."

"It's a pretty way you've chosen to honor his memory," Rafe said flatly. He had dropped his hands from her shoulders.

A wash of shame tumbled over Imogen's body. "You have no idea—"

"No, none," he said. "And I don't wish to know. If I ever have a widow, I certainly hope she doesn't mourn me in your fashion."

Imogen swallowed. Thankfully, they were at the end of the room, because she could feel the tears swelling in her throat. She turned on her heel without another word and walked through the door. Rafe came behind her, but she ignored him, heading blindly for the front door.

At the side of the room, Annabel sighed. Her little sister had always been passionate to a fault, and unfortunately Rafe, comfortable Rafe who liked everyone, had taken a sharp dislike to Imogen almost from the first. As the two of them left the room, the storm of gossiping voices around them reached a high cackle, like hens experiencing a visit from the neighborhood fox.

"If Rafe wanted her to marry that Scot," Griselda remarked, "he couldn't have done more to force the match."

"She won't marry Ardmore," Annabel said.

"She may not have a choice," Griselda said darkly. "After Rafe put on such a paternal performance, Ardmore will likely guess that given a modicum of scandal, Rafe will force a marriage, and he could use her estate, if the tales are true."

"She won't marry him," Annabel repeated. "Have you seen Rosseter tonight?"

Griselda's eyes brightened. "Ah. All that land in Kent and no mother-in-law. I approve, my dear." Griselda was always to the point.

"He's a nice man," Annabel reminded her.

Her chaperone waved her hand. "If you believe that silence is golden."

Annabel settled her scrap of gold silk around her shoulders. "I see nothing wrong with his lack of verbosity. I can talk enough for both of us, should the need arise."

"He's dancing with Mrs. Fulgens's spotty daughter," Griselda said. "But have no fear. Rosseter is not a man to overlook imperfections, is he?"

Annabel looked in the direction of Griselda's nod to

find Rosseter leaving the ballroom floor. He wasn't the sort of man who immediately struck you as handsome: certainly he was no big, burly man who tossed women around the ballroom as if they were bags of wheat. In his arms one floated around the floor. He had a narrow, pale face with a high forehead and gray eyes. He tended to look expressionless and rather detached; Annabel found that a refreshing change from the puppies who begged her for dances and sent her roses with rhyming poems attached.

Rosseter had sent her only one bouquet: a bunch of forget-me-nots. There was no poem, only a scrawled note: *These match your eyes, I believe.* There was something deliciously offhand about his note. She had made up her mind on the spot to marry him.

Now he dispensed with Daisy, as Griselda had predicted, and drifted in their direction. A second later he was bowing in front of Lady Griselda, kissing her hand and saying in his unemotional way that she was looking particularly lovely.

When he turned to Annabel he didn't bother with a compliment, simply kissed the tips of her fingers. But there was a look in his eye that warmed her heart. "Madame Maisonnet?" he asked, indicating her costume with one slim hand. "A superb choice, Miss Essex."

Annabel smiled back. They didn't speak as they danced. Why should they? As far as Annabel could tell—and she could always tell what men were thinking—they were in perfect harmony. Their marriage would be riven by neither tears nor jealousy. They would have beautiful children. He was extremely wealthy and so her lack of a dowry would not bother him. They would be kind to each other, and she could talk to herself if she lacked breakfast conversation.

For someone with as little tolerance for inane chitchat

as she had, the prospect was entirely pleasing. In fact, the only drawback she could think of was that conversation with oneself held few surprises. Neither did Rosseter's farewell to her that evening. "Miss Essex," he said, "would it be acceptable to you if I spoke to your guardian tomorrow morning?" His hand was snow-white, slim and delicate as he pressed her fingers in a most gratifying manner.

"That would make me quite happy, Lord Rosseter," Annabel murmured.

She was having trouble suppressing a grin. Finally—finally!—her heart's desire was within reach. She had longed for this moment for years, ever since her father discovered that she had a gift for figures and promptly dumped the entire accounting of the estate in her lap. From the time she was thirteen years old, Annabel had spent her days bargaining with tradesmen, shedding tears over a ledger book that showed far more minuses than pluses, pleading with her father to sell the most expensive animals, begging him not to spend all their money at the track . . .

And was rewarded by his dislike.

But she had kept at it, well aware that her financial management was often the only thing between her sisters and true hunger, the only thing holding off the ruin of the stables her father held so dear.

Her father had called her Miss Prune. If she approached while he was standing with friends, he would roll his eyes at her. Sometimes he would take out a coin and toss it in her direction, and then joke with his friends that she kept him on a tighter string than the worst of wives. And she would always pick up the coin . . . bend down and pick it up because that was one coin saved from the huge maw of the stables. Saved for flour, or butter, or a beautiful hen for the supper table.

So she had turned to dreaming of the husband she would have someday. She had never bothered imagining his face: Lord Rosseter's face was as acceptable as that of almost any wealthy Englishman. What she had imagined were sleeves clad in gleaming velvet, and cravats that were white as snow and made of the finest linen. The kind of clothes that were bought for beauty, not to last. Hands in that flawless state that screamed manual labor was unnecessary.

Rosseter's hands would do perfectly.

Three

Grillon's Hotel
Early that morning

Ewan Poley, Earl of Ardmore, was fairly certain that he was obeying Father Armailhac's instructions to the letter. "Go to London," he had said. "Dance with a pretty girl."

"And just what am I supposed to do with this pretty girl?" Ewan had inquired.

"Surely the spirit will move you," Father Armailhac had said. For a monk, he had a wicked twinkle at times.

And so far, Ewan had met a multitude of pretty girls. Due to his terrible memory, he couldn't remember any of their names, but he reckoned he must have danced with half of London by now. Thanks to his title, he had been showered by invitations within a few days of his arrival; it seemed that the English were not quite so blasé about Scottish titles as was rumored in the north country. Yet it seemed to him that Father Armailhac had meant he should meet a *particular* girl, one whom he could contemplating wooing and bringing back to Scotland.

He had no objection to marrying, although he couldn't say he felt passionate enthusiasm for the idea. His mind slid easily from marriage to the long, clean rows of his stables, the golden fields of spring wheat just beginning to sprout. He could give this marrying business another fortnight. Then he would return home, married or no.

The black-haired lass he had danced with this evening seemed more than ready to hop before the altar. But what was her name? He couldn't remember. She had clung to him like a limpet, which he didn't care for much. Yet perhaps the lady was desperate, widowed as she was, and likely with naught more than a small dowry.

His manservant appeared at the door, a silver plate in his hand. Ewan might not be enjoying London much, but Glover was ecstatic. All his ambitions were fulfilled by being in the city, as he called it, during the season. "Your lordship, a card has arrived."

"At this hour? Just put it over there," Ewan said, nodding at the mantelpiece. It was crowded with cards and invitations from people he'd never heard of.

Glover bowed but didn't move toward the fireplace. "Your lordship, this card is from the Duke of Holbrook. And"—Glover lowered his voice to an awed whisper—"His Grace has condescended to wait."

Ewan sighed. A duke. Perhaps the man was desperate to send one of his daughters off into the supposed wilds of Scotland. He'd figured out soon enough that the English thought of Scotland as a wilderness of crazed warriors and grim religious dissenters.

He glanced at his cravat in the mirror. Glover was brokenhearted at his refusal to change his customary black for the gaudy waistcoats Englishmen wore to balls. But he looked fine and, more importantly, Scottish. Scotsmen wore kilts if they felt the need for a little color, even if they weren't allowed to wear them in this country.

"His Grace awaits you in the sitting room," Glover said.

"Aye."

"If you'll excuse the boldness, my lord," Glover said, hesitating.

Ewan raised an eyebrow. "Yes?"

"A duke of the realm," Glover said, trembling with the excitement of it. "Try to avoid Scottish phrases such as *aye*. 'Twill make an unpleasant impression on His Grace."

"I'm not marrying him," Ewan said, but then softened. "But thank you for the advice, Glover. I shall do my best to appear reasonably English." Not that he would ever wish to mimic an Englishman, not in a hundred years.

The duke was a messy sort, Ewan saw with some relief. In fact, the sort who would take no offense at an occasional *aye*. Ewan had already had several conversations with the perfumed, sleek type of English nobility, and he didn't care for them. No more did they him.

This duke was dressed in clothes that looked comfortable rather than elegant. His stomach strained comfortably over the waist of his pantaloons, and as Ewan stood in the doorway of the room, his guest threw back a glass of brandy that Glover must have given him with all the enthusiasm of one of Ewan's laborers greeting the evening.

"Your Grace," Ewan said, entering the room. "This is indeed a pleasure."

The duke straightened like a bloodhound and turned around. Ewan almost took a step back. Bloody hell, the man looked enraged. And now he remembered precisely where he'd met him before. If you could call it a meeting; the duke had snatched the black-haired lady from his arms and danced with her himself.

"Do you know who I am?" he said. His voice was as deep and burly as his figure.

"According to your card, you are the Duke of Holbrook," Ewan observed. He moved over to the sideboard. "May I offer you another drink?" He dropped the *Your Grace* part as it made him feel faintly servant-like.

"I am the guardian of Lady Maitland," the man announced.

"Quite so," Ewan murmured, pouring himself a stiff glass. "Well, I am the Earl of Ardmore, hailing from Aberdeenshire, if you were not already aware of the fact."

"Lady Maitland," Holbrook insisted. "Imogen Maitland."

Imogen must be the black-haired charmer from the ballroom. "If I have offended you or the lady in any way, I offer my sincere apologies," Ewan said, striving for diplomacy.

"Well, I should say you have!" the duke huffed.

"How?" Ewan inquired. He kept his tone easy and even.

"All London is talking of the two of you," Holbrook snapped. "Of your tasteless exhibition of waltzing."

Ewan thought for a moment. He had two alternatives: to tell the truth, or to take responsibility. Honor demanded that he not reveal the fact that Holbrook's ward had clung to him with all the expert passion of a Bird of Paradise. He was no fool: the black-haired Imogen was far less moved by his beauty than she had pretended to be. He caught some sort of emotion in her eyes, but it didn't seem to be pure lust, even if that was the emotion that she was flaunting.

"I apologize in every respect," he said finally. "I was bowled over by her beauty and I gather it led to my actions being interpreted in an unpleasant light."

Holbrook narrowed his eyes. Ewan gazed back at

him, wondering if all dukes in England were so undisciplined in their emotions and dress.

"I'll have that drink now," the duke said.

Ewan picked up his personal decanter and poured him a healthy glass. Holbrook had the distinct atmosphere of a man who enjoyed a good brandy, and Ewan had brought with him several flasks of the best aged whiskey to be found in Scotland.

Holbrook took one large sip and then looked at Ewan in surprise. He sank into a couch and took another sip.

Ewan sat down opposite him. He could see that Holbrook understood exactly what he was drinking.

"What is it?" Holbrook said, his voice hushed.

"An aged single malt," Ewan said. "A new process and one likely to change the whiskey industry, to my mind."

Holbrook took another sip and sat back. "Glen Garioch," he said dreamily. "Glen Garioch or—possibly—Tobermary."

Ewan gave him a real grin this time. "Aye, Glen Garioch it is."

"Bliss," Holbrook said. "Almost, I could let a man who knew his whiskey marry Imogen. *Almost!*" he said, opening his eyes again.

"I've no particular desire to marry her," Ewan said agreeably.

He realized his mistake when Holbrook's eyebrows drew into a ferocious scowl.

"Although I would consider myself immeasurably lucky to do so," Ewan added. "She is a lovely young woman."

"Rumor has it that you're in England precisely to find a wife," the duke growled. But he was sipping his liquor again.

"The rumor is correct," Ewan said. "But not necessarily your ward."

"Ah."

They sat in silence for a while, enjoying the whiskey.

"I expect the truth of it is that Imogen threw herself at you, and you're being too polite to tell me so to my face," the duke said as gloomily as was possible when one is holding a glass of '83 whiskey distilled by Glen Garioch.

"Lady Maitland is an exquisite young woman. I'd be more than happy to marry her."

The duke caught his eye, and then: "Damned if you don't mean it. Don't care who you marry, is that it?"

"I take a reasonable interest in the subject," Ewan protested. "But I will admit that I'm rather anxious to return to my lands. The wheat is sprouting."

The duke looked as if he had never heard the word *sprout*. "Are you telling me that you're a farmer?" he asked. "One of those gentlemen who dabble about with experimental methods. Turnip Townshend, isn't that his name?"

"I'm not quite as engrossed as Mr. Townshend," Ewan murmured, letting another sip of liquor burn its complex, golden way down his throat.

"This is delicious," the duke said, clearly discarding a subject of little interest to him. "This whiskey is utterly—" he stopped. "Wheat? Do you have anything to do with whiskey production, then?"

"My tenants supply some grain for the distilleries in Speyside," Ewan said.

"No wonder you know your drink so well." The duke seemed quite struck by this. "Been thinking about giving up the tipple," he said suddenly.

"Indeed?" Ewan had to admit that the duke was putting away the best whiskey there was to be had in Scotland at a fantastic rate, and showing little signs of it. Perhaps he had fallen into the way of drinking too much.

"But not tonight."

Ewan decided the appropriate response to that revelation would be to pour the duke another generous portion, so he did so.

"Your estate is in Aberdeenshire?"

Ewan nodded.

"There's a lovely horse up there," the duke said, thinking it over. "I haven't seen him for a year or so, but—"

"Warlock," Ewan put in. "He strained a fetlock last July."

"Exactly! Warlock. Belongs to a friend of yours, does he?"

"I own Warlock," Ewan said.

Now the duke's eyes were definitely warm. "Good man. Out of Pheasant, wasn't he?"

"Pheasant by way of Miraculous," Ewan said.

"I don't suppose you're thinking of breeding his line, are you?"

"I already have a yearling who's showing definite possibilities."

The duke had shed his sleepy, pleasant manner and was sitting bolt upright, looking more awake than Ewan had seen him, except perhaps at the ball when he was in such a rage. "I've three offspring of Patchem sitting in my stables, two mares and a colt. The daughters are my wards, and each one of them came with a horse for a dowry. Their father was a bit of a featherhead and he doesn't seem to have thought carefully about the business. I was thinking of breeding the mares, since neither shows much racing ability."

A horse for a dowry? He'd only heard of such a thing once, and that was from the golden-haired beauty at the ball. Who had told him to look elsewhere, because she only had a horse for a dowry. Apparently she didn't think it important to note that the particular horse was from the line of Patchem.

"I should like to see a horse with Warlock's and Patchem's bloodlines," he said.

They sat in comfortable silence for a few moments, the duke slumping back into his boneless, indolent stance.

"You've gone about finding a wife the wrong way," Holbrook said, after a while.

"I've gone to fourteen events in the last week," Ewan observed. "Four balls, a number of afternoon gatherings and one musicale. I did ask a young lady to marry me this evening, but she declined." He didn't think it necessary to note that the woman was apparently one of Holbrook's wards, not when the duke had only barely gotten over his annoyance at Ewan's behavior with another of those wards.

"That's not the way of it. These things are handled between men. The key is to figure out which woman you wish to marry *before* you go to the ballroom." The duke's voice had just the slightest husky edge now, a golden burr of whiskey. But all in all, Ewan thought he held his liquor better than any man he knew except old Lachlan McGregor, and McGregor had given his life to the practice.

"I'll take you along to my club," the duke continued. "We can have it all fixed up in a moment." He rose and Ewan was rather amazed to see that the man wasn't even unsteady. "*Not* that you can have Imogen," he said with a sudden roar, "even if she does come with a mare for a dowry. We'll do the horse breeding on the side."

"I wouldn't think of it," Ewan said, looking around for the card case that Glover had bought for him. He didn't find it, so he simply followed the duke out the door. The only sign that Holbrook had imbibed the better part of a flask was a certain talkativeness.

"You see," the duke said in the carriage as they were trundling off to his club, "the poor girl lost her husband a mere six months ago. The man fell on the racetrack, racing one of his own horses: a yearling that should never have been put to the bridle."

"Aye," Ewan said. He'd heard that story somewhere, but as was often the case, the name of the rider eluded him.

"Imogen had loved him for years." Holbrook was leaning back against the cushions, having no problem whatsoever keeping his balance as the carriage swung around corners and rumbled down cobblestone streets. "She picked him out when she was a mere nursling, and they ended up eloping. And then he died but a matter of weeks later."

"Weeks!" Ewan said, struck by the misfortune of that. And then: "Of course, that would be *Draven* Maitland."

"The same."

"Ah," Ewan said. He had met young Maitland a few times, since the man used to race the Scottish cycle before returning to England for the English racing season. Maitland was a rash, foolish young man whom Ewan had rather disliked.

The duke took a little flagon out of his pocket and took a sip, but shook his head. "This is like drinking pisswater after that whiskey of yours. At any rate, poor Imogen is not quite herself, due to the shock of the whole thing, as you can imagine."

The carriage stopped in front of an imposing, pillared building. Ewan had no idea what part of the city they were in. "Aren't these clubs for members only?" he asked.

The duke waved his hand dismissively. "No one will question my bringing a guest in for a drink. I'll put you up for membership, if you'd like. But it is a hell of an expense," he tossed over his shoulder. "Not worth the money, I should think."

Ewan agreed with him. Surely men stewed in liquor

all offered the same tedious company, and if it was their society he wished, the men in his local tavern would do.

The duke seemed to know precisely where he was going. They were greeted by a solemn-faced individual, who bowed deeply and intoned a welcome to "White's." Then the duke trundled past a few rooms that seemed to be filled with gamblers and finally arrived in a library.

It was a magnificent room. The few bits of wall that weren't covered with books were papered in a deep crimson. There was a fire burning in a generous hearth, and comfortable chairs scattered about the room in groupings that offered intimacy. The duke didn't hesitate. "Come," he threw over his shoulder, heading to a corner.

Four high-backed chairs were grouped with their backs to the room. In one of them was a scion of English nobility of just the sort that Ewan disliked. He had black curls tossed in one of those styles that Ewan had just figured out *was* a style, rather than the effect of an unexpected rain shower. And he was wearing a waistcoat of such riotously embroidered beauty that Glover would have grown weak at the knees. Ewan could only be glad that his manservant was not with him: the last thing he wanted was to find himself dressed in a garnet-colored jacket, as if he were a man milliner.

Ewan saw with one glance that the gentleman seated next to the man milliner was a man of power. He had a face that bespoke the ability to move nations, if he wished. His very quietness radiated power and presence. Perhaps he was one of those royal dukes, although he had heard tell that the dukes were on the plump side.

"I've brought along a Scottish earl," Holbrook said without ceremony. "Seems a decent fellow, and keeps a whiskey in his chambers that's full of the devil. Plus he's the owner of Warlock, who won the Derby two years ago, if you remember. Ardmore, that sprig of fashion is Garret Langham, the Earl of Mayne. And this is Mr. Lucius Felton. As for myself, I go by Rafe amongst friends."

Without waiting for a response, he signaled to a footman. "Ask Penny if they have any aged Glen Garioch whiskey in the house."

"They don't," Ewan said, bowing to the gentlemen, who had stood up and were doing the pretty. "Aged malts aren't exported for sale yet."

The duke collapsed into a chair. "I suddenly have a deep interest in visiting our northern neighbors."

Now that the Earl of Mayne was on his feet, Ewan could see immediately that the man was no man milliner, for all his deep red jacket seemed to catch the gleam of the firelight. He had tired eyes and a dissolute droop to his mouth, but he was a man to be reckoned with.

"Ardmore," Mayne said. "It's a pleasure." He had a strong handshake. "Didn't I see you dancing at Lady Feddrington's house?"

"You and the rest of London," the duke put in darkly.

"I danced most of the evening," Ewan noted, shaking hands with Felton.

"He's in need of a wife," Rafe said. "And since I'm not giving him Imogen, for all she's thrown herself at his head, I thought we could find him someone ourselves. After all, we didn't do badly with you, Felton."

"Least said about *that,* the better," Mayne muttered.

The duke was finally showing the effect of all that whiskey and he grinned rather owlishly at Ewan. "What Mayne is trying to say is that after he jilted one of my four girls, Felton stepped in and married her."

Mayne was looking at Ewan with just a faint curl of a

sardonic smile on his face; Felton was grinning outright. Englishmen were far stranger than he'd heard. "How many wards do you have?" he asked finally.

"Viscount Brydone had four daughters," the duke allowed, his head falling back. "Four, four, four. All sisters. One is still in the schoolroom, that's Josie. Imogen is one of them, and Tess was the eldest, until Felton here took her away."

Felton was smiling. Yet a Scotsman would never stay in the company of a man who had jilted his wife. Never. One look at Mayne's face and you knew he was a dissipated trifler.

Felton must have seen that fact in his eyes, for he said easily, "Unfortunately, I had to force Mayne to jilt his bride. I decided she would do better married to me than to him."

"Ruined my reputation," Mayne said.

"Nonsense," the duke snorted. "The jilting was merely one in a line of scandals you've tossed to the wind. So who can Ardmore here marry? You know the *ton*, Mayne. Find him a bride."

Ewan waited with faint curiosity for Mayne's response, but at that moment a plump waiter appeared.

"Your Grace, we haven't a drop of Glen Garioch in the house. Would you like some Ardbeg or Tobermary?"

Rafe looked at Ewan.

Ewan bent toward the man and said, "We'll try the Tobermary."

The plump man bowed and took himself off, and Rafe said dreamily, "A man who knows his liquor is more precious than rubies."

"In that case, may I point out that Miss Annabel Essex is doing the season," Felton said. "The second of Rafe's wards," he explained to Ewan. "Dowried with Milady's Pleasure, and since I gather that you are likely putting Warlock to stud, the combination would be quite interesting."

So the golden-haired Scotswoman was called Annabel. But the duke shook his head. "It'll never fly. Begging your pardon, Ardmore, but Annabel has a penchant for rich and titled Englishmen. She'd be an uncomfortable wife for a penniless Scottish earl, and that's the truth of it."

Felton opened his mouth but Ewan caught his eye and he closed it.

"Ah, a dowry problem," Mayne said thoughtfully.

The waiter returned with a decanter of the Tobermary, which was just as good as Ewan remembered.

"Do you like poetry?" Mayne asked.

It seemed an odd question. "Not particularly."

"Then Miss Pythian-Adams won't do. She's got a hefty dowry, but I've heard she's memorized the whole of a Shakespeare play. At any rate, she does drop bits and pieces into conversation. Maitland used to complain when they were engaged that she made him read aloud the whole of *Henry VIII*. Apparently it took an afternoon."

"No," Ewan said. "That won't do."

"So that's why you're in London." Rafe stared at him over a mere inch of brandy left in his glass.

"To find a wife," Ewan agreed. "As I told you earlier, Your Grace." The duke was definitely showing his whiskey now.

"Sometimes I think that I need one of those too. She could take care of all these wards of mine. They're going to have me in Bedlam."

"Don't be a fool," Mayne said to him. "No one would marry a drunken sot like yourself unless she wanted your title and money."

Somewhat to Ewan's surprise, Rafe took no umbrage at his friend's harsh assessment.

"You're probably right," he said, with a yawn that appeared likely to break his jaw. "I have to go to bed. Come up with a few names for Ardmore here, Mayne."

"Miss Tarn," Mayne said, his eyes narrowed in thought. "She's quite beautiful; her dowry is more than adequate; by all reports, she's an expert horsewoman."

"My wife says she's in love with a Frenchman named Soubiran," Felton said. "Her father doesn't approve of the connection, but Miss Tarn has dug in her heels."

"In that case, Lady Cecily Severy," Mayne said. "Eldest daughter of the Duke of Claire. Not bad-looking and the dowry is obviously magnificent."

"This is her third season," Felton put in.

"She does lisp," Mayne admitted. "But her dowry surely trumps the lisp."

"She pretends that she's approximately five years old," Felton said crisply. "Talks in baby talk to her suitors. Puts some men off."

"I would consider myself one of them," Ewan said.

"Third choice, then," Mayne said. "Lady Griselda Willoughby. She's a young, beautiful widow, with a large estate and a cheerful disposition. She thinks she doesn't want to marry, but in fact she would make a happy wife and mother. And her reputation is impeccable."

Silence followed this suggestion. Ewan thought Lady Griselda sounded just fine. He nodded.

"Lady Griselda is Mayne's sister," Felton said.

Ewan looked at Mayne. "Your sister?"

Mayne nodded. "Mind you, she's been courted by many a man, and none of them has had the least success." He eyed Ewan narrowly. "But I have a feeling that you might have more luck than most. She's only thirty, and there's more than enough time for children."

"He doesn't have an estate," Rafe said, his voice turned to a dark-toned growl by exhaustion and liquor.

"She doesn't need it. Her jointure alone was excellent, but Willoughby's estate is also extensive."

Felton nodded. "I would agree with your assessment of Lady Griselda's holdings."

"She says she doesn't want to marry again," Mayne said. "But I'm fond of her."

Ewan translated that into a typical English understatement of a loyal love for his sister. Lord, but Englishmen were strange. Here was a man who looked like a rake-hell if he ever saw one, and yet . . . it seemed he was truly being offered a wife.

"I would be honored to meet Lady Griselda," he said.

"Good, that's settled," Rafe said, with another yawn. "I'm off. Ardmore, would you like me to drop you at Grillon's, or will you find your own way home?"

Ewan rose and bowed to the two men.

"Perhaps we could talk about your stables at some point," Felton said.

Ewan recognized the spark in his eye as being that of a man with an abiding passion for horses. "I would be delighted," he said, bowing again.

Mayne rose in turn. "Have you been invited to Countess Mitford's garden party tomorrow afternoon?"

"Yes." Ewan hesitated. "I thought not to go. I found the last garden party painfully tedious."

"This won't be. Countess Mitford models herself on the ancient Renaissance families of Italy. She holds only one party a year, and it's not to be missed. I shall escort my sister."

"Come along," Rafe said grumpily. "Aged whiskey gives one the same headache as its younger brethren, damn it."

Ewan bowed again.

Four

Everything had changed since Tess married. For years, the four of them would curl up in bed, huddling under threadworn blankets in the winter, wearing chemises because they had no nightgowns . . . talking. Josie was the baby, who sometimes sounded the eldest of all of them because of her biting wit. Imogen next youngest, with her passion for Draven Maitland that had thrived for years before he even noticed her existence. Annabel was two years older than Imogen and had spent her adolescence managing the finances of the household, exhausted by the burden of it and tired, bone-tired, by the poverty of their father's house. She had talked incessantly of London, of silks and satins, and of a man who would never make her count a penny. And Tess was the eldest . . . Tess, who had worried about all of them and kept her fears to herself.

But Josie was in the country under the care of her governess, Miss Flecknoe, and Tess was in her husband's bed. Which left only two sisters to squabble, Annabel thought gloomily.

Imogen was in a sullen mood tonight, sitting with her lips pressed together, scowling at the bedpost at the end of the bed.

"He's got no right to act in such a fashion," she said. "He has no *right!*"

Annabel jumped. Her sister's voice was as sharp as the north wind. "Rafe is our guardian," she pointed out.

"I can do whatever I wish, with whomever I wish," Imogen said. "He may be your guardian, but he is not mine, since I am a woman of independent means. I never liked him, drunken sot that he is, and I never shall. And I shall never forgive Tess for not bringing us onto the season herself."

Tess's husband traveled a great deal, checking on his holdings all over England. Tess had taken to traveling with him, and was away from London as often as she was present, so Rafe, with Lady Griselda's help, was bringing Annabel out this season.

"You came out when you married Draven," Annabel pointed out. "You have no particular need for Tess's help."

"Draven . . ." Imogen said, and her whole face and voice changed, softened and looked like the old Imogen, before she became so harsh, so hard and shrill.

Annabel held her breath, but Imogen didn't dissolve into tears. Instead she said, after a moment, "He *was* beautiful, wasn't he?"

"Very," Annabel confirmed. Just don't ask me whether he was a reasonable person or a rational man, she added silently.

"I loved his dimple," Imogen said. "When we married, I . . ." she stopped.

Annabel saw a glimmer of tears in her sister's eyes

and surreptitiously pulled a handkerchief from her bedside table. She kept a supply there. But Imogen shook her head.

"Do you know the problem with being married only a matter of two weeks?" she asked.

Annabel figured that was a rhetorical question.

"The problem is that I don't have many memories," Imogen said, her voice tight. "How many times can I remember kissing Draven for the first time? How many times can I remember his asking me to marry him? If we'd just had more time, even a month or two, I would have feasts of memories, enough to last me for years."

Annabel handed her the handkerchief. Imogen wiped away a tear snaking down her cheek.

"There will be other memories to treasure, someday," Annabel ventured.

Imogen turned on her with a flash of rage. "Don't try to suggest that anyone could replace Draven in my heart! I loved him from the moment I reached girlhood, and I shall never, ever love another man as I loved him. Never."

Annabel bit her lip. She always seemed to say the wrong thing. Perhaps she should inform Lord Rosseter that she wished to marry him immediately; at least it would get her out of the house. "I didn't mean to imply that you would forget Draven," she said, controlling her voice so that no shade of irritation entered. "But you're very young to talk of *never*, Imogen."

"I've never been young in that respect," Imogen said flatly.

Annabel decided to try for a new subject. "I have decided to marry Lord Rosseter," she said brightly.

Imogen didn't appear to have heard her. "Rafe said something similar to me, this very evening in the carriage. He actually implied . . ." she turned to Annabel and hesitated. "I probably shouldn't say this to you, since you're unmarried."

Annabel snorted.

"He accused me of missing the pleasure of the marital bed!"

"Oh. And are you?" Annabel inquired. It seemed a reasonable, if impertinent, inquiry, given Imogen's behavior on the dance floor.

"Of course not! I miss Draven. But not . . . or rather—if Draven were . . ."

Annabel rescued her. "Well, I can see Rafe's point. I should think that anyone could reasonably have assumed that you were missing those particular pleasures, given the way you looked at Ardmore on the dance floor."

"Nonsense!" Imogen snapped. "I was merely being seductive. The same as you always are."

"I never act in that way," Annabel stated.

"Well, of course, you don't have the knowledge that I do," Imogen said pettishly. "You're just a maiden, after all. I was able to be much more direct because I understand what happens between a man and a woman in the bedchamber."

Annabel did not trust herself to speak.

"At any rate," Imogen continued, "I have definitely made up my mind to take Ardmore."

"Take him?" Annabel inquired, giving her a direct look.

"Make him part of my retinue," Imogen said, waving a hand in the air. "That's all I'll say on the subject to a maid, even if you are my sister."

Annabel ignored her provocation. "Be careful, Imogen. I would be very, very careful. That earl does not look like a tame pussycat to me."

"Nonsense," Imogen said crossly. "Men are all the same."

"All right," Annabel said. "Make him your cicisbeo,

if you wish. But why put on such an exhibition while dancing? Why embarrass yourself in such a fashion?"

"I was expressing our mutual—"

But they had been siblings for a long time. "Whatever it was you were expressing, it wasn't a desire to bed Ardmore."

"Yes, it was!" Imogen flared, and then the words died in her throat. She had been so certain that she was being inviting and sensual. But perhaps she had failed at that too. She glanced at Annabel. It was tempting to confide in her . . .

No. She couldn't bear to tell Annabel of her marital failures, Annabel who had the ability to make any man within ten yards start panting.

"You could talk to Tess about it," Annabel said now, showing that uncanny ability that sisters sometimes have to guess what another is thinking.

"There's nothing to discuss," Imogen said, coughing to cover the rasp in her voice. "I thoroughly enjoyed myself dancing with Ardmore, and I look forward to more happy hours with him."

"You sound like a vicar accepting a new post," her sister observed.

What did Annabel know about anything? Imogen couldn't talk to her, and she couldn't talk to Tess either, because for all Tess was married, she was *happy*.

She took a deep breath. "I am enthralled by the pleasure I shall share with Ardmore," she said.

"Perhaps not a vicarage . . . a bishopric," her sister mused, clearly unimpressed.

Imogen turned away.

Five

Lady Mitford's garden party was savored by each member of the *ton* lucky enough to receive an invitation. Of course, they savored it for different reasons. Mothers of nubile girls found that the romantic bowers Lady Mitford placed around her gardens were excellent enclosures for nurturing intimacies that were not too intimate.

Those who were, for whatever reason, uninterested in mating games enjoyed Lady Mitford's considerable efforts toward producing true Renaissance cuisine. There was the year, for instance, when a pie was split open to reveal five cross and extremely undercooked doves who promptly flew into the air. When one of them dropped a noxious substance on the head of an upstart young lord, the pie was deemed an enormous success.

Finally, the day was appreciated by those with a sense of irony. Ewan Poley, Earl of Ardmore, would have put himself in the latter category. In fact, this was by far the most entertaining gala he had yet attended in England.

Lady Mitford had positioned herself and her husband at the far end of a great stretch of lawn, the better so that entering guests could admire the spectacle. They were a plump couple stuffed into brilliant Renaissance clothing; Lord Mitford's canary-yellow stockings were particularly noteworthy, as they were echoed by some thirty servants stationed about the lawns. The couple sat on gilded armchairs that had a suspicious resemblance to thrones, under a sky-blue silk canopy that rippled in the breeze. Around their feet frolicked a number of small dogs and a real monkey, tied to Lady Mitford's chair with a silk ribbon. Ewan tried not to mark the fact that the monkey appeared to be squatting on Lady Mitford's silk slipper and enjoying a private moment.

He bowed before her. "This is a tremendous honor, Lady Mitford. I cannot thank you enough for including me in your invitation."

"Wouldn't have missed you," she barked at him, sounding for all the world like one of her small dogs. "I do believe I had at least eight requests for your inclusion—all from mamas, of course."

Lord Mitford gave him a conspiratorial smile. "Our gala is quite known for the matches that have ensued."

They were an odd couple; Lady Mitford was wearing a high coned hat more suited to the reign of King Richard than that of Queen Elizabeth. Lord Mitford looked as kingly as a carnival barker, and the monkey, the dogs and the silk canopy spoke of that carnival as much as a Renaissance fête. But the Mitfords' eyes were merry, and it was clear that they enjoyed their own eccentricities as much as did everyone else.

Lady Mitford raised a beringed finger and pointed off in the distance. "I understand that you have a particular interest in a lovely widow. She is over there, next to the rose arbor."

For a moment Ewan blinked. How could she know that Lord Mayne had recommended his widowed sister as a possible spouse?

"Lady Maitland has grieved enough," his hostess said with a benign smile. "She would do well to forget the tragic death of her young husband and turn to you."

With a smile and a bow, Ewan turned and walked toward the rose arbor where, presumably, the passionate Imogen was to be found. Then, as the Mitfords turned to greet another guest, he walked in the opposite direction.

He had just spied Holbrook's other ward, and strangely enough for his lamentable memory, he even remembered her name: Annabel. She was the one who wouldn't dance with him, who called him a lad. He hadn't been called a lad since his grandfather died, and that was years ago.

He slowed to watch her. She was all honey and gold. Soft loose curls were pulled to the top of her head and then tumbled onto her shoulders. Her dress was that of an unmarried lady, from what he could see: cream silk and lace that flowed from just under her breast and made her legs seem as long as a colt's. But she was no youngster. Her eyes glowed with wit and intelligence . . . so why was he just a lad to her?

Ewan strolled over, mentally dismissing the man she was smiling at so brilliantly. *He* was the sort of man who would always be ruled by others.

"Miss Essex," he said, bowing.

She turned to him, her eyes dancing. "Ah, Lord Ardmore," she said. "May I introduce Lord Rosseter, if you have not already met?"

Rosseter bowed rather punctiliously. Before he realized what he was doing, Ewan shifted his body slightly, just slightly, so that he stood with a wider stance. And

Rosseter caught the message. Ewan saw in one glance that he was a man of innuendo and secret messages, the type who would never express himself openly.

With an unhurried, overly elegant sweep of his cloak over his arm, Lord Rosseter made some practiced excuse to Miss Essex and walked away. She blinked after him, looking quite surprised. There were likely very few men who walked away from her, Ewan thought with some amusement.

"He'll be back," he said to her, discarding the idea of offering a practiced gallantry.

She answered with a twinkle in her eyes. "I certainly hope so."

Well, she couldn't have said that more clearly. Apparently she intended to marry the sleek little coward she'd singled out from the herd. Which was entirely her prerogative, Ewan reminded himself. Naturally he would prefer to see a countrywoman make better choices.

"I met your guardian last evening," he said.

"I saw that you did," she answered, the smile disappearing from her face.

For a second he didn't follow her, then he remembered Rafe's furious interruption of his dance with her sister. For the life of him, he couldn't see a single resemblance. The black-haired lass was all ice and fury, while her sister's face was as beautifully shaped as an Italian Madonna and fifty times more sensuous. He'd never seen such a deep lower lip, nor eyes of that particular shade of blue. He pulled himself together. "In fact, your guardian visited my chambers last night."

Now her smile was truly gone. "I'm very sorry to hear that," she said stiffly.

He found himself grinning at her. "He took me to his club, a place called White."

"White's," she corrected him.

"I have a terrible memory for details." And why was he grinning at her like a lummox who'd had too much sun?

"Mine is the opposite," she confided. "Sometimes I think it would be a blessing to be able to misplace a name or a number."

"I should think that would be a useful trait in a place like this," Ewan said, giving the garden a cursory glance. It was filling with Englishmen, clustering under the fluttering silk pavilions that housed food and drink.

"It is useful," she agreed.

They seemed to have finished that subject. "So you are the daughter of the late Viscount Brydone?" he asked, knowing the answer.

She nodded.

"I bought a horse from him once."

"Blacklock, grandson of Coriander."

He blinked at her.

"I never forget names, remember? Your factor managed the transaction. Father asked for sixty pounds and your factor managed to buy the horse for forty. Disappointing for papa, but still lovely for the rest of us." She bit those words off as if she never meant to say them.

"Why on earth was it lovely for you?" he asked. From the corner of his eye he saw a determined-looking gentleman in lavender breeches heading directly toward Annabel, holding a glass of champagne as his admission ticket.

She raised her eyes, and there was a wry companionship in them. "Because we ate meat at night for three months. Ate our fill," she clarified.

Ewan blinked at her. She was a polished glowing statue of perfection, as beautiful as Venus and five times more sensuous. "Your father's stables were known through Roxburghshire up to Aberdeenshire for their magnificence," he noted.

"Indeed," she said. "Every man has his virtues."

She was not only beautiful, but she had an ironic turn of phrase. He would quite like to bring her home, if only because he felt a smoldering heat in his loins at the very sight of her. So, in fact, it was better that she had decided on Rosseter. For she was one to put a man into a feverish sin of the flesh, beyond the natural, respectable love of a man for his wife. She looked as if she might drive a man to despair if she closed the door even one night.

The very thought filled him with horror. He bowed smartly. "Miss Essex. It's been a pleasure."

The gentleman in lavender started up at her right shoulder like a puppet. "Miss Essex," he simpered, "I've brought you a glass of heaven. You do know that champagne is nothing more than a glass of stars, don't you?"

She turned to him and smiled so kindly that Ewan expected to see the poor lad melt at her feet. If he didn't die of the embarrassment of being condescended to in such a manner. "Just what I was hoping for," she said.

Ewan bowed and walked away. He needed to find Mayne. Mayne and his cheerful, widowed sister.

Imogen Maitland was well aware that she had transformed into a fury out of a classical play. She knew she was behaving abominably toward her sisters, snapping at them like an untamed dog. She knew she ought to be grateful to Rafe for his kindness and generosity, taking her back into his house after she eloped in such a scandalous manner. Instead, she wanted to kill him, every time she saw his indolent manner and the drink he always held. And she wanted to kill her sisters too: Tess because her husband loved her, and he was alive. Annabel because she so effortlessly made men adore her. Josie . . . well, Josie was in the schoolroom, so Imogen exempted her from her gallery of hatred.

It was shocking, how all that grief inside her had turned to hate. She saw their shocked eyes when she snapped at them, the rage in Rafe's face when she taunted him. And yet . . . there it was.

They simply didn't understand.

None of them had ever had anything terrible happen to them. Never. Rafe had lost his brother and parents, but he probably just drank an extra glass in their memory. That didn't seem quite fair, but she didn't want to think about it. Annabel had her whole life in front of her, and Tess—

Tess made Imogen's heart hurt so much that she couldn't stand it. Tess's husband loved her. Really loved her. Felton looked at Tess with the emotion so stark in his eyes that it was enough to make Imogen vomit. He couldn't even wait to be private; he kissed her in public. He . . .

Imogen bit her lip savagely. Lord knows he probably cherished his wife in the bedchamber.

She stared intently at a boy dressed as a Renaissance page, who was putting on a demonstration of archery. Don't think about it . . .

If she had just had more time with Draven, he would have loved her the same way.

Tears were pressing hotly at her eyes, but she wasn't going to cry here, in Lady Mitford's garden. Of course Draven loved her. He said so, just before he died, didn't he? He did. He *did*. He loved her.

The truth of it was as black as the coldest ice. He just didn't love her the way that Lucius loved Tess.

The eternal circle chased in her mind: if they'd had time . . . if she'd been more seductive, more knowing, more beautiful . . .

She turned from the archery tent and began to walk quickly in the opposite direction. Lady Whittingham was strolling toward her with her feckless husband; Imogen smiled, fighting the tears. Lady Whittingham turned her head away and walked on.

For a moment Imogen paused as if she'd been struck in the stomach. Then she remembered that she'd burned her bridges at the ball the night before . . . Ardmore . . . their dance . . . Rafe. But she couldn't bring herself to care. Likely she wouldn't have been invited to this garden party had the invitations not gone out the previous week. But who cared for that?

The question, the eternal question, flooded back into her mind and she walked on, Lady Whittingham's snub forgotten.

She was beautiful. Everyone said so. Her modiste said so; her maid said so; she saw the truth reflected in the eyes of men who passed her. If only it was a problem with the way she looked, she thought bitterly. Then she could simply resign herself to a loveless life and become a nun.

What good was beauty when she'd failed to make Draven love her? Beauty wasn't enough. She needed the quality that Annabel had, that melting, sensual look that she had. It wasn't fair that her sister had it, since Annabel was a virgin.

Since she was about to bump into a table offering glasses of ratafia, she took one even though she despised the drink.

Surely Draven had been happy enough. Except . . . the doubts followed her. Perhaps if she had been more enticing, Draven would have loved her, really loved her. She could have made that Scottish earl want her. She saw it in his eyes when she pressed against him.

There was a whisper of protest in her mind, but she ignored it.

Perhaps she could learn how to please a man in the

bedchamber. How to make him delirious with desire for her so that he loved her, whether he wished to or no. That's how Tess had done it. Imogen had seen her: she let her husband kiss her at the racetrack, surrounded by people. Lucius had kissed Tess in the open, where anyone might see them. She herself would never have allowed Draven such a liberty.

Fool! She was a fool! If she had enticed Draven into such liberties, perhaps he wouldn't have left her and walked down to the track, and found out that his jockey didn't want to ride that devil of a horse, and decided to ride him . . . he would have stayed at her side.

Safe.

Alive.

The ratafia was so sickly sweet that the danger of tears receded. She drained the glass. Why should she sit about mourning Draven when she could be—

The pain caught her heart and wrenched it so hard that she almost gasped aloud.

How could Draven be dead? Automatically she started to count to ten but it was too late. She could feel a sob tearing its way up her chest.

The only person who loved Draven besides herself was Draven's mother. And when Lady Clarice had seen that Imogen was not carrying a child, she simply gave up. She stopped eating, caught a chill . . . leaving Imogen in a world of fools who didn't know Draven, who didn't remember how exquisitely funny he could be, how full of life, how . . .

Tears made the world blurry but one of Lady Mitford's pavilions loomed before her, offering a bench and a canopy of fluttering white silk.

She sat down and launched into a familiar routine. First, she sat rigidly upright. She had discovered that one was less likely to dissolve into tears if one's backbone was straight. Then she counted her breaths: one, two, three. Finally, she turned her thoughts to Rafe's behavior the previous night. How dare he? How *dare* he presume to say anything to her about her behavior? He wasn't her brother, nor an uncle, nor anything to her. He was simply the guardian she had before marrying. He was nothing to her now, and yet he presumed—he *presumed*!

Her eyes narrowed and the tears were gone.

Thank goodness. There was nothing she hated more in the world than letting people see she was crying. She had enough pity from her own sisters. Pity or patronization: it was all the same, and none of it helped this awful bitterness that she could taste in her mouth. Like metal. It wasn't exactly grief; grief tasted more like tears.

Draven was gone. She pushed herself off of the bench.

Six

Annabel was just growing a trifle impatient when she saw Lord Rosseter strolling back toward her. There he was.

She had dressed carefully, given that Rosseter had made a formal offer that very morning. As per her instructions, Rafe had accepted, and all that remained was for Rosseter to personally request her hand.

She was wearing a dress of straw-colored muslin, trimmed in silk tassels. It was demure yet flattering. Rosseter was dressed in a morning coat of pale brown stripes lined with yellow. His cravat was not too elaborate: just precisely right for a garden party. The rightness of it all, even down to the polished tips of his extremely expensive boots, warmed her soul. This was a man who would understand her desire to wear silk next to her skin at all times: understand it, and never question her. She would never have to count pennies again.

She gave him a lavish smile on the strength of it. He

smiled faintly in return and turned to meet her chaperone. But Lady Griselda sent him off to bring her a glass of lemonade.

"I wanted a moment," Griselda said, giving her a smile bright with conspiratorial pleasure. "I think the pavilion to the far right corner of the garden is the proper place. I strolled by earlier and there's no entertainment planned for that pavilion, so you won't be interrupted by a caterwauling singer abusing a lute. It's covered in rose silk, which has a most flattering effect on the complexion—not that you need it, my dear. And finally, if you wish to allow him a small expression of his devotion, you are unlikely to be seen by more than twenty or thirty, and that should ensure that the news travels far faster than an announcement in the *Times* would do."

"An excellent suggestion," Annabel murmured. Now that the moment was at hand, she just wanted to move on. To be safely married, and never have to even think of worrying about money again.

"Remember, your married life begins now," Griselda said. "Be kind but firm. Your every expression will inform Lord Rosseter what liberties he may or may not take. You must train him to understand your every glance. Do you understand, Annabel?"

"I think so," Annabel said.

Rosseter had begun walking back toward them, trailed by a page carrying a tray with a glass of lemonade for Griselda.

"Now, look at that," Griselda said. "You've made a good choice, dear. He acts decisively."

"I suppose so," Annabel said.

"It's not every man with the providence to think ahead and avoid the possibility of staining his clothing,"

Griselda told her. "And I like the fact that he's a bit older than you are. It gives him a sense of depth."

"How old do you think he is?" Annabel said, watching him drift toward them, raising a white hand in response to a remark tossed to him by a friend.

"Oh, at least—well, let's see. I was married to Willoughby when I first met him, but he was by no means a newcomer to the season . . . I would guess forty-three or forty-four. Seasoned but not antique. Perfect!" she said brightly.

Twenty years older than she was . . . it was a bit more of a gap than Annabel had thought. Rosseter's face was ageless, though, so perhaps it didn't matter. After all, men didn't age the way women did.

"No one's ever caught him," Griselda said. Rosseter had stopped and was exchanging greetings with one of the royal dukes, Clarence. "But you seem to have taken him effortlessly, my dear. A true triumph."

"Thank you," Annabel murmured. Rosseter seemed to be truly engaged in talking to His Royal Highness. He wasn't even glancing her way in apology. Annabel felt a prickle of annoyance. He knew perfectly well that she was awaiting his proposal. Was it too much to ask that he actually *do* that particular deed, rather than chatter nonsense with a fat overgrown lummox of an English prince?

As she watched, Rosseter turned to the boy following him and murmured something, and the boy started hurrying toward them with the lemonade.

Annabel turned to Griselda, but Griselda spoke before she even opened her mouth.

"I absolutely agree. Absolutely. Clarence is no reason to delay a proposal of marriage. Rosseter needs to be taught a lesson."

Annabel knew precisely the man to do it. She had just happened to notice that the Scottish earl had shown up again and was standing off to her right, watching an exhibition of tumbling.

"Perhaps you should—" Lady Griselda began, but Annabel ignored her. She didn't need to leave her chair. Instead she looked directly at Ardmore, allowing a little smile to play around her mouth.

His rumpled dark red hair and sculpted shoulders made him look like a medieval knight. In fact, she wouldn't mind seeing him pull back an arrow at the archery . . .

Not for Ardmore, the drifting, sophisticated walk of Rosseter. Ardmore walked through the crowd directly toward her, not even taking his eyes from hers.

"Do you remember what I said about him?" Griselda squeaked next to her. "That is *not* a man to toy with!"

Annabel wrenched her eyes away and smiled at her chaperone. "I'm not going to toy with him, Griselda. He's a countryman, and I think he can be a friend. I'm simply going to ask him to accompany me to the archery stand."

"Ah, archery." Griselda watched Ardmore walking toward them. "I do like a man with a broad set of shoulders."

Annabel noticed from the corner of her eye that Rosseter had seen who was approaching. Undoubtedly, he would now conclude his conversation with the duke. Without thinking about it, she rose and walked toward Ardmore. He truly was a complete opposite of her chosen husband. Every inch of him was Scots, from those sturdy, muscled legs to his strong chin and angled cheekbones. She had no problem imagining him as an ancient Pict, painted blue and wearing just a—

No. She snapped her imagination back where it belonged. The man walking toward her was a Scottish earl in exactly the same cast as her father. In fact, if it turned out that he had a set of racehorses into which he poured every penny in the house, the similarity would be complete.

His smile was all in his eyes. "I have been watching a demonstration of jousting. I begin to imagine myself in a suit of armor," he said, those eyes glinting with laughter.

"And here I was imagining you a Pict," she said, putting her hand on his arm and walking away from Rosseter as if he didn't exist.

One eyebrow shot up. "One of my naked and bloodthirsty ancestors?"

"And mine," she said sedately.

"In that case, why don't we try our skill at the bow and arrow?" he asked, playing directly into her hands.

She glanced back over her shoulder and found Rosseter bowing unhurriedly before Griselda, doubtless apologizing for sending the lemonade by servant rather than his own hand. She turned slightly so that Rosseter could see her face and smiled up at Ardmore.

His eyebrow went up again. It was a good thing that she would never even consider marrying him, because that eyebrow could be really annoying in the long run. There was nothing about Rosseter that was irritating, thank goodness.

If Ardmore had any brains at all, he'd know precisely what she was doing and as her countryman, he should be supportive. Helpful, even.

Sure enough: "Do you want me to walk more slowly so that he can catch up?" Ardmore asked. There was laughter glinting in his voice. Apparently he had decided to be helpful.

"No," she said tranquilly. "I think an exhibition of archery should do it."

"I see what you mean," he said. "Englishmen are distressingly slight in their frames, aren't they? Weedy, almost. But you needn't worry about your children," he added. "After all, you have a Pict or two in your background. Most likely the boys won't get *too* weedy."

"My children will not be weedy! At any rate, women dislike being towered over, you know."

"I've never noticed that," he said, and she thought with annoyance of all those Scottish women who had built up his confidence to these unprecedented heights.

They stopped at the archery tent. A breeze flapped the silk roof, carrying with it a smell of April flowers. There was a pile of bows in the corner. The attendant took one look at Ardmore and handed him one that appeared to have been made out of half a sapling.

Ardmore squinted at the targets, posts with circles painted on them. They were adorned with silk flags, the better to look antique, one had to suppose, and positioned at farther and farther distances.

Then he stripped off his jacket. He was wearing a shirt of thin linen. Annabel had to admit that it wasn't threadworn and actually appeared to be quite lovely material; perhaps it was woven on his estate. He stretched the bow back experimentally. Great muscles rippled on his back, clearly visible through the clinging linen. He turned to the attendant, taking a handful of arrows. He handed all but one to her and gave her a lazy smile. "In case you haven't noticed, your chosen one is approaching. He seems to have found himself an escort."

Annabel looked about. "Oh, that's my chaperone, Lady Griselda. You met her last night when we were first introduced."

"I told you I can't remember anyone's name." Then he blinked. "Did you say Lady Griselda?"

She nodded.

He turned. Griselda was chattering with Rosseter, and looking far too pretty and young to be a widow. In fact, if Annabel hadn't loved her so much, she would have been jealous of her perfect ringlets and lush figure. She looked precisely like what she was: a merry, gossip-loving, adorable lady. A perfect—

Annabel glanced up at the medieval knight next to her, who was all but standing with his mouth open.

"The Earl of Mayne's sister?" he asked.

Griselda and Rosseter moved into a patch of sunlight. Her hair gleamed like the proverbial gold.

"Do you know Mayne?" she asked.

"I met him last night," Ardmore muttered. He turned about and drew the bow back again, but without fitting an arrow.

At that moment, Griselda walked up to them with a twinkling smile. Rosseter bowed with all the tempered nonchalance of an irritated Englishman. Ardmore seemed to be in an excellent mood. He flexed the bow again; Annabel was quite certain now that he was only doing so to show off his muscles, and not for her benefit either.

If Griselda stretched her blue eyes any wider, they'd likely fall out of her head.

"Shall we have a friendly match?" Ardmore said to Rosseter.

"I have no interest in sports," Rosseter said evenly. Characteristically, there was no disdain in his tone or anything that a man might take insult from.

"In that case, how about a match between country-men?" Ardmore said to Annabel.

Griselda laughed. Rosseter shifted his weight from one foot to the other. He said nothing, but she felt his disapproval.

"All right," Annabel said. She turned to the attendant

and gave him a melting smile. The boy scrabbled about and handed her a bow. It was ash, with a pretty curve, but good for nothing. Annabel took a closer look at the bows. "I'll try that yew," she said.

It had a sweet curve. She pulled back the string experimentally. Luckily, the small sleeves of her dress didn't impede her arms in any way.

Ardmore was grinning now, obviously as aware of Rosseter's disapproval as she was. And Griselda was laughing. Then Ardmore drew back his great bow again, muscles flexing through his shirt.

Annabel looked away and met Rosseter's eyes. She read approval in his face: Rosseter thought she was avoiding a display of gross masculinity by looking to him rather than Ardmore.

She picked up her bow and Rosseter put a gloved hand on hers. "You needn't do this," he said.

"I enjoy archery," she said noncommittally, turning so that his hand slid away. The boy handed her a clutch of arrows.

Rosseter lowered his voice. "There's no need to put the Scot in his place. Leave him to his grotesque posturing; Lady Griselda seems to enjoy it."

She glanced over and, sure enough, Griselda's dimples were in full play. She was handing him arrows and Ardmore was plunking them into the target, one after another.

"Kind of her," Rosseter remarked. "I'm sure they won't even notice if we go for a stroll." He put his hand on her bow this time.

"That would be impolite," she said, matching his expressionless tone perfectly.

"Ah," he said.

She took that as assent, not that she need it. Ardmore turned around and said, "Now, then, Miss Essex, what's our challenge?"

She walked over to him, eying the targets. "Three arrows each. You're for that far one, and I'll take the one with the red flag, in the middle."

"Go for the blue one; it's closer," he said generously.

Annabel glanced up and saw that he thought to win. A smile touched her lips. "The center of the target, of course, is that black dot," she told him.

"I'm aware of that."

"Good," she said sweetly. "I just wanted to make sure, given that you seemed to have some trouble hitting it during your practice run."

A slow grin spread over his face. "But there must be a forfeit if this is to be a proper competition, Miss Essex."

Rosseter intervened. "Of course there will be no forfeit. That would give it the coarse air of a public exhibition."

"But you see," Ardmore said, "we Scots are quite coarse."

Annabel frowned at him. Rosseter clearly wasn't entranced with her nationality, and she didn't wish to remind him of it.

"The forfeit is a request," Ardmore said. "A favor that can be demanded at any time and must be paid without question."

"Miss Annabel has no need whatsoever to ask you for a favor," Rosseter said, and now she could hear a thin disdain behind his well-bred tones.

"One never knows," Ardmore said, selecting an arrow. "She has already made several requests of me, and of course I am always glad to help a countrywoman."

Annabel fitted her own bow. Griselda was giggling and helping Ardmore draw on the archer's glove handed to him. Naturally Rosseter just stood to the side as she drew on her own glove.

Suddenly there was a spray of those high, arching trumpets that Lady Mitford liked so much. "A contest!"

shouted the trumpeter. "An archery contest commences at once!"

Rosseter's thin nostrils flared as he stepped back. Annabel realized that he was really angry now. In fact, if she didn't back out of the contest, he might simply stroll away in his elegant striped morning coat and dismiss the idea of marrying her. That was likely how he had remained single all these years.

In a moment they had an audience, a circle of women in fluttering dresses of white and pink, a sprinkling of gentlemen with admiring eyes. Ardmore drew back his bow and let it fly. Annabel suddenly realized that drawing back her bow would make her breasts push forward in an unseemly manner. She glanced at Rosseter. He was still there, waiting for her to make a decision. Didn't it bode well for their marriage that the two of them had no need to exchange a word to know precisely what the other was thinking?

She moved forward to take her shot.

"It appears you didn't quite hit the target," she said to the Scot, allowing just a trace of regret to deepen her voice.

He squinted at it. "It looks good to me."

"Hmmm." She drew back her bow and paused for a moment, looking for that black spot in the center of her target. Then she let fly and the arrow flew like a bird to its nest. She smiled and glanced up at her opponent. He wasn't looking at her target, but at her, and he looked a bit distracted. She glanced down. She had felt her gown strain over her chest when she drew back; after all, such light muslin wasn't designed for sport.

Rosseter was still there, his mouth thin with distaste. Apparently he had decided to give her a second chance.

The attendant hurried over to the targets, his yellow

tights flashing in the sun. He stooped next to her target and then rose. "Miss Essex wins!" he cried.

"Second," Ardmore said, drawing back his bow again.

It was a good shot; Annabel had to give him that. But he was holding his elbow just a fraction of an inch too high in the air. Sure enough, to her eyes the arrow was slightly off target, although he turned to her with a smile that suggested he thought it was square.

"I have heard that spectacles can be quite helpful as one grows older," she said to him sweetly. She drew back her arrow and let it fly immediately. Truly, she had chosen a target that was too easy.

There was quite a cheer when the attendant announced the winner of that round.

But when she looked at Ardmore and thought to see him showing the strain of competition, or even a flash of competitive spirit, he was just laughing. "No matter how this attempt goes, you've won my forfeit. I believe my mistake was in not allowing you to go before me."

"That would have been more polite," Rosseter put in.

Ardmore bowed and motioned to her.

She moved forward, aware of the two men watching her intently. She shook her curls back over her shoulders; they could be distracting. Then she pulled the bow back, slowly, slowly. She could feel her breasts coming forward and up, straining from the bodice of her muslin gown. Finally she let the arrow slip and it sailed home. It was slightly off its target because she'd held the arrow too long.

Ardmore took her place. He drew back the bow just as slowly as she had. Broad shoulders flexed, and he flashed a glance at her. His eyes were almost—almost—guileless, but not quite. She nearly burst out laughing but instead she gave him a delicious smile, one of her very best. For a moment he looked as if he'd been clopped in the forehead. She stepped back. Unless she'd missed her bet, he had held that arrow too long, *and* his elbow was jutting high again.

Sure enough, he missed the target altogether.

Lady Mitford popped up in front of them, beaming happily. "I do so love it when my guests fall into the *spirit* of the times!" she trilled. "Now Lord Mitford and I have a most lovely surprise for the two of you."

She beckoned wildly with her arm and a flower-covered pony cart came into view, being dragged along by two miserable-looking donkeys. Flowers had been woven into their manes and tucked behind their ears.

"You shall be the King and Queen of May!" Lady Mitford said happily. "Of course, it isn't quite May yet, but we thought this was so appropriate to our festival. Lord Mitford and I had planned to be the king and queen ourselves, but since the two of you entered so fully into the spirit of the day, we looked at each other and with one breath, we decided to crown you instead!"

Griselda was laughing and clapping her hands, so Lady Mitford's suggestion must be acceptable from a chaperone's point of view. Annabel hesitated but Ardmore took the decision from her. Without pausing to ask her, he put his hands around her waist and swung her into the pony cart. She gasped but the next second he was in the seat next to her, and the trumpets were blowing again. Lady Mitford handed up a wreath of flowers.

"You must do it," Ardmore said to her, sotto voce. "Look how happy it's making her!"

Surely enough, Lady Mitford was cackling with pleasure.

"There's something wrong, though," Ardmore said. He narrowed his eyes. "You don't look exactly right."

Suddenly his hand darted out and with an unerring touch he pulled three hairpins from her hair.

Annabel gasped. Her hair fell down around her shoulders, rolls of soft golden curls that had taken her maid a full hour to pin to her head. "How dare you!" she said, looking up at him.

But he was settling the wreath of white flowers back on her head. "Hush," he said. "You're a queen."

His thigh brushed against hers as the donkeys started off with a jerk around the garden.

"This is so humiliating," she hissed at him.

But he was grinning broadly. They began a circuit of the garden, Annabel smiling at all the guests and silently cursing her companion. Lord Rosseter looked up at the cart and then turned away. Annabel added a particularly virulent curse to her silent tirade. But actually, she wasn't terribly worried about Rosseter. He would come back, if she wished him to. Or he wouldn't, and she'd find someone else. His censoriousness was a bit worrying.

Then they were back at the beginning, and Lady Mitford was begging to send the cart around the back of the house. "It's just to show the household. They all take such interest in our little Renaissance festival, bless their hearts. I know they'd want to see the king and queen."

So Ewan sent the donkeys around the back of the house as commanded. But it seemed Lady Mitford had misjudged the enthusiasm of her household, for there wasn't a soul to be seen, just curtains drawn against the afternoon sun. The donkeys stopped and began chomping on a rosebush that flanked the kitchen door.

"Perhaps she's alerting the staff to our presence this very moment," Ewan suggested. There was something about Annabel that made him feel reckless, as if champagne were pouring through his veins.

She folded her hands primly. "I believe we should turn the cart about. It's not proper for us to be alone."

He put down the reins. No man of blood and bone would turn down this opportunity. That wasn't innocence he glimpsed in Annabel's eyes, but awareness of him as a man. And Ewan was a man of action, rather than words.

He lowered his head so slowly that she had time to squeak, or say no, as proper maidens did when they were about to be kissed. But she didn't say a word, just looked at him with smoky blue eyes.

His lips brushed hers. They were soft, like the petals of the roses the donkeys were eating, and he wanted to eat her, all of her . . . He rubbed his lips across hers again, stronger now. But she didn't say anything, or make a sound, so he let his lips wander down from that little curve in the corner of her mouth, thinking of her neck, that creamy soft neck, but he didn't want to leave. So he came back and she parted her lips a little and he slipped in between one breath and the next.

And then he had her in his arms, cradling her, and the air was thick with the smell of roses and their tongues were tangling. Her mouth was hot and not at all like that of an innocent maiden but rather— He pushed aside the memory of his first kiss with Bess, a friendly milkmaid. Because this kiss was nothing like Bess's, had nothing in common with Bess's . . .

Annabel had her arms around his neck before she knew what was happening, before she realized that her heart was beating so rapidly that she couldn't breathe— that must be why she couldn't breathe—because she couldn't. Breathe, that is. Not with the way he was kissing her, as if time had stopped and there was nothing left in the world but the King and Queen of May and a cart full of flowers.

Perhaps it was because he was Scots. He kissed long and slow, and there was none of the jostling sense she'd had from Englishmen, as if they kissed while thinking about how to get hold of one of her breasts and wring it like a pump handle. Ardmore's hands were on her back, but they hadn't moved since drawing her close, and he didn't seem to have anything else in mind than the slow tangle of their tongues. It was almost maddening.

In fact, it was maddening. Annabel had been in London for precisely two months, and she'd already been kissed by several men. All of whom punctiliously asked Rafe for her hand in marriage. But their kisses were enough to make her reject their proposals. They pawed and breathed hard, and she couldn't see sharing a bed with someone who sounded asthmatic.

As far as she could see, Ardmore had the opposite response to her. Here they were, just sitting and kissing, and kissing, and her blood was racing but he seemed as calm as ever. He had those great laborer's hands spread on her back but he didn't pull her close to him. And yet she—she—she felt boneless and as if she were about to slump against his chest.

The inequality was unnerving. She pulled back. When he opened his eyes, she revised her idea that he was untouched by the kiss, because there was something deep and hot in his eyes that sent a tingle straight down her thighs. "We must return," she said, keeping her hands around his neck.

He didn't even say anything, just smiled his lazy Scottish smile and bent his head to hers again. And she couldn't help it: she opened her mouth to him and he started kissing her again. And now she could see the attraction of just kissing. Just letting his tongue . . . well. She was trembling. Trembling from a kiss.

This time he pulled back. And his eyes were even

darker and wilder but he had a thoughtful look too. "Will you marry me?" he said. His hands still hadn't moved from her back.

"No," Annabel said, feeling a pang of regret. It'd be nice to marry a man who kissed so well. But kissing wasn't a prerequisite for marriage, and money was.

He didn't say anything, just looked at her. "I spent years dreaming of getting out of Scotland," she said awkwardly, not wanting to mention money because it was too—unpleasant.

He nodded. "I've seen that happen with lads in the village."

"Well, then," she said.

He looked at her once more. "Are you sure? Because I won't ask you again. I need to finish this marriage business and return home."

She smiled at that. "I am sure."

"You could never marry a Scotsman."

"No."

"I regret your decision."

Then they were back in the garden, and Imogen was waiting for them. Her eyes were alight with a brilliant glow that made Annabel uneasy just to see her. But she looked exquisite, like a black-haired princess in a fairy tale.

Before Annabel quite knew what had happened, the King of May had wandered off on the arm of her sister without a backward glance. Annabel took off the wreath of flowers and tossed it into the pony cart.

Two gentlemen bounded up to her like overgrown hounds and demanded the pleasure of bringing the Queen of May to the pavilion for supper.

Willy-nilly, she glanced over her shoulder. Ardmore had got himself between Lady Griselda and Imogen now. He was bending his head toward Griselda.

"I'd love to come," she said coolly. "Why don't you both escort me?"

They bobbed around her, showing every sign of men who would kiss and grab, kiss and pant. Englishmen, both of them.

Seven

Ewan had almost made up his mind. The one lass he could truly fancy didn't want him, or so she said. And he had enough sense to know that dragging a woman back to Scotland when she was bent on marrying an Englishman with a title was not a good start to a marriage. But the black-haired Imogen had such potent despair in her eyes that he felt it in the pit of his stomach.

Even now she seemed determined to drag him off to some solitary bench, as if he were a prize pig at the fair. He didn't mind, as long as all those tears she was saving didn't overflow and drown the two of them. She would be a good choice for wife, surely. She was beautiful, and if he gave her time to recover from her grief, she'd likely be a pleasant partner in all respects. He certainly didn't want a wife who started increasing on the spot: he had more than enough to do without worrying about children for a few years.

All in all, Imogen seemed a suitable alternative. Of course, her guardian was fiercely against the idea, but perhaps the duke would be more amenable on seeing how much his ward wanted to marry him. Why, she looked at him as if she wanted nothing more than to bed him on the spot. She must be desperate to return to Scotland.

He could appreciate it; he felt the same way. London was nothing more than a smoky, smelly mess. His carriage had become tangled in traffic that morning and they ended up standing still as a stock for over an hour.

This party wasn't so bad. But all the high-pitched voices and the repeated shrilling of trumpets were like to give him a headache, if he'd been prone to them. Likely it was a rain-soaked day in Scotland, the kind where you can almost see the lush grass reaching up to meet the branches of trees. And the only sound would be the rain, and perhaps a bird singing, and it would seem as if the very dog daisies were praising God for the beauty of it all. For a moment he closed his eyes, but—

"Lord Ardmore," she was saying, and the misery in her voice was written plain. The poor lass was in a bad way.

He opened his eyes and looked down at her. Imogen, her name was. Imogen, Lady Maitland. He felt a spark of gratitude at being able to remember. "Lady Maitland," he said.

"I'd like to speak to you privately, if I may."

"Of course. There's a bit of land down at the bottom of the garden that's marshy and less frequented by all these folk," he told her.

She gave him a dewy smile that almost had him convinced that she was longing for him to drag her down there and have his way with her. "How very astute of you to remark the place," she cooed.

He thought about defending himself—after all, he

hadn't been searching out trysting places—but gave up. Instead he held out his arm and they tripped along together in silence.

"Has your husband been gone long?" he asked. For all his reasoning that she would be a good candidate for marriage, he felt a queer reluctance to deepen the conversation.

"Long enough," she said, giving him that look again. "I hardly think of him."

Well, if that wasn't a lie, he'd never heard one before.

They walked along some more, she taking little mincing steps because her dress was so narrow it was binding her at the knees. "Perhaps I'd better carry you down this last bit," he said as they neared the slope. "That is, if it won't create a scandal." He glanced back toward the party, but no one appeared to be watching them.

"I don't care about scandal," she said. An idiot could tell that was true. So he scooped her up and carried her down the hill until they reached an wrought-iron bench under a large willow. The tree hung over the riverbank, emerald-green strands meeting the surface of the water and dropping below. It looked like an old dowager trailing her yarns behind her.

But Imogen was looking at him again, all fiery invitation. Ewan felt supremely uncomfortable. This was worse than the day when Mrs. Park, down in the village, caught him stealing plums and threatened to tell his papa. He cleared his throat but somehow the marriage proposal just refused to word itself.

She leaned toward him, and her bosom rubbed against his arm. She was a nicely proportioned woman, though she hung it out for all the world to see. Then she started running a finger over his chest.

He cleared his throat again. She looked at him, all expectant. The offer of marriage just refused to come out.

So she spoke instead, and of course her voice was all low and husky, like the Whore of Babylon's, Ewan had no doubt about that. "This affair is so tedious," she said, slipping a finger under the buttons of his jacket and caressing his shirt.

"I've been enjoying it," he said awkwardly, trying not to move backward. He didn't want to hurt her feelings. She was as vulnerable as a newborn calf.

"I haven't," she said, and she forgot that husky innuendo in speaking the truth. But it was back a moment later. "I'd very much like to . . . get to know you better, Lord Ardmore. May I call you Ewan?"

Now, how in the world had she learned his first name? He'd practically forgotten it himself, he'd been Lord Ardmore'd so much in the past few weeks. "Of course," he said. "And I'd like to know you better as well."

"In that case . . . why don't we spend some time together?" The silky whisper was almost mesmerizing, as was that hand wandering over his chest.

He swallowed. "Of course."

"Good." She straightened. "I'll come to you at eleven o'clock." She looked about to stand up and leave.

"Wait!" He grabbed her wrist. "Are you saying . . . what do you mean, you'll come to me?"

A little scowl knit her brow and perversely, he felt the first pang of attraction for her. "I'll come to you," she said painstakingly. "Since I'm not currently living in an establishment of my own—although I mean to buy a townhouse just as soon as I have a moment on my own— I shall come to you, rather than the other way around."

"At eleven o'clock," he repeated.

She nodded, quite businesslike now.

"At *night*?" he clarified.

That scowl was back. "Of course. I'm generally quite busy taking calls in the morning."

"Ah." Well. They appeared to have different ideas in mind. "I'm not the man for that," he said, rather apologetically.

"No?" She looked stunned.

"No. I've come to London to find a wife, you see."

Now the scowl was really ferocious. In fact, it wasn't adorable anymore, and reminded him dangerously of his Aunt Marge who once broke half a set of Spode china. Against his uncle's head.

"We've no real desire between us," he said gently.

"Yes, we have!" she snapped.

Ewan glanced up the hill, but there was no one watching. Then he reached out and tilted her head back, lowered his mouth to hers, and kissed her. It was pleasant enough, but nothing more. To compare it to that kiss he shared with her sister would be blasphemy.

"You see, lass?"

She glared at him. "If you don't wish to bed me, you needn't make a song and dance about it."

The pain in her eyes was so great that he instinctively put an arm around her shoulder. "Don't touch me!" she shouted. "There are men out there who are more than eager to—to do whatever I wish."

"I've no doubt of that," he said, but she had pulled away from his arm.

"Don't you *dare* pity me!" she hissed. "The Earl of Mayne will do just fine. He's not a limp Scotsman. I can guess why you traveled to London to find a bride! It's because all my countrywomen knew that you had problems in the bedchamber, didn't they? I've heard that sort of news travels fast."

"Thankfully, no," he said. But a sense of alarm was growing in his chest, and he grabbed her hand. "You can't turn to Mayne; I met him last night."

"He wants me," she said, struggling to free herself. "He wants me, and you don't, and that's all there is to it."

"He's too old for you."

Her lip curled. "Mayne is in his early thirties. Since he was engaged to my own sister, I know all about him. And believe me, in all the pertinent facts, he's in prime working order!"

"He's not old in years, in other things," Ewan said, knowing the truth about Mayne without hesitation. It was written on his face . . . a man didn't reach thirty and above without leaving his scandals in his eyes. "Mayne's a rakehell, a man who's slept with far too many women. He's tired."

"Ha!" she said. "*Tired* may be how you'd excuse yourself, but I assure you that Mayne has never disappointed a woman."

"And there've been so many of them."

"Which means it will be all the more pleasurable for me," she said defiantly. "If you don't let go of me, I'm going to scream."

"In that case, you'll have to marry me," he said, and finally the words were easy enough. This poor girl needed rescuing more than any waterlogged kitten he'd ever pulled from the millpond. She was in a desperate way. "Marry me, Imogen. Marry me."

She rolled her eyes. "I'll never marry again, so would you please let go of my hand?"

"Not until you promise to consider marrying me."

"Absolutely not. Release me, if you please."

"I'll release you if you come to my chambers at eleven o'clock tonight," he said.

Her eyebrows rose. "Have you changed your mind, then?"

"A woman with such spirit is always worth a second

thought," he said, hoping she would fall for that non-sense. Which she did. A more naive scrap of a girl he'd never met. Now the only question was whether he could keep her from doing herself some sort of injury to her soul from which she'd never recover.

"I'll come to your chambers, but I'll never marry you," she said clearly.

He let go of her wrist. "I'm staying at Grillon's Hotel. Is this your first tryst, Imogen?" As if he didn't know the answer to that.

She raised her chin. "Yes, it is."

So he was as crude as he could be, to shock her into thinking about what she was doing. "*Affaires* aren't like marriages, you know. You needn't bring a nightgown, because we'll sleep naked, of course. And I do hope that your husband taught you how to pleasure a man."

Color crept into her white cheeks, but he was re-morseless.

"I'm fond of the coney's kiss, if you catch my mean-ing, lass. Of course, a woman of the world, such as you are, won't need any instruction in such matters."

But she had more courage than he gave her credit for. "I don't know everything about pleasuring a man, or perhaps I know nothing," she said.

He could have cried at the look in her eyes.

"I'm willing to learn."

"Then say it: coney's kiss." He bent toward her, knowing how large he was, deliberately looming over her. "Say it, why don't you?"

"No."

"Do you know what a coney *is*?"

"No!"

"Then why won't you say it? Go on: coney's kiss. Say it." He shaded his voice with a dark erotic desire, giving her a liquorish smile, the kind the villain in a melodrama always gives to the poor serving maid. "*Coney's* kiss."

She stared at him, all anger, confusion, and revulsion.

"If you're embarking on a life of ill repute, you'll have to learn many such a phrase."

She jumped away and flew up the slope, so fast that her slippers hardly touched the ground.

Had that worked or not? And if not, what the devil was he to do at eleven o'clock? A stupider idea he had never had.

What the devil was he to do?

The Herb Garden

Common wisdom had it that there were few things more disagreeable than coming face to face with a woman whom one has jilted.

But the Earl of Mayne had never felt that reluctance when it came to Tess Essex, now a happy Mrs. Felton. In fact, he considered himself quite the injured party, given that he had traded in the shreds of his reputation after Felton told him to get out so he could marry Tess himself. Now everyone thought him a despicable rake, who had left a woman at the altar, whereas Felton was hailed as the knight who stepped in to save a lady's reputation and future.

And considering that the Feltons were nauseatingly happy, he rather thought he should take credit for the match. In fact, it was amazing how he seemed to leave a trail of happily married women in his wake. First there was Countess Godwin—and he counted it quite a success that he could think of her without wincing, a full year later—and now there was Tess. Both of them were, by all accounts, blissfully happy, and never mind the fact that he was turning into a permanent bachelor.

Since the countess had rejected him, he hadn't had even a simple intrigue. Nor a mistress. People didn't quite realize it; sometimes he couldn't believe it himself. At this point, he hadn't been in a woman's bed in a year, and given the apathetic state of his interest in the female sex, it was likely to be years more.

Tess smiled at him as he kissed the tips of her fingers, and that made him think about how well they would have got along as a married couple, if only his best friend hadn't decided to take her away.

"Feeling sorry for yourself again?" she suggested sweetly.

"I could have been a happy man," he grumbled.

She smiled at that and walked on, her fingers light on his arm. "I need to ask a favor."

In his experience, when a married woman asks you for a favor, it's often something that leads to pistols at dawn. Still . . . "Has Felton been misbehaving?" he asked with some surprise. It was positively unnerving to sit about with his old friend, the way that smile kept creeping onto his face.

"Not yet," she said. "No, it's about Imogen."

"I met her Scottish beau last night. Rafe was doing his best to persuade the man to marry elsewhere, but I gather Imogen has her own plans. What's the matter, don't you care for him?"

"It's not him that I'm worried about," Tess said. "She would do better with you."

Mayne blinked. "With *me*?"

"Yes."

"Are you talking about marriage or something other?"

"Other," she said, just as calmly as if she were discussing raspberry syllabub.

He cleared his throat. "I'm not quite sure how you missed this pertinent fact, m'dear, but I'm not exactly a proper matron's first choice. And, more to the point, your sister hasn't chosen me for that honor."

"Yes, but you're quite experienced in all that . . ." She indicated *that* with a wave of her hand. "And Imogen—"

"Does your husband have any idea you're speaking to me on this matter?"

"Of course not," she said tranquilly. "Lucius is much occupied with affairs of business."

"I think he would still be interested to know that you're—you're—" But he couldn't think of a polite way to phrase exactly what she was suggesting.

"Let me be more clear," she said. "You haven't had a mistress since the Countess Godwin returned to her husband, am I right?"

He waited for that sour twinge of bitterness, but it didn't come. "I have not."

"Imogen does not truly wish to take a lover. But she seems willfully self-destructive at the moment . . . I'm not sure why. At this rate, she will bankrupt her reputation and ruin herself. She's throwing herself out of the *ton*. Perhaps so she'll never be eligible for marriage again."

"Ah," Mayne said. He could almost understand that kind of grief.

"But hardly anyone takes notice of your *affaires*, and if they do, the scandal seems to wear off within days."

"Humph." It wasn't an attractive picture.

But she didn't stop there. "I'd like you to dislodge the Earl of Ardmore, if you please. You can reuse some of those compliments you wasted on me."

"Tess—"

Quick as a cat, she turned on him before he could even voice all the reasons why this plan of hers would never work. "You *owe* me."

He opened his mouth, but she raised her hand to stop him. "I know that you were merely obeying Lucius when you jilted me, but the truth of it is that you acted as you did from loyalty to your friend, and not loyalty to me, your betrothed. And when Lucius asked you to say nothing to me, you simply galloped away without a second thought. What if I hadn't wished to marry Lucius? What then?"

"That's an absurd line of questioning, because you *did*." But he didn't need her frown to see that she had a good point. "All right," he muttered. "I'll cut out the poor Scot. He probably thinks to marry her, you know. I rather liked him last night, and I'm fairly sure that he said he has to marry well."

"He'll find someone."

Another thought struck Mayne. "What about Rafe? He'll slay me."

"I'm sure you two can work it out between yourselves. Perhaps a fistfight?" She needn't sound so condescending.

"Right. A fistfight. Maybe I can get Rafe drunk first and just trip him up."

She patted him on the arm. "You males know precisely the best way to solve these little problems amongst you."

"Tess. You do realize what this is going to do to my reputation, don't you?"

She cocked her head to the side and looked at him thoughtfully. "Imogen is an extremely beautiful young woman, but also a grievously sad one. If you could see your way to having this *affaire* without engaging in any intimacies, I'd be very grateful."

"That's off the subject. I was pointing out that my reputation is going to be destroyed by first jilting one Essex sister, and then having a highly improper affair with a second, widowed Essex sister."

"Yes," she said thoughtfully. "But darling, if you were

going to miss your reputation, you should have noticed years ago, when it first went missing. Now, if you could get right to work, I'd be very grateful. Because so far today Imogen hasn't shocked anyone, but she has a gleam in her eye that I don't like."

Mayne sighed. "And just how do you interpret that gleam?"

"She had just this look when she went riding over to the Maitland house, and the next thing I knew she had sprained her ankle, and a day after that she'd eloped with Draven Maitland, and the devil take the hindmost. Imogen simply doesn't consider reputation very important. You two should get along very well."

That was another slur, but Mayne let it pass. Obviously, he was being pointed like a bullet in the direction of Imogen, and since there was no way to escape it, he might as well give in.

Eight

Mayne found Imogen was sitting at the banquet next to her sister Annabel. There was a strange sense of isolation about her. Mayne had seen that time and again; he knew precisely what was happening. Imogen was being given the cold shoulder by the *ton*.

He walked over and sat down next to her. She was eating pigeon pie, and (thankfully) looked unperturbed. Some women dissolved into tears at their first snub; others felt deprived if they didn't receive at least one cold shoulder of an evening.

"May I join you?" he said, giving her the special smile he reserved for future *chères amies*.

"Of course." She looked indifferent.

"I am so happy to see that you are out of mourning," he said softly.

"In that case, you'll be disappointed to learn that the fact I'm wearing black means I'm still in mourning."

"Black suits you like no other woman," he said, gazing soulfully into her eyes. She did have beautiful eyes, with bewitchingly long eyelashes. In the old days he would have been after her like a hound scenting a fox.

"Actually, black makes me sallow," she said. "But once I told my modiste to lower my bodice as far as it would go, every man I meet seems to find it a satisfactory color."

Of course, his gaze automatically shifted to her breasts, and then flew back to her mocking face. "There was no need to call my attention to such a lovely aspect of your figure," he said, with just a touch of asperity.

"Actually, there was," she said, taking a deep draught of wine. "You hadn't noticed, had you?"

"I was entranced by the cupid's bow of your mouth," he said.

"Nice phrase," she said, obviously unimpressed.

He suppressed a sigh. Apparently he'd lost his touch, but he couldn't bring himself to give a damn. He could report failure to Tess, and this little episode would be over. After all, in his experience a woman bent on sending her reputation into flames usually succeeded. There was no reason for him to burn to a crisp with her.

But then Imogen glanced at him over her shoulder and said, "So who put you up to my seduction?"

"*What?*"

"You don't know Annabel well enough, so my guess would be Tess." She must have read the truth in his eyes. "Tess! Who would have thought that she could stop thinking about her delectable husband long enough to give me a thought?"

The thought of Tess and her husband seemed to give her a pang, because she got a queer look on her face, like a little girl lost in a storm, and Mayne felt some of his resolution to walk away slip.

"Thank you for the letter you sent after Draven died," she said, abruptly changing the subject.

"I was sorry to miss the funeral. Maitland was a good man with a horse. And a humorous story," he added.

"He was funny, wasn't he?" Imogen said. "I—" She looked away from him and drank some more wine.

Someone brought him a plate of food. He took a bite and choked on its sweetness. Imogen looked back at him, all mocking again, and said, "In the Renaissance, spices were the only way to preserve meat. I think there might be quite a lot of nutmeg in this food. The recipes are all authentic."

"God." He signaled the waiter for wine. Which wasn't quite normal because there were strange, small objects floating about in his glass, but he could live with that.

"How well did you know Draven?" She asked it very casually, as if the answer meant nothing to her, but Mayne hadn't spent his twenties sleeping with married women without learning the ins and outs of a casual question. Imogen very likely knew the answer; she just wanted to talk about her husband. His mother had been the same, after his father died.

"I didn't know him well," he said, wracking his brain for some sort of story he could tell her.

"How did you meet?"

"We met at the Ascot in '12," Mayne said. "Maitland was racing . . ." He paused, trying to remember.

"Seashell," she said. "Remember? He was a chestnut who ran like a dream."

"That's right," Mayne said. "Excitable, wasn't he?"

"He should have won, but he bit his jockey in the ear just before the race, and Draven said it put the jockey off."

"But that was long before you married."

"I had known Draven for years," she said with a lop-sided little smile. "He trained his horses at my father's stable." Then she looked directly at him, and he felt as if he were being struck by her eyes: they were that passionate. The thought drifted through his head that no one would ever look as unbearably sad when he was dead.

"So shall we have an *affaire*, then?" she said, as if the question followed rationally from their talk of her dead husband. "I would guess that Tess placed your jilting of *her* against your seduction of *me*," she said, as cool as a icehouse in July. "It'd be a pity to waste her request. And as it happens, I had initially considered you as a companion."

Mayne repressed a wish to laugh. He was used to choosing his own partners, a fact that the Essex sisters seemed to discount. "Yes. Well—"

"Moreover, I've gotten myself into an entanglement that I would quite like to end," she said. "As a man of the world and one who, as I understand it, has had hundreds of these little trysts, I'm sure you understand what I'm saying."

She was already involved with another man?

Suddenly he felt rather glad that he hadn't married Tess. Scottish girls were too much for his hidebound English soul. "Of course, I'd be happy to aid you in any fashion whatsoever."

"Good. In that case, why don't you take me home, because this food is inedible. Tomorrow I should like to start looking at townhouses. You may escort me."

"Escort you?" The very idea was inconceivable. Didn't she have any idea of the implications of him accompanying her on such an errand? He had never, in all his misspent years, engaged in something so scandalous.

Then she turned to him and said softly, "You didn't think that having an *affaire* with me was going to be a matter of a few rides in the park, did you?"

He cleared his throat again. This woman had such a way of drying up one's words that she should be in the House of Lords.

"Tess likely informed you that I am determined to ruin my reputation," she said, tasting one of the small objects floating in her wine and then spitting it out. Come to think of it, he'd never seen a lady spit in public. "I'm not. I'm simply going to the devil, and if you wish to come along for the ride you may. I'm going to buy a house, and then I'm going to live there, and I don't give a damn what this whole tedious pack of people who call themselves the *ton* has to say about it."

He opened his mouth and closed it again. Suddenly he saw one thing clearly: he did owe Tess something. But this task was Herculean. He had to save Imogen from herself, somehow.

And if he did that—if somehow, by hook or by crook, he saved this woman—perhaps he wouldn't feel so . . . tarnished.

Because he did. He felt tarnished, shabby and dirt-cheap, and not worth his own time in speaking to. And if he were honest with himself, he'd been feeling like that for quite a while now. Deep down, it didn't surprise him that Countess Godwin—the one woman he'd ever truly loved—had rejected him and returned to her husband, even though that husband had a mistress and God knows what other terrible habits. In the balance, he, Mayne, wasn't any better than her husband. But perhaps, just perhaps, he could do amelioration. Was that the right word? Penance.

Trust me, he thought, to find charity work that involves bedding a beautiful woman rather than founding an orphanage. He looked at Imogen again. She was fishing out little pieces of orange rind and cloves and putting them into a straight line.

She didn't need bedding. She just needed time.

Time . . . now, *that* he could buy her.

"Did you say that you had made a previous engagement with someone?" he said. It had to be the Scotsman whom he met last night. Ardmore was a decent fellow.

She nodded, not looking up.

"You'll need to tell him that it's off."

"Don't tell me what to do, *ever.*"

He shrugged. "I don't poach on other men's territory."

For a moment, she smiled. "That's rich, coming from you. The only virtue you have besides your clothing is your ability to seduce married women. My sister Tess always goes to experts when she needs something."

That stung. Apparently he'd taken on a woman who was halfway to being a raving bitch and it looked as if they'd probably be together for a good period of time. A scourging, that's what it was.

The key was to be patient and kind. That was how you were supposed to behave with a bereaved person. "As a matter of fact," he said, schooling his voice carefully, "I have only seduced women whose husbands were all too willing to share."

She laughed shortly. "And that's why you've been in so many duels?"

"Only two." And how in the hell had she heard about those, living in the wilds of Scotland? "When I was young and stupid. So I'd like you to clear out my rivals, if you please, Imogen."

She narrowed her eyes at him. "I didn't give you permission to use my first name."

"Under the circumstances, I took the liberty. Would you like to call me Garret?"

She thought about it. "No. I prefer Mayne. I'll write Ardmore a note."

"In person," he clarified. "These things are done in person. You made something of a fool of him, by all accounts, at that ball last night. You certainly damaged his chance to marry a proper young lady. You might want to offer an apology as well."

"I'll apologize when hell freezes," she said, stung. "You didn't hear what he—he said to me—he—"

"Frightened you, did he?"

"Never!"

"Offended you, then," he guessed. "Ardmore must not have much experience of tenderly raised women who decide to go wrong. I've found that married ladies remain just as squeamish and proper as they were in their husbands' beds. It's one of the things that makes *affaires des coeur* stale so quickly."

She shot him a murderous look.

"I can take you home, but I can't escort you to look at houses. If I did so, Rafe would likely murder me, which is a distinct possibility even so. Where is Rafe?"

"He stayed home, the better to drown himself in a barrel of brandy," she said unemotionally.

Mayne coughed. "Do you always aim for the jugular?"

"Why bother with flummery? Rafe is a sot, and has been for years. We had someone in the village like that. He won't live long, at this rate."

"He doesn't drink that much."

"Watch him. He does."

"He never used to drink to excess until his brother died."

"Perhaps I should take up brandy," she muttered.

"It'll make you fat and give you red veins in your nose."

She seemed struck by that.

"If we're going to do this, we might as well do it with finesse. I suggest we join the dancing. But no hanging on me the way you did with Ardmore last night."

She opened her mouth but he kept talking. "No finesse. Nothing interesting for the *ton* to talk about except the excesses of a shameless trollop. And *that's* a tedious story, and oft told."

Her eyes looked so murderous that he almost choked, but he plowed ahead. "We're going to stage something altogether more interesting: a pursuit. I'm going to pursue you, and you are not going to simply fall into my arms."

"Why not?"

"Because you're a novice at this business," he said.

"I'm a fast learner."

He leaned over and tipped up her chin. "One of the secrets of the human race, Imogen. Easy women are tedious. I *never* bed tedious women. Everyone knows that. So you need to be a little less forthcoming than you appeared to be last night. I'm prepared to throw away the last shards of my reputation, but I am not prepared to have it said that I've sunk to taking on a woman so desperate that she hung herself out like washing on the line!"

She turned a little white. "You are very blunt."

"We will dance, and I will flirt with you, but you will not flirt back. As the music is ending, I will lean toward you and whisper something in your ear. And you will slap me, as hard as you can, and then proceed to call for your carriage."

"Are you recuperating my reputation?"

"Only in order to take it away," he said. "I mean to have you: but I have to make you into someone worth having first, if you see what I mean. After last night, no one would believe that I would spend a night with you. I have my own kind of reputation, and if we're going to make this believable—"

"I need to be more attractive," she said flatly.

"Interesting," he clarified.

"Because trollops are tedious."

"Precisely."

Imogen was about to tell him to go to the devil, when the truth slid into place with a devastating jolt. Easy? She'd been nothing more than easy for Draven. She'd put herself in his way for years, fell out of an apple tree at his feet, fell off her horse so that she could get into his house . . .

If she hadn't been so easy, perhaps he would have— The truth blinded her and made her feel unable to breathe.

She turned back to Mayne. He held out his hand and she rose.

Naturally, complicated old-fashioned dances were being played, the kind where you see your partner for two seconds and then twirl away into the hands of another. But Mayne caught the eye of the orchestra leader, and a second later, a gold coin was snugly nestled in the man's pocket. The master of ceremonies called "A waltz by Franz Schubert!"

Imogen curtsied. Mayne bowed. He held out his hand and she took it. "Don't come close to me," he said to her, sotto voce. "At some point I'll try to pull you against my body; I'd like you to visibly resist."

She nodded. The music lapped around them, Schubert at his sweetest and saddest. He glanced down and found her eyes were dark and teary.

"Don't you dare cry!" he hissed. "That would ruin everything."

"Draven and I never danced together," she whispered.

"Good thing. You're not keeping the beat very well, are you? That's the second time you've trod on my feet. It might have been enough to put Maitland off."

Thankfully her chin rose and she glared. He smiled down at her, the serpentlike smile of a man preparing a seduction. From the corner of his eye he saw Lady Felicia Saville, one of his less lovely conquests of the past, eyes wide.

Deliberately he spread his hand on Imogen's back and pulled her toward him. She sprang back as stiff as a spring and glared at him.

"So why can't you dance?" he asked, giving her a smile as sizzling as he could make it.

She frowned at him. "Because my father didn't have enough money to keep a dancing master, that's why!"

He moved his hand caressingly just as he twirled her about, so that Felicia could have an eyeful. Then he smiled again, the cool, calculating leer of a rake.

"I don't like your face when you do that," Imogen said suddenly. "It makes you look quite dissolute."

"Getting your own back for the trollop comment?"

"Telling the truth." Her eyes fell. "As you were, I suppose."

Thankfully the dance was drawing to an end; he was feeling quite battered by Imogen's loving comments. Perhaps he'd crawl off and join Rafe in his barrel of brandy. Then he remembered how enraged Rafe would be when he heard of this dance.

"All right," he said to her, "I'm going to whisper in your ear, and then you slap me."

He leaned in to her just as the music stopped, brushing her hair aside with a tender hand, whispering, "I'll come for you tomorrow, at three o'clock in the afternoon."

She sprang back, eyes flaming. Then she drew back her hand and whacked him in the cheek, jerking his head back.

When he straightened, she leaned toward him with an assassin's smile on her face. "I enjoyed that," she said. "And I just want to make one comment." Her eyes were so sharp that they could have cut stone. "I don't mind

slapping you, but if you ever think that I'm doing anything by the name of a coney's kiss, you're wrong!"

"A *what*?" he said, but she was gone.

He rather of liked the sound of it, although it was
probably something he knew of under a far more pedan-
tic title.

Perhaps something Scottish?

He grinned. Perhaps his penance would not be entirely
cheerless.

Nine

Griselda had promised to attend a debut ball being given for the daughter of a friend, and she was justly irritable at the idea that she must delay her departure and accompany Imogen to Grillon's Hotel.

"A hotel!" She said it with all the loathing of a woman who would never enter a hotel of her own volition.

In her voice Imogen heard the echo of Mayne's label, *trollop*. "I can't go alone, Griselda," she said steadily. "Annabel will come with me, but it's not proper for the two of us to make that visit alone."

"Of course it's not!" she snapped. "Dragging your sister into a place like that."

"So I'm asking you. I made a mistake," Imogen admitted. "You were right." Tears welled up in her eyes. "You were right about Ardmore and I was wrong, and I'm sorry. Please help me to get out of this, Griselda."

"I suppose you can't just send him a note," she muttered.

"Mayne said not."

Griselda's head swung up. "Mayne? So my brother is involved in this, is he?"

"He's the one who—who told me that I had to apologize to Ardmore in person," Imogen said, a tear spilling down her cheek at the humiliation of it all.

"Mayne is always right in these matters," Griselda said resignedly. "Lord knows, he's had years of experience. And you did put the earl in an awkward position last night. I expect Ardmore will have to explain you away before he can make a proposal to a decent girl's father."

Imogen swallowed. "I didn't think about him."

"No." And then: "All right. We'll be unfashionably late to Lady Penfield's ball and doubtless I'll have to hear about it for the next month or so. She's so anxious to have this ball of hers a success. Perhaps Mayne could accompany us . . . that would at least ensure his presence. Lord knows why matchmaking mamas still want him around, but they seem to."

"He might fall in love someday," Imogen said doubtfully, picturing Mayne's Lucifer-like exhaustion. After their conversation, she no longer had the faintest belief that he would fall in love with her.

"One can always hope," Griselda said. "Now, what are you going to wear tonight, darling?"

"Black," Imogen said.

"Not too low in the bosom. You don't want to entice a man when you're begging his pardon."

Imogen never wanted to *see* Ardmore again, let alone beg his pardon, but she stiffened her back. Maybe she'd make him beg her pardon too. For saying such a horrible thing in her presence. That horrible . . . word. Whatever it meant.

By a quarter to ten that evening, Imogen, Griselda and

Annabel were bundled in their pelisses against the chill of an April night and trundling toward Grillon's Hotel. Griselda was fretting that they would be seen. "I've never entered such a place," she kept saying.

"It's just a hotel," Imogen said.

"No one stays in hotels," Griselda snapped. "The implication is that you have no family in the city. No one in London to stay with! You're an outcast."

"Ardmore doesn't seem to be an outcast," Annabel put in, picturing the way the *ton* had welcomed him with open arms.

"Oh, he's a man, titled, and from the north country. It's all different for men. Besides, he's clearly staying in a hotel because he's too short in the pocket to rent a townhouse, or at the very least a suite of rooms, for the season, the way someone with a reasonable estate might. His residence is one of the clearest signs of his impoverishment. No one would stay in a London hotel unless he had to: robbery and theft are commonplace, as I understand it. They'll take the very linens from your bed while you're lying in them!"

"But Griselda," Annabel objected, "you yourself read us that piece of news about the Russian ambassador, and he was staying at this same hotel, if I'm not mistaken."

"Ardmore is not a woman," Griselda said. "For a woman even to be glimpsed in a hotel is to risk her reputation." The carriage began to slow down and she pulled up the rosy hood of her pelisse, tucking her curls inside. "With luck, we'll be in and out of that building without meeting a soul. Surely everyone who counts will have already embarked on their evening."

"What could anyone possibly think we were doing, if we *did* encounter someone we knew?" Annabel asked. "Three women, two of whom are widowed, do not enter hotels together for nefarious purposes, Griselda."

"Believe me, the implication is all that's needed!" she snapped. "Widows are particularly vulnerable to this sort of ugliness. Do you know how many jests there are about lusty widows? And the ballads! There's a horrid one about widows who have *sipped bliss* before. Something like, *If you'd win a widow, you must down with your breeches and at her!*" She was getting more and more agitated but the carriage was at a halt now. They had taken a hired hack so that Holbrook's crest wouldn't be recognized.

"Wait for us!" Griselda commanded the driver. "Don't you *dare* go anywhere! We'll only be a moment."

Annabel looked at his smirk and realized exactly why three hooded women would enter a hotel. He clearly thought that they were on business, so to speak. "I'm at your service, ladies," he said cheerfully.

"Rafe will kill us for this," Griselda moaned.

Annabel thought that Rafe would have a point. Still, the antechamber of the hotel was beautiful, with huge arching ceilings and various pieces of statuary that were as fine as any she'd seen in any formal garden.

Griselda clutched Imogen's arm. "What are we supposed to do now?"

Imogen shook her head. "He didn't say anything. I suppose we have to be announced."

Luckily, as they stood like an indecisive group of country bumpkins, an officious-looking man strode over to them. "Now, then, ladies, what can I do for you?"

There was a shading in his voice that suggested he had jumped to the same conclusion as the driver, at least until Griselda drew herself up to her full height, pulled back her hood slightly and gave him a look.

A second later he was bowing so low that his nose could have touched his knees, and apologizing for keeping them waiting, and asking if there was any possible way that he could aid them.

"We must speak to these ladies' cousin for a moment," Griselda told him, giving him a measured smile. "And since we have condescended to even *enter* this establishment, Mr. . . ."

"M-Mr. Barnet," he stammered. "We are honored by your entrance, my lady."

"Just so," she said, unimpressed. "As I was saying, since we have condescended to enter this establishment, Mr. Barnet, I am naturally worried about the consequence of our rash action. Therefore, I would request that we be shown to the Earl of Ardmore's chambers immediately."

"I shall do so myself," Mr. Barnet said.

Griselda gave him a slightly bigger smile, and he began walking toward an imposing staircase.

"His lordship has the best suite of chambers in Grillon's," he said, ushering them up red-carpeted stairs that were as grand as any found in a duke's palace. "I assure you, my lady, that hotels have changed a great deal from merely twenty years ago. This is a most respectable establishment, with only the very best clientele."

"Humph," was Griselda's only response.

A moment later they were ushered into a sitting room by Ardmore's manservant, who seemed delighted to welcome ladies to his master's chambers, even ladies inadvisably visiting late at night. Once he left to bring Griselda a glass of ratafia, Annabel threw back her hood and wandered over to the mantelpiece, which was adrift with invitations.

"This is a lovely room," Griselda said, clearly feeling much better now that they were snugly inside without having been seen by anyone of consequence. "Quite nice. I do like Hepplewhite's early furniture. Annabel, do not take off your pelisse. We will be here for only a moment."

Two seconds later the earl himself strolled through one of the five doorways leading from the sitting room. "What a pleasure," he said, seemingly unmoved by the fact that instead of one widow, bent on an errand of wicked pleasure, he was faced by three women, one of whom was known throughout London for her impeccable reputation.

But Griselda wasn't going to waste any time with pleasantries. "Lady Maitland has something to say to you," she announced, with all the preemptory tone of a governess. "And after she's said it, we shall leave you to your evening, and you will kindly forget that we were ever here."

"To hear is to obey," Ardmore murmured, but he glanced over at Annabel and there was a twinkle in his eye that made her think he remembered their kiss. Or was remembering their kiss. Or— Annabel turned away and examined one of his invitations as if it were passionately interesting.

"Lord Ardmore," Imogen said, moving forward into the center of the room and clasping her hands, "I wish to inform you that I shall not pursue the relationship that you and I discussed."

He bowed, most graciously it seemed to Annabel, who was pretending to read yet another invitation. "I am most happy to hear that," he said, and the ring in his deep voice seemed sincere enough.

"Excellent," Griselda said, bustling out of the corner of the room and taking Imogen's arm.

"I have one more comment," Imogen said, stopping Griselda from pulling her from the room. "I'm not quite a ninny, Lord Ardmore. I realized this afternoon that—"

There was a knock at the door and a nearly simultaneous moan from Griselda.

His manservant bustled out of one of the side doors and said, without opening the door, "His lordship is not receiving."

"It's Mr. Barnet, sir," came the voice of the hotel manager, sounding quite harassed. "I'm afraid his lordship has an urgent visitor."

"The visitor can wait," the valet said, after a glance from his master. "Keep him downstairs, if you please, Mr. Barnet."

"I'm sorry, but this cannot wait," Mr. Barnet replied, and to Annabel's horror, the knob began to turn.

"It must be Rafe!" Griselda hissed, her eyes wide. "Quick!" She pulled Imogen through one of the doors to the side of the room.

Ardmore looked at Annabel and he had that funny little half-smile again, so she felt quite safe and rather as if she were acting in a poorly written melodrama. She slipped behind the huge velvet curtain next to the fireplace—because that, after all, is just what a heroine in a melodrama would do.

That very second the door slammed open.

It wasn't Rafe.

Ten

There were two of them, and they both held large, murderous-looking calvary carbines. Annabel stood as quietly as she could behind the curtains, watching through a gap. One of them had his gun poking into poor Mr. Barnet's back, and the second pointed a gun at the Earl of Ardmore. Ardmore looked as unconcerned as he had the moment before.

"Was there something that you wished, gentlemen?" he asked.

It seemed that the very nonchalance of his voice irritated them, because they scowled. Even though she had a growing feeling of fear, Annabel found it interesting. She would have thought that ruffians of this nature came with unshaved faces and rough-and-tumble clothing. They would swear and spit on the ground. At least those were the men that her father had always indicated were dangerous.

Mr. Barnet was babbling an apology, something about being caught in the hallway . . .

These must be London criminals. They looked like gentlemen, really. One was slender and dark-haired. He was wearing a velvet coat, and had a watch chain slung across his waistcoat. He smiled, and she could see clearly that he had every one of his teeth.

"We came across this upstanding man doing a bit of eavesdropping outside your door, my lord," he said. Annabel hoped that Griselda hadn't heard that comment. "I'd be most grateful if you would sit comfortably on the settee," the robber continued. His voice was as educated and respectable as she'd ever heard. Still, since her father had trained his daughters to speak without a Scottish burr, one had to suppose that anyone could learn to speak like an English gentleman.

Ardmore strolled over to the settee in question, his manservant and Mr. Barnet following when the second robber motioned with a wave of his gun.

"You see, my lord," the suave robber said, "I'm going to ask Mr. Coley here to enact a brief search of your bedchambers."

Annabel gasped. Mr. Coley was heading directly for the door leading to the room into which Griselda and Imogen had vanished. She hoped they had had the sense to hide. She started to breathe again when there wasn't a sound except for the slam of a wardrobe, and what was likely a desk drawer.

Annabel could feel anger growing in her. Poor Lord Ardmore didn't have any money and already had to stay in a hotel. And now these men were going to take what little funds he had, and probably any jewelry he had as well? Yes, they definitely were.

"I'll trouble you for your signet ring," the suave robber said. "And any other finery you have about you. I'd hate to have to lay hands on a peer of the realm." There was something mocking in his voice that made Annabel even more enraged.

If she could just strike one of the robbers from behind, then . . . She stepped back from the velvet curtains and looked about her. She was standing in a deep window leading to a balcony, and there wasn't even a lamp she could throw. But perhaps . . . the window was ajar. She pushed it open with the tip of one finger and peered over the balcony.

Below her was a carriage, horses stamping, steam coming from their nostrils. A burly carriage man was standing at their heads. Unfortunately, it wasn't Griselda's carriage. And how was she to get the coachman's attention without warning the robbers?

She could try to drop her reticule directly onto the head of the coachman. But then he was sure to simply shout something up to her, which would cause the robbers to realize her presence—and that would merely lead to the loss of her ear-bobs.

The only thing to do was scream. Loudly. Then the coachman would dash into the hotel, and—

The door to the coach swung open and out stepped an unmistakable figure, from the tip of her lorgnette to the pointed toes of her slippers: Lady Blechschmidt. Annabel gasped and drew back from the railing. Lady Blechschmidt was one of the most moral ladies in London, her reputation for upstanding behavior only matched by her pious indignation at the behavior of less prudent mortals. Moreover, she was one of Griselda's friends, although even Griselda thought she was occasionally harsh in her assessments.

At the moment, Lady Blechschmidt seemed to be talking to her coachman. She was probably going to send him away, and that would be the end of Annabel's chance to attract attention before the robbers took every penny belonging to the earl. But if she screamed, what would Lady Blechschmidt think of her presence in Lord Ardmore's chambers? It didn't take a genius to answer that.

She tiptoed back through the door and put her eye to the crack between curtains. The robbers were back together now and—

It was awful. Even as they watched, the first robber laughed and said something, and Lord Ardmore, his face so grim that it made her quail to look at it, started pulling off his cravat. His cravat? They were going to steal his cravat?

Then she heard what the robber was saying. "You see, my lord, in my extensive experience, I've found that gentlemen don't willingly give me every gewgaw they may have around them. There might be something in your pockets that we'd like to take with us. Your coat will fetch a pretty penny, and the time it takes you to pull your smalls back on will be just long enough for us to stroll out of the hotel without fuss. Because I *do* dislike unpleasantness, and I'd hate to have to shoot anyone."

Annabel took one look at Ardmore's furious, set face, and the way he tossed his cravat onto the settee, and she dashed back to the railing. Her mind was made up. Ardmore couldn't lose everything he had, down to his very clothing, to these villains. What would he do? How could he possibly find a rich bride to marry without a coat to his name? Imogen had already dented his reputation.

Besides, Griselda was in the next room . . . surely her presence would quell Lady Blechschmidt's sharp tongue.

Lady Blechschmidt was just turning from her coachman. Leaning over the balcony, Annabel threw back her hood and screamed, "Robbers! Up here! *Help!*"

Lady Blechschmidt looked about confusedly, but her

burly coachman jerked back his head, took one look and ran into the hotel, followed by two groomsmen. Annabel opened her mouth to shout an explanation to Lady Blechschmidt, when a rough hand fell on her shoulder and pulled her backward so quickly that she dropped her reticule over the side. Which meant that at least the robbers couldn't steal her handkerchief.

The man practically threw her into the sitting room. She spun across the room and was about to slam to the ground when a pair of large hands caught her and the earl pulled her back against his chest.

"He had a ladybird on the balcony," growled the second robber.

"We should have searched the bloody apartment," the first robber said, not sounding so gentlemanly anymore. "There had to be a reason that damned fool was listening at the door." He pointed his carbine at Ardmore. "Don't try any heroics, my lord."

Then they were gone, before Annabel could even blink.

"Are you all right?" Lord Ardmore asked her, spinning her around and smiling, even though all his money and his ring were gone. His voice didn't have a trace of disquiet in it . . . it was the same husky, compelling Scottish burr that—

She snapped her eyes shut. "Your clothes!" she moaned.

His hands dropped from her shoulders and she heard his deep voice say, "Throw me my pantaloons, Glover." At the same time, the door slammed open on its hinges and she heard men running heavily in the corridor. But her hands didn't fall from her eyes until she heard the acid tones of Lady Blechschmidt in the corridor, demanding to be told the explanation for *all this*.

Annabel dropped her hands. Thankfully, the earl had

his pantaloons on. He was just pulling on a shirt, though, and she couldn't help noticing that his chest looked like that of the statues of Roman gods she'd seen in the British museum at Montagu House, all rippled with thick muscle, narrowing to a taut waist. But white, still marble looked very different from golden skin, dusted with the faintest shadow of hair—

He looked over at her, and she felt a blush rising in her cheeks. Then his shirt came down over his head, and Lady Blechschmidt's coachman walked into the room, saying, "They've caught two men downstairs with some rings and such."

Annabel swallowed. It was over. Almost. Lady Blechschmidt was staring at her, and there was a pucker between her brows. "Just what are you doing in these chambers, young woman?" she said. There was an icy tone in her voice that made Annabel shiver.

But she raised her chin. "We paid a visit—"

Lady Blechschmidt broke in. "*We?*"

Annabel gasped. "Imogen! Imogen, are you all right?" She ran back to the door that led to Lord Ardmore's bedchamber and flung it open. The room was empty. The door of the wardrobe slung open, the arm of a shirt hanging from the shelf. The drawer of the little writing desk had been thrown to the floor.

There was only one possible place for them to be. She fell to her knees and lifted the heavy counterpane that hung to the floor on three sides of the bed. "Griselda? Imogen?"

Sure enough, something was moving in the darkness. "Annabel, is that you?" Imogen squeaked.

"Come out, darling, it's all over."

A second later Griselda and Imogen scrambled out.

"What happened?" Imogen cried, at the same time that Griselda looked down at herself and realized that she was covered with dust and bed fluff and stray cotton from the mattress. Her shriek was far louder than Imogen's question.

Lady Blechschmidt appeared in the doorway in a moment. "Lady Griselda!" she said, coming to a stop so quickly that the earl bumped into her from behind.

"Is everyone all right?" he asked, looking over Lady Blechschmidt's head into the room. "You weren't hurt, were you?"

"All right!" Griselda said on a rising shriek. "Of course I'm not all right, you—you nincompoop! Look at me! I was due at Lady Penfield's ball hours ago and—and just look at me!" A dust curl hung from her pelisse button; she was covered with a thin layer of whitish-brownish dirt, and there was a huge smudge on one cheek where she had clearly rested it against the floor.

Mr. Barnet entered the room behind the earl. "*You!*" Griselda said, pointing at him with a rising shriek. "This is all your fault! How dare you allow robbers into the room when we were there. How *dare you!*"

"They had a gun at my back," Mr. Barnet said, nervously rubbing his hands together.

"I'll have your position," Griselda said, advancing on him. "I'll have your position due to the extreme uncleanliness of this hotel, if not for putting myself and my wards into extreme danger."

"But precisely what were you and your wards doing in a gentleman's chambers at this hour of the night?" Lady Blechschmidt inquired. "I should not have expected such behavior of *you*, Lady Griselda."

"Nothing untoward!" Griselda said, turning away from the hapless Mr. Barnet. "I find it hard to believe that you would even imply such a thing after our long years of acquaintance."

"Since I was responsible for halting the robbery in

midprogress," Lady Blechschmidt observed, "I believe that I am owed a reasonable explanation."

"You are owed nothing," Griselda said magnificently. "If you cannot respect me enough to accept without a second's thought that I would never involve myself in an injudicious action, then we are friends no longer!"

"My carriage broke down on the way to the ball," the earl said, stepping forward. "Lady Griselda and her charges merely escorted me to the hotel, when we were caught by armed men."

Lady Blechschmidt looked at him. "I know who you are," she said slowly. "You're that Scotsman who made such an exhibition of yourself on the dance floor. You are—or were—considered something of a catch."

He bowed. "At your service."

She turned back to Griselda. "While I have the utmost sympathy for your plight, Lady Griselda, and particularly for the deplorable state of your clothing at the moment, I just wish to note that the presence of these young ladies, one of whom"—she nodded toward Imogen, who was trying to brush dirt from her pelisse and only making it look worse—"created a scandal but two nights previous with *this particular man,* is suspicious. That's all I shall say about it. I shall make no suppositions, I shall simply—"

She faltered and stepped back as Griselda advanced toward her. Normally Griselda resembled a lush female angel rather than an avenging Archangel Michael. But at the moment her face was so chilly that it would have taken a stronger person than Lady Blechschmidt to withstand her. "Emily Blechschmidt," she said through clenched teeth, "if you ever say a word about this evening, or if one of your servants ever murmurs something to a friend, there will be hell to pay!"

Lady Blechschmidt tittered nervously. "Well, I hardly

think that I would say anything, but as for the servants, you know what—"

"Don't even finish that sentence," Griselda snapped. "Your servants are as well trained as mine. You will ensure that they say nothing, *if* you please!"

"I certainly don't know why you're taking this so much in affront! Naturally, I shall caution the servants to share nothing of this unusual evening. I shall particularly direct them to ignore the fact that Miss Essex was in the company of the earl, who was *disrobed,* while you were ensconced under the bed in quite a separate room!"

But Griselda's eyes were narrowed. "What were you doing here?" she demanded.

"I?" Lady Blechschmidt said indignantly. "Why, my coachman dashed up here to rescue your friends from these ruffians, and—"

"What are you doing at Grillon's Hotel?" Griselda's voice was much calmer now, but still remorseless, and Annabel, tightly holding Imogen's hand, thought she saw the shadow of a smile. "You are due to Lady Penfield's ball, just as I was."

"I have been to Lady Penfield's ball, and a pitifully thin affair it was. I left with a headache."

"You left with a headache," Lady Griselda said, "and then somehow you ended up at Grillon's? Really, Lady Blechschmidt, you surprise me."

The room was so quiet that Annabel heard herself breathing.

"I shall ensure my servants' silence," Lady Blechschmidt said. "Peters!" Her coachman appeared from the adjoining room. "It is time to go home."

And she stalked from the room a moment later, without further farewell, apology or comment.

Griselda turned to the hapless Mr. Barnet. "I shall return tomorrow," she announced. "I shall return tomorrow and I shall speak to the owner of this hotel, who I believe is a distant acquaintance of my husband's uncle. A Mr. Reardon, is it not?"

Mr. Barnet was blinking rapidly. "I assure you, madam, that—"

"I have nothing more to say to you," she snapped. "Imogen, Annabel. Follow me to the carriage, if you please. And put your hoods up!"

Obediently Annabel and Imogen pulled up their hoods and followed their chaperone from the room. For someone who usually strolled in such a way as to accentuate her entirely feminine curves, Griselda could stalk like the best sort of avenging angel when she wished.

In the carriage, she twitched a dust curl from her pelisse and said, "This evening never happened. Do you understand?"

Annabel nodded.

Imogen said, "I'm so sorry, Griselda—"

But Griselda cut her off. "Never. Speak. To. Me. Of. This. Again."

Annabel exchanged glances with her sister. Imogen squeezed her hand, and leaned over. "I was so frightened for you," she whispered. "I don't care in the least about my reputation, and I'm a widow anyway. But you—"

The very thought made Annabel's throat tighten. "We were lucky," she whispered back.

"I can scarcely believe it. I thought there was no escape from Lady Blechschmidt."

Annabel glanced with affection at their chaperone, who was sitting with her eyes closed as if the very effort to stay upright were leading her to faint. "I have the feeling that Griselda generally gets what she wants, don't you?"

Imogen smiled and squeezed her hand.

Who but Griselda could save Annabel from a situation

in which one of the most prudish members of the *ton* walked into a bedchamber to find Annabel in company with a half-clothed earl? She had worked a miracle.

Until the miracle stopped working, that is.

Eleven

The blow descended, as bad news so often does, in the form of *Bell's Weekly Messenger,* a gossip sheet delivered promptly at eight o'clock every Thursday morning.

The Duke of Holbrook's butler, Brinkley, accepted the sheet from the hands of a delivery boy and walked in his measured way back to his parlor, where he intended to iron the gossip sheet and deliver it crisp and fresh to the bedside of Lady Griselda, accompanied by a cup of rich hot chocolate and an unbuttered rusk, since her ladyship pursued a rather erratic policy designed to reduce her hips. But after one glance at the sheet, he almost burned the newsprint with his iron.

Brinkley wouldn't have been surprised if the article had talked of Lady Maitland. The whole household had heard of the state in which *she* returned to the house the previous night: her pelisse filthy, according to her maid, fairly covered with smudges, as if she'd been lying on the ground. The implications of that statement were too scandalous to be countenanced, and Brinkley had felt it necessary to give a round scolding to all members of the household who even heard the account.

For a moment he paused, hands fluttering in uncharacteristic dismay. The piece didn't mention Lady Maitland. Which meant there were two scandals lurking about to disrupt the peace of the household.

It should go to the master, even though the master never rose before noon, and would have a terrible head from the brandy he'd downed the night before. Brinkley took the precaution of having the cook fix a restorative draught to take with him.

So, with a silver tray laden with a gently fizzing drink and a crisply folded newspaper, Brinkley walked into the master's darkened bedchamber.

He was greeted by a moan. "Who the hell is that?"

"Brinkley, Your Grace," he said, averting his eyes while the master fought himself out of a tangle of linen sheets. Sleeping in the buff, he was. Leave it to the nobility to act like the poorest in the nation. "I am most sorry to disturb you."

"What are you doing in my room?" the duke finally said groggily. "Is the house burning down?" He must have thought his head was on fire, from the way he was clutching it.

Brinkley felt a flash of sympathy. He held out the salver. "*Bell's Weekly Messenger* has arrived," he said, in a tone of suitable gloom.

"Damn that to hell," the duke said, lapsing back and pulling a pillow over his head. "You've lost a cog. Bring it to Griselda."

"Your Grace will wish to see the *Messenger* personally."

"No, I won't." The butler waited. After a few moments the pillow fell to the side and the duke snatched the paper from his salver. "Open those curtains, Brinkley."

He drew back the drapes. His Grace was staring, red-eyed, at the gossip sheet. "What in the bloody hell am I supposed to be looking at?" he demanded. "Not that I can ever understand the way they phrase things."

It was true that the duke never paid attention to gossip. Unfortunately, the rest of London would decode precisely who was being referred to. "The second item in the right column, Your Grace," he said.

Holbrook squinted at it. "Damn this head of mine . . . *A certain golden-haired Miss A. E——* . . . I suppose that's Annabel . . . *was discovered with a certain red-haired earl, in his bedchamber* . . . Nonsense! Pure lies! Annabel was at a ball with Griselda last night."

Brinkley's mouth twisted sympathetically. The master had done his best as guardian of four penniless girls, and it wasn't his fault that they had turned out to be the sort of young women who create scandals with the ease with which other ladies embroider handkerchiefs.

Rafe continued reading in stark disbelief. ". . . *he being, as they say, buck naked, and she prettily begging that their 'relationship' not continue. We are happy to report that the gentleman was perfectly acquiescent in her plea and behaved with all the courtesy appropriate to the unfortunate situation. We who only stand on the fringes of society cannot help wishing that titled gentlemen of the north would not stray from their mountains; this particular person was reportedly engaged in scandalous behavior only last week with a close relative of Miss A. E——!*"

"Damn it to hell!" Rafe bellowed, throwing the paper to the side. "A pack of villainous lies, fudged up to sell the paper. I'll have their skins!"

He looked up at Brinkley, who was holding out a tankard. The very sight of it made sweat break out on his forehead, and drinking it made him shake all over. But after a moment or so, the pain receded and he was able to open his eyes without seeing dancing imps. "Got to cut back on the brandy," he said to himself. Even though the very thought of the scandal brewing in the pages of this damned gossip rag was enough to make him call for spirits, no matter the hour of the morning.

"Have to talk to Griselda," he said, staggering a little as he got out of bed. "Where the devil was Griselda? Didn't they all go off together to some debutante ball last night?"

Brinkley nodded.

"Well?" the master roared. "Did they return together, or not?"

"They were most certainly together," Brinkley said with dignity. "All three ladies returned to the house at a perfectly respectable hour . . . I believe around midnight."

"A mistake," Rafe said, dragging an unsteady hand through his hair. "Must be another Miss A.E. I'll make them print a retraction. I'll burn down their offices. I'll sue them for slander."

Brinkley didn't think that those ideas would solve the dilemma before them, but he kept mum. "Your manservant is waiting to run you a bath, Your Grace," he said soothingly. "Meanwhile, I shall ask Lady Griselda's maid to deliver the *Messenger*. I am certain that her ladyship will wish to speak to you about this unfortunate dilemma."

His Grace had dropped onto the side of the bed and was sitting with his head in his hands. Brinkley beckoned silently to his valet, and gratefully left the room.

* * *

Ewan had raised the knocker twice before the door was opened by a distracted-looking butler who took one look at his red hair and pulled open the door. "The Earl of Ardmore," Ewan told him, but the butler was already ushering him into a sitting room.

"May I bring you something, my lord?" he asked. "Some refreshment, perhaps? A cup of tea? I'm afraid that His Grace has just risen and he won't be able to greet you for at least a half an hour."

"I don't wish to see His Grace," Ewan said, pleasantly enough. "I've called to see Miss Essex, and I'd be grateful if you'd let her know that."

"Oh, but—"

"Miss Essex," he said firmly. The butler looked even more frazzled, but Ewan was a man used to getting his own way. "Immediately," he added.

"Miss Essex," the butler said, "has not yet seen the journal in question, my lord."

Ewan smiled. "All the better," he said. "Then may I count on you to summon her to this room without revealing the existence of that benighted article?"

The butler seemed to cock an ear toward the upper regions, but Ewan couldn't hear anything. "Lady Griselda may have informed the young lady," he said finally. "I shall ascertain if that is the case. Perhaps Miss Essex will join you, with her chaperone, naturally."

Ewan caught the butler's arm. "Without the chaperone."

The butler's eyes widened.

"Too late for that," Ewan said cheerfully, which probably confirmed the man's worst thoughts about Annabel, but it couldn't be helped.

The butler gone, Ewan sat down and thought about mundane things like jointures and the sprouting wheat, and (incidentally) how very nice it was to have a special license in his pocket and all this wife-catching business on the way to being sewn up tight.

Annabel walked through the door to the sitting room twenty minutes later, well aware that something had gone terribly wrong. For one thing, Griselda's fit of hysterics could be heard all over the house. For another, she had heard Rafe bellowing as well. On the rare occasions that Rafe rose before noon, he certainly never raised his voice. Thus, whatever had occurred, it was of sufficient gravity to trump Rafe's morning headache.

Their adventure of the previous night had surfaced, somehow. Perhaps they were all ruined. Or perhaps only she was ruined, having been found in a hotel room with a semi-clothed Scottish nobleman.

When she had the message that the Earl of Ardmore was below, Annabel was sitting at her dressing table, summoning up the courage to find out that she was no longer a candidate for any decent Englishman to marry.

Ardmore was asking for her. Not for her guardian, but for her.

She'd spent years and years dreaming of getting out of Scotland. Dreaming of leaving all the poverty and the disgrace behind, and coming to London with her beauty and her lush curves and trading them to a man who would keep her in silk forever. A man of ample means who had nothing to do with horses. That was all she ever asked.

It seemed that had been too much.

She felt numb. Surely, she could survive this. Maybe the earl didn't drown all his money in the stables. After all, he pulled together the money to come to England for a wife. Their father had never been able to give them the season that he talked about.

She opened the door to the sitting room so quietly that

the earl didn't hear her. He was standing on the other side of the room looking at a Constable landscape. He was tall. She knew that, but for some reason it seemed important to note his characteristics. Tall actually wasn't the first thing that sprang to mind when you saw him: Ardmore was more powerful-looking than tall, with large shoulders and legs that looked like tree trunks. At least he's getting enough to eat, Annabel thought with no humor. In fact, if things became particularly unfavorable, he could always hire himself out as a day laborer. Even that thought didn't make her smile.

His hair was a russet color, like autumn leaves just turning brown, and it turned up at his neck. He was wearing black, as he had both times she had seen him. Black had its virtues, she thought drearily. It could be turned, and re-turned, and the seams never showed that they had been re-dyed.

She walked into the room. "Good morning, Lord Ardmore."

Ewan turned around. For a moment, he thought that the wrong sister had come to meet him, even though they looked nothing alike. Surely it was Imogen whose eyes were so tragically unhappy, who looked as if she were holding herself upright merely so that she didn't collapse into tears. Annabel was the one whose eyes danced with humor, who had laughed at his proposal of marriage.

"Annabel . . ." He took her hand. It was ice-cold.

She pulled her hand gently from his and curtsied. Then she folded her hands before her and waited.

And what the hell was she waiting for? Obviously, the butler was wrong and she *had* read that benighted gossip column. Should he begin with a proposal? She looked so—uninviting. And yet . . .

"I'm afraid that Mr. Barnet has decamped from the hotel," he said finally.

She blinked at him.

God, but she was beautiful: all soft, rumpled curls of a gold that had nothing to do with the brassy colors that people often attribute to the metal. This was real gold: soft, sensual, beckoning gold curls, matched with the creamy skin of a Scotswoman. And her eyes . . . they were beautiful. Almost too lovely to catalogue, as if the good Lord had made that smoky blue just for her and then thrown away the paint box. They tilted a bit at the corners, and her lashes swept her cheeks—

He wrenched his mind away from that nonsense.

"Mr. Barnet, the hotel manager," he explained.

"What about him?"

"He was the person who provided *Bell's Weekly Messenger* with information about the events of last night," he explained. "He was eavesdropping, and I'm afraid that when he realized that he would lose his position due to Lady Griselda's wrath, there was no reason for him not to sell the information."

"The *Messenger*," she said dully. "So that was the source."

He walked over and stood just before her. "We're going to have to put that nasty rag out of our minds, lass. We've a life to start together, and that sort of ugliness has no part in it."

"Of course," Annabel said. "That makes a great deal of sense." She could read the article later. At the moment . . . she just wanted him to get his proposal over with, so that she could retreat to her room and cry. She hadn't cried since Father died. Not even when Imogen eloped, nor yet when Draven died. But this felt like the moment to resurrect the habit.

He took her hands in his. Go ahead, Annabel thought. Get on with it!

But he didn't.

After a moment or so, she raised her eyes and looked at him. He had interesting eyes: deep-set and green. They made him look quite unlike the glossy Englishmen of her recent acquaintance, and more like the old farmers who used to be her father's tenants, before he sold off all the land except the horse pastures.

"Annabel," he said, "I don't expect that you wish to marry me."

True, she thought. She looked at his boots. They were nicely polished, at least.

He sighed, and when he spoke, his voice had taken on an even deeper, rumbling Scottish brogue. "What's done is done. And I can't pretend I'm unhappy about it, because I find you very beautiful."

Annabel bit the inside of her lip. She'd always thought of her beauty as a gift from her mother. The gift that would get her out of Scotland and a life of poverty. "I'm very glad to hear that, Lord Ardmore," she said.

Ewan didn't know what to do. Her voice was utterly lifeless. She wouldn't meet his eyes for more than a moment. "Am I such a bad bargain, Annabel?"

"Of course not," she said. But then: "I have not read the article. Please do not take this amiss, but is there any way at all that my reputation could be recuperated without this drastic step?"

He shook his head. "To tell the truth, even our marriage may not quell the scandal. It's a nice thing, I'm thinking, that Scotland is a good space from London. We can let this whole fervor die down. You see, Mr. Barnet confused Miss Imogen and yourself, and had you asking to end our liaison, and then when that was put together with my disheveled state . . ."

He didn't need to continue. He was probably right about the need for them to disappear into Scotland. Annabel had a momentary streak of fear that she would cry every step of the way. She took a deep breath. "In that case, had you something you wished to ask me?"

He took her hands back. "I should like to marry you," he said slowly. "I should like you to come with me to my land, to be my wife and a mother to my children, to live with me, for richer, for poorer, in sickness and in health."

Annabel fought a wild urge to flee. Somehow her slippers stayed nailed to the floor. "Yes," she whispered.

He let go of her hands and pulled a thick piece of parchment from his inside coat pocket. "The moment I read that rag of a paper, I woke up a bishop and obtained a special license." He gave her a sudden grin. "I had to show him the *Messenger,* but after that he agreed that the situation was quite urgent."

She nodded.

"But I'd like to ask you a favor," he said.

"Since you are saving me from a lifetime of disgrace," she said, making a vain attempt to sound amusing, "I should think that you may ask many favors and I shall grant them."

He ignored her pitiful attempt at humor. "With your permission, I would like to leave this special license unused."

"Unused?" She frowned at him.

"You see, lass, I find the idea of marrying in such a godless, harum-scarum way not to my liking. But if we leave all these London folk with the impression that we have indeed married, and we travel to Scotland . . . perhaps we could marry there. There's a church on my land, and a priest who lives there. And 'twould mean a great deal to me if Father Armailhac could wed us."

"Will he have to call the banns?"

"No. We'll have a hand-fasting, an ancient thing in Scotland, and none the worse for its antiquity. 'Tis a simple ceremony before friends, though Father Armail-hac will make it a true ritual."

"I don't have a dowry," Annabel said suddenly.

"I've heard quite the opposite."

Her heart sunk. He thought she was wealthy. It was Rafe's gifts, fine feathers given to a peahen who had scarcely a chemise of her own. She couldn't even bring herself to speak or to look at him. Between them, she and Imogen had ruined him.

In fact, they were both ruined. Her dreams of a fine, rich groom were stolen from her by happenstance, Imogen's foolishness and the intervention of a pair of robbers. His dreams of a rich bride were stolen away by the same factors.

"I'm sorry," she said finally. "You are mistaken. I do not have a dowry."

"Milady's Pleasure?" he asked, raising her chin.

"Oh, Milady's Pleasure . . . I have a *horse*. But I have no *dowry*. No proper dowry."

"We shall do without it," he said.

It had to be said. "I am truly sorry that my sister and I brought you to this pass," she said, putting a hand on his sleeve. "If it weren't for us, you would have found a young lady with a formidable dowry. An heiress. We have destroyed your hopes."

"But I asked you to marry me before this even happened," he said to her.

He really did have remarkable eyes, especially when he smiled. His eyes smiled more than his mouth. "You thought I *was* an heiress," she pointed out.

"No, I had no such idea. I just liked your face, and that's the truth of it."

Annabel thought about the fact that she had been clothed in a gown that cost more than a yearly laborer's wage, and that she had been wearing pearls in her ears and around her throat (a gift from Rafe). Ardmore would have had every reason to expect a notable dowry.

But he spoke first. "People have been talking about dowries ever since I got to this benighted town. I assure you that there were factors far more important to me—"

"I know," she said. "The first being that your wife be Scottish."

"And the second that she be Scottish," he said, and there was that smile in his eyes again. It made gold flecks shine against the green. "But that was a mere jest. If I had been set on a Scottish bride, I'd not have come to this country. If you were English . . ." He tipped up her chin. "I'd be right where I am." Then his head was coming toward her and warm lips descended to her mouth.

Annabel was miserable. She was ready to scream with the frustration and rage of it all, to burst into tears at the unfairness, to sob at the loss of her every dream for the future . . . and yet there was something immeasurably comforting in the gentle touch of Ewan's lips. His arms came around her and she felt for a moment as if . . . as if . . . it was hard to think about it. His lips were drugging her mind, caressing her as if they were asking something.

She sighed and leaned against him . . . just for a moment. A moment's comfort. And his arms tightened as if she were indeed sheltered from the world, being saved by a knight in shining armor who would sweep her off her feet, and put her on the back of his horse, and take her to his castle. She sighed again, at the foolishness of her old dreams . . .

And he took advantage of that sigh, slipped into her mouth and suddenly their kiss changed to something altogether different. Not thinking about it, Annabel put a hand on the back of his neck. His hands tightened on her back and suddenly she felt the hard press of his body against hers.

Annabel felt his inquiry through her whole body. Instinctively she closed the last fraction of an inch that lay between their bodies. She felt a shudder go through his hard body. It was an extraordinary feeling to be so intimate with another person. It was as if he could taste her sorrow, and her fear, and her reluctance, and he was telling her silently that he would make it better—he would solve everything, and all that without words.

It made her want to do nothing more than nestle against his chest and simply . . . let him. But at the same time, the very generosity of it made her conscience awake, and even as his mouth slanted hungrily over hers again, and again, and her body started to tremble in his arms, her conscience kept beating at her, a small voice that wouldn't be silenced until she finally tore her mouth away and said, "I'm not jesting, Lord Ardmore. I truly have no dowry."

He had his large hands spread on her narrow back, and now he slid those hands slowly, slowly up to her shoulders. His eyes had an indolent smile in them that made Annabel shiver just as much as the fact that his thumbs were tracing lazy circles on her shoulders, where the little sleeves of her morning gown ended.

"You have a horse," he reminded her.

"*Only* a horse." She swallowed. "Surely you've heard of my father's will. Our dowries have become somewhat infamous."

"The rumor had not reached me, but then, I'm not much for gossip. I shall welcome your dowry to my stables. I can't say I share your father's skill, but I do have an ample training program. 'Twill be like coming home for you."

Annabel swayed on her feet, and all the rosy glow she felt from his kiss disappeared from her body like a mist in the night.

She was marrying a horse trainer, a man with her father's enthusiasm for a horse.

She *was* going home, in every sense of the word.

Twelve

They were all together again. Tess was leaning against one of the bottom bedposts; she and her husband were spending the night so as to be able to see Annabel off in the morning. Josie, just arrived from Rafe's country estate, was curled up against the other bedpost, and Imogen was next to Annabel.

Annabel leaned against her bedpost and tried not to even think about tears. She'd been poor before, and she could be poor again. Only a weak-spined ninny would cry over such a paltry thing.

Instead she tried to feel happy that her sisters were with her. But in reality she felt a numbing, selfish sense of the unfairness of it all. Imogen and Josie would stay in England in Rafe's comfortable house, and Tess would stay in the luxury of her husband's house, while she had to return to Scotland. She, who hated Scotland more than any of them.

Josie would have taken her place in a moment. Josie

had just turned sixteen and was beginning to blossom
into a beauty who would be irresistible in a year or so.
Now she was prey to spots, bouts of nostalgia for Scotland and fits of temper. The temper might well be a life-
long characteristic, Annabel had to admit. Certainly
Josie's sense of humor would be.

"If you'd like to have a wedding-night conversation
with Annabel," Josie said to Tess, "I would be glad to
lend my advice."

Tess snorted. "Your advice, shrimp? And just what
marital advice would you offer?"

"Plutarch has a great deal to say about marital relations," Josie said with a grin.

"Plutarch!" Tess said. "I thought Miss Flecknoe kept
you on a strict diet of ladylike pursuits."

"You've forgotten. I obediently practice dancing and
curtsying and paying morning calls in the mornings, and
then I am allowed to read as I wish in the afternoon.
Rafe's library is stocked with classics. Miss Flecknoe
considers those books to be far too *old* to be dangerous
and unladylike . . . she is most worried that I will somehow obtain a copy of one of the novels printed by the
Minerva Press. Miss Flecknoe seems to consider that
Minerva is staffed by devils bent on ruining ladies'
virtue."

"I'll give you mine," Annabel said, smiling faintly. "I
think I have acquired every volume put out by the Minerva Press, thanks to Rafe's generosity."

"You'll want to take those with you," Tess objected.
"Keep your books, Annabel. I'll send Josie some novels."

"I won't need them," Annabel said, realizing that her
tone was bleak. She never had any time for reading novels when they were growing up, although they probably
didn't remember that. She used to watch Tess going off
to the river to try to catch a fish for dinner, Josie hanging

on to her hand and Imogen trailing after . . . but she could never go with them. She had too much to do.

A wave of bitterness caught her and Annabel had to bite her lip, hard, so as not to cry.

"I have something important to say," Tess was saying. Tess had mothered them all, after their mother died, and Annabel was a little afraid of her perceptiveness. So she summoned up a smile.

"Good!" Josie said happily. "Now, Plutarch says that a bride should nibble a quince before getting into bed." She turned expectantly to Tess. "Do you have any idea why? I don't like quinces because they're so sour, but I'm willing to—"

"Stop this foolishness," Imogen said, and now she wasn't curled under the covers anymore, but sitting upright. "*I* have to say something first, and it's the more important." She took Annabel's hand, and Annabel saw with a pulse of exhaustion that tears were making their way down her cheeks. "I've ruined your life . . . my own sister's life, and I just—I just have to say that—"

But tears were choking what she wanted to say, and so Annabel scooted over in the bed and gathered her into a hug. "My life is not ruined, Imogen," she said, stroking her hair. "Hush, now."

"You don't get—get to choose who you wish to marry," Imogen choked. "And I only had Draven for two weeks, but I chose him, and even if he's gone, I'll always know that I—that I gave myself to someone I loved—"

"Darling, think about it," Annabel said gently. "Falling in love has never been very high on my list of priorities. You know that. I think I'm simply missing that romantic side that you have in such abundance."

"That's—that's just because you don't know how wonderful love can be," Imogen stammered, gasping for breath, she was crying so hard.

"What one doesn't know, one doesn't miss," Annabel pointed out.

But it was no use. Imogen launched into a tangled explanation of love, and how she knew she was in love with Draven the moment she saw him (as if she hadn't told them at least one hundred times), and how important she thought—

Until Josie leaned forward and said, "Imogen, this conversation did not begin by focusing on *you*. May I suggest that you actually try to think of someone else's feelings for a change?"

Imogen choked to a halt, and Annabel frowned at Josie.

"Oh, stuff it," Josie said impatiently. "Imogen needn't be coddled forever. By her own account, she was lucky enough to have two weeks of heavenly bliss. This evening is supposed to be about *you*, Annabel, not an endless tearful reiteration of Draven Maitland's less-than-obvious virtues!"

Imogen and Josie always sniped at each other, but this time Imogen didn't respond in kind. She just rolled out of the bed and stood up, her face smeared with tears. "I was trying to say something important!" she said fiercely to Josie. Then she turned to Annabel. "I just want to say that I am so *sorry* that my stupidity led to you being forced to marry Ardmore. I want you to know that. And now please have your conversation. I know I'm not fit company." She turned and fled.

Annabel sighed and started to get off the bed. She was Imogen's chief comforter, although she had to admit that there was a certain weariness about her efforts, after nearly six months practicing consolation.

But Tess reached forward and pinched her toe. "Don't go," she said. "I think Imogen could use some time alone. Perhaps she's been coddled a bit too much."

"I expect you're concerned that she'll snap at you next," Josie said. "Didn't you two make up your differences?"

"Of course," Tess said. "Imogen is quick-tempered, but she can be magnificently apologetic."

"She's had plenty of practice with the latter," Josie said. She caught Annabel's eye and raised her hand. "I know she's a widow and she lost the love of her life, but to be honest, Draven was a lummox stupid enough to ride an unbroken horse just to make an extra penny at the races. I simply *can't* see the grand tragedy of it all. He was no Agamemnon!"

"That's true enough," Tess agreed.

"You'd think she was in a Greek tragedy, from the way she carries on," Josie said. "*Now,* shall we have that discussion you began? Because everyone sent me away when you discussed all this before Tess married. But I am sixteen, as I said before."

"Barely," Tess said.

"Old enough. I'll be coming out next year. I need to know what lies ahead of me." She looked fascinated and horrified at once.

"As a matter of fact, I have no need for any sort of premarital conversation," Annabel said. She didn't want to think about bedding the Scot. For many reasons, only one of which was the way he kissed her.

"That wasn't what I wanted to say," Tess said, catching Annabel's eye and leaning forward. "You know that Lucius has a great deal of money, Annabel."

"An underestimation, surely," Annabel said. Everyone in England knew that Tess's husband was as rich as William Beckford, even though Beckford prided himself on being the richest man in the country.

"We've more houses than we know what to do with. Would you accept one of those houses, and funds to support it, Annabel? You could live there in perfect ease, and when all this dies down, you could come back to London."

Now Annabel really felt as if she were going to cry.

But Josie was shaking her head. "Are you demented, Tess? If Annabel went off and lived in some house in the country without marrying the earl, the reasonable assumption would be that the earl had paid her to do so. Her *only* future would be as a concubine."

Annabel swallowed. Of course Josie was right.

"One has to presume that you would be extremely well paid," Josie said thoughtfully. "Plutarch says that—"

"That's enough!" Tess snapped. "I think that is a very ugly construction of what people would think."

"People always think the worst," Josie pointed out.

"I'm afraid she's right," Annabel said, hearing the bleakness in her own voice.

"Do you mind, very much?" Tess asked.

Then, seeing the answer on her face: "Oh, darling, don't go!" Tess reached out and gathered Annabel into her arms.

"I—I—" Annabel said, but the tears wouldn't be stifled anymore.

"This settles it," Tess said firmly. "You shan't go to Scotland. We all know how much you hate the country. We'll think of something."

"I have to go," Annabel choked. "He's been kind—"

Josie snorted. "Ardmore is a lucky man and likely he knows it."

"It's just that he has *stables*," Annabel said, her voice breaking with tears. "And he told me that his stables were as magnificent as Papa's. I just can't bear it, I can't *bear* it. He'll put all the money into—into hot mash in the winter—" Her voice disappeared in a huge sob.

"I know," Tess said, her hand rubbing circles on Annabel's back. "You always took the worst of Papa's foolishnesses. I never had to worry because of you."

Annabel took a deep breath and wiped away her tears with Tess's handkerchief. "We all worried. I remember Josie crying when all the beans caught a blight, and she was just a little child."

Josie was leaning forward and rubbing Annabel's foot. "But I never had to worry very much," she offered. "You took care of everything, Annabel. You always found enough money to buy something to eat."

"I don't want—" The tears were coming again, so Annabel took a deep breath. "I don't want to do that again. I just don't want to spend my whole life trying to pry pennies from a stable maintained by someone who can truly afford only a brace of rabbits." The tears were coming again. "I just—I just can't bear it!" She took a shuddering breath and managed to regain her composure. "I'm sorry. I'm acting like a heroine in a melodrama."

"You shan't have to bear it!" Tess said passionately. "My husband and I shall—"

But Josie interrupted. "I've thought of a compromise."

"You go and I stay?" Annabel managed a watery smile. "I'd quite like to be sixteen again. I've enjoyed my debut."

Josie ignored this foolishness. She leaned forward. "Marry the earl in Scotland, as he wishes. Bear it until the scandal dies down, after the season is over. Then come back to London as a countess!"

"You are forgetting—"

"Don't tell me I'm forgetting about your husband," Josie said. "Do you know that my governess's secret vice is the gossip columns? London seems to be perfectly littered with ladies living apart from their husbands. And if your husband won't provide you with an allowance, Tess will simply do it instead."

Annabel bit her lip. "I couldn't do that to him," she

said uncertainly. "If it weren't for Ardmore, I'd be looking at utter disgrace."

"Yet if it weren't for Ardmore, there'd be no disgrace to talk about," Josie said. "And anyway, he'll probably be glad to see the back of you. There aren't many happy couples in literature, I can tell you that."

"It's a good idea," Tess put in. "There's something almost respectable about separated couples these days. We'll provide you with an allowance, of course, Annabel."

"That will work perfectly," Josie said with satisfaction.

"But Ardmore—"

"Shouldn't have propositioned Imogen in the first place," Josie said flatly. "He's made his bed and he must needs lie in it."

"Harsh but practical," Tess put in. "There's our Josie. How do you feel about the earl?" she asked Annabel.

"As I understand it," Josie said, "it was more a question of what *Imogen* felt for the earl."

"Your understanding of it isn't important, Josie," Tess said. "Annabel?"

"I like him," Annabel said. "There's nothing objectionable about him." In fact, his kisses kept teasing at the corners of her mind. Less the kisses than the shocking pleasure she felt . . . It was rather unnerving. And Annabel was never unnerved, any more than she wept.

Tess's eyes narrowed. "You do like him, don't you?"

"Who wouldn't? He's given up his hopes for a wealthy bride, and accepted me without a word of reproach," Annabel said, tossing her handkerchief onto the bedside table.

"Sounds like a milksop to me," Josie said dispassionately.

"That's because you haven't met him yet, you little termagant," Tess told her. "Ardmore is—well, Annabel, how would you describe him?"

"He's a Scot. He's not as complex as an Englishman, and yet more honorable. He says what he thinks. I would guess that he is kind in his dealings with servants and that he cares for his tenants."

"But do you like the way he looks?" Tess insisted.

Annabel shrugged, trying to push away an image of the earl's gleaming muscles when he stood shirtless in the hotel room. "He's not objectionable."

Suddenly her elder sister was grinning like a cat with a saucer of cream. "I take back my offer of a house," she said. "I think a dose of Scottish air is just what you need. Whenever you wish, you shall come back to London and we'll all be comfortable. All right?"

"All right," Annabel said slowly.

"Now, darling, here's what I wish that Mother had been alive to say to me before my wedding night."

"Splendid!" Josie exclaimed.

"It's nothing you'll find terribly interesting," Tess said to her.

"How can you say that? I find everything interesting!"

"As regards the marital bed . . ."

Josie leaned forward. "Yes?" she asked breathlessly.

"It is my firm opinion that gentlemen have some trouble expressing what they would like," Tess said. "Perhaps because it is difficult to speak to ladies. And it's not just my Lucius who—"

"Who is rather on the expressionless side," Josie interrupted.

"Not always," Tess said, with an impudent grin that made Annabel laugh for the first time in three days. "At any rate," she continued, "the solution is to observe that a man will do to you exactly as he would wish you to do to *him*."

Annabel blinked at her sister. She had a fairly good understanding of the mechanics of marital consummation, and there was no way that she could—could—she didn't have the equipment, for one thing.

"Not *that,*" Tess said, understanding her expression. "And I'm not going to be more explicit because you are barely sixteen," she said to Josie. "Just watch what Ardmore does . . . He will likely treat you to exactly the kind of behavior he would most like to see, except his good manners won't allow him to ask for it directly."

Annabel thought about it. She had some trouble imagining Ardmore not asking for anything he wished. But perhaps people became more tongue-tied in the bed. "Thank you, Tess," she said finally.

"Thank you for nothing!" Josie cried. "I certainly hope that someone will be a little more forthcoming with me next year. I fully intend to marry within my first season, you know." She looked down a little uneasily at her body. "Miss Flecknoe knows of a reducing diet, and she's going to put me on it four months before the season begins."

Annabel shook her head. "Don't do it, love. Your figure is exquisite."

"No, it's not," Josie said. "I'm plump as a Bartholomew chicken, just as Papa used to say."

"Papa," Annabel said, "could be unkind."

"He was truthful," Josie said.

A memory darted into Annabel's head of her father in a fury, staring her down over a ledger of her own carefully recorded figures. "You'll never be the woman your mother was!" he had shouted at her then. "Your mother would never have spoken to me in such a churlish fashion. You'll never make a biddable wife!" She sighed.

"Father was not always right," Tess said. "And when it came to the way he teased you over your figure, Josie, he was always wrong. And the way he was so unkind to you as well, Annabel."

A faint smile touched Annabel's lips. She was unlikely to be a biddable wife, so their father was right in that respect.

"I'll give it six months," she said suddenly.

Tess blinked. "What?"

"I just can't do it. I can't face the misery of a lifetime of poverty," she said, the truth bursting out of her. "But"—she steadied her voice—"if I just think that it's only a six-month exile, and that perhaps I could return and live with you, Tess, I think I could bear it."

"Oh, darling, you could always live with me."

"I wouldn't be in your way," Annabel said. "I just need a—a refuge to think about."

"I will always be your refuge!" Tess said, clutching her so tightly that it was almost as comforting as Ardmore's hard arms around her. "You know that, darling."

"Then I shall be off to Scotland in the morning," Annabel said, swallowing back more of those unruly tears. "And I'll see you very soon . . . perhaps for Christmas!"

Thirteen

It wasn't until they had trundled on their way clear out of London that Annabel thought of a problem. That wasn't quite true; for the last three days she had thought of nothing but problems, and only a few of them solvable. But this was a true problem, and it had to do with the world and everyone in it thinking they were man and wife. Lord and Lady Ardmore. Thinking she was a countess, an empty title if there ever was one.

"We're not yet married," she ventured to say.

Ardmore sat opposite her, hair tossed by the wind, looking boneless and indolent, as if he hadn't pounded alongside the carriage on a magnificent thoroughbred for the first three hours of their journey.

He flashed her a grin. "We will be."

"But we are not at the moment. Yet we'll be stopping at an inn for the night. How—how shall we arrange ourselves?"

His grin grew wider. "I'm afraid you're right, lass. We'll have to share a room. But the happy side of it all is that you can't be ruined."

"Because I already have been." Her heart sank. She was no Puritan, but she had thought to marry before . . .

"No, no, you can't be ruined because in the eyes of the world we're married."

So this would be her wedding night. In a manner of speaking.

But he was leaning forward. "When we're truly married, Annabel, a night in a shared bed will be quite different from that we'll have tonight, I promise you that."

Not her wedding night, after all. She could feel color stealing up her cheeks. It was something about the way he grinned at her.

"What we should do is get to know each other better," he said. "In the normal course of events, I'd be courting you now, trying to discover whether you sing off-key, whether you drink tea or coffee and, of course, whether I could bear to look at you every morning over breakfast. And you'd be doing the same for me."

"In fact, I have been wondering if you have any relatives, my lord?" It was appalling, how little she knew of the man she was to marry.

"I dislike formalities," he said, sidestepping the question. "My name's Ewan, and I'm hoping that you'll call me by it."

"Ewan," she said, nodding.

He leaned forward at that, and kissed the very tips of her fingers. "This is the very first time that my future wife has called me by my given name," he said. He was smiling with his eyes, in that way he had . . . as if she were everything he ever wanted in a wife. Still watching her, he turned her palm over and put his lips to her palm.

"You have such small hands," he said. The touch of

his lips on her palm made a sudden thrill shoot through her stomach. "I feel like a great, awkward farm boy next to you."

She laughed, and he pressed another kiss into her palm. His touches were like wine, a heady pleasure. "So it's already occurred to you that I look like a laborer, has it?" he teased. And kissed her again.

How could her palm feel so unbearably sensuous? A hundred men had held that palm and kissed her fingers during the last month, and yet . . . His eyes were steady on hers as he brought her hand to his mouth again. And this time she felt his tongue touch the center of her hand, and the shock was so great it burned down her legs.

"I would labor for you, Annabel," he said, watching her. "Shall we move to a small cottage and keep goats?"

"I'm not very good at gardening," Annabel said. And she was suddenly cool as could be, broken free of the spell of that husky voice of his. She pulled her hand away.

He leaned back in his seat, showing nothing more than an amused acceptance of her rejection. "What do you know of gardening? I should think young ladies do little more than snip roses, when the gardener bids her welcome."

"Something like that," Annabel murmured, closing her heart against the memory of Josie weeping when their beans died in the blight. She was determined not to be sullen with the earl, nor let him know just how great her reluctance to marry him was. None of this was his fault. Offering her his name was the act of a true gentleman.

She straightened on the seat and gave him a smile. "And *do* you have family, Ewan?"

"I do."

She waited, and finally he said, "I have them, and I don't have them. My close family is no longer living."

"I am sorry," she said.

"It's difficult to know how to phrase it. My Nana is always trotting out a bit about how they're waiting for me in heaven. But I very much doubt that they have naught to do in heaven but wait for my arrival, should I be lucky enough to end up at the right address."

"How many of your family were—were lost?"

"My mother and father died in a flood," he said, and for the first time, his eyes weren't smiling. "And my brother and sister died with them."

Annabel swallowed, and he answered her unspoken question. "I was six years old. Our carriage was caught in rising water. It didn't seem dangerous at first. My father took me to high ground. He went back for the others, but . . ."

To her horror, Annabel felt tears pressing at the back of her eyes. She truly was overemotional from the events of the past few days. "I'm so sorry," she said. There wasn't much more to be said.

Besides, now—strange man that he was!—her husband's eyes were smiling again. "I do believe that my mama has been watching the last few days, Annabel, and I'm quite sure she approves of you."

There was no point in saying something cynical, which was the only sort of comment that came to mind. Finally, Annabel searched around for some sort of phrase one would say to a child, and came up with: "I'm naturally glad to hear of your mother's approbation."

His smile grew wider, almost as if *he* were mocking *her,* but he didn't say anything more of that. "So when my parents died, that left my grandmother, Lady Ardmore," he said. "My Nana, as I call her, is still alive, and a feisty Scotswoman to the bone. She'll like you."

Annabel doubted it. Wait till the feisty grandmother heard about her whinnying dowry.

"And there's an uncle on my father's side," Ewan continued. "His name is Tobin. He spends most of his time hunting . . . I'm afraid he has a somewhat bloodthirsty nature. The household eats a great deal of venison, thanks to Tobin."

Annabel smiled grimly. Well, that was better than her sisters' rather dubious fishing skills.

"And then we have Uncle Pearce," Ewan said, "although by all rights, he's truly my great-uncle. He's almost ninety but clear-minded. His favorite activity is cheating at cards."

"Cheating?" Annabel echoed.

"Aye. And for money," he said, nodding. "He'll take every penny you have, if you allow him to deal the cards."

"Oh. Thank you for the warning. Anyone else?"

"Certainly," Ewan said. "There's still the reason I came to London to find a bride."

Annabel blinked. "I thought you wished for an heiress."

He frowned at her. "You seem to have dowries on the brain. Nay, I didn't come to London for such a flimsy reason. If I wanted an heiress, I could have married Miss Mary McGuire, whose lands march along mine. Nay, I came to London for another reason altogether. Well, for two reasons," he said.

Annabel waited.

"He's eleven years old," Ewan said. "His name is Gregory, and I'm afraid—"

He seemed to be choosing his words, but she jumped ahead. "You have a *son*?"

"Not exactly. Could we just say that he's a member of the household?"

She frowned at him. Her oh-so-honorable husband had a by-blow living in the house? But she suddenly realized that she didn't care all that much. If he'd had a child out of wedlock and thrown the poor lad to the parish—now, that she would have disliked. "What is Gregory like?" she asked.

"He's a pain in the rear," Ewan said, picking up her hand again. "At the moment he has great ambitions for his future and he won't accept the least opposition. I thought perhaps a wife might be able to soften the lad's stubborn character."

"That must be difficult," Annabel said sympathetically. Life could be quite limited for those of illegitimate birth, precluding them from positions of power and responsibility.

"You have no idea," Ewan said with a shudder. "He's up at the crack of dawn, singing lauds at the top of his lungs. And believe me, while I'm well aware of the existence of boy choirs, Gregory would not be a happy addition to such a group."

"Lauds?" Annabel said blankly.

He nodded. "He sings for almost an hour, up on the battlements. But you can hear him for a half mile. I'm sympathetic—"

She couldn't help it; she interrupted him again. "What *are* Gregory's ambitions?"

"To be a monk."

"A monk! We don't have monks in Scotland!"

"Nay, now, there you're in the wrong," he said. "There's any number of monks in Scotland since Napoleon kicked them all out of France. And we've three of them on my land."

"You have a monastery?"

"No, no, just three monks. They're part of the household, not living off on their own."

"Wait a moment," Annabel said faintly. "If I'm correct, your household consists of your grandmother, an ancient uncle, an uncle, a young boy and three monks?"

He hesitated.

"And?" she asked, eyebrow raised.

"There's Rosy McKenna," he said. "I'm not quite certain how to explain Rosy."

"Is she a relative?"

"No. She's Gregory's mother."

"Gregory's mother?" Annabel repeated faintly. He had—had—"That won't do," she said. "If you're taking a wife, Ardmore, you must send other women from the household. Unless you—" A horrible suspicion blossomed in her mind. He looked so innocent, but . . .

"Why, who do you think Rosy is to me?" he asked, bantering with her as if such a thing were the subject for a tea party. He was not a simpleton, but a madman.

She didn't know how to answer. The words that came to mind were such things as she'd heard around the stable, and not appropriate to be said aloud.

"Never a lover of mine," he said, and there was definitely laughter shining in those green eyes. "I wouldna bring you home to meet my lover." He had her hand again, but she pretended not to notice.

"Well, then," she said, resisting a sudden urge to grin back at him.

"*If* I had a lover," he said. "Which I have not."

"Oh. So who is Rosy?" she asked hastily, trying to move away from the subject of lovers. "And Gregory?"

"Rosy was my betrothed," he said.

She snatched her hand away, but a second later he was sitting next to her on the seat, and sure enough, he was laughing at her again. "Ach, but you're a suspicious one, you are," he said. "Now, do you truly think I'd bring home a wife if I had a fiancée all of my own waiting for me?"

"Then who is she?"

"We were to marry, many years ago," he said. And

now he had both her hands. " 'Twas a marriage that my father and his great friend McKenna had worked out when we were wee bairns. So when the time came, Rosy was sent to me in a carriage." He stopped and his eyes darkened. "On the way that carriage was stopped by some ruffians. She wasn't found until a week later."

"Oh, no," Annabel said softly.

"She hasn't been in her right mind since. Some nine months later Gregory was born. I would have married her, once we realized she was carrying a child, but back then she couldn't even give a straight yes or no in the church. And she didn't like me, you see. She couldn't even get near me without screaming. I was too big."

"And too male," Annabel said, her heart aching for the sadness of it.

"That as well," Ewan said, kissing her hands one by one, on her curled knuckles. "She's better now, although a strange man will always upset her. She can play spillikins."

"Her father?"

"Came to see her once and didn't want her back. He thought she should be sent to a nunnery, where they care for such poor creatures. Rosy's half French, you see. But of course, we were at war with France. We sent off a letter to the nunnery anyway, but it turned out that Napoleon had sent all the nuns hither and thither. Instead of sending Rosy to them, we ended up with three monks of our own. They've been a great help with caring for the poor girl."

"So she's the second reason you came to London for a wife?" Annabel guessed, trying to ignore all those butterfly kisses he was putting on her hands.

"No. The second reason would be Father Armailhac," he said.

"One of your monks?"

Ewan nodded. "He sent me off to London to dance with a girl."

"*Dance* with a girl?" Annabel repeated. "Only that?"

"Well, I interpreted that as finding a wife," Ewan said. "I hadn't wanted one, you see. And Father Armailhac disagreed with me. And now I rather see his point." He was uncurling her fingers like the petals of a flower and he was going to start kissing her palm again . . .

"You never danced with me," she said quickly. "Only with Imogen."

"The Lord moves in mysterious ways," he said. "Because 'twas you I wanted to dance with, Annabel, ever since the moment I saw you. And 'twas you I wanted to marry as well. Never Imogen."

The carriage rocked around a corner and Ewan took a quick glance out of the window. "We're in Stevenage," he said, "and we've made excellent time. We'll stop at the Pig and Cauldron for the night."

Annabel pulled her hands away, feeling uncommonly shy. But he turned back to her. A second later his hands cupped her face and he started brushing his lips back and forth against hers. "You're like the finest wine," he said, his voice sounding bemused.

Annabel knew just what he meant. His very touch had her heart thundering in her chest. His hands slid over her cheeks, across her hair, and he was going to kiss her, she could feel it— He pulled back.

"We've a problem, lass," he said.

Annabel felt such a severe twinge of disappointment because he hadn't kissed her that she almost pulled his head down to hers.

"I'm wanting to kiss you, *all* the time."

That made her smile.

"Even seeing your lips curve like that," he said, his

voice deepened to a husky velvet, "makes me feel like—"

"Then why don't you?" she asked, and the provocative smile that curled on her lips was not one shaped in the mirror and practiced to catch a rich husband. In fact, Annabel wouldn't even have recognized it herself.

She wanted more of his kisses. When they kissed, she didn't—couldn't—think about anything but him.

And Ewan clearly wasn't a man to disappoint a lady. His lips crushed hers in a drugging kiss that seduced and demanded. This time, Annabel shuddered at the very first touch of his mouth, and her body seemed to mold itself to his, hungrily, as if it already knew the hard lines and—

His hands were moving down her back, and she strained forward against him, feeling her breasts crushed against his chest. Instantly that feeling of peace flooded through her. There was something about being in Ewan's arms, being held by Ewan . . . it felt like the most protected place in the world. Except that his lips were ravaging hers, moving over them again and again until his tongue finally slipped between her lips. By then, Annabel was ready to cry out because she wanted—she wanted—

She wasn't even sure. She simply held on, accepting that the world had narrowed to the tight circle of his arms.

When the door swung open and light flooded into the carriage, Annabel didn't even realize it. Her entire being was focused on the feeling of Ewan's thick hair sliding through her fingers, the demand of his mouth, the fire racing down her legs, the mindless pleasure of their kiss—

It was Ewan who pulled away, putting his faux countess from him with a reluctance that almost made him laugh aloud. He was like a possessed thing around Annabel. Possessed. He threw a glance at the groomsman holding open the carriage door and the man shut it again instantly. The carriage fell into twilight, but he could still see her. He could reach out and—

He had the feeling that he would always be able to see her. Even in the darkness his hands would know which patch of it held the curvy, delicious body of his bride.

"We're—" he caught himself. "This is a dilemma," he finally said.

She was pushing hairpins into that gorgeous mop of curls she had. For a second an image of those curls draping her breasts flashed into his mind and he almost groaned aloud. For God's sake, he'd been rock hard for the last four hours. At this rate, he'd be dead by the time they made it to Scotland.

She looked up at him, a woman who liked kissing, he could tell that. Every time he kissed her, she got a softer look about her and lost that hovering little anxiety she had in her eyes. He itched to pull her against him, kick open the carriage door and head straight into the inn. Into their best bed and—

"Hell and damnation," he muttered, disgusted at himself.

Her eyes danced with merriment. "A problem?" she asked, obviously pleased with herself.

"I can't keep my hands off you," he admitted.

He liked her smile now. It made him ache, it looked that welcoming.

"We can't go on like this for another two weeks," he said. "Let alone tonight." He had a sudden image of her stretched out next to him, sleeping peacefully, while he stared hungrily at her all night long. "Do you wear a nightcap?" he asked hopefully.

She shook her head.

"Is your nightgown the type that covers you from neck to toes?"

She giggled at that. He'd never heard her giggle . . . It

was a deliciously feminine sound. Of course, it made desire explode down his groin. He wanted her to giggle against his skin. He wanted to hear that delicious, breathy sound turn to pure pleasure, turn to a gasp and a moan.

"I'll not make it to Scotland."

She raised an eyebrow.

"I'll be dead first," he clarified. "And yet I'd never dare change the way we've planned things. Your guardian promised me last night that if I laid a hand on you before solemnizing the wedding, he'd come to Scotland and do some very unpleasant things to my limbs."

She laughed outright at that. "It's hard to imagine Rafe as the avenging warrior."

Ewan saw in his mind's eye the rigidly furious face of her guardian when Ewan explained that Annabel had agreed to wait for marriage until they reached Scotland. "He trusted me," he said. "The man didn't like the idea, but he was good enough to trust me."

"Of course he did," Annabel said, smiling at him. "You didn't have to save my reputation, you know. You could have disavowed all knowledge of Miss A.E. My whole family is indebted to you."

He knew he shouldn't touch her, but he tipped up her chin. "They can think as they like," he said, "but you owe me nothing, Annabel. I wanted you from the first moment I saw you, and to tell the truth, I should have written that article in the *Messenger* myself. Would have too, if I'd thought of it."

"What do you mean?"

"After you left the hotel, I thought it over—" But he couldn't tell her yet. "I knew you'd seen me without any clothing, and that meant you were ruined for all other men. Naturally, I was going to have to marry you, if only to save you from a lifetime of disappointment."

"*Now* I know you're Scots," she said impudently, grinning at him. There wasn't a trace of anxiety in those gorgeous eyes of hers.

"To the bone," he growled at her, and dared to just drop a kiss on the corner of her mouth. But: "We have to talk."

"Among other things, because this carriage is standing in the inn yard," Annabel pointed out. "And all the inhabitants of the inn must be properly mystified as to why we haven't left the carriage."

"No, they're not," he said, dropping another kiss on the other side, just to balance the ledger. "They think we've jumped into our marriage night right here. The carriage is probably ringed with spectators waiting to see if the vehicle starts rocking back and forth."

"Starts rocking?" she repeated, looking fascinated and deliciously naive. "Rocking?"

He couldn't explain it to her. Not without grabbing her, and then the carriage *would* be rocking. If not tipped over. "I'll have to sleep in the stables," he said with a groan.

"You can't do that," Annabel said, eyes sparkling with mischief. "The news would leak out and everyone would think that we were estranged, before we've even wed. That would never do."

"Eve, to the life," he said, staring at her with fascination. She'd merely ask him to eat the apple and it would be gone in a moment. "Fornication without God's blessing is a sin," he said, as much to himself as to her.

He wasn't sure she'd know the word, but she did. Her little nose went into the air. "Eve, am I?" she said with a toss of her curls.

"Aye. And I think we'd better set ourselves some limits."

"I have no need for rules," she scoffed. "You're not as

interesting as all that, Lord Ardmore, for all you consider me ruined for other men."

"Then the rules are for me," he said. "Because I'm definitely ruined for other women, and I haven't even had the pleasure of seeing you in the buff."

She blushed at that and said nothing.

"I think we'd better stop kissing," he said with a sigh. "Because I know where this is leading."

Annabel felt an acute pulse of disappointment. Kissing Ewan was the only thing that made her confusion and fear evaporate. "Of course, if you're not able to control yourself," she said loftily.

"Eve!" he said. But she could see him weighing his male wish to claim control against this fear of her that he had.

"As you said, this is our courting period," she reminded him. "In the normal course of things, you'd be trying to lure me into any handy garden."

"I would, would I? So were many men trying to pull you off the garden path, then?"

She grinned at him. "And what do you think?"

"I think that gardens came into my mind the very moment I saw you. You were cheated of a courting, I'll give you that. How about if we simply count all the efforts of those men toward my courtship?"

"Mr. Lemery asked me to ride in Hyde Park, and then he drove down an empty path, but he had a very *wet* mouth." She made her eyes tragic. "Does his kiss count in your favor, then?"

He laughed. "Surely all Englishmen aren't wet kissers?" He was liking that idea, she could tell.

"Certainly not. Lord Simon Guthrie kissed me before he asked me to marry him and it was quite pleasant."

For a man who seemed generally good-natured, he had a ferocious scowl. "Asked you to marry him, did he?" But then he realized. "And why did you say no, if he was such a splendid kisser, then?"

"He was a third son," Annabel said. "We'd be living on the parish. But his kisses . . . perhaps he'd had a great deal of practice . . ." She let her voice trail off provocatively, even though it was all poppycock because Ewan's kisses were in another class from poor Simon Guthrie's.

He knew it too. He gave her a derisive look through his lashes and said, "Perhaps just kisses. But no kisses in the bedchamber, mind."

"I'm not begging you," she said with a sniff. "I can do perfectly well without kissing you at all."

"You know, we Scots are different from yon English," he said to her.

"I've noticed that!"

"Then you'll have noticed that we have no fear of saying the truth. And the truth is, lass, that you just tricked me into keeping on with our kisses, which means that you can't do without those either. And another truth is that I've got no control when I'm around you."

"None?" she asked, with some curiosity.

He shook his head. "So it's going to be up to you, Annabel, love. You'll have to rein us in. Kisses only. And nothing in the bedchamber, mind. I think we'd better set a limit. Ten a day should be more than enough."

Annabel grinned at him. There was something enormously satisfying about having this great mountain of a man admit that he had no control around her. It went some way toward making up for the humiliation of the way they got engaged, and the humiliation of his not wanting to marry her immediately. "In that case," she said, "I'll thank you to open that door, Lord Ardmore, and we'll disappoint the crowd."

"*Not* Lord Ardmore," he said.

"Ewan."

At his smile, she almost kissed him again.

He seemed to guess her thought before it even flashed in her mind, and his smile deepened. "By my count, we're up to five kisses today."

She leaned forward and rapped on the door. "Perhaps we should start with half measures," she told him. "Given your lack of control."

"Nay, I'll have my full share," he promised her.

Fourteen

At first glance, the inn yard of the Pig and Cauldron was a flurry of activity. Far from there being a ring of people around their carriage, no one seemed to be paying attention to it at all, except for the groomsman holding open their door. And his eyes were rigidly fixed on the sky, Annabel noticed.

Then, as she walked down the steps, she realized that a great deal of the activity was the result of their arrival. The courtyard seemed to be full of men wearing Ewan's colors, black and dark green, leading horses hither and thither and hoisting trunks.

She turned to her husband. "How many outriders came with us?"

"Six before and six after," he said, looking around. "Oh, there's Mac."

A slight, bespectacled man holding a few papers in his hands came toward them through the organized chaos.

"And how many groomsmen?" Annabel inquired.

"The usual number," Ewan said. "Four behind each carriage."

Annabel had been so benumbed that morning that she had hardly noticed the color of their carriage, let alone that it wasn't traveling alone. Now she slowly turned around. They had ridden in a gleaming coach, painted dark green and picked out in black. There were two additional coaches drawn up at the side of the courtyard, both in the same colors, if slightly more serviceable-looking.

She was starting to have a very peculiar feeling. Either her future husband was a spendthrift, or—or— She turned to him, but the bespectacled man had appeared and was talking to Ewan.

"Annabel, I'd like to introduce you to Mr. Maclean, my factor," Ewan said. "Mac and I have been together these twelve years now, and I don't know what I'd do without him. Mac travels ahead of us, and will meet us at each stop. You'd better call him Mac as well, if he doesn't mind."

Annabel held out her hand. Mr. Maclean had rather sweet brown eyes and a harassed expression. He took her hand rather tentatively, then dropped it and bowed. So she curtsied.

"Lady Ardmore," he said. "Welcome to the Pig and Cauldron. The inn eagerly awaits your arrival." He turned to Ewan. "You've the best chamber, my lord, and the innkeeper's wife is preparing a special dinner for you, in honor of the occasion. They're quite excited, so if you could spare a moment to greet them, it would be most appreciated."

"Of course we can," Ewan said. He tucked Annabel's hand under his arm. "Come along, then, *wife*." The glance he sent her was full of mischief.

"How did you obtain the best chamber, given that you hadn't even intended to travel to Scotland until a few days ago?" she asked. "Did the innkeeper send whoever was originally in the chamber away?"

"I'm not sure of the details," Ewan said, steering her around a cobblestone knocked out of its place. "I leave all that to Mac."

When they reached the door of the inn, the innkeeper strode toward them. He was a tall man with a bald head, a cheerful smile and a strong smell of cider about him. "It's an honor to have you choose my inn for your wedding night, Lord Ardmore, my lady. May I escort you upstairs to your chamber? Your private dining room is here to the right."

Two minutes later Annabel was sitting in a comfortable armchair. Her husband was talking with Mac. His valet had arrived and then Elsie, her maid. There was talk of hot baths. And a minute after that, the room was empty but for her husband, who was coming toward her with a most purposeful look in his eyes.

"Ewan," she said, "why do you travel with so many outriders?"

"Because of what happened to Rosy. I would never risk anything of that nature happening to you. It's worth spending a whole year's harvest to travel in safety."

"Oh," Annabel said, confused.

He leaned over her chair, bracing himself on the arms, and said, "Kiss number six?" He was quite appealing, this almost-husband of hers.

"I think not," she said primly. "I would like a bath. In *my* chamber, if you please."

"Now, Annabel, you know this chamber has to be shared by the two of us." His eyes had an unholy glee about them.

"Then out the door with you!"

He laughed and strolled to the door. "I'll send your

maid up with the hot water and await you in our dining room . . . *wife.*"

Of course, he had his kisses. There was one behind the dining room door, just before the landlord's daughter brought in a second course. There was another in the curve of the stairs, when they heard cultured voices in the anteroom below and Ewan thought they shouldn't go down the stairs just yet. He had another outside their room.

That left two kisses.

And that left the two of them.

He went below while Elsie helped Annabel change into her bedclothes. Then she jumped into bed and waited. After a half hour or so, he strolled in, and now he had the same cidery sharp apple smell as the innkeeper.

"The man makes excellent cider," he told her.

"It's a good thing Rafe isn't here," she said, just to make conversation.

He looked as if he couldn't remember who Rafe was. "Are you planning to wear that scrap of silk to bed?" he asked, his voice gone still and deep.

Annabel looked down at herself. She was wearing a French nightgown of pale pink silk, the color of the youngest of spring roses. Surely he'd seen a fashionable nightgown before? She pulled up the sheet a bit higher, almost to her breasts. It was a large bed, after all. "That I am," she said. " 'Tis the nightgown that Tess gave me for my wedding."

"I'll be going through that door into our dressing room," Ewan said firmly. "And you'd best change into something cotton, my girl, and up to your ears as well. Or we won't last a night together. I'll have to jump out the window and run to the stables, and that will cause more gossip than our marriage did in the first place."

He closed the door behind him and Annabel just grinned at the ceiling. After a second, he poked his head around the door and growled, "I'm warning you."

So she slid out of bed and stood up and saw the shock of it in his eyes, the way they darkened and turned tiger-hungry. Annabel knew she had a lovely body, from a man's point of view. She had always thought of it as her personal dowry, to be offered in a trade for a man of sustenance. But now she felt the swell of her breasts in a different way, measured by the sudden rasp of Ewan's breathing, by the way he stood so rigidly by the door. The silk of her nightgown caught between her legs for a moment and he closed his eyes. As if he were in pain. Annabel could have laughed with the pleasure of it.

He felt for the latch behind him and left without another word. Luckily, there was a starched and ironed cotton nightgown near the top of her trunk. She took off the silk and folded it into a shimmering square. Then she pulled on the cotton. It billowed around her legs like the sails of a ship as she ran back to the bed.

When Ewan came back into the room she was peeping at him from under the covers, cotton buttoned up to her chin. He was wet, his hair back against his head. But he was still dressed. She raised an eyebrow.

"I bathed at the sluice in the back," he explained. "And there's something I didn't think of."

"Yes?"

"I don't sleep in a nightshirt. I never liked them."

"But what do you—" Her eyes widened.

"In the buff," he said. "Obviously I can't do that at the moment."

"Obviously not!" she snapped.

"Although you have already seen my chest," he pointed out.

"I have no wish to see it again."

He sighed. "In that case, I'll wear a shirt and my smalls." And without further ado, he pulled off his boots and tossed them to the side. And then he put his hand to his pantaloons, but she realized her cheeks were turning fiery red, so she turned on her shoulder and stared at the wall.

After a moment she felt a large body settle into the bed next to her.

"I canna fathom how I got myself into such a stupid situation," Ewan murmured, and she had to turn over to look at him.

He was lying on his back, staring up at the beams, arms crossed behind his back. He'd rolled the sleeves of his linen shirt up, and it was open at the neck. Annabel could feel her heart beating in her chest, for all the world as if it were trying to escape.

"I should have marched you over to a bishop, special license in hand, and had done with it," he said. "Don't you agree?"

"No. I like being courted," Annabel said. She felt unaccountably shy. It was as if her whole life had led up to this moment of finding herself in bed with a man. And yet it was happening under such strange circumstances!

"I don't even dare look at you," he said after a moment.

Annabel felt like laughing aloud. "Well, close your eyes, then," she said. She turned her shoulder to him again.

"Two more weeks of this," he groaned. She felt him moving around and risked a peek. "I'm putting a pillow between us," he told her. "I'm not risking you rolling over in your sleep and ending up in my arms. There are limits to my endurance." He found a bolster pillow of at least a half body's length to put between them.

Annabel settled down again and tried to think about sleep, but suddenly he was there, looming over her. She looked up at him. "I've two kisses left," he reminded her. "I'm keeping one for tomorrow."

"But you said never in the bedchamber," she said, feeling a flutter of excitement mixed with apprehension.

"Then this is a goodnight kiss only," he said. He bent his head and kissed her, a sweet, small kiss. "It doesn't count in my ten. But I want to tell you that I thank God your sister Imogen draped herself around me on the dance floor."

She smiled at him, and then he turned over. And after a while, listening to his calm breathing, she went to sleep.

Fifteen

"You hold yourself very dear," Imogen said to the Earl of Mayne. He was following her up the grand flight of stairs that led to Almack's ballroom.

"I *am* very dear," Mayne replied. "It's a pity you don't account yourself at the same value."

"There's no need to be sarcastic simply because I tried to kiss you," Imogen tossed over her shoulder. "You must have shared a hundred kisses in carriages before." On the way to Almack's she had suggested that since most of London thought they were involved in a torrid *affaire*, it was his duty to at least kiss her on occasion. Mayne, apparently, felt otherwise.

Imogen was rather surprised to find herself pleased that he continued to elude her advances. He was a challenge, and having a challenge took her mind off Draven.

"I am used to the choice of location and activity being my prerogative," he said now.

"Then I am rendering you a great service by bringing

you into the modern age. Widowed ladies in particular no longer have to act like pious nuns."

"All these newfangled notions might be too much for me," Mayne said pensively.

"Oh, I doubt it. Lax morality suits you far better than this prudishness, you know. You have a reputation to keep up. People will start thinking you're marriage material, if you don't watch out. Matchmaking mamas will add your name to their private lists, rather than shuddering if their daughter catches your eye."

"I surprise myself," Mayne admitted, joining her at the top of the stairs.

"As a matter of fact, you should be showering me with grateful kisses. Here am I, a beautiful young widow allowing you to partner me about. Why, if the *ton* weren't convinced that you were engaged in an extramarital affair, they might think the worse of you."

"That I am considering marriage?"

"That you have the pox," Imogen retorted.

"Your ladylike nature constantly astonishes me," he said acidly.

Imogen grinned. She felt more cheerful than she had for months. Something about bantering with Mayne made her feel less hopeless. And less grief-stricken. She paused and put a hand on his arm. "Prudishness is an affectation that doesn't become you. Since the *ton* is convinced that we are conducting an *affaire,* why is it that you have never even kissed me? Don't you find me desirable?"

"You are all that is desirable, as you very well know." He looked over her head and nodded in greeting to an acquaintance. "But should we really discuss the lack of intimacy in our friendship at this particular moment?"

Imogen looked around. Almack's was full of people, all of whom were undoubtedly fascinated by their arrival.

She grinned at him. "Everything important should be discussed within the full view of the *ton*. It stops people from trying to exercise their imagination on their own."

"In that case, I'd like to note that no one is entirely convinced that we are having an *affaire*; in fact, they don't know what to make of us, which is why they are so interested."

"People always believe the worst," Imogen said, "especially of young widows. Why, Griselda told me about a fascinating ballad; the refrain insists that if you wish to court a widow, you need to pull down your breeches." She sang a few lines for him.

"I am sure there is a great deal of talking going on behind our backs," Mayne said. "And there will be even more if you sing any louder. Young ladies, even widows, are not supposed to know such verses. I shall have to speak to my sister about providing sterner chaperonage for you."

"I make it a habit not to worry too much about what people say behind my back," Imogen said. "I might get conceited."

"Quite clever!" Mayne said, raising an eyebrow.

She giggled. "I heard it in a play."

"Well, you certainly cannot complain about your reputation. You were in a fair way to being utterly disgraced when I took you up. Now look at you: positively the talk of the town, and all because you constantly rebuff me. If only they knew the truth!"

"I shall definitely rebuff you again this evening; it creates so much amusement. It would be cruel of me to neglect it. Perhaps you should ask me to waltz with you."

"Just don't slap me again," Mayne said. "I wish I'd never suggested it. I think my jaw is still tender."

"I promise that I won't," she said, slipping her arm under his and nestling close.

"Let me guess, Lady Blechschmidt just entered the room."

She smiled up at him, a blindingly adoring smile. "No."

"Your sister Tess?"

Imogen laughed. "No! Why would I want to impress Tess with my affection for you?"

"Oh." Mayne stopped. "Damn it, Imogen, you could have told me that Rafe was coming to Almack's tonight."

"I had no idea until this moment," she said, watching her former guardian thread his way across the dance floor straight toward them. "It's very odd of him, actually. I don't think Rafe is fond of Almack's, do you? They don't even serve spirits."

"I'm going to tell him the truth about our relationship before he murders me," Mayne said.

"No, you will not! I don't particularly care that you are puritanical in your conduct around me, but you would embarrass me to reveal it to others, especially to Rafe!"

"There would be no embarrassment involved," Mayne protested. "Rafe will be grateful to learn that his closest friend has not seduced one of his wards, especially when the ward in question has been widowed only these seven months."

"*Six*," Imogen said.

He looked down at her. "And how many days?"

"Twenty," she said softly.

"Precisely," he said with a sigh. "What kind of a monster does he think I am, anyway?"

"Oh, for goodness' sake," Imogen said crossly. "Rafe is no longer my guardian. He lost that privilege—if one could call it that—when I married Draven. And as for you, you're a lecher, Mayne; all London knows you to be one. Rafe knows that of you as surely as you know that he's a drunkard. Why on earth did you have to choose *now* to start having all these scruples?"

"You put things so prettily," he said. "I always find myself soothed by your ladylike phrasing."

"I am known for the sweetness of my disposition," Imogen said, grinning at him. Rafe had almost made it to their side of the room, and even from here Imogen could see how angry he was. Perhaps it was cruel of her to allow him to think Mayne had been so despicable. But there was something about Rafe that made her wish to annoy him.

Sure enough, he swept between them like a cold wind, taking each of their arms and giving them a snarling smile that would have fooled no one. Rafe never had much social finesse. Two seconds later, they were all in one of the little sitting rooms off the antechamber and Rafe was engaged in his favorite activity: bellowing at Imogen.

She wandered over and rubbed a finger against the mantelpiece. Her white kid glove turned gray. Perhaps she would drop a word in Mr. Willis's ear. He would surely wish to know that his establishment was not being kept to proper standards.

For a moment she focused on Rafe's voice. "I cannot believe your debauchery!" Apparently he was taking it out on Mayne, then. Imogen thoughtfully made the shape of a four-leaf clover in the dust. It didn't seem quite fair to poor Mayne that he bear the brunt of his friend's wrath. Why, here was Rafe, calling his friend far worse than a lecher. In fact—

"Goodness me!" she said, putting her smudged glove over her heart. "Could I have heard that word correctly, Your Grace? Did I truly hear you say the word *hellhound* in my presence?" Imogen thought her horrified simper was all that it could be.

Mayne rolled his eyes at her, from behind Rafe's back.

"You're a fine one to throw insults at Mayne—my darling Mayne," Imogen said with relish. "He is a fruitful member of society, whereas to all appearances you exist merely to keep the whiskey industry alive and thriving!"

But Rafe had got himself into a pair of knee breeches just so he could be admitted to Almack's and find the two of them before they created an even greater scandal. He was determined to stop making a hash of this guardian business. Somehow he had to stop his wards from ruining themselves right and left.

"A man is measured by his responsibilities," he said stonily. "Mayne has none, and I, God forgive me, count you among mine. So please"—he turned to Mayne—"don't do this. Imogen's insolence is nothing more than a very fragile shell covering her grief. I'm certain that she was quite active in the seduction, but I'm asking you on the strength of our friendship to leave her be."

Mayne looked at Imogen.

Imogen looked at Rafe.

"If he isn't prepared to stop this foolishness," Rafe continued grimly, looking steadily back at Imogen, "I'm taking you away from Almack's now—physically, if need be. You'll come to the country with me. You need to recover, not frolic about!"

"If I come to the country, can Mayne come with me?" Imogen said it provocatively, just to see Rafe's eyes darken from gray-blue to black.

"No, he cannot." He bit the words as they came, and turned his shoulder on Mayne. Behind him, Mayne was looking quite peeved.

"Oh, all right! If you must know, Mayne is doing nothing more nefarious than escorting me about! He has utterly refused to make our relationship more intimate. At least," she added with a roguish smile at Mayne, "so far."

"I can escort you, if you need a companion other than Griselda."

Imogen gave Rafe a point-by-point examination, starting at his unmanageable hair, lingering on his slightly paunchy belly, ending at the tip of his unpolished boots. Then she remarked, "I have a reputation to uphold."

"Mayne may be prettier," Rafe snapped, "but the whole world thinks you're sleeping with him."

"Not yet, they don't," Mayne said, speaking for the first time.

"Most of them do," Rafe retorted. "The rest of them think you're actually courting Imogen. So unless you're planning on leaping into matrimony, I'd suggest that you temper that *courtship* a bit."

At that, Mayne's mouth fell open. "They do?"

"Well, what did you expect? You haven't pursued an *affaire* in months—almost a year, isn't it? And now Imogen is alternately rebuffing you and leading you on. The bets are at five hundred to one that she'll accept you before the end of next month."

Imogen took out her fan and waved it before her face to hide her delighted grin. "I had *no* idea."

"Neither did I," Mayne said with a scowl.

"Well, don't worry," she said. "I wouldn't have you, so you needn't fear for your marital future. I was rather under the impression that you were shunning the idea of marriage."

"I am."

"Then I am providing an excellent cover for your lack of intentions," she said, turning to Rafe. "There. You've delivered your little warning." He was looking at her with a look—a look that—could it be that he was pitying her again? Rafe, old sodden Rafe? Anger stiffened Imogen's back. "I suggest we continue just as we are," she said sweetly. "And merely so that you know precisely where we are, Rafe, I might as well tell you that the only thing standing between me and enjoyment of Mayne's bed are his own scruples." She wrapped an arm around Mayne's neck. "I shall, naturally, continue to try to change his mind."

Sure enough, Rafe's eyes turned black with fury. "You just don't understand, do you?" he said, his voice a low growl.

She smiled at him, her heart beating fast at the rush of rage in his eyes, courting the excitement, the feeling that she was alive. Then she deliberately reached up and pressed her lips to Mayne's cheek. "Oh, but I think I *do*."

"Don't mind me," Mayne said, shaking her arm off from his neck.

"You're just trying to curb me from having any pleasure!" she said to Rafe. "You're nothing but a killjoy, so swilled in whiskey that you can't stand the idea of sober people taking pleasure in something other than liquor!"

"That has nothing to do with it," Rafe growled at her. "When my brother died, I tried to throw myself to the dogs, the way you're doing."

"Oh?" she said. "When did you stop the practice? After so much experience, your advice must be of great practical value."

Mayne groaned and walked away, throwing himself into a chair. Imogen paid him no attention.

Rafe's jaw clenched. "I'll give up the whiskey if you give up this shameless attempt to ruin yourself."

"I see no reason for shame," Imogen said, her voice dripping with disdain. "I think you forget that I am no tender miss, frightened by the sight of a man's—"

Mayne interrupted her. "That's—"

But Rafe spoke right over him. "You know as well as I do, Imogen, that you are simply trying to drown out your grief by making yourself notorious. I told you: I did the same thing, and I see it in you."

"You—" Imogen said, but suddenly her fire was fading away because his eyes were too kind. Too pitying. She turned around sharply and sat down on Mayne's lap, ignoring his startled noise. "I shall go to the dogs in my own fashion," she said, leaning her cheek against Mayne's black hair, but watching Rafe. "I've never been kissed with such passion by any but Mayne. I adore him."

Suddenly Rafe looked like the duke he so frequently forgot to be. His eyes blazed at her. "If that's your choice."

"It is," she said, half wishing he would grab her by the wrist and pull her from the room. "After all, you didn't avoid the whiskey, did you? So why should I avoid Mayne? He's a far sweeter drink."

Mayne groaned. "Don't ever take up poetry, Imogen."

"Notwithstanding your trite analogy, I take your point," Rafe said, sweeping a hand through his hair so that it stood straight up on the top. "Perhaps I haven't a right to criticize you, given that I'm not the best model. But I care for you, God knows for what blighted reason. I'm the guardian your father chose. He wouldn't wish to see you go down this route."

"How would you possibly know?" Imogen said stonily. "If I'm correct, you met Papa only one time."

Rafe's jaw set and he looked at Mayne, who was trying to keep Imogen's hair out of his mouth. "Take care of her," he warned.

"I—" Mayne said.

But Rafe was gone.

Imogen let her head fall back against Mayne's shoulder.

"You bungled that properly," he said, pushing her hair away from his face again.

Imogen could feel the tears coming, now that the excitement was draining away. "I didn't mean—I—"

"Oh, God," Mayne said, fishing about in a pocket. "Here." He handed her a large handkerchief.

"I'm sorry," Imogen wailed.

Mayne settled her into a more comfortable position on his knee. She seemed to have launched into a proper rainstorm, but if there was one thing that every English gentleman knew, it was that a rainstorm always passed eventually. He started thinking about his stables. The Ascot was coming up, and a man couldn't be too prepared.

Sixteen

It was at the end of their first week of traveling that Ewan made up the game. He wanted more than ten kisses. *Annabel* wanted more than ten kisses. Somehow, kissing Ewan made her thirsty, so much so that she spent hours in the coach stealing glances at him, only to find that he was looking back at her, and the expression in his eyes—

It was only two of the clock, time for luncheon, and they'd already spent all ten kisses, starting that very morning, when Ewan stole one over the bolster, breaking his own rule about no kissing in the bedchamber.

"We'll just stop in the next village and ask the priest to marry us," he said.

But Annabel resisted that notion. "No," she said, shaking her head. "I don't wish to. I want to be married by your Father Armailhac." They had whiled away the time—at least when Ewan wasn't riding alongside the carriage—by talking, and Annabel was more and more curious about this serious, tender monk whom Ewan described as something of a father to him. "Besides, we don't reach a village until this evening, don't you remember? We're having a picnic luncheon."

Mac had arranged everything, loading great baskets into one of the carriages that went before them, promising that all would be ready when they arrived. Life with Mac, Annabel was finding, was a very pleasant thing.

"A picnic," Ewan groaned. "And no—"

"None," Annabel said firmly. She wasn't sure why she was enjoying this game of the kisses so very much. But she was. There was a huge pleasure in the way they could and couldn't touch, in the way she could tell him no, again and again, and then finally let him crush her into his arms. The only problem was that they were having some trouble distinguishing the end of a kiss. In Ewan's mind, one kiss took at least a half hour. "I *am* a Scotsman," he kept telling her. "Obviously you're used to the English, and we all know what a hasty species they are."

She wasn't quite certain what he was referring to, but she didn't inquire. Obviously, haste was an undesirable quality in the bedchamber.

The carriage was drawing to a halt for luncheon when Ewan had his idea. "The goal of this journey is to come to know each other better," he said, a wicked grin in his eyes. "So I suggest that we make a more concerted effort in that direction."

"Certainly," she agreed.

"We'll ask each other questions."

"But we already do that," she objected.

"Difficult questions. And every question that's answered truly and openly, with honesty here"—he put his hand on his heart—"earns a kiss."

"So if I don't answer a question honestly, then there's no kiss?" she asked.

"None. But you have to ask me questions as well."

"Who decides whether an answer was honest or not?"

"The person who gave it, of course. I'll start. Now, Miss Annabel Essex, imagine you're before the mighty recording angel himself. What is your worst fault?"

"I have none," she said flippantly.

The footman cast open the door and Ewan handed her out. "And were you honest?" he asked, when she was squarely on her feet, to the side of a charming meadow.

"No," she said. "Oh, Ewan, isn't this lovely?"

Mac was there, bowing and clutching a sheaf of papers. "Lord Ardmore, your picnic is set up in the glade just beyond those trees, if you and your ladyship wouldn't mind walking through the meadow. It is quite dry."

"Mac, this is lovely!" Annabel said, beaming at him.

"And yourself and the men?" Ewan said.

Mac nodded across the road, quite in the other direction. Annabel could see a rough table set up in the sunshine, with what looked like a keg of ale next to it. "Since we have a long drive before we reach Witham Common, I thought it best if we take a comfortable pause here and perhaps an afternoon rest before continuing. We won't supper until ten or even later."

A slow smile spread over Ewan's face. "Mac, remind me that I am doubling your salary," he said. And then he offered an arm to Annabel.

For early May, the weather was utterly lovely. The sky was a high, pale blue, like faded linen hung in the sun. Just a few clouds floated high in its arch. The meadow itself was littered with cow parsley whose white flowers stood vividly against new grass. They crossed the meadow and entered a line of alders that divided the meadow from a little glade. Under the alders were blue-bells, dark blue, blue flowers hanging their little heads from the beauty of their blossoms.

"Oh, look," Annabel cried, sinking to her knees and gathering bluebells. "There's so many of them, I've never seen so many!"

Ewan crouched down beside her. "They're almost the color of your eyes," he said, holding one up next to her cheek. "No, not quite. You have extraordinary eyes, do you know that?"

She caught a smile back, but it trembled in the air between them. "You're a flatterer," she said severely. "I shall ask you for your worst fault, and then be able to judge the truth of your answer for myself."

He smiled at her, a crooked smile, and didn't answer. And she had a lap full of bluebells, so she pulled up her skirts before her to hold them and they walked over to the blankets Mac had laid out in the shade of a oak tree. The sun danced through the small leaves of the oak, turning them saffron and dappling the blankets with the ghosts of baby leaves. Ewan very seriously filled all the glasses with bluebells, and gave them water from the stream, so the picnic turned from a very formal affair, all heavy silver and starched linen, to a child's tea party.

And then he stretched out across from her and Annabel realized that he had hardly said a word since she said she had no faults.

"What is your greatest fault?" she asked him.

"My faults are legion," he said. "And I think I may be in the process of changing the king, as it were."

"Oh," she said, rather disconcerted to find him so serious on the subject. "And what is your newest fault, then, pray?"

"Lust," he said, and grinned wolfishly at her. "I've earned myself a kiss for my honesty."

She could feel laughter bubbling up in her chest. "That's a short-lived fault," she said. "From all I heard from the wives in the village, lust is something a man feels for his wife only briefly, if at all."

"Not I," Ewan said, ignoring her jesting tone. "I expect I'll be lusting for you to the day I meet my Maker."

Annabel raised an eyebrow, but somehow Ewan seemed immune to sarcastic comments. It was hard to be cynical around him; the words just seemed to die before they could be spoken. So she picked up a dainty cucumber sandwich and ate it.

After a while he still hadn't said anything, and she was beginning to feel the silence was oppressive, so she said, "I'm not sure that *lust* even counts as a sin when it's between a man and his wife. Not that I'm your wife, but—"

"But you will be," he said. "I was just thinking of the same thing. I'll have to ask Father Armailhac that."

"You take the question awfully seriously," she said.

"We've no glass," he said, handing her an open bottle of white wine.

She looked at him in astonishment. "I can't drink without a glass."

"Can't you? Why not?" He took the bottle back and swung it into the air.

She laughed. "I can't drink that way."

"Ladies have a tiresome number of restrictions," he said, pulling bluebells out of a wineglass and stuffing them into a water glass with a number of their brothers. Then he poured her a glass of wine. "And I do take those questions seriously."

"Why?" she asked. The wine was lightly sparkling and slipped down her throat with a smell of flowers.

"Why? Because I care for my soul," he said, drinking from the bottle again.

She stared at him, trying to figure out exactly what he

meant. But it was hard to keep her mind on the task. Now she knew how soft his hair felt against her fingers, and the way it curled at the nape. And she knew the feeling of his face when a beard was just beginning, as it was now. And the softness of his lips, the way they turned her weak at the knees and made her collapse into his arms. And his eyes—

"If you look at me like that, lass," her husband-to-be said quietly, "we'll have to rely on God's grace to forgive us for disregarding our vows."

She blinked. "I was only trying to decide what you meant by your soul," she said, but she could hear how her voice seemed to have turned husky.

"I meant that I care about my soul," he said. "There's no other way to put it, that I can think of. 'Tis a valuable thing God gave me, and I've no mind to mar it."

Annabel frowned and absentmindedly drank the rest of the wine in her cup. "Are you saying that you're— you're *religious*?"

He looked mildly surprised. "I'm not entirely sure what you mean by that, but I suspect the answer is yes."

Religious? She and her sisters had gone to church every week of their lives, but she would never call herself more than observant. She had hardly exchanged more than a word or two with their priest in the past few years; their father had said that he was a dagger-cheap beggar, and left the church before the organ quieted. Which meant the priest had made the mistake of asking her father to tithe part of his income.

Once they moved to England, Rafe rarely made it out of bed in time to join them on Sundays, and although Griselda had her own little pearl-encrusted prayer book, when she returned she talked of friends she'd seen, and never of the sermon.

Ewan drank again. "My revelation seems to have

halted the conversation," he observed. "You're looking at me as if I'd grown an extra head. I shall count myself as having earned another kiss; after all, you asked me the question."

Annabel tried to figure out what to say. Of course there was nothing wrong with being religious. She knew that perfectly respectable men often went into the church and became archbishops. But that was because they were second sons. And of course she knew that laborers often practiced a kind of superstitious piety. It was an excellent thing for a child to believe in heaven, and she'd found it quite helpful when her mother died. But since then . . .

"I take it that you would not describe yourself as religious," Ewan said.

"No," Annabel said, "although of course I have no concern with the fact that you are—I mean, I'm glad that—" But she got tangled in her sentence, and couldn't think what else to say.

"So do you think I answered you honestly?" he asked, rolling over so that he was quite close to her.

"What? I suppose," she said, still flustered.

"Since I was the one answering the question, I can tell you that I did. Answer honestly." He looked at her expectantly.

"Oh," she murmured, "a kiss. Well." And she leaned forward and pressed a small kiss on his mouth. The kind of thing you'd give to a man who has kept his childish beliefs intact.

Then she pulled away, but he followed her. "An English kiss was not in order," he growled, and suddenly she found herself tipping backward and there she was, like a floundering fish on the riverbank, and this great Scotsman looming over her.

But there was a look in his eyes that made Annabel

forget all about the question of churches and priests and belief in general.

"You owe me a kiss, Miss Annabel Essex," he said to her, his breath warming her cheek. "Two, if my counting is correct." The very nearness of him was making her heart thump in her chest. Yet at the same time, she felt a lazy peace creep over her, the feeling of calm that she always had when she was near him.

He was braced on his elbows now, and leaning over her. Then his head descended and Annabel closed her eyes, blotting out the faint blue of the sky, and the sheen of his hair, and simply allowing her world to become his lips, and the touch of his hand on her cheek. His mouth was warm and persuasive, shaping her lips slowly, patiently, asking a silent question until she opened her mouth and welcomed him.

"You like to keep me out, don't you?" he whispered in a husky murmur.

She couldn't help smiling with the pure glee of it. "Only for a time, so that—"

But she gasped. His mouth had locked on hers, and her cry was unheard. His kiss was scorching in its possession, arrogant in his dominion . . . and all she could do was tremble, and then run her hands into his hair and kiss him back.

It was an eternity later, when her whole body felt ablaze, that he wrenched himself away and said in a growl, "We've one kiss left."

Annabel smiled at him, laced her arm even tighter around his neck and arched up to meet his mouth. "Then come back to me," she breathed.

This time her mouth met his openly, with a wild sweetness that made both their breathing ragged within seconds. She heard a little breathy moan and knew it was hers. She couldn't feel the hard curves and ridges of his body, so she tried to pull him down to her.

But he laughed at that, though the sound caught in his throat, and said, "Nay, not on a kiss."

But then one of his big hands suddenly touched her waist, and she shook with the pure pleasure of it. His mouth came away from hers, but she didn't open her eyes. Because if she opened her eyes, he would take away his hand, and it was inching higher and higher . . .

For a moment, a blissful moment, a large hand cupped her breast and she instinctively arched into it, a cry torn from her throat. A thumb rubbed across her nipple. Annabel had never felt such a thing, as if that small motion scorched her whole body. He did it again, and her eyes flew open, seeking his face. He was leaning over her, his jaw hard, and then just as their eyes met he rubbed across her again and she cried out, pulled his head to hers and pulled him down to her in the process. So then there they were, his lips ravaging hers, and his hand trapped between them.

And then Ewan wrenched his mouth from hers and rolled away. She heard his ragged breathing over the thumping in her ears.

Finally she opened her eyes and stared at the bleached sky. She wasn't sure what to do. She'd behaved like a wanton. And wouldn't he be horrified, a man of God as he was? "That kiss is over," she said finally.

A feeling of shame was creeping over her. She knew well enough what she'd been wanting. She'd wanted him to pull down her bodice and touch her naked breast with his hand. And if she hadn't been so embarrassed, she would have asked him to do it. Shameful. She bit her lip and wished she never had to open her eyes again. Wished she could just pretend that this all never happened.

"I think," he said, and his voice sounded almost normal, "that we should pretend that never happened."

He agreed with her! Annabel felt a flash of acute shame, and then shook it away. What was done was done.

She sat up, avoiding his eyes, and fussed with her hair. Then she saw her wineglass and reached for it, appalled to find that her hands were shaking. She drank the whole glass and it helped, some. Its faint flowery bitterness was cool on her throat. But she couldn't meet his eyes.

He poured her another glass of wine. "You'd best eat something before drinking more wine," he said, sounding amused again.

It was rather tiresome, how he always sounded amused, Annabel decided. Finally, she looked over at him. Naturally, he looked as calm as if nothing had happened. She was beginning to think that nothing rattled Ewan's calm. She cast around in her mind for a nice, innocuous question to ask, one that would show that she too was utterly unconcerned about—about that.

"How many days would you estimate are left on our journey?" she asked, and then realized her mistake the moment he laughed.

Her cheeks stained scarlet, but Ewan only said, "Eight."

She nodded and ate a cucumber sandwich.

"Now I'm afraid to ask you any questions," he said conversationally.

"Go ahead," she said. "I won't answer with honesty, and then there's no call for alarm."

"Very well, then," he said. "Did you like my kiss, Annabel?" The very sound of his lazy voice sent tingles down her spine. It was maddening.

"I think that you are improving. Lord Simon Guthrie was strong competition, but you are quite good as well."

He gave a shout of laughter. "The only good news about your answer is that I don't earn another kiss."

She bit her lip and tried not to feel stupid.

"I couldn't take another kiss like that. I'm not answering a question, so I don't mind telling the truth. I've never felt like that while kissing a woman, and I never thought to. And," he added, "I'm rather worried that when we finally get that blasted set of vows out of the way, we'll suffer spontaneous combustion. I've heard it can happen."

A smile prickled at her lips but she couldn't look at him. She *couldn't*.

"Since I'm being so honest here," he continued, "I'm also a bit worried that you hate me now that I touched your breast. I didn't mean to do it." And then he wasn't sitting on the other side of the picnic cloth, but kneeling just before her. "Forgive me, Annabel? I know I should never have touched you in such a fashion before we were married, let alone in the out-of-doors. I—I lost control and you're likely thinking it's because I'm an uncouth man but—"

There really was anguish in his voice. "Ewan," she said.

"Yes?"

"Do you like kissing me?"

"In God's truth, lass, it's the only thing I think about from morning till night."

"I just won a kiss," she said achingly, finally meeting his green-flecked eyes. What she saw there made her smile tremble with the pure force of it. Then she reached out and pulled him toward her and fell backward, and his heavy body followed hers. It was as if they had never stopped kissing, that's how fast the heat returned. In less than a second, she couldn't catch her breath, and she couldn't think, but she did do just one thing.

She took his hand from her cheek and she moved it.

He groaned aloud when his hand cupped her breast, shaped it as if it were made for no other purpose. But he didn't touch her nipple again. He just kissed her, all that wild hunger sweetened with a promise, and the truth between them.

And when he pulled back his head this time, she smiled up at him.

"I think my hand is frozen in place," he said to her.

"Mac will be very surprised, then," she said, gurgling with laughter.

He reluctantly rolled away and sat up. "No more questions."

"None."

"At least not today," he amended. "Would you like a piece of chicken?"

Perversely, the only things that came into Annabel's mind were questions. She ate an apple, and eyed Ewan, and all the questions she had in mind had to do with whether his chest was truly as muscled as she remembered, and whether it was a golden color, or whether that was just a trick of her memory. The rest of her questions couldn't even be put into words.

The wine tasted like clear water spiced with flowers; it was making her feel uncivilized and free.

"Of course," he continued, "you *do* have one question, so to speak, left to you."

"And that is?"

"You won the archery contest. You won a forfeit of me. Remember?" His eyes were dark and shamelessly seductive. "You could ask me anything, Annabel, and I'd have to do it for you."

In one smooth motion, Annabel slid down so that she was in a most unladylike pose, lying on her side just as he was, her head propped up by an elbow. It was scandalous. She grinned at him with the pure pleasure of it.

"You'll have to give me some suggestions," she said, and her voice poured out like slightly burnt honey. "You know, Lord Ardmore, that I am not as experienced in these things as you are."

"There you make an assumption."

He was grinning at her. What could he mean? Annabel opened her mouth to ask him a question, but they'd said no questions.

"No questions at all?" she queried.

"Perhaps I can guess what you'd like to know," he said, eyes dancing.

"Quite likely," she returned.

"There aren't many likely candidates for my affections in the wilds of Clashindarroch Forest," he said, using his eyes shamelessly. "When I was a lad, I did practice my skills for a short while with a willing young lady from the village. But then my Uncle Pearce pulled me to the side and said some strong things about the nature of responsibility and what would happen if a woman came with child. I'm their earl, you see."

She nodded.

"I was tutored at home, and in the normal way of things I would have found myself at a university and there would have met many a young woman who might be able to train me in the ways of women. But unfortunately, before I could do such a thing Rosy was sent to me, under the terms of my father's agreement with her father. Rosy would have stayed with us for a few years before we consummated the marriage, while I was off at university. She was only thirteen, you see."

"Thirteen!" Annabel gasped, forgetting her languorous pose and sitting up. "That's awful. Poor, poor Rosy!"

His mouth was a tight, straight line. "I couldn't leave her, especially when we discovered she was with child."

"Did she even know what was happening?"

"Not really. And the night she gave birth . . ." his eyes had an anguished look. "By then she was able to tolerate my presence. She liked me, even. But when the pains came, she decided somewhere in her tangled-up little brain that they must be my fault. And even though I took myself away, she kept breaking free of the chamber where they had her and looking for me. Finally Nana—my grandmother—decided it was better for her to be able to express herself. So I came to the birthing room."

Annabel pushed the picnic things to the side and sat down next to Ewan's reclining body. She wound her fingers into his thick, beautiful hair, and said, "Tell me."

"As long as she could stand up, she beat at my chest with her fists," he said expressionlessly. "Then, when she could no longer stand up, she cried. And bit my hand."

"Bit your hand?" Annabel repeated, stunned.

He rolled onto his back and held up his right hand. There was a deep scar below his thumb.

"Poor you! And poor girl . . . that's awful. Did she have any idea what was going on?"

"Not that we could see. Clearly she thought I was inflicting that pain on her."

Annabel swallowed. "The baby?"

"Was quite healthy. I can't say it was a very pleasant experience being there at his birth, but Gregory was a fine bouncing boy who screamed himself purple. And that's how I lost my chance to take university courses in the art of seducing women."

Annabel had lost track of his reason for telling the

story in the pain of its details. "Rosy was only thirteen when Gregory was born?" she asked.

"She was fourteen by his birth. She's never been a mother to him, but she did play with him a great deal when he was younger. I'm hoping that she'll never develop the fear of him that she has of other men."

"Does he know that she's his mother?"

"Well, he knows and doesn't, if you see what I mean. He's fond of her, I'm sure of that. He's a good-hearted boy, and generally kind. But he doesn't see her as a *mother,* no."

"You are a good man," Annabel said to him. He was lying on his back next to her. All that thick russet-colored hair had fallen into a patch of sunshine, and he was manifestly beautiful. "It was truly good of you to keep Rosy with you."

"Don't go thinking that I took care of her myself," he said, reaching up and tugging on one of her curls. "She couldn't bear the sight of me for a good while after the birth, for one thing. 'Tis my grandmother and the monks who've done the most for her."

"But you didn't leave," she said. "You let her bite you." She picked up his hand and kissed it, running her lips along the white scar.

"I've scars in other places," he said, his eyes crinkling with wicked laughter. "Perhaps you'd like to kiss all of them?"

Suddenly temptation was running in her veins like the flowered wine, making her feel brave and curious. "You owe me a forfeit," she said. "Anything I care to ask."

"True." The whole sunlit meadow seemed to be holding its breath, waiting for her to say something. Even the lazy hum of bees had faded away.

And yet she hadn't lost her senses. The sweetness of this lazy afternoon was undercut by a sharp current of desire, strung between them as tight as wire. "Then I'd like you to remove your jacket," she said, throwing caution to the winds. "And your shirt as well."

His lazy eyes swept over her with a blatant invitation. "And if I'm unclothed—here—in the outdoors, what of you?"

"What of me?" she asked. " 'Tis I who am owed a boon. By you," she added, in case he'd forgotten.

With a mock sigh, he sat up and pulled off his coat. It was finely made, to wrap close to the body, and Annabel almost leaned forward to help him, but the gesture felt too intimate. She stayed where she was.

He undid his cravat, watching her the whole time, and threw it to the side.

"You'll have to tell your valet it was uncomfortable," she chattered, feeling slightly dizzied by—by something.

He smiled at her but said nothing, undoing the buttons at his neck. Then slowly he stood up and pulled his shirt over his head. It billowed for a moment, like the sails of a great ship, and fell to the side.

"And what do you think, Miss Annabel Essex?" he inquired. Amusement and desire entwined in his voice in a wine more spicy than that in their glasses.

He stood above her, dappled with the shadow of saffron oak leaves. And she had remembered correctly: his chest was thick with muscle, beautiful, covered with skin that looked like rough satin kissed by the sun.

In one smooth motion he came to his knees by her side. "When you look at me like that," he said, "I truly feel that I am one of God's creatures."

Annabel couldn't see what God had to do with it, but never mind. Close up, his stomach had no extra flesh, just rippled muscles that made her long to touch him.

"Put on this earth for no other reason than to adore

you," he said. "Do you know the lines we use in the Scottish marriage service: *With my body, I thee worship*?"

A smile uncurled on Annabel's lips. "Isn't that rather pagan for one as Christian as you?"

"Never. By worshiping you, I worship God. You are one of His most beautiful creatures, after all."

Annabel liked the compliment, if it was a bit over-mixed with theology for her taste. He could call it what he wanted: she saw hunger in his gaze. Hunger for *her*.

Ewan saw that little self-satisfied smile on his future wife's face and it made him feel reckless and drunk, naked in the afternoon. *She* was the pagan, his wife, a glorious, deliriously beautiful pagan. He reached out without even realizing what he was about to do.

His fingers were deft, quick as lightning. Annabel's traveling dress buttoned up the front, to make it easier for the traveler to unclothe herself in the absence of a maid. Those buttons flew apart at the touch of his fingers and Annabel—Annabel quivered like a newborn fawn, but she didn't stop his hand. He told himself that if she said *no,* he would stop. But she made no sound other than the sound of a shaky breath . . . and that was so entrancing that he unbuttoned even faster.

One second, two seconds later, he eased the dress back over her shoulders. Of course, she was wearing more layers.

"Doesn't that—" His voice caught in his throat. For she was smiling at him, the mysterious, timeless smile of a woman, and unlacing her corset.

Still without saying a word, he pulled her chemise up. Her cheeks took on a wild-rose color, but she said nothing, allowed him to tug the chemise over her hair . . . and there she was.

Sitting with her legs curled to the side, her dress still

modestly clinging to her hips, but bare from the waist up.

And she was lovely. "Ach, lass," he whispered, "you *are* the finest of God's creations." He wanted to kiss every inch of her skin, make her ache inside as he was doing. Her body was ripe in the sunlight, curved and shadowed with such delicious skill that his hands trembled to touch her.

"I daren't come near you," he said, his voice strangled in his throat.

Something about that seemed to give her cheer, and she grinned at him with a flash of her usual impudence. "I shan't touch you either." And then: "Do you really mean to say that you haven't seen a woman since you were a lad?"

"I was older than a boy. But you were worth waiting for." There was a note in his voice that she heard as the deep bell of truth.

He picked up one of her bluebells, its little bonnets hanging heavy, and drew it slowly over the delicate curve of her shoulder, blazing a path where his tongue could follow when they got to his lands.

She shivered and looked down. They watched together as dusky blue blossoms trailed over the generous curve of her breast, over her rosy nipple—

"Stop," she breathed.

But he was entranced, watching her shiver under the flower's caress, dazzled by the flash of creamy skin against deep blue.

She reached for her chemise and pulled it over her head so quickly that the flower flew to the side and landed in his glass of wine.

Ewan sighed. She was right, of course. As it was, his breeches were strained in an agonizing fashion.

"That did not happen," Annabel said. By the time she dared look at Ewan, he was tying his cravat. His fingers looked perfectly steady. "We will not discuss it, ever."

"There's no need to discuss it," he told her, his voice sending a quiver of pleasure down her legs. Or perhaps it was that look in his eyes. "I'll never forget it."

Annabel threw back her head and looked up. By evening, the sky might—just might—echo the beauty of the bluebells. But there was nothing in nature that came close to the beauty of Ewan's green-gold eyes. Nothing.

Seventeen

Annabel woke at dawn. There was something nagging at the back of her mind, an elusive thought. Ewan was breathing next to her, long slow breaths. He slept like a cat: as quiet and contained as he was while awake.

Light was stealing through curtains of their bedchamber. For a while Annabel watched sleepily as the rays crept across the polished mahogany of their bedchamber in the Queen's Arms . . . the very *best* bedchamber. Ewan had laughed last night when he discovered that the chamber pot was made of bronze, decorated by delicate satyrs chasing about the rim. Annabel had blushed and looked away; there were some aspects to the intimacy of marriage that she wasn't prepared for, such as Ewan even mentioning such an object in her presence.

The chamber pot was bronze. The desk was mahogany. These sheets were linen; well, they were Ewan's own sheets, put on the bed fresh every night.

Her mouth fell open.

The truth was blindingly clear.

Ewan was rich.

Very rich. He had to be. Her husband rode in a coach with twelve outriders. He was no improvident, penniless Scot along the lines of her father. Everything she knew about Ewan told her that he would not waste his substance on luxuries, unless he had so much that such luxuries were insignificant.

For a moment she just blinked at the pearly morning light. Of course Ewan was a wealthy man. It spoke in every movement he made, in the gleam of his boots, in the casual way in which he trusted Mac to handle everything, in the beauty of his carriages. She'd been blinded by her own fear.

A surge of pure joy washed over her, followed immediately by shame. But she shook the shame away. Just because she married a man who believed in God didn't mean that she had to start worrying about her soul right and left. It was perfectly sensible to wish to marry a rich man. She'd never thought it greedy while in England, and she wasn't going to turn into a Puritan just because she married one.

At that moment, Ewan woke up, in the same silent, contained way in which he did everything, moving straight from sleep to wakefulness.

"Tell me about your home," she demanded.

"And good morning to you," he said, giving her his lazy smile.

"Your home?" she asked again, batting away a hand that stretched over the bolster and seemed to have improper ideas in mind.

He gave up and rolled over, stretching. "It's an old pile of stones that's been the family seat for ages. Luckily for all of us, my great-grandfather was a bad-tempered fellow who stayed put when Prince Charles summoned the clans. Apparently he said that he didn't give a damn who was on the throne, and a Hanoverian would be as witless as a Stuart."

"It's a castle, isn't it?" Annabel said, knowing the truth.

"Of course," Ewan said, yawning. "If you wish to make some changes, I'd be happy. No one's touched the furniture since my mother died, and that's over twenty years ago now. My grandmother's not a very domestic type of woman."

Annabel couldn't think of a word to say. She was marrying a man who lived in a castle. She couldn't help it. There was a grin on her face that had nothing to do with virtue, and everything to do with castles.

"Nana likes to be out and about," Ewan was saying. "She's not the type to sit around the castle and think about upholstery. She spends most of her day visiting the cottages."

"The cottages," Annabel repeated, congratulating herself on remaining so calm.

"Quite a few people live and work on my land. They're the cottagers and crofters, or so we call them. And Nana runs about interfering with their lives and generally making herself a nuisance, but I believe they like her, for all that. She's very good at birthing babies."

Annabel tried to focus her attention on a sweet-faced Scottish grandmother, bringing everyone jars of home-made jelly and strengthening broth. "She sounds like a lovely person," she said. "You were fortunate to have her when your parents died."

"I was lucky," Ewan agreed. "Although I'm not quite certain most people would describe her as lovely. She's— well. She's just Nana."

He swung out of bed. "I'll go downstairs to bathe and

then meet you for breakfast, shall I?" he asked. Ewan was a very clean person: every morning he bathed at the sluice, and in the evening he had a full bath. Annabel liked that. She liked the way his shoulders tapered as he pulled on a clean shirt. And then there was the castle. She was a little afraid of just how happy she was feeling.

So she sat on the edge of the bed, watching as he moved around the room. Quite unusually for a man, he was swiftly putting everything into order, rather than waiting for the servants to do so.

Apparently her fears about this marriage weren't true. She wasn't marrying an improvident Scotsman who would gamble away their breakfast. There was—there was nothing to be afraid of when she was with Ewan. It made her feel as if she were light as air, almost as if she couldn't breathe.

"You look very serious," he said, pulling on his breeches.

"What are you most afraid of in the world?" she asked.

He turned about with a wry grin. "A serious question . . . Are you trolling for kisses, so early in the morning?"

She made a face at him.

Now there wasn't an object out of its place in the room; the only unkempt thing in it was Annabel herself. So she picked up a brush from her side table.

"I'll do that," Ewan said, taking it from her. He sat down on the bed and began drawing the brush through her long hair.

"I'm most afraid of losing my soul," he said a moment later. " 'Tis easily said, and, I hope, easily prevented. And the fear of it certainly doesn't keep me up at night."

"What could cause you to lose your soul?" she asked, frowning at the wall. She was starting to think that perhaps a more thorough education in the church might be helpful in making her way through this marriage.

"Only a terrible fault," he said, turning her face so he could drop a kiss on her lips. "I shouldn't lose it for lust, for example." His eyes lingered on her, and Annabel knew suddenly that it didn't matter whether she was wearing a high-necked cotton nightgown or even a burlap sack. Ewan always wanted her. He *lusted* for her.

"Then?" she prompted.

"Oh, something terrible," he said lightly. "I'm telling you, lass, I don't worry about it. Perhaps adultery. So the marvelous thing is that by marrying you, I'm saving my immortal soul. I could never sleep with another woman after you."

"Who's to say that?" Annabel said, pulling back. "I've always thought that adultery was something that gentlemen practiced with some ease. And other types of men as well," she added.

"Not all gentlemen." He paused. "Did you think to practice adultery? And that's a question, Annabel."

"I thought to marry for practical reasons," she told him, and only then did she realize that she was going to tell him the truth. "For comfort and ease. I thought to marry a man who desired me, and trade his desire for my security. And then, after I had fulfilled the obligations of marriage, I thought that he would likely turn to others and I might, someday, find pleasure for itself."

"You actually planned to be adulterous," he said, seemingly fascinated.

"It wasn't like that," she said crossly. "'Twas only a practical look at the way people truly behave. Imogen could afford to be romantic, but I never could."

"Poor love," he said, and gathered her into his arms. Her arms slipped around his waist as if they had always belonged there. She leaned her head against his chest and listened to the strong thump of his heart. "Obviously you haven't been spending your time worrying about things as ephemeral as souls. What's your greatest fear, then?"

"The kisses are piling up," she murmured.

"Mmmm . . . tonight," he said, and she shivered against him with the promise of it. "What does one fear if you don't believe in the hereafter?" He sounded genuinely curious.

"It's not that I don't believe in heaven," she told him (although she didn't, not very much). "But I don't worry about it."

"What *do* you worry about?"

"Being poor again," she admitted. "I would hate that."

His arms tightened. "Hunger is a terrible thing."

"We weren't ever really hungry," Annabel said. "There was always enough to eat; it was just the same food day after day. No, I'm afraid of the exhaustion of it. The strain of not being able to pay a bill when it comes due. The humiliation of trying to convince someone to wait for his justly earned payment. Of not having a single chemise without a hole in it."

He said nothing.

"You're rich, aren't you?" she demanded fiercely.

He kissed her. "I am."

"Why didn't you tell me?"

"I wanted you to like me for myself first. And you do, don't you? At least, you like some of the things I do *to* you."

He laughed at her blush, but she felt ashamed, to the very tips of her toes. She felt shabby and small.

"I estimate that we owe each other at least five extra kisses," he said, smiling down at her. There wasn't an ounce of condemnation in his eyes.

"Don't you mind?" she asked him.

"Mind what?"

"Mind that I—I wanted to marry a rich man, and now I'm marrying you—"

" 'Tis an example of God's gifts, isn't it? Money has never meant much to me; I grew up with lots of it, and without family, and I hadn't the heart to attach myself to the coins. But for you this money was important, and perhaps that's the reason I have it."

She buried her head against his middle and thought about how simple his view of life was, and then, with a kindled fire, how easy it would be to love a person like him. Like Ewan. "But if you're only afraid for your soul," she asked suddenly, "does that mean you're not afraid for your person?"

"What do you mean?"

"Well, when the robbers were in the hotel room, you looked furious, but you undressed without putting up a fight."

"I was furious. And I was worried about you and your sister. But there wasn't any real reason to start a fight. If I did so, they might shoot off one of those guns, and then someone would be hurt. Whereas if I just gave them what they wanted, they would leave without violence."

"Even though they tried to humiliate you by making you take off your clothing?"

He grinned. "I got to see your eyes widen when you realized what you were looking at. That moment paid back any humiliation. Besides, Annabel, what if I had fought?"

"You were much bigger than either of them."

"I could have taken one of their guns away," he said. "And then what would I have done with it?"

"Threatened them?"

"Do I look like someone who would hold a gun to your head and threaten to kill you?"

"Why not?" she asked uncertainly. "Anyone can do that."

"You have to mean it. I would never point a gun at a person because I would never mean to kill him." He paused. "And there's an answer to what would kill my immortal soul: killing a man, and all because I wouldn't share my money with him. How many kisses is *that*?"

She had to laugh. Until he took her breath away with a kiss.

Eighteen

The Earl of Mayne put down a detailed account of a promising yearling being offered by the Grafton stud and sighed. His butler stood at the door of his study, his body stiff with annoyance. Rimple was a highly principled individual who had made it clear that he would countenance his employer's debauchery only as long as proprieties were observed.

"Is she here?" Mayne asked, knowing the answer.

"A carriage with the Maitland coat of arms is drawn up at the front door," Rimple said, his lips barely moving. "If you wish, I will ascertain whether Lady Maitland is within. Since she has not emerged herself, I would conjecture that her ladyship wishes you to join her in the vehicle."

To Rimple's mind, gentlemen paid visits to unmarried ladies, and not the other way around. The London *ton* agreed with him. Yet somehow Mayne couldn't manage to convince Imogen of that fact: she had already visited him twice this week in the broad daylight, which gave the servants up and down St. James's Street ample opportunity to gossip as well as delighting scandal rags in need of material to print.

Mayne rose. Life had been easier when he was bedding a number of ladies, rather than *not* sleeping with only one lady, Imogen. His previous consorts had precisely understood the power of reputation, the need for a guarded show of chaste behavior and the delicious piquancy of secrecy. Imogen was like some sort of puppy, rushing in wherever she wanted, and the hell with the consequences.

Rimple offered Mayne his greatcoat. "Perhaps her ladyship wishes you to join her for a brief drive in the park," he said.

Mayne understood. If he himself entered the carriage, rather than allowing Imogen to enter his house, little scandal would result. He shrugged on his greatcoat, selected a hat from the three offered by a footman and walked into the morning sunshine. It was still rather startling to find himself up so early in the morning.

Until the previous year, he had rarely gone to sleep before five in the morning, spending his evenings dancing and his nights snug against the curves of a beautiful woman. Consequently he had dodged morning sunshine for years. Now he looked around and shrugged. He wasn't going to fool himself that the sight of dew shining on the spiky leaves of daffodils at his front step was compensation for the pleasure of watching a woman's eyes close in ecstasy.

The footman waiting at the door of Imogen's carriage opened the door as he approached. Had he promised to go for a drive this morning? Surely not. It was only nine o'clock, and he generally maintained the delusion that he was still leading a fashionable life, even though these evenings he found himself sitting at home with a book more often than not.

He took off his hat and entered the carriage. But instead of a minx hell-bent on impropriety, an oddly respectable party met his gaze.

"Why, Grissie," he said, bending to kiss his sister's cheek. "And Miss Josephine." He nodded to Imogen's little sister, and finally to Imogen herself. "I regret to say that my engagement to drive with you this morning somehow slipped my mind."

"We had no appointment," Imogen said blithely.

"Then to what do I owe this pleasure?" Mayne asked. "I thought you were laid up with a cold, Grissie." He sat down opposite his sister.

"I'm over the worst of it," she said. To a brother's eyes, Griselda still looked rather hagged. Of course, this was likely the first time she'd been awake at this hour since the season began.

"To what do I owe the pleasure of your presence, given your malaise?" Mayne asked. The carriage jolted and started down the street without further ado. "May I ask where we are going?"

There was an odd moment of silence in the carriage.

Mayne raised an eyebrow and looked at his companions' faces. Griselda had closed her eyes and was obviously pretending she didn't hear the question. Therefore, despite her denial of responsibility, he inferred that she approved of the expedition.

Imogen favored him with a wicked grin. He was starting to see that mischievous look more and more as her grief for her husband receded. One had to assume that her true nature was emerging, a thought that would fill any sane man with trepidation.

"I'm not going to like your answer," he stated.

"Myself," Imogen said, "I like surprises. Why, when Annabel and Tess surprised me on my eighth birthday—"

"Imogen."

She pouted at him, luscious, dark red lips as plump as raspberries. Moments like these made him wonder whether something was physically the matter with him. He didn't seem to feel a flicker of desire, and Imogen was eminently desirable.

The thought made him scowl. "Cut rope, if you please. Where are we bound?"

"Scotland," she said brightly. "Isn't that an adventure?"

"If you meant that by way of an invitation, I'm not accompanying you. The Ascot is nearly upon us. I'm far too busy, and far too uninterested. When are you planning to travel? And why?"

"Please accompany us?" Imogen begged, making her fine dark eyes tragic. Faced with that appeal, another man, Mayne thought dispassionately, would grovel at her feet. One moment Imogen looked like a naughty imp, and the next she was all woman, looking at him as if he were the only man in the world capable of saving her from the guillotine. Her eyes shone with tears, her mouth pouted and her breast heaved—

"Absolutely not," he said. And then, out of pure curiosity, "Were you planning to take that little performance on the stage?"

"What performance?" she asked, looking like a cat who had never smelled cream.

"That one you gave me just now."

Her grin was (if she but knew it) fifty times more entrancing than her practiced repertoire of seductive glances. "I hadn't thought of the stage, but perhaps you're right. I could become an actress!"

Mayne almost groaned. Wonderful. He'd given a woman bent on ruining herself yet another avenue to disgrace herself.

"But not yet," Imogen said. "First we have to save Annabel."

"Annabel? Is that why you're talking of Scotland?"

"We are going to Scotland!" Griselda snapped, opening her eyes and giving him a pained look. "Do you think anything other than utter necessity would get me into a carriage on its way to Scotland? *Anything?*" Griselda suffered from a weak stomach and loathed lengthy carriage rides.

"If you're asking whether I have forgotten how frequently you vomited on my feet when we were children, the answer is no," Mayne said testily. He was starting to get a very nasty feeling. Why was Griselda wearing a traveling dress? Why was she up so early? And—most importantly—why had the carriage stopped for him?

"Imogen," he said. "Where is this carriage headed? At this very moment?"

She met his eyes without a drop of shame. "Scotland," she said. "Aberdeenshire, Scotland. To the holdings of the Earl of Ardmore."

Mayne's eyes narrowed. "You can let me out here," he said, his voice as cold as polished steel.

"I shall not," she said, folding her arms over her chest.

Mayne leaned forward so he could rap on the box, summoning the coachman.

"Oh, for goodness' sake," Griselda moaned, her face already looking a bit green. "Just give him Rafe's note, would you, Imogen?"

Without trusting himself to speak, Mayne took the note that Imogen extracted from her reticule and ripped it open.

Mayne,

*Something extraordinary has happened; it appears
I have a family member of whom I knew nothing.
I can't explain at the moment, but I must beg you
to help me with a problem that has arisen with my
guardianship of the Essexes. Felton has managed
to solve the fiasco of Annabel's scandal in a way
that does not necessitate her marriage, but you
must be in Scotland before she and Ardmore arrive, so as to head off that wedding. Unfortunately, Felton can't make the trip, and I am tied up
with legal affairs at the moment. If you could see
your way clear to accompanying Griselda, Imogen, and Josie, I would be most grateful.*

Rafe

"Who the hell has showed up in Rafe's family?"
Mayne asked, looking at his sister.

She moaned.

"We're still in the center of London," he pointed out.
"You have no reason to pretend to a stomach malaise
already."

"I'm not pretending!" she said indignantly, her eyes
flying open. "Merely the *thought* of two weeks in this
carriage makes me feel ill."

"Rafe's family?" he asked, with all the impatience of
any younger brother. Still, he didn't neglect the prudent
removal of his booted feet from his sister's proximity.

"An unsavory fellow has claimed kinship," she said,
closing her eyes again. "Wrong side of the blanket, of
course. I only caught a glimpse of the man, but he had a
marked resemblance to Rafe."

"I didn't get to see him at all," Imogen complained.

"This is a most improper subject, especially in Josie's presence," Griselda observed. "We should all forget his existence."

"I'm enjoying it," young Josephine observed. "Unfortunately, I didn't see the man either." Her eyes had a naughty sparkle; clearly she and Imogen were apples from the same family tree.

Imogen paid no heed to Griselda whatsoever. "The improper bit of it is that according to Rafe, he and his half-brother were born within a week of each other."

"Be that as it may," Mayne said, biting off his words, "why on earth did you abscond with me in such a fashion?" From the sound of the wheels he could tell that they had, indeed, left the cobbled streets of London and were heading toward the Great North Road.

"We need you," Imogen said. "We must save Annabel from this marriage; we *must*." There was no sign of humor in her eyes now: she was fierce with sisterly devotion.

"It's too late to save her from anything," Mayne said flatly. "I don't care what solution Felton has come up with. Annabel has been traveling with the Scotsman for days. If that situation doesn't warrant the loss of her reputation, I don't know what would."

Griselda opened her eyes. "Ah, but I've had a chill. I did send you a note telling you so, but I received no expression of sympathy, no flowers, no—"

"For God's sake, Griselda," Mayne said, exasperated, "you take a chill at the—" Suddenly he saw her point. "You're going to say that you traveled with them."

"Of course."

"The truth will leak."

"I doubt it. I have kept to the house for days. My nose was red." She seemed to consider that adequate explanation. "And since we have Josie with us, the whole expedition takes on the flavor of a family trip to the country."

"Well, of all the harebrained schemes—"

"We have Rafe's fastest horses," Imogen said, leaning forward and putting a hand on his knee. "What's more, Rafe has horses housed all along the North Road, whereas Ardmore will presumably be employing job horses. This carriage is beautifully sprung. We can easily beat them, if we put up with a little discomfort and travel a longer day than might be expected."

"Discomfort!" Mayne's mind was reeling. His servants thought he'd gone for a ride in the park. He had no—

"I have no clothes!" he almost shouted.

Imogen patted his knee, precisely as if he were a small child who'd lost his favorite bobble. "Don't worry. I told Rafe's manservant to pack a valise for you."

Rafe's clothing? Was she mad? "Where is your maid?" he snapped at his sister.

"She follows us," Griselda said. "Believe me, Garret, if I could think of another way to save Annabel from this marriage, I would have."

"There's nothing so terrible about the match," Mayne objected.

"The poor girl cried before she left for Scotland. She cried," Griselda said.

"Women always weep at weddings."

"Annabel never cries," Josie put in.

"I wept when Father told me I was to marry Willoughby," Griselda said reflectively, not meeting her brother's eyes.

"Willoughby was a fine fellow," Mayne said. Then, when Griselda said nothing, "Wasn't he?"

"Of course he was," she said. "I can't think why I brought up such a dismal subject as my short-lived marriage. Poor Willoughby."

Mayne could hardly remember his brother-in-law's face; after all, the fellow had fallen dead at the supper table only a year or so after marrying. Overeating, or so his parents had said at the time. He'd always thought Willoughby was a jolly fellow. But perhaps Griselda would have preferred to marry someone else.

"You could have remarried anytime these ten years," he said, staring at his sister.

"True enough." She closed her eyes again. "I can't think why I haven't bothered to do so."

"Sarcasm has never been your forte, Griselda," Mayne observed.

"Annabel cried on hearing that she had to marry Ardmore," Imogen said pointedly. "And she only stopped once we came up with a scheme for her to return to us in six months. That marriage is doomed before it has even begun. Saving her from such a fate is worth some small disruption in our schedules and a little discomfort!"

"Why would you talk of a *little* discomfort, when apparently you think I am comfortable wearing Rafe's clothing? You could have sent me a message last night. My manservant might then be in the carriage with your maid."

"You wouldn't have come with us," Imogen said.

"Yes, I would have!" he retorted.

"No. You would never bestir yourself for something that concerns you so little," Imogen flatly contradicted him.

Mayne ground his teeth.

"Unfortunately, I agree with Imogen on that point," Griselda said. "We're a selfish pair, the two of us. I myself would manifestly prefer not to be traveling into the wilds of Scotland."

"But here you are," Mayne pointed out. "*With* your maid. Whereas apparently I am expected to make the trip without my servant or even a change of clothing."

"It will do you good, Garret," she said, staring at him with all the arrogance of an elder sister. "You've grown too attached to your attire. You don't want to turn into a man milliner, and all out of boredom."

He felt such a surge of rage that there was no speaking about it. So he lapsed into his corner and closed his eyes. Maybe he'd just sleep all the way to Scotland.

Nineteen

For the next few days, Annabel and Ewan kept resolutely to ten kisses per day and no questions. Every once in a while one of them would start to ask a question and stop. And sometimes the other would answer, just for the pleasure of it and although it was not a kissing question.

Annabel felt as if somehow she ended up doing all the talking. Ewan got out of her, by turns and twists and sympathetic eyes, the truth about her father's circumstances.

"So he gambled away all the money in the house?" he said one afternoon, when they were rumbling along the road.

"It wasn't like that!" Annabel protested. "Papa never gambled."

"Aye, but taking the money from the estate and backing a horse, whether it's on the track or in your own stable, *is* gambling." He eyed her over the cribbage board.

"And I'll tell you, lass, that I don't like the fact he made you into his bookkeeper either."

"I like keeping track of numbers," Annabel said rather lamely.

"Then he should have kissed your feet for it," Ewan said. His eyes were laughing again, and he dropped to the carriage floor between them and started on with some nonsense about kissing her feet.

But Annabel couldn't help thinking about it. Ewan would never gamble, not at the track, nor with his own horses. He was a different sort of man from her father.

They were into the highlands by now. "I'm thinking that perhaps we might ask Father Armailhac to marry us on the very day we arrive," Ewan said at luncheon. "Would you be agreeable, darling?"

There was something about the way *darling* rolled from his tongue in a Scottish burr that made Annabel think that she could never say no to him, not if he called her that. A fact that should be concealed obviously. So she pretended to think about it.

"Rafe would be happy to hear that you had followed through on your obligations," she said.

"Yes, and just imagine. The more time that passes, the more likelihood that I'll lose interest and run for the hills."

She had to smile at the look in his eyes. " 'Tis a serious consideration," she agreed.

"Of course, Uncle Pearce would likely step in and marry you, just to save the family name, and given as you're such a ruthless cardplayer."

"I've always thought maturity was an excellent thing in a spouse."

"Damn it, Annabel," he groaned, running his hand through his hair so that it stood straight up. "Will you marry me immediately? Please? I'm dying here."

"I thought you didn't care who you married."

"Now I do," he said flatly.

"Then I shall," she said. "And that's an honest answer."

The smile on his face flew straight to her heart. "I'm saving my kisses for tonight," he said. "And Annabel— I'm giving you warning right here that I'm breaking that foolish rule about no kissing in our bedchamber. You're mine. I shall consider this the moment I asked you to marry me, and forget entirely that business in London."

She swallowed.

"I'll ask Mac to send a message to Father Armailhac," Ewan said. "And then I'll ride outside this afternoon, because otherwise I won't be able to keep my kisses until evening."

Annabel was startled at how much her heart lightened at the sight of long stretches of dark forest. She liked England's tidy green fields and neat little thickets. But there was something glorious about looking out of the carriage window at a rolling hill covered with thick fir. Great birds—kites? hawks?—flew in wide circles over the deep green treetops. Ewan rode by her window, his hair blowing back in the wind, looking red-haired and brawny and Scots to the bone.

Annabel's heart sung. "You're turning into a fool," she muttered to herself. "He's making you into a fool."

But there seemed nothing wrong with foolery, not on a crisp day in May when her near husband had smiled at her in such a way. The problem was that while he rode next to the carriage, all she did was think of questions that she wanted to ask him.

"This is *not* a kissing question," she told him that evening. They were in an inn so old and magnificent that it boasted King James VI once slept there, before he moved down to England. They had eaten like kings, and were finally alone. Bowls of fruit in silver bowls glowed dully in the light from the candles. Annabel regarded Ewan thoughtfully over a tiny glass filled with golden cognac. "How old were you when the flood took your parents?"

"Seven."

"And your siblings?"

"They were twins and still just babies. I only remember the way they used to cry at night. If one stopped, the other would start. My mother and their nurse would run between their cribs and I would laugh."

"So you remember your parents? I have hardly any memories of my mother."

His eyes were shaded by the candlelight so that she couldn't see them clearly. "I remember my mother, but not my father."

There was something about the way he said it that told her Ewan hated not remembering his father. "I'm sorry," she said. "Imogen can't remember Mama at all, and I know that she wishes dearly that she could. When she was small, she always asked for stories about her."

"That's likely part of your sister's problem."

"What do you mean by that?" Annabel scowled at him.

"She's a reckless girl who'll come to grief if she's not lucky, and you know it, darling. After all, first she eloped with her poor husband—and I get the feeling she probably forced the man over the border herself—and then she threw herself at me. A dangerous woman."

Annabel knew she should defend her sister, but something in her liked the fact that Ewan showed no signs of wishing that Imogen had been the one to marry him. "You're not one to talk. After all, you invited Imogen to your hotel."

"But I asked her to marry me first."

Annabel frowned at him. "Did you ask every woman you met to marry you?"

"Not at all," Ewan said. "I only asked two . . . or perhaps three, now I think of it."

"But marriage is a serious consideration!" Annabel cried. "How on earth could you treat it so cavalierly?"

He shrugged. "I don't find the question earthshaking."

"Do you mean," she said slowly, "that it didn't make any difference to you whether you brought home myself or my sister as your bride?" She had a queer, empty feeling in her stomach.

But Ewan grinned at her as cheerfully as ever. "Actually, as I recall, I thought your sister would be a better bride than you."

She scowled at him.

"You're a woman to drive a man insane with desire. And I didn't want that." He didn't even move, but there was something in his eyes that gave her the hot, melting feeling she felt when he kissed her.

"Why not?" she managed.

"I'm not the sort to run after my wife like a tame lapdog. As a rational man, I have no fear that I couldn't make myself compatible with almost anyone. But you . . ."

"You thought I was shrewish and would beat you about the head?" she said, smiling.

His gaze was like a caress. "I thought I ran the risk of making a fool of myself over you," he said. "Prescience on my part, I have no doubt."

"But you wouldn't have made a fool of yourself over Imogen?" Annabel persisted, wanting to hear it said aloud.

"I thought your sister would make a handy wife because she was Scottish, she was miserable and I could give her the heart's ease that she needed. But no, she certainly wouldn't drive me to distraction. I have no doubt we would have become comfortable together, after she'd had time to grieve."

"You thought of Imogen as some sort of charity case!" she said, staring at him in fascination.

He raised an eyebrow. "And isn't she, then? The poor lass was threatening to sleep with the Earl of Mayne. He isn't a man to be toyed with. He's clearly had many a lover, and I didn't think she should be indulging in such antics with Mayne."

"So you asked her to marry you—"

"Which didn't work because the girl was set on debauchery."

"So you invited Imogen to your room," Annabel said with a scowl.

"That was just to dissuade her."

She snorted. "A kind of dissuasion that every rake understands, then."

"I was as coarse to her as I could be, thinking I'd scare her off. I did my best to give her a fear of debauchery. And my plan worked like a charm."

"How did you do it?"

"I suppose these are all relevant points, in the long run," he said. There was a sinful glint in his eye. "I told her that she would have to sleep with me naked. That there'd be no nightgowns between us. Of course," he added, "I wasn't thinking about scraps of silk."

A surge of desire swept over Annabel's body at the look in his eyes. No nightgowns! "You mean adulterous women don't—"

"Never," he said, shaking his head. "Didn't you know that, lass?"

"No, in fact, now that I—"

"*Never*. No more than do man and wife wear clothing in bed together. And then I told her that I hoped she knew how to pleasure a man."

Annabel frowned at him. "That wasn't a very nice thing to say!"

"I didn't want to be nice," he said painstakingly. "I wanted that silly girl to reject the idea of forgetting her husband and risking her soul in the bargain. And then I said something else, and I do think that the last was what changed her mind."

"What was it?" Annabel demanded.

He looked at her.

"Oh, all right, it's a question," she said.

"I told her that I was particularly fond of a coney's kiss."

She blinked at him. "A what?"

He shook his head. "So much to learn . . . and only a lifetime to do it in." He was laughing at her again, but Annabel was possessed by curiosity.

"Imogen knew what this kiss was? I can't believe it!" Annabel was the one who had talked to women in the village, since she did all their bargaining. Imogen had stayed at home, mooning over Draven. How could *she* know what this kiss was, if Annabel had never heard of it?

"Have we done this kiss already?" she demanded.

He laughed even louder. "No. I'm sorry to tell you, Annabel, that you didn't learn quite everything there was to learn from the gossips in your village. And now I believe you owe me any number of kisses." He was beside her seat so fast that she hadn't even seen him move.

At the end of his kiss, she felt mad, maddened by desire for him. "Was *that* a coney's kiss?" she asked, falling back into her chair.

He just grinned. "No." He pulled a pack of cards from the mantelpiece. "Do you want to play? I'll teach you speculation, so that Uncle Pearce can fleece you without feeling guilty. Not that he ever shows signs of such a worthy emotion."

"I know how to play speculation," Annabel said,

thinking that they should stay away from talk that led to kisses. "It's Josie's favorite game."

"In that case," Ewan said with a wicked gleam in his eye, "we'll play for a forfeit."

Annabel smiled. "Best of five hands?"

He won the first game; she won the second. He won the third game; she won the fourth. "If I didn't know better," Ewan grumbled as he laid down the cards, "I'd swear you were cheating, my girl. I had that game."

"Shall it be pistols at dawn?" she asked, giggling.

"I shall win this hand," Ewan said, looking at his cards. "You see"—he looked up at her and there was a wild look about him that made the blood suddenly thunder in her veins—"I want your forfeit."

Annabel looked down at her cards, but he'd destroyed her composure. When he looked at her with that light in his eyes, it was as if a different Ewan had stepped forth. One that made her think of bedchambers and private things. She put down a card at random.

He reached out and drew a finger down her cheek. She shivered, and put down another card without thinking of the consequences.

"I seem to have lost a forfeit," she noted, a few minutes later. "What will you ask for?" He smiled slowly, and she felt suddenly scorched by his heavy-lidded gaze. "You're so different like this," she said suddenly.

"Different how?"

"Normally, you look at me as if I amused you. In fact, you seem to view the entire world as an amusing spectacle."

"You don't amuse me," he said, a wry smile curling his lips.

She could feel herself turning pink. "Not when . . ."

"Not when I want you as much as I do now," he said.

Then he added conversationally, "I can hardly think of anything else, you know."

She turned even pinker.

"There you sit, wearing a dusky blue dress—a color rather unsuitable for traveling, but it looks quite dramatic with your hair—and I can recite every detail of your clothing, from the brocade around the sleeve to that affecting little tassel at the shoulder."

"Imogen gave the gown to me," Annabel said, trying to turn the subject. She felt instinctively it was going beyond her control.

But his smile just got deeper, somehow. "All I can think about is taking it off." There was such a tone of husky conviction in his voice that Annabel gasped.

"It's time to retire," she said hastily, standing up.

He stood up too, his eyes on hers. "As you wish."

"With the bolster between us," she said, frowning at him. Then she froze. "Are you—are you going to ask for your forfeit tonight?"

He tipped up her chin. "Do you wish me to do so?"

"No," she breathed, seeing his lips come to hers. "No." There was a plea in her voice.

And there was a groan in his throat, but he lost it in kissing her. It was a long time before she pulled back. He turned away, running a hand through his hair. "*Damn.*"

"What?"

"I'm on the verge of losing control," he said, and the amusement was back in his voice. "I pride myself on never losing control."

"You know what they say about a fall," Annabel observed. "The truth is, there isn't much in your life that would make you lose control, is there?"

"I suppose not."

"It's so easy," she said, watching him gather the cards into a neat pile and replace them in the precise spot from which he'd taken them. "Mac takes care of everything. That's why you're always amused."

"Yes," he said. "Mac is a treasure."

"So you never lose your temper because there's no call to," she finished.

He smiled at her wryly. "You must be good for me."

But Annabel was suddenly cross that she'd lost the forfeit. She should have concentrated and kept her mind on the game. Now he'd make her undress in the outdoors or some such scandalous action. "'Tis easy to curb one's temper when there's nothing to disturb it," she said sharply.

"Except you," he said, standing just before her, but not touching her. "*You* disturb me."

She had to smile at that.

They had a routine now, like any married couple. Annabel undressed with the help of her maid, and then tucked herself into bed. Some time later, Ewan came in, all sluiced down from washing at the pump, and took off most of his clothes and slid into bed. Then he usually got out of bed and found some sort of pillow and put it between them, because he was still adamant that it would be a disaster if he woke with her in his arms.

"A man," he had told her one night, "would be happy to make love morning, noon or night. But in the morning he's primed for the exercise, if you take my meaning."

She had. All those hours spent listening to the women in the village complain about their marriages were truly paying off.

Tonight didn't feel like the other nights, though. Somehow the stiffness Annabel usually felt after sitting in a coach all day long had melted away, replaced by a racing excitement and trepidation. For one thing, she couldn't figure out what Ewan meant to ask for his forfeit.

He walked in and Annabel tried to look at him objectively, the way she had back at Lady Feddrington's ball when she didn't know him from Adam. He was tall, and powerfully built . . . but checking off those characteristics didn't work anymore. Because glancing at his chest made her think about their picnic. And—

"Ewan!" she said. "What are you *doing*?"

"I'm not wearing this shirt to bed," he said calmly. "I'll keep on my smalls, to protect us both. But you've seen my chest before, lass, and after we're married, you'll see it many a time."

Annabel swallowed. Ewan pulled his shirt over his head, and his shoulders and arms bunched with muscle. Rather than making her embarrassed, it gave her a peculiar melting feeling in her stomach. His chest tapered to narrow hips, to which his white smalls clung as if they were about to fall down . . . Annabel closed her eyes. Her body felt suddenly all curves and softness, a natural match to his.

That night their bed was a great carved monstrosity that looked to have been built in the Middle Ages. He got in and the mattress listed to that side with a mighty creak.

"It's a good thing we're not married yet, because this bed couldn't survive a bout of shaking sheets," he muttered, pulling the covers over himself.

There was no bolster in the bed.

"Didn't you ask me what a coney is, Annabel, my love?" Ewan asked softly.

She bit her lip, looking at him in the hazy light of the candles on the bedstand. His eyes were very, very green.

"A coney's a rabbit," he whispered, moving closer to her. "A soft, velvety rabbit."

Annabel tried to think about rabbits and kisses, but his body was just next to hers, and the only thing between them was her nightgown. She felt as if she could feel the heat of his chest although he wasn't yet touching her.

Ewan looked at his bride-to-be and told himself for the hundredth time that he would be able to control himself. She was breathing in a shallow way, and earlier he'd seen her looking at him with a stealthy pleasure that suggested she wasn't thinking of kicking him out of bed. Except—

"Annabel?" he inquired. "Why have you closed your eyes? You're not afraid of me, are you?"

Thankfully, he saw a glimmer of a smile on those luscious lips of hers. "Is that a question?"

"Yes," he growled. And then he couldn't wait any longer: he gathered the delicious body of his almost-wife into his arms. He kissed her until she was trembling in his arms, until they were both near senseless, until her tongue was as bold as his. And then he slowly, slowly rolled onto his back, bringing her with him.

Annabel's eyes popped open. She had direct contact with his groin now, and he wasn't quite certain she understood the implications of what she was feeling. Not that his Annabel ever showed any particular signs of virginal innocence.

Sure enough, she obviously knew precisely what she was feeling. She was staring down at him with a little frown between her brows and he could practically see the objections racing through her mind.

"It'll fit," he said, pulling down her head for a kiss. "I promise. There's no need to fear me, Annabel." Then he slipped between her lips with all the hunger for her taste that he felt in his body, kissed her until she was clutching his hair and kissing him back, and until she'd cradled herself between his legs in a way that told him that they would be a marvelous fit for each other.

He pulled away from her mouth only when he found that his hands had stopped caressing her narrow back and had shaped themselves to the most beautifully round bottom he'd ever felt in his life.

So instead of continuing with that caress, which would surely lead to madness, he rolled her over, keeping one leg over hers, determined to gain control of himself before he touched her again. She was exquisite, this bride of his, even with her smoky eyes closed tight.

He dropped kisses on her eyes and the rosy tilt of her mouth, but she still didn't open her eyes. "Don't you want to know what a coney is, then?" he whispered in her ear, giving her a little bite.

She gasped, and opened her eyes. She was a great one for seeing the world blind, this lass of his. "You told me," she said. "It's a rabbit." Her voice was all husky and low, and made Ewan's groin throb so that he almost lost control again.

He took a deep breath. "Aren't you a bit more curious about the origins of the phrase?"

"Yes," she whispered.

He slid his leg down the long smooth length of her legs, and surprised himself by wondering if he truly would be able to stop in time. Surely he would. He hadn't practiced restraint for all these years to have it desert him when he most needed it. Slowly, reverently, he put a hand on her breast.

The warm curve of it made him almost moan aloud but he stayed rigid, instead watching Annabel, who, of course, had her eyes closed tight. He dared to rub a thumb across her nipple and her body instinctively arched up. Her hand flew to his wrist and she said, her voice shaking, "Ewan!" But she didn't open her eyes, and he counted that as a welcome.

"Yes, love," he whispered, keeping his hand—and his

thumb—right where it was. Then he let himself kiss her again and desire exploded like fury between them. She was writhing under his hand now, making little squeaking sounds that inflamed his blood. Slowly, slowly, he ran his hand from her breast to her flat stomach, over a hip, down a long sleek leg and finally to the edge of her nightgown, bunched at her thighs.

Her eyes flew open. "What are you doing?" she cried, grabbing his wrist again.

It was time for another kiss. He kissed her until her eyes closed in helpless surrender, until she dropped her fierce grasp on his wrist and wound her arms around his neck. And then, before she could stop him, he ran his hand up the sweetness of soft skin at her inner thigh to . . . *there.*

She went rigid. "I thought we weren't—" she said with a gasp.

"We aren't," he told her, at the same time he warned himself of the same thing. "We aren't. This is just another kind of kiss, Annabel."

But her eyes were open, and narrowed at him. "I've never heard of such a thing!"

"You didn't learn everything there is to learn in the village," he said to her, trying to keep his voice even while his fingers were wandering over the softest tangle of hair he'd felt in his life, and his breath felt as it were exploding in his chest.

"I don't think this is proper," Annabel insisted. "We're not—"

She squeaked, and Ewan covered her mouth with his. And in the middle of that fevered kiss, he touched her until her legs relaxed and she cried out against his lips again and again, finally hiding her head against his shoulder and twisting against him.

"But the kiss, Annabel," he said, knowing that his

control was growing weak. Another moment of this and he'd simply roll over and—"Our last kiss, and my gift . . ."

She mutely tried to pull his head down to hers.

"Nay," he said gruffly, "that's not it."

And then quickly, before those beautiful eyes of hers could fly open and she could leap off the bed, he moved down.

Annabel was in a haze of heat and desire. Against her thigh she could feel Ewan's—Ewan's—and though he said things would fit, she had a nagging suspicion that they wouldn't. But every time the suspicion grew firm in her mind, he would kiss her senseless again and she would forget her worries, lost in a haze of ecstasy.

At least he'd finally taken his hand off her breast, but—

"What are you *doing*?" she said, surprised by her own ragged voice.

He was lying between her legs and there she was, like a wanton, with her nightgown pulled up almost to her waist. "Stop that!" she cried, trying to sit up, but a huge muscled arm slid up her stomach and held her down. And his other hand . . .

He touched her there. She couldn't help it; a whimper broke from her lips. But he could *see* her. He shouldn't be in such a position. "Ewan!" she said, trying again for rationality, for decency, for—

She lost her train of thought. His fingers were—

That wasn't his finger!

"Ewan!" she choked, but he didn't answer, and his hand was holding her down—well, it was caressing her breast—and there was nothing to do but close her eyes tight and sink into a velvet darkness that had nothing in it but his tongue and the flames licking around her body, sending her arching helplessly against him, trying to cry his name but managing only cries, her voice cut into ribbons by the sweetness of his kiss.

This—this—but she couldn't remember what it was called. She couldn't remember her own name. Every sensation in her body was focused on the decadent, rough touch of his mouth.

"I can't—I can't—" she managed . . . and then she shuddered, twisting up against him, bursting into a spasm more intense than she had ever felt before, an all-consuming, raging explosion that had her gasping and crying out, and then falling back, limp, to the bed.

Twenty

Two days later they were trundling along the road in the early afternoon. Annabel had succumbed to a haze of boredom and weariness, and when Ewan decided to ride, she curled up on the seat and fell fast asleep. What woke her was the sensation that the carriage was listing steeply to the left. She blinked, trying to decide whether the box was actually sloping to the side, and then, before she could brace herself, a violent lurch threw her against the wall, followed by shrieking, scraping noises as the carriage slid down some sort of embarkment. The last sound as the carriage settled was the violent *snap* of a thick piece of wood giving way.

Annabel landed with a hard bang against the carriage door, which was now serving as the floor. In the sudden stillness, she heard shouts and whinnies. With the instinct of someone raised in the stables, she held her breath and listened for the sound of horses screaming. But no. They were frightened and angry, but not in pain.

Then Ewan shouted above the clamor: "Annabel! Annabel, can you hear me? Are you hurt?" There was a clear strain of panic in his voice.

"Ewan!" she called out. She was on her knees, since the seats now stretched vertically into the air. "I'm merely shaken." Her bonnet was squashed over one ear, so she pulled it off and put it to the side. "What about the horses?"

"Jakes managed to cut them free just before the carriage slid. So all we have to do is get you out." And then, very close to the carriage wall, "Don't worry, I'm right here."

"I'm not worried," Annabel called back. To be honest, she was tired of traveling in the carriage. Now she would be able to stretch her legs while they mended the vehicle.

"We have to turn over the carriage," Ewan said. She could still hear an echo of fear in his voice and it gave her a queer pang of pleasure. "It might take me a few minutes to decide how to do it best. I don't want to jostle you too much in the process, and there's some water in this ditch that might make it difficult to brace ourselves."

Annabel had just discovered that herself, since water had started seeping through the doorframe on which she was kneeling. She scrambled up and leaned against the side of the carriage.

"How much water?" she asked with a credible show of calmness. It was pouring in now, swelling around the door and creeping muddily toward her slippers. She reached over and grabbed her squashed bonnet before it was inundated.

"Not enough to drown you. Wet to your ankles at the most."

Annabel scowled. The window was above her, but she could certainly fit through it.

"Ewan!" she called. "Does the carriage window open?"

"You couldn't fit through a window," he said, before shouting something unintelligible up the slope at his men.

"Yes, I could," Annabel shouted back, a bit indignantly. The water was at her toes now and it was cold as ice and filthy. "But I can't reach high enough."

"Wait a moment!" The coach shuddered with Ewan's weight and a moment later his face appeared in the muddy glass above her. "Hello!" he said, grinning. "Your hair's a mess."

She made a face at him and pointed at the black water lapping at her slippers. She saw him look down and frown, and then he said, "Turn around."

She turned about and hid her face against the coach seat, but no flying glass struck her. Instead she heard the splintering, screaming sound of wood being torn from its moorings. When she turned about again, sunshine was pouring down. Ewan had ripped the entire window frame from the carriage and lifted it into the air. There was a crash as it landed in the ditch. "Wait a minute," he said. "I'll just brace myself. . . ." And then he reappeared, lying down and leaning half through the window with his arms stretched out to her.

"Come on, darling," he said, "easy as pulling a babe from its crib, I'm thinking."

"I'm glad you find this amusing," Annabel said, but she reached up to him. His large hands closed on her hands and then with a powerful, smooth movement, he pulled so hard that she literally flew upward, and his hands closed again on her waist. Then with a grunt he pulled her through the window and sat her down, skirts hanging into the coach's cavity.

Annabel just stared at him. She had to remind herself

to close her gaping mouth. "How in the world did you do that?"

" 'Twas no trouble at all to lift a featherweight such as yourself."

Annabel had never wasted any tears over the fact that she had a lush, rounded figure. She'd always liked it, and frankly, men showed every sign of liking it as well. But she was no slender, fragile waif who could be wafted through the air on a breeze.

At some point Ewan had taken off his jacket and rolled up his sleeves. His forearms were bulging with muscle, and his shoulders appeared likely to rip through the thin linen of his shirt. Annabel swallowed, thinking of Ewan without his shirt at their picnic. He wasn't even breathing hard.

"Where do you get all these muscles?" she asked.

"Lifting damsels in distress." He grinned at her, and there was a slight lurch as he leaped off the carriage and landed with a splash in the ditch.

Then he held up his arms. "Jump!"

Annabel couldn't help smiling. If that were any normal Englishman standing below her—a normal gentleman of any nationality—she would be afraid that her weight, hurtling off the top of a carriage, would drop him to the ground like a stone. But Ewan . . .

She pulled her legs out of the destroyed carriage window and stood up. From here she could see miles of dark emerald forest with just a few birds erupting from its depths like flying fish skimming an ocean. The air was cool and crisp and smelled of fir trees, deep, loamy earth and spring.

"Annabel!" Ewan called.

She looked down. He *was* standing in water, after all. So without a moment's trepidation, she launched herself from the downed carriage, coming home to his arms with all the security and the pleasure of a child leaping from the second stair.

His arms closed around her and for a moment she felt nothing but the heat of his body. He smelled of soap, and clean sweat, and linens dried in the sun. Dimly she could hear Ewan's men cheering her recovery. But he was tipping up her chin and looking down at her with those sea-green eyes. "Ask me a question, lass," he said. "We're out of kisses."

"Do you want to put me down now?"

"The answer is no," he said, covering her mouth with his own. His lips were as hard and as powerful as his body. He looked like a great, innocent farm laborer but he kissed like a sinful lord, a rake who knew her heart's darkest secrets, desires of which she'd known nothing until his kisses awakened them.

Finally he drew back and she blinked at him, realizing it was a good thing he was still holding her up; her legs had turned liquid and she was trembling all over.

He wasn't smiling. She liked that.

"My lord," Mac called from the road. "The man we sent ahead has returned and says there's a small hamlet three miles down the road. Perhaps you may wish to go there while we work with the carriage. The slower vehicles can't be more than an hour behind us and I'll send them on to you directly."

Ewan held out his hand. Annabel took it and he pulled her up the slope to the road. She glanced back to see their sleek, fine carriage scratched and broken, lying on its side like a bird shot down in midflight.

"Annabel and I will take one of the horses and ride to the village," Ewan was saying. "Send the other carriages to pick us up, and we'll continue until we find an inn for the night."

She shook her head at him, and he said, "We don't have a sidesaddle, Annabel; you'll have to ride before me."

"Those horses aren't strong enough for the both of us. We'll take two horses, and I can do quite well without a sidesaddle."

Ewan's eyebrow shot up but he only said, "Excellent," and turned back to Mac.

Annabel listened until she heard him making plans to bring several men to the village with them. Then she put a hand on his sleeve. "The men should go before us," she said.

He looked rather confused but accepted her comment without question. Annabel stood and thought about that for a moment; it was a rare blessing to find a man who would accept a word of advice without querying it. Certainly her father had never seen the point of such a thing.

A few minutes later four outriders set off for the village at a good clip, directed to bring back more men and some sort of farm cart in case the carriage wasn't immediately usable.

Annabel turned to the horses milling about the edge of the road, cropping grass with their blunt teeth. She walked among them, stopping to pat a rough dapple coat and scratch the ears of a twitchy job horse. Finally she found a red-brown gelding with a black mane and large, soft eyes. She held out her hand and he politely stopped eating grass and blew air into her palm with his velvety nose.

"What's your name, beauty?" she crooned at him, but he just lipped her fingers and shook his bridle. "I'll call you Ginger, then," she said. "Ginger was my very first horse and you have a similar look about you."

He accepted a gift of grass with courteous attention.

Ewan threw a saddle on Ginger and turned to her. "May I give you a hand up?"

"No, thank you," Annabel said. Outriders and groomsmen were milling about the road, waiting to figure out precisely how Mac wanted to retrieve the carriage. Mac was prowling around and around the vehicle, splashing in the mud while he decided what would cause the frame the least damage. "I'll just walk this sweet gentleman for a moment," Annabel said.

Ginger liked walking and blew in her ear in a companionable sort of way. A second later Ewan caught up with her, his horse on a long rein. The sun felt warm on Annabel's face. Its rays were catching Ewan's hair and made it look as if prisms of ruby light were caught in its strands.

Slowly they drew away from the shouts of the men working on the coach, and then the road turned a corner. Annabel glanced back and saw that they were thoroughly out of sight.

"Will you give me a hand now?" she asked.

She swung up into the saddle and rearranged her skirts with some care. After a moment she realized that Ewan was still standing at her horse's shoulder as if he were frozen. She cocked an eyebrow.

"Lovely stockings," he said calmly enough, but there was a flare in his eyes.

Annabel looked down at her lacy, woolen stockings. They gleamed snowy white in the shadowy light, all the way from her slender ankles to just above her knees. "You can see why I didn't wish to mount this horse in front of your men," she said, grinning at Ewan.

He didn't say anything immediately, just curled his hand around her ankle. "You have beautiful legs." His voice had a deep, almost hoarse note.

Annabel grinned at him and hitched her skirts a little higher. His eyes wandered over her thighs, closely gripping the horse's back, and he got such a strange expression on his face that she raised an eyebrow.

"Is there some problem, Ewan?"

"I may not be able to mount a saddle myself," he said, and his voice was definitely hoarse now.

"Try," she said impudently. With a slight movement of her knee she prompted Ginger to start walking down the road.

"You didn't tell me you could ride!" Ewan called after her.

"You didn't ask!" Annabel called back. She could feel swells of joy rising in her heart as Ginger gave a little tentative prance under her. He was stretching his legs, hoping that he wouldn't be kept to the endless trot and walk maintained by the outriders.

So she leaned over his neck and loosed the reins. "Go!" she said, and he needed no encouragement.

She felt his great muscles bunch and leap forward as he gave a snort of satisfaction and threw up his head as if to smell the wind. And then they were whipping past the dark stands of fir trees, racing down the dirt road. Annabel sat up and laughed aloud, holding on to the reins with one hand, keeping Ginger at a gallop with a faint pressure of her knees.

From behind came a pounding of horse hooves. Annabel looked back and grinned. Apparently Ewan had managed to mount after all. He probably thought her horse was running away with her. No lady rode like this. If he leans over to grab my bridle, Annabel thought, I'll—I'll pull him off.

He caught up with her, of course. But he didn't make a move toward her reins, just laughed, and even over the pounding of the horse's hooves and the whipping of her hair around her ears, she heard the deep pleasure of it.

They rounded a curve and galloped down a shady bit
of road, and around another corner and out into the brilliant sunshine again. When Ginger started to blow,
Annabel pulled him up, took him to a canter and then to
a walk. Ewan and his mount kept pace beside her.

Then Ewan nosed his horse over so that it was walking a hair's breadth from Ginger and their shoulders
were almost touching.

"The longer we spend together, the less I feel I know
about you," he said, shaking his head at her. "You're so
different from the woman I thought I met in London."

"What did you think I was like?" Annabel asked, not
quite sure that she really wanted to know the answer.

"A lady," he said promptly. "A true lady."

"I *am* a lady!" Annabel said, scowling at him.

"You know what I mean. I was shocked when you
didn't slap me after I kissed you in the May cart at Lady
Mitford's garden party. I finally decided you must have
been suffering from the heat. There you were, all dressed
in lace, and looking melting and soft—"

Annabel laughed at him. "I beat you at archery, if you
remember. Was that a ladylike thing to do?"

"I forgot that," he said. "You do have some very useful skills."

"Nothing is more useful than looking *melting,* as you
call it," she said, giving him a little smile.

"Oh? Why?"

"Because if a woman looks fragile and melting, the
men in her vicinity do errands. Plus, they think that she
is helpless, and they defend her. They think that she is
adorable, and so they want to cuddle her. Before they
know it, they feel a desire to take her home and keep her
safe forever."

"I feel like taking you home, and you won't be safe
there," he growled at her.

Annabel giggled. "Another useful skill."

"*What?*"

"If I make you desire me, you'll do my errands in the hope that I'll pay you a favor in return. Or, to take a larger example, you'll give me jewelry, specifically a wedding ring."

"So make me desire you," he said, watching her.

She looked at him over her shoulder and let her eyes drop to his lips, and her eyelids droop a little. Then a tiny smile curled her lips a smile she'd been practicing since she was fourteen years old and discovered that smiles occasionally inspired the butcher to give them free cuts of meat. That a smile would confuse the baker so that he would give them extra loaves of bread.

Ewan whistled. "I can see how that might be effective."

"Oh? Should I take it that you'll give me jewelry?"

"A question!" He pulled up his horse. Automatically she stopped Ginger as well. He wrapped a large hand around the nape of her neck and gently pulled her toward him. These days their kisses started as if they had never left off the last one. Their mouths met, hungry, open, seeking each other's taste . . . He kept his hands to himself, though. And she kept her hands tangled in his hair and didn't try to direct him. And they never, ever embarked on a coney's kiss or its like.

In the back of her mind, Annabel kept trying to figure out which of Ewan's kisses she liked the best. There were those times when she kept her mouth shut, and made him beg and plead silently for entry until he could slip past her guard. Sometimes she thought those were the best kisses, and sometimes she thought a wild tangling, in which they were both shaking within a second or two . . . sometimes she thought *those* were the best kisses. And then there were the ones that Ewan didn't count: the little morning touch on her cheek or an eye, the sweetness of their lips just touching over the bolster at night.

"I would do your errands for a smile," Ewan said softly a moment later. "For a kiss like that—"

Annabel looked away, suddenly shy. Kisses of that nature had no part in the schema she'd worked out for her life, in the precise trade of her body and accomplishments for a man's ring and his fortune.

He switched his reins to his left hand. Then he curled his fingers around hers. They walked down the road sedately, letting their horses snort at each other. Annabel didn't look at Ewan again. She had a feeling that all her preconceptions of men and women were tumbling at her feet. He had breached her defenses.

When they came to the little fork that led to the hamlet, Ewan helped Annabel from her mount and they walked beside their horses, still without saying a word.

A few moments later they met Ewan's outriders, returning the way they'd come. Apparently there were no carts to be had, so they were headed back to the site of the accident.

The village was not merely small; it was no more than a motley collection of three houses arranged around a dusty square. There was no store, no pub and no inn, just a broad-shouldered young man with a snub nose and a cheerful grin to greet them.

"My name's Kettle, my lord. I had no expectation of seeing gentry today, and I'm afraid we're not prepared." He waved his hand at the little patch of ground between the wattle-and-daub houses, scaring a few chickens who started up in protest.

"May I beg you for the courtesy of a drink of water for my wife?" Ewan asked, bowing.

Kettle beamed. "We've better than that. I'll ask my

wife to bring out a glass of ale for her ladyship." He went into one of the houses, returning with a woman carefully holding a tin cup. She had fiery red hair, braided away from her face, two dimples that made her look as if she were about to laugh and a belly that arched before her as if it were defying gravity.

She managed to bob a curtsy without spilling a drop of ale. "I'm so sorry," she said shyly. "We've only the one cup, but if your lordship could wait a moment, I'll refill it in a jiffy. And I've some oatcakes on the fire, if you would care for one."

"Oh, no, Mrs. Kettle," Annabel said, at the same moment that Ewan said, "We'd love one. Thank you!"

A huge smile spread over Mrs. Kettle's face. "Mrs. Kettle! I guess that's me!"

Kettle himself put an arm around his wife's shoulders. "We don't get many visitors, and a circuit-riding Methodist preacher came through just last month. I reckon you're one of the first to call her that."

"But you don't live here alone, do you?" Annabel asked.

"Not normally," Mrs. Kettle said, bobbing another curtsy. "There's three houses, as you can see. But Mrs. Fernald took poorly in the last winter, and so they've gone to her relatives for a bit, until she feels better. And the third house belongs to Ian McGregor. He's gone to find work in the fields for the summer. He has no wife at all." Clearly, from Mrs. Kettle's point of view, poor McGregor was cursed.

From Annabel's point of view, McGregor was absolutely right not to take on the responsibility of a wife when all he could afford was a shack. She sipped her ale. It was clear, thin and cold.

They all stood together awkwardly for a moment and then Mrs. Kettle gasped. "I never thought—" Her voice disappeared into the depths of her house, and she appeared a moment later with a chair. Both her husband and Ewan started toward her immediately, but Ewan was at her side first. Then Mr. Kettle fetched a stool, and then they put the two chairs together in the middle of the dust and chickens. Annabel sat down on the chair, and Mrs. Kettle on the stool. The men drifted off to the side and began talking about hops and ale and how the wheat was sprouting.

"This is so kind of you, Mrs. Kettle," Annabel said.

"Do you know," she replied with her dimpled smile, "I'm not sure but what I enjoy plain Peggy better. Would you mind calling me Peggy?"

"Of course not," Annabel said. "And you must call me Annabel."

"Oh, no, I couldn't do that," Peggy said, dismissing the idea with utter certainty. "But I've been naught more than Peggy me whole life, and I expect that's why it's hard to get used to having two names. *Two* names!" She laughed. "That's riches!"

"Of a sort," Annabel managed. But then Peggy leaped to her feet again. "I've clean forgotten my oatcakes!"

Mr. Kettle said something to Ewan about his woodshed and then he disappeared as well.

One of the chickens was so desperate that it came up and pecked at the bedraggled ribbon hanging from Annabel's slipper. She shivered.

"Are you cold?" Ewan asked.

She shook her head. "I can almost smell the poverty."

"And you don't like it?"

Annabel nudged the chicken with her foot. "No. No, I don't. It would be a terrible thing to be this poor."

"They don't seem unhappy," Ewan said.

"Mrs. Kettle has one tin cup," Annabel said. "One chair, and likely one stool."

"Almost certainly only one dress," Ewan put in.

"And one baby on the way," Annabel pointed out.

"Hmmm. Still, they seem happy."

"It's impossible to be happy under those circumstances."

"I don't agree."

Annabel felt a surge of irritability at the calm conviction in his voice. "If you think that, you know nothing of it. Think of how much you enjoy bathing. That poor woman likely hasn't had a hot bath since she was married, if then. It's too exhausting to heat all that water. Actually, I doubt they have a bathtub at all."

"True," Ewan said. "It's a rare cottager who has a tin bath, and I don't believe these poor folk are attached to any laird."

"She's probably eating gruel for her main meal," Annabel said, not quite sure why her voice was so accusing. "Even though she's carrying a child! She should be having a nice fat chicken every night." Annabel kicked away the scrawny hen, who was back, pecking at her shoe ribbons. "You shouldn't have told her you'd like an oatcake. Now she'll likely have nothing to eat for supper."

"To refuse it would have been an insult to her," Ewan said. "She wants to offer us something."

Annabel frowned.

Just then Peggy came out and offered them all slightly burned cakes. "I'm still learning to cook," she said, waving one of them in the air. "And I'm sorry there's no honey. We're hoping to find a honey tree. I know they're here somewhere, because bees come into the sun. But whenever I follow a bee into the woods, I get lost!" She laughed.

"Well, I think these cakes look wonderful," Annabel told her. "I can't cook a bit."

"Oh, no, of course you can't!" Peggy said.

"I should learn."

"I agree," Ewan said, finishing his second cake. Annabel scowled at him as he reached for a third. "If you could make cakes like Mrs. Kettle's, you'd never have to fear my displeasure."

"I don't fear your displeasure!" Annabel told him roundly, turning back to Peggy. Ewan was laughing, and Peggy looked as if she wanted to giggle but wasn't quite certain whether that would be allowed in the presence of gentry.

"I don't want to keep you from what you were doing; might I help you, perhaps?" Annabel asked.

Peggy looked at Annabel's beautifully tailored traveling gown. "That's a daft notion," she said with a chortle of laughter. "I'm warming the cream for butter. There's nothing for a lady to do."

Annabel's face cleared. "I may not know how to cook but I can churn butter! My sisters and I used to help Cook every week."

Peggy blinked at her. "You must be jesting?"

But Annabel was already heading into the house, dragging Peggy behind her. Ewan heard her voice disappear inside the door. "Are you using carrot, or . . ."

"Why don't I go see how Mr. Kettle's woodshed is faring?" Ewan asked the air. Clearly Annabel was going to give Nana a run for her money when it came to poking about in his crofters' business.

An hour later the carriages had still not made an appearance. Ewan wandered back to the clearing to see if he could find his almost-wife. He stopped in the door of the cottage before she saw he was there.

The house was fashioned of one room. A large bed was tucked against the wall, and a rough-hewn table stood in the center. Annabel was standing at the table, washing a large piece of butter in water. Peggy was sitting on the one chair.

"No, you just keep resting," Annabel was saying to Peggy, for what was likely the twentieth time. "I can mold the butter." Deftly she turned the lump of butter out of a wooden bowl and sprinkled salt on it. "Now, where do you keep your press?" she asked, looking about.

At that moment Peggy caught sight of Ewan leaning in the doorway, and jumped to her feet. "What you must think of me!" she cried. "I simply couldn't stop your lady wife, my lord, I couldn't!"

Ewan grinned at her. Annabel had found the mold hanging on the wall and had begun packing it with butter.

"I've been telling Peggy that she needs to rest," Annabel said to him. "Here she is, a day or so from giving birth, and she's on her feet from morn till night! Peggy, you lie down on that bed this minute. You've sat up long enough."

Peggy gave Ewan a hopeless look, and he winked at her. She lay down on the bed with the helpless attitude of someone who just met a hurricane and was blown off her legs.

Annabel turned the mold upside down on a plate and pushed on the loose bottom. A pat of golden butter popped out. The top of the butter pat was marked with a *P*.

"That's pretty," he said to Peggy, watching as Annabel started to pack down more butter in the mold. He'd never paid any attention to the look of butter, but now he thought of it, the butter that appeared on his table had his coat of arms on top.

Peggy looked pleased. "The orphanage gave me the butter mold as a good-bye present," she said.

"When you left to marry Mr. Kettle?" Annabel asked.

"Yes, exactly."

Ewan had to admit that Peggy looked rather tired now that she was lying down. Her belly stood out from her thin body like an island rising from a stream.

"Of course, when I left the orphanage I wasn't sure whether I would marry Mr. Kettle or Mr. McGregor."

"What?" Annabel said, pausing in the middle of turning another butter pat onto the waiting platter.

"The peddler brought word to the orphanage that Mr. Kettle and Mr. McGregor were wanting wives," Peggy explained. "I was the only one of age who was willing to go into the north woods. So I traveled along with the peddler. The orphanage gave me the mold, and then the peddler was nice enough to give me a cheese hoop because I helped him on the way here." She beamed. "I'm planning on making cheese next time I have some extra milk."

"So you arrived here with the peddler, and then you chose Mr. Kettle?" Annabel asked, obviously fascinated.

Ewan settled himself more comfortably against the doorframe, crossing his arms over his chest. "What if you hadn't liked either Mr. Kettle or Mr. McGregor?"

"By then the peddler had offered for me as well!" Peggy said, obviously delighted by her popularity. "But I knew Mr. Kettle was the one for me the moment I saw him. The peddler tried to change my mind. Course, I could have had as many pans as I wanted if I'd stayed with him. But he didn't take it at all badly when I chose Mr. Kettle. In fact, he was good enough to give me a piece of cloth for a wedding present, and when the baby comes, I'm going to make it into a wee dress."

Annabel didn't say anything, just packed more butter with a little frown.

Ewan caught back a smile. "So the peddler had lots of pans, did he? But Mr. Kettle has a cow."

"That was a consideration," Peggy said. She was looking quite sleepy now, lying down in the bed with her head on her hand. "But the peddler had a belly." She giggled drowsily. "Aye, and a long beard too. Mr. Kettle is a proper man."

Annabel smiled at her, and Peggy gave her a naughty smile and added, "Every inch of him!"

Peggy giggled, and Ewan's low rumble of laughter echoed in the little house. And then after a second Annabel joined in. Peggy's eyes were closing, so Ewan put a finger to his lips and backed out of the house.

Outside, he caught Annabel's hands in his and said, "So you can make butter, can you? And you shoot arrows with precision, and you ride like an angel. Is there anything you can't do?"

Annabel looked at him with a crooked smile. "I couldn't make the choices that Peggy's made. I don't want to choose between pans and livestock."

"You needn't," he said, nuzzling her cheek. "I hear the peddler in these parts is looking for a wife, but I won't let him have you, for all the pots and pans in the world."

"I have a question," Annabel whispered, pulling him farther away from the house.

He led her over to Kettle's woodshed and shifted his stance so that he was leaning against the wall and he could tuck Annabel's body against his. She gasped but let him.

"What's proper about inches?" she whispered.

"What?"

"Mr. Kettle is a proper man," she said, keeping her voice low although the curiosity leaked through. "Every inch of him."

To Ewan's disappointment, he didn't get to explain the jest, because saying it aloud seemed to bring the meaning home. She gasped, and a tiny giggle escaped. "Lucky Mr. Kettle," she said.

"Yes, I expect the poor peddler just couldn't measure up," Ewan whispered back.

"That's wicked!"

Ewan kissed her neck. "So how do you like churning?"

"It's fierce work," Annabel said, leaning against him in a boneless fashion that he entirely approved. "Poor Peggy. It's too hard, all this work and the baby on top of it. Do you know that the baby might come along any moment, Ewan? And what will she do, with no woman for miles about?"

"I expect Kettle will help her," Ewan said. An idea was beginning to sprout in his mind. A wicked one, for sure.

"It's a disgrace," she grumbled, as if she didn't even realize that he was kissing her ear. But she did; he could feel the little tremor through her body when he nipped her. "Kettle should take her somewhere where she can be properly tended."

"He'll take care of her," Ewan said.

"A woman needs another woman at times like this! And she shouldn't be lifting a heavy butter churn either."

Ewan threw caution to the wind. "You owe me a kiss," he said.

She met his eyes and tilted up her strawberry-red mouth, as tempting a mouth as had any self-respecting siren in the Mediterranean Sea.

But he held back, just touching her with a whisper kiss, as light as silk and fine as down.

"You owe me a forfeit," he stated.

A little flush of pink rose in her cheeks. "Yes."

"I think I shall claim my forfeit here," he said thoughtfully.

She looked around the dusty, sunlit clearing, alarmed. "*Here?*"

But he didn't feel like talking. Their tongues touched and for a moment Ewan heard her breathing, all shallow and fast. The blood surged to his groin. Slowly he pushed his knee between her skirts and then pulled her up and against him. She was like molten wax in his hands, soft and hot. She had her eyes closed, of course, and she had that luscious dazed look that he was starting to get addicted to.

"Annabel," he said, and his voice came out so raw and low that it surprised him.

"Yes?" She didn't open her eyes, though, just leaned against him.

"My forfeit. May I take it now?"

"Do you want to take my clothing off?"

The question hung in the lazy afternoon air. They were surrounded by the sound of bees, and a faint clopping as Kettle's cow moved uneasily around its stall. "Of course I do," he growled into her ear. "But I won't ask for that."

"Are you going to take your clothes off?" There was a thread of hopefulness in her voice that set his heart to pounding again.

But he shook his head. "No. It's nothing to do with clothes."

She turned her cheek and rested against his chest. "Then of course you may have your forfeit. You won it fair and square, after all."

Ewan grinned against her hair. It was like that play by Shakespeare, the one a company of traveling players had put on in the castle courtyard. He hadn't liked it all that much at the time, but now he saw it differently—now that he had a wife of his own.

"Have you read Mr. Shakespeare's plays?" he asked.

"What?" And then: "Yes, most of them."

"There was a play in which a man marries a woman whom no one else will have," he said, tightening his arms around her. "She has a beautiful younger sister, I remember that."

"She's a shrew," Annabel said, leaning against him. "It's called *The Taming of the Shrew,* and I certainly hope that you don't think I'm akin to the shrew in question."

"Nay, you're no shrew," he said.

"What's the play got to do with anything?" she asked. "I haven't thought about it for a few years . . . Isn't he quite unpleasant to his wife?" And then: "Don't you think the coaches have been a long time coming?"

But Ewan had decided it would be better if he didn't remind Annabel of the details of that particular Shakespearean plot. Not when he had in mind to use the same stratagem himself. The husband in *The Taming of the Shrew* took his wife off into the country and cured her of being shrewish. Likely the same stratagem would work to cure Annabel of her fear of being poor. Anyone could see that the Kettles were as sweetly set up as any couple in Christendom. If he and Annabel stopped a day or two here, she would learn what it was like to be poor but not prey to the whims of a gambling man. They could rely on each other. A slow smile curled his lips. Because there wouldn't be anyone else there to rely on.

As if in answer to Annabel's question, he heard a rumbling sound in the distance that sounded like one of his heavy, slow luggage carriages coming to bring them to the next village. So he didn't hesitate.

"I'd like to put Kettle and Peggy into that carriage," he said.

She opened her eyes. "Oh, Ewan, that's a lovely idea!"

"Mac can settle Peggy at the inn, or with the midwife, and stay with them until the baby is born. You said it was a matter of a day or two."

"That's what Peggy thinks," Annabel said. "I haven't the faintest notion about babies myself."

"Well, as long as it takes," Ewan said.

Annabel beamed at him. "That is a *wonderful* thing to do!"

"But . . ." Ewan said.

She frowned. "But?"

"Someone has to stay here and take care of the cow, the chickens and the house," Ewan pointed out.

"One of the footmen? Surely one of them came from the country," Annabel said promptly.

"I claim my forfeit," Ewan said. "*We* stay."

"We *what*?"

"We stay and take care of Peggy's butter and Kettle's cow." His lovely, luscious girl was looking utterly confused. "It'll only be a day or two," he told her. Then he gave her a butterfly kiss, one of the ones that didn't count. "It's not as if we're in any particular hurry. Think of us as Good Samaritans."

"Good what?"

"Never mind. We're in no hurry. We have a week or more of traveling left before we reach my lands, you know. A break would be enjoyable."

"*Enjoyable!*" She seemed stunned.

He shrugged, loving the way her breasts jiggled against him.

Unfortunately, she drew away and stood up straight, staring at him as if he'd grown another head. "You think it would be fun to live here, in this place—in that house? Are you cracked?"

He bit back a grin. "No. 'Twould be a good thing to do."

"Ewan Poley, if you think I'm some sort of self-sacrificing hymn-singer who's going to follow you all over creation while you tend to savages, you should think again! I'm no missionary. I've no wish to travel to India!"

At that Ewan had to laugh. Anyone farther from a missionary than his silk-adorned, luxury-loving fiancée couldn't be imagined. "I'm no missionary either," he said finally. The coach was rumbling into the clearing. He caught her hands. "To help Peggy," he said. "And because . . ."

"Because?" she said, glaring at him.

"Because we might enjoy it."

"You are cracked," she said with utter conviction.

"I'd like to be alone with you," he whispered, taking her hands up to his mouth. "I'd like to watch you make butter." He kissed her, even though it was breaking the rules of the game, since he hadn't asked a serious question first. "I'll show you how to milk a cow," he whispered against her mouth.

"Well, that's a mighty enticement," Annabel grumbled.

The coach had stopped, and Ewan's outriders were filling the quiet air with boisterous conversation. He could see that Mac was waiting to speak to him.

"Please?" he said, not touching her again.

She bit her lip. "Just for a day or two?"

He nodded.

"Do you really mean all alone? Without my maid?" She looked horrified.

He hesitated. What did he know about ladies? Perhaps she couldn't get along without a maid.

"Oh, never mind," she grumbled. "I had no maid for twenty years. I suppose I can survive a day or two."

He smiled at her. "Your maid can help Peggy when her time comes."

"But I want my own sheets," she said suddenly.

Ewan nodded. "Of course. We use our own sheets in inns; why not here?"

"Do you truly wish to stay here *all alone*?" The idea

seemed to both fascinate and horrify her. "It's so scandalous." She half whispered it. "We're not married."

He nodded, still not touching her. "But we will marry. And we already share a bed every night."

"Staying here will be good for you," she said finally, staring at him with narrowed eyes. "I can see that you've no imagination, Ewan Poley. None. You've no idea how hard it is to live under these circumstances, and I think this will be good for you!"

He swallowed his grin and turned to Mac.

She caught his arm. "I want my trunk with my clothing!" she said urgently.

Ewan nodded. Of course they would wear clothing.

Most of the time.

Twenty-one

Annabel watched the two carriages trundle their way down the road with an overwhelming sense of disbelief. She was standing in the middle of a dusty, deserted little square, and her only companion was a man to whom she was not married.

"I must have lost my mind," she said, stunned by the truth of it.

Ewan looked rather surprised as well. "Mac clearly thinks I've lost mine. I should warn you that I've never known him to be wrong on any subject. Do you know, I actually had to order him to stay away until the baby is born? I never order Mac to do anything."

"Perhaps the child will arrive quickly."

"The shock of entering an inn might do it," Ewan said. "Peggy looked ready to collapse with excitement." Her eyes had glowed with fierce joy on being told that she was being sent to an inn and would have a midwife to attend her.

"What shall we do now?" Annabel asked, staring around the clearing.

The forest pressed on all sides rather cozily, as if it were protecting the little houses. Without the outriders and the carriages, there was no sound but some birds in the woods.

"We should milk the cow," Ewan said. "Kettle said it was overdue for attention. Apparently the animal finds its way to the field and then comes back to its stall when it's time for milking."

The cow turned out to be a rusty brown animal with an annoyed look in her eye. She slammed the wall of her stall with her rear hoof by way of greeting.

"She seems annoyed," Annabel observed. "My father always said to avoid a horse's stall when they have that look in their eye."

"She's annoyed because it's past milking time," Ewan said, taking off his coat.

He moved toward her and the cow launched another solid thunk that could easily cave in a man's chest.

"I would suggest she wait," Annabel said, backing up a little. "Perhaps she'll be more accommodating in the morning."

"Wait?" Ewan said. His hair was all rumpled. He was rolling his sleeves past his elbows. "Cows don't wait." He walked into the space next to the stall and began feeling along the wall. "Here it is."

He slid open the bottom section of the low wall. "Obviously Kettle has himself a cantankerous animal, so he's fixed it so that he can milk her without being gelded in the process." Ewan reached his hands through the open space to milk the cow.

"You're quite good at that," Annabel said after a time.

"Between the two of us, we can handle the milk," Ewan said, looking up at her. "I can milk the cow and you can make it into butter. This will be easy."

"Hmmm," Annabel said. Ewan's hair curled into the white linen of his shirt in a very distracting way. "Have you ever cooked?"

"Never!" Ewan said cheerfully. "You?"

"No."

" 'Twill be an experiment, then." He pulled the pail of milk toward him and slid the panel shut. Finally he forked some hay into the manger and they left.

As they walked down the path, Ewan wrapped his free arm around Annabel's waist. "I'm rather astonished by how improper this is."

"So am I!" Annabel said, turning her mouth so that his kiss landed on her cheek. "We are not married."

"Fool that I am," he lamented. "I should have trotted you off to that bishop before you even combed your hair."

Annabel could feel her cheeks growing rosy. If anyone knew her circumstances, she would be disgraced. More disgraced than any lady she could remember hearing about in her life.

"Look!" she said. "It's one of Peggy's chickens!" A scrawny white chicken missing a number of feathers around its neck was scratching around to the side of the clearing. "There must be a coop. The chickens should go inside for the night. A fox might eat them."

The chicken looked at them suspiciously. Annabel took a step nearer and it clucked angrily and flew onto a short stump. "That chicken looks like a wild chicken," Ewan said. "It doesn't want to go into the coop for the night."

"There's no such thing as a wild chicken. We can't let it be eaten; Peggy only has three hens. Come here, you stupid bird." She tried clucking to it, but the chicken just turned its bony head and fixed her with an uncivilized eye.

"That is not a tame animal," Ewan said. "I think—"

But at that moment Annabel made a lunge for the chicken and caught it by one wing. The chicken opened its red throat and squawked as if it were being made into stew on the spot. "Help!" Annabel yelped. "Take it, take it!"

"Absolutely not," Ewan said, laughing. "Throw it in the coop."

"Where is the coop?" Annabel asked, looking around wildly.

The woods were falling into peaceful twilight, and Annabel couldn't see any structure other than the little houses and Kettle's stable.

The chicken was twisting and snapping viciously. "I think she means to bite you," Ewan observed. He opened the door to the house. "Here!"

A flurry of feathers swept through the air in tune with the chicken's infuriated cackling. Annabel slammed the door and jumped back, losing her balance. She was halfway to the ground when Ewan caught her around the waist.

"Thank you!" Annabel said, gasping. "Do you see Peggy's other chickens?"

"No," Ewan said, his hands lingering at her waist. "But she has one less pail of milk than she had a moment ago."

Annabel looked down. Foaming milk was spreading over the dusty ground. "You dropped it!"

"It was you or the milk. I chose you."

Annabel pulled away and gave him a frown. "I was going to make that into butter. I thought I might make so much butter that Peggy wouldn't have to worry about it for weeks."

Ewan tried to look remorseful.

"The first thing we should do is heat some water," Annabel said, going to the door of the house.

"For baths?" Ewan said. It was his devout wish that Annabel would find it necessary to take a bath. Of course, he would serve as her maid . . .

"There's no bathtub," Annabel reminded him. "For cooking. I'm growing hungry, aren't you?"

Now he thought about it, he was ravenous. He followed her into the house. "What shall we cook?"

"Potatoes," Annabel said, pointing to a box by the wall.

"We could roast the chicken," Ewan said, thinking of how hungry he was.

Annabel looked at the white chicken. It was sitting on top of Peggy's butter mold with its wings fluffed up. It looked very comfortable. "You'd have to *kill* it. We can't do that."

"I could do it," Ewan said with conviction. "I'm hungry."

"That chicken was Peggy's wedding present from her neighbors," Annabel said, pouring water from a bucket by the door into a pan. "Potatoes will have to suffice." She added them to the water and hung the pot over a little hook that swung into place over the fire.

Ewan threw on another log. Annabel was trotting about the house, putting Peggy's things neatly into their places. Then she threw open her trunk. "I know I have something in here . . ." She pulled out a towel and soap, and kept burrowing. Finally, with a happy noise in her throat, she pulled out a length of cloth. "Look at this, Ewan!"

He looked. It was dark red and seemed nice enough.

"This is going to be a tablecloth and a curtain!" Annabel said triumphantly. He started to laugh and she scowled at him. "No scoffing." She rooted around some more in the trunk and pulled out a small sewing box. In a few moments she had the cloth ripped and was sitting on a chair by the fire, her head bent over a seam.

"If only the *ton* could see you now!" Ewan said.

She turned to the next seam. "You'd be surprised at the things I know how to do, Ewan Poley!"

"I'm more fascinated by what you don't know," he said, and was gratified to see a sweep of warm color rise in her cheeks.

An hour later, the lantern glow was reflecting rosy light back from a neatly stitched curtain over the one window. The chicken had gone to sleep.

Annabel was sticking a long fork into the potatoes, trying to scoop them out of the pot, when she poked a bit too hard and the support that held the pot over the fire collapsed.

Ewan jumped back, just avoiding being splashed by boiling water. With a great hiss, the fire went out. The potatoes bounced and rolled about the floor getting covered with ashes, and the chicken woke up and fluttered its wings like an eagle, screeching at them irritably.

"Oh, no," Annabel cried, running after a potato. "Catch them, Ewan!"

"They won't make it as far as the woods," he said, but he started chasing them.

"My goodness, they're filthy," Annabel moaned, putting potatoes onto the table. "Will you get me some water?"

He walked to the bucket next to the door and then paused. It was pitch-dark outside. "Annabel, where *is* the water?"

"What do you mean, where—" She turned around. "You mean that you don't know where to find water?"

He shook his head. "Mac was right. I must have lost my mind. I didn't ask Kettle if he had a well."

"How much water is in that bucket?" she asked. Ewan could visualize his grandmother's reaction to this disaster. He would have deserved every moment of her harangue. But Annabel just looked rather surprised, standing there with a potato in each hand. She had pinned her hair up again, but she had a black streak of ash on her cheek.

"We have enough to drink tonight," he said, dropping the pail and coming over to her. "As long as we drink wine with supper."

"Wine!" she squeaked, but he couldn't wait for a taste of her sweetness, and so he took her mouth with all the gladness of a man who deserves to be shrieked at and instead finds his future wife blinking at him in surprise. And she let him rock against her body without shrieking over that either.

There was a small thunk as first one of her potatoes dropped to the ground, and then the other. It was a while later that he let her fall away from him, once her eyes had gone all sleepy and she was limp. He was trembling with hunger for her. He felt depraved, wild—and just close enough to madness to know that they had to stop kissing. He couldn't take this much longer.

"Wine?" Annabel asked a moment later. "*Wine?*"

Ewan picked up a potato on his way over to the bed. Then he bent down and pulled out a large wicker basket.

"The picnic basket!"

"It's always full," he told her. "In case we lose a wheel on the road." He hoisted it onto the table, bumping a blackened, misshapen potato that fell over the edge and bounced on the floor.

Annabel was humming happily in her throat as she unpacked. "A whole chicken, that's lovely, bread and—"

"A bottle of wine," Ewan said, pulling out the corkscrew.

"But I needn't have made the tablecloth!" Annabel said, an unmistakable pang of regret in her voice. "There's a linen one here."

"I like yours much better." He wasn't very good at describing things, so he just waved his hands lamely. "The house looks all red and homey."

She looked so happy that he broke his new kissing prohibition. And then they ate supper and Ewan had four potatoes with fresh butter, and insisted they were the best potatoes he'd eaten in his life.

Annabel perched on the stool and watched Ewan eat his fifth potato. She was searching for something to say that wasn't a question. She had a growing feeling that their kisses were edging toward some corner from which there would be no return. And she didn't want that . . . or so she told herself.

But she couldn't help peeking at the bed. It seemed to have grown twice as large in the last hour.

"Peggy doesn't have a bolster," she finally said.

"We'll have to sleep without one, then," Ewan said. He wasn't looking at her, but his voice was rough and tender.

Desire streaked down Annabel's legs and the breath seemed to disappear from her lungs. She opened her mouth to say—to say . . . ? A refusal? But why? They were as married as a couple could be without saying rites before a priest. Ewan stood up and went to fetch a large armload of wood that he carried as lightly as a baby.

"Those were very good potatoes," he said over his shoulder. "A man could live on potatoes like that."

"Poo!" Annabel said. "They tasted like ash."

"All the better for a little seasoning."

Then Ewan was gently pulling her to her feet. "Annabel?" he asked. There was a question in his voice that didn't need to be spoken out loud.

For a fleeting second, Annabel thought about what she was about to give up. She had always scorned young women who found themselves in the family way and without a husband. But none of that was relevant to Ewan; to the hunger in his eyes, and the ragged sound of his voice. Nor did it seem relevant to the ache she felt.

She didn't want any more kisses—or at least, not only kisses. She was tired of going to sleep with her heart pounding, her body squirming against the sheets, feeling unsatisfied, curious and desirous, all at once.

She turned her lips to his throat and kissed him softly, but the taste of him made her shake with excitement. "Yes," she whispered. "Yes, Ewan . . . Yes. Please."

Twenty-two

They were sitting in the courtyard of the Pig & Sickle, waiting for a light supper before they climbed back into the carriage for three more hours. Josie was braving a scolding from Griselda by taking off her bonnet and sitting in the last rays of afternoon sunshine reading. Mayne had found to his delight that the innkeeper had an only slightly out-of-date copy of *Racing News,* and he was reading every line. Naturally, Imogen was devoting herself to irritating him.

"Draven loved Scotland," she was saying, thankfully without that edge of grief that often haunted her voice. "He always said that horses trained better here. He thought the air was bracing, and that when you took them back down to England they would run faster, because their lung capacity had grown from breathing Scottish air. Do you agree, Mayne?"

He muttered something. Anachronism had won the Newmarket Stakes; he couldn't believe it. He'd consid-

ered buying the roan and decided she needed too much
work. Apparently the Syvern stud had seen the same po-
tential and done the work. If Anachronism was in top
form, the horse would certainly beat his own entry in the
Ascot.

Imogen broke into his thoughts again. "One thing you
can say about Draven was that he did things with all his
heart."

"What are you talking about?"

"*You,*" she said pointedly. "You and your flirtation
with horses. Anyone can tell that you're utterly obsessed, just as obsessed as Draven ever was."

Mayne cast her an irritated look. "I'm not planning to
take a race so seriously that I leap on the horse's back
myself, if that's what you're suggesting."

"Uncalled-for," Imogen remarked, tapping her finger-
nail against the table and eying him in a way he didn't
like. "For all Draven made mistakes, he was no dilet-
tante. He took his study of horses seriously."

Mayne turned over his racing sheet. "Thank you for
your suggestion," he said, controlling his voice to an
even keel.

"I'm just thinking that you might take more pleasure
in life if you allowed yourself to actually *be* interested in
horses," Imogen said, showing no reaction to his rebuff.

Mayne bent his head to read a squib about Burling-
ton's stables at Raby.

"I think you're bored. You're all of, what? Thirty-
seven years old?"

"Thirty-four!" he snapped.

"You've more money than you know what to do with,
no ambitions to take a wife or set up a family and no
particular interest in your estate."

"I take all proper interest in my estate."

"I'm sure you do," Imogen said in a soothing voice

that wouldn't have fooled a child. "Likely the roofs are mended, but that's not my point. It doesn't interest you."

"And what precisely *could* interest me about it?" he asked, irritated beyond all bearing. "Are you suggesting I take up farming?"

She shrugged. "Lord knows, I don't know what gentlemen do. Some of them seem to find it all quite engrossing. Look at Tuppy Perwinkle."

"Tuppy fishes," Mayne said flatly. "I cannot imagine anything so tedious as sitting on a riverbank in the rain."

"In all probability, he would feel the same about the stables," Imogen persisted. She opened a sewing box and was beginning to pull apart the tangled mess inside.

"Just what are you going to do with that?" Mayne said in a feeble attempt to change the subject.

"Sort Griselda's embroidery yarns," Imogen said, and then she turned directly back to the subject. "You're in a malaise from pure boredom. You've nothing to do."

"I've a great deal to do," he answered, nettled beyond all bearing.

"No, you don't. You have an excellent man of business, and I happen to know that Tess's husband advises you on what to sell and such things, so you needn't make any decisions there."

"Only a fool would reject Lucius's advice," Mayne said. "What's your point?"

"You're bored. That's my point." Her rosy-tipped fingers danced over the skeins, selecting a plum-colored one. She started to tease it from the tangle.

Mayne considered going for a walk, anything to get away from her.

"Perhaps you should take up your seat in the House of Lords," Imogen suggested.

He tried to imagine himself standing up on the floor,

lecturing to all and sundry about the Corn Laws. And then his imagination failed. "No."

"It *is* difficult to imagine you in such a place," Imogen agreed. "It's unfortunate that you have developed such a distaste for dalliance, since that kept you happily occupied for the last ten years."

Mayne didn't like that statement, however casually it was delivered. He didn't like it that his memories of the last ten—no, the last fifteen—years were made up of little more than a glittering sweep of intrigues, stolen kisses, furtive erotic encounters and the odd duel with an enraged husband. Meetings with complacent husbands who didn't give a damn had become routine. As had a few tears dropped on his sleeve once he made it clear that he had decided to move to another woman. Another woman, and another, and another.

Thinking over those years gave him a sour taste in his mouth.

Imogen had managed to free the plum-colored yarn and was starting on a sky-blue one. "There's no use in bemoaning the past," she said, without even looking at him. "I expect you enjoyed yourself at the time."

Mayne's lips twisted. In retrospect, those perfume-saturated evenings seemed tediously similar, tawdry and shallow, fueled by too much wine and a hearty sensual appetite.

Until the sensual appetite deserted him . . . and left him with nothing.

"But you seem to have lost your predilection for illicit dalliance," she said, as if she read his thoughts. "Consider me, for example. You look at me with all the interest of an altered tomcat."

"That's disgusting," Mayne snapped, at the same moment that Josie inquired, "What's altered about a tomcat?"

"You must be the most indelicate female of my acquaintance!" he told Imogen, ignoring Josie's question.

"Do you really think so?" Imogen said, utterly unmoved by his criticism. "And here I thought gentlemen had such a variety of acquaintances."

"There's been nothing so adventuresome about my life. Generally speaking, I've had the pleasure of knowing ladies whose language matched the delicacy of their minds."

"Ha!" Imogen said. "If that is what you believe, then it doesn't take much speculation to realize that you have never really had an intimate conversation with any woman in your life."

Mayne had a flash of near-homicidal rage, a reaction that was becoming common around his supposed mistress. "I have had many intimate conversations," he said. "Not that such intimacy or a lack thereof is a suitable topic to discuss before your younger sister."

"I may be young, but I have a great deal of common sense," Josie said, looking over the top of her book. "I am perfectly aware that Imogen has made you several proposals of a less-than-honorable nature, and that you have rebuffed her. I expect that explains her impertinence; Plutarch says there is nothing sharper than the sting of rejected affection." She turned back to her book without further ado.

Obviously Josephine would be just as much trouble as her sister once she reached her majority; Mayne shuddered a little at the thought.

"Why don't you set up your own stables?" Imogen asked.

"I *have* stables. How many times have I told you that I'm missing the Ascot and I'm running two horses there?"

Griselda appeared from the door of the inn, leaning

on the arm of her maid and looking marginally better than she had an hour ago. "I have steeled myself to return to that vehicle," she called to them, her face as set as that of a French aristocrat facing the guillotine. "Josie, put on your bonnet. How many times must I tell you that freckles are most unattractive? If you would all enter, please, the innkeeper tells me that he has prepared a light repast."

"I know you have a stable," Imogen said, winding up the blue yarn and scooping the tangle back into the box. "Why don't you let yourself take it seriously? Hire a proper training crew. My father talked of his competition for years, of you, as well as every other man in England who might be persuaded to buy a horse from him. You're a gentleman dabbler, buying a horse here or there, selling it if it doesn't win its first race. You've never taken your own stables seriously. Well, how could you? You were always in London."

And I was never awake until afternoon, Mayne thought. He picked up the ribbon box and headed after Imogen toward the door of the inn. Her traveling dress hugged her every curve. He eyed them deliberately and discovered—

Nothing.

He was completely uninterested. An altered tomcat indeed.

She was right. Without women, what was he? What would he do?

Twenty-three

She gave him a smile she had practiced and never used, the smile of a siren beckoning Odysseus, the smile of Venus hailing Adonis, the smile of any pagan goddess faced with male beauty. "We're marrying as soon as we reach your lands," Annabel stated.

"That is not tonight," Ewan replied. But she could see that his eyes were black, and his voice hadn't even a thread of amusement. "We would be anticipating the bonds of matrimony. I shouldn't—"

"Tonight," she whispered achingly. "I want you, *tonight*, Ewan. I want you to make love to me. I like the coney's kiss. I did. But there's something more, isn't there?"

It was as if all sound had drained from the room. "Oh, God, Annabel, of course there is. And you know it."

"Show me. Please." She caught his face in her hands, pulling him down to her, brushing her lips over his.

"We're alone," she said into his mouth. She put little kisses on the strong curve of his lips, on the angle of his jaw, on his ear.

Then, just when she thought that he might have changed his mind, that his principles were stronger than his desire, he turned his face and captured her mouth. She could read the truth in the possessiveness of his touch.

"You won't regret it?" he asked her, his voice hoarse. "We aren't married."

"Never," she gasped.

He turned her toward the bed, keeping her body against his, and then stopped short.

"What is it?" she asked.

Ewan eased her away from him. "The bed," he said, voice tight with need. "I forgot to ask my man to put on our sheets." He looked around. "In fact, I forgot to have our sheets taken off the carriage."

"Oh," Annabel said, pulling back the thin coverlet. The sheets were a grayish color. "I expect Peggy finds it difficult to do washing."

"I can take care of it," Ewan said. "Just let me find the linen closet."

A little smile played around Annabel's mouth as she watched him prowl around the cottage. "Ewan," she said finally, "there *is* no linen closet."

"Well, where does Peggy keep clean linen?"

"She doesn't have any."

"For God's sake," Ewan said. There was a soft growl in his voice. He was so beautiful that Annabel's body tingled all over just looking at his broad shoulders and the square line of his jaw.

"The tablecloth," she said, hearing the tremor in her own voice. "We can use the tablecloth that was in the picnic basket."

Ewan jerked the cloth from the basket so fast that

crumbs flew through the air. Annabel stripped off the bed, and they found that the beautiful linen tablecloth—generously embroidered with Ewan's crest all around the hem—fit the Kettles' bed perfectly.

"Now," Ewan said, with a note of slumberous satisfaction in his voice. "Come here, Annabel." He sat down and held out his arms.

She moved toward him, suddenly shy.

"My wife," he said, pulling her toward him.

"Not yet," she whispered.

"In my heart. You know that I believe in the soul, Annabel. But"—he paused and skimmed a kiss along the edge of her mouth—"not all the teachings of the church. You are my wife in my heart and soul, from this moment forward."

Annabel drew a shaky breath. In truth, she wasn't even thinking in words. She craved Ewan with the depth of her being, craved his mouth and his touch, and the weight of his body.

Two seconds later she was lying on cool linen. Her clothes were gone, stripped away by Ewan with the ease of someone who had disrobed many a woman. And yet . . . The stray thought made her body suddenly rigid. She didn't have much idea how to do this, and if everything Ewan said was correct, neither did he.

The village women had told her that consummation needn't be painful, if she married a man who knew what he was doing. "Marry a tired rake," Mrs. Cooper had said. "They know everything, and yet they're worn out and ready to settle down. As long as he doesn't have the pox." The pox was something she didn't have to worry about. But Annabel's thighs tightened at the thought of pain.

He knew instantly. "Ach, lass, are you frightened?" he whispered against her skin.

"There are ways to make it not painful," she said hopefully.

"Old wives' tales, or so Nana says."

"You *asked* your grandmother such a thing?"

"Nana knows all there is to know about a woman's body. She told me once that some women suffer quite a bit, and others don't even notice and might as well not be virgins at all."

It was too late to change her mind, so Annabel nodded, a little jerkily.

Ewan looked down at his bride-to-be. One moment she gave him the most temptingly seductive smile he had ever seen on a woman's face, and the next she was trembling and clearly scared out of her wits. She had her eyes shut tight; they tilted at the corners with an exotic little curve that was at odds with the practicality of planning adultery before she even decided whom to marry. The very thought of it made him grin. But he had to admit that for a woman this passionate, and yet so set on marrying a man of wealth, adultery was likely just a practical suggestion.

Now she lay before him like a feast of raspberries and cream, and desire was surging through him like molten fire. Disjointed thoughts about the sanctity of marriage flew through his mind, but none of them mattered. She was *his*, and she would be his until death.

In fact, it was a great thing they were doing, because their wedding night could be a proper celebration, once they'd gotten all the fear out of the way beforehand. He could see her breast rising and falling with little pants but she said nothing. And she didn't take her hands from her eyes.

"Are you all right?" he whispered, coming on his knees over her. Ewan didn't know anything about the art of seducing virgins, of taking virginity, of introducing a woman to the pleasures of the bed. But he knew one kind of kiss they had both enjoyed, and one at which he appeared to be quite able. He let one hand slide between her rounded thighs and pushed them apart slightly, then began to kiss his way down her creamy stomach, down to that buttery patch of hair again, down—

"You needn't do that," she said, her voice stifled by her hands, which covered her whole face.

"I want to," he said simply. And then, two seconds later, her moans were flying into the night air again. One hand even fell from her eyes, and her legs slid restlessly up to form a perfect cradle for his body. *Soon,* he promised her silently, soon. Tremors were wracking her now, and she was whimpering, crying, coming to him—and then she flew free again, hands over her head, her body arched into the air . . . and falling back down, gentle as thistledown.

It took everything he had to stay in control. She was sweet, swollen, ready for him . . . He said, "Annabel, could you open your eyes now?" And then: "Please?"

So she did, dewy, smoky blue peering at him. He nudged against her, and her eyes grew wider.

"Don't shut me out, sweetheart," he breathed. "I want to see you . . . if only this time. This first time."

A shaky smile curved her lips. "I—"

Annabel caught back her words, shut her eyes tight, remembered and opened them—because he was there, he was sliding inside her, and there was no pain—

"Ewan!" she cried. Then she arched and he came to her, all the way.

"Thank God," he said, as if it were wrenched out of him, and then: "Does this hurt?"

And it didn't.

And none of it did. Not even when he started taunting her, pulling back and smiling down at her as she tried to pull him down to her, then choosing his moment and thrusting home. Not when she decided to taunt him and, dimly remembering Tess's advice, let her hands slide to his hard buttocks and linger there . . .

He groaned and then took her mouth, hard and purposeful, the wild kind of kiss that meant something quite different now. Annabel tasted the moment Ewan lost control. He plunged deeper and deeper, his breath coming in gasps. He was grasping her hips, driving forward as if they could grow ever closer.

At first she just enjoyed looking at him, but then a feeling started growing and growing, a kind of molten desire that spread from their joining through her whole body, and she found herself rising to meet him, her fingers clenching on his muscled shoulders.

"Annabel," he said, in a growl that was half a moan. "Oh, God!"

And she didn't think he was referring to a deity now. The feeling was growing and growing, and finally Annabel just let herself slide into the chaos of it, into the sweat and rhythmic madness of it . . .

Until she cried out against his shoulder and he thankfully let his jaw unclench and drove home, home to her, to his still center, to his wife.

Twenty-four

It was the middle of the night. They'd fallen asleep curled together, but Annabel woke after an hour or so to find that Ewan had lit the candles on Peggy's table and built up the fire.

"What are you doing?" she asked sleepily.

"Looking at you," he said, and there was such a deep languorous satisfaction in his voice that she smiled. So much for all her plans to trade her body and her bankable kisses for a man of wealth and title. Now she knew with a bone-deep instinct that her body was always meant to be here, adored by Ewan, even—even worshipped.

"I'm thirsty," she whispered.

He tried to hold the tin cup to her lips, as if she were a child with a fever, but water ran down her neck. He kissed the damp away, and then Annabel suddenly realized that she could have all the kisses she wanted from Ewan, for free, without asking questions.

"Kiss me," she said.

"Annabel—"

She pulled his head to hers. "I am not marrying you because you have a castle," she said against his lips.

Of course there was laughter in his voice. "Nay, I know all too well that you will marry me because you have to do so. Although now you have a double reason."

"I just want you to know that I had no idea you were so rich," she said. "None!"

"I know *that*," he said. "It was obvious in your desperate eyes when you accepted my proposal. Plus, no one in London seemed to know a thing about me, except your sister's husband, Felton. He knows everything about finances, it seems."

"Lucius Felton knew you were rich?" Annabel said.

"You can't move stocks and such without encountering a few of the men interested in doing the same thing. We'd never met, naturally, as I send my secretary around to do such things as have to be done in person—"

"Ewan," Annabel interrupted. "Just how rich are you?"

He smiled at her, and there wasn't much of the simpleton about him now. "I expect I'm the richest man in Scotland, give or take a castle or two," he said.

Annabel let her head fall back. "I don't believe it."

"Because I am willing to take risks," he said, looking at her, amused. "I have had little trouble increasing my possessions. Father Armailhac always says that possessions bring with them responsibility. And sometimes I think that I try to shed responsibility by shedding possessions."

"But everything you make comes back to you tenfold," she guessed.

He nodded. "If you don't wish for money, it comes to you easily. And if you don't wish for responsibilities, they come in droves."

"I don't believe you. How would you feel, would you really feel, if you were no longer the Earl of Ardmore?

It's such a part of you, almost as if you were a medieval feudal lord, with the crofters and cottagers, and all the people who live in the castle, and the way they depend on you."

He took her questions seriously, even when there was no question of kisses, and she loved that.

"So I lose the earldom . . ."

"Yes."

"And the castle . . ."

"Yes."

"And all the trappings, all the possessions—"

"More than that. You lose all the people who love and depend on you."

"Gregory and Rosy?"

She nodded. "And the cottagers, your staff, Mac. All the people and things that make you formidable in the eyes of the world."

"Are Gregory and Rosy safe and well-cared-for?"

"Of course."

"Then . . . do I get to keep you?"

There was a note in his deep voice that made her shiver, and she said, rather breathlessly, "I suppose so. I thought I was marrying a penniless earl."

"Then I don't care." He wasn't even touching her and she felt as if she'd received the sweetest caress of her life. "If I had you, Annabel, I could start in this little cabin and make us a living."

Annabel tried to smile, but it trembled on her lips. "I'm glad we don't have to live here," she said finally.

"I could eat your potatoes with butter every day and be happy."

"You would have to," Annabel said with a little gurgle of laughter, "since that's all I know how to make."

"It isn't so bad, is it?"

And she was silent, thinking about the rosy, clean little

house, and the way Ewan caught her when she fell, and the way he laughed when the milk spilt. "No," she said finally, "It hasn't been the way I would have thought."

"Father Armailhac says that one should be able to give up the things of the world without a moment's regret," Ewan said, turning over and nuzzling her shoulder.

"Good for him," Annabel said, a bit crossly. "I don't believe that you could do it, for all you say so. This is only for a day or so."

"Believe it," he said, but his voice was muffled by kisses. He was kissing his way down her throat, past her collarbone . . .

"What if you didn't have me either?" Annabel asked. "What then?"

He didn't even hesitate. "If I had no responsibilities and I had to live without you, I'd become a monk. Or a priest. Something of that sort."

His lips were drifting across her breast; Annabel was terribly glad that Ewan hadn't disappeared into a monastery. "I have another question."

"Mmmm," he said, not paying her close attention.

"If you haven't been with a woman for years . . . how on earth did you know about that kiss?"

"Which kiss?" he asked with maddening obliviousness. He was running his fingers over the curves of her breasts as if he would never get enough.

"You know! That coney's kiss," she said.

"Oh, that."

"How did you know how to do it? How did you know what it was?"

He was stroking the undercurve of her breast with his lips. "I made it up."

"You *what*?"

"I made it up . . . well, part of it. Men are always

telling jokes about coney-catchers, you see. *Coney* being a rabbit, but also—"

"I know," she said hastily.

"So I was trying to think of a way to horrify your sister, and I made up a coney's kiss. It worked, didn't it? And as for how to do it . . . 'twas instinct, darling. I trust my instinct a great deal." His mouth closed around her nipple and she squeaked aloud. "My instinct tells me that you like that," he said, smug as a cat by the hearth. "And I know *I* do."

She swatted him.

"It's a God-given gift I have, obviously."

He was laughing against her breast and kissing her at the same time, and Annabel, for once, had to agree with him on a matter of theology. It was, indeed, a God-given gift.

In the end, they had no sleep at all. They were cuddled together in an exhausted, boneless state when the sun began stealing under the curtain. By then Annabel had decided that her new favorite activity was to make the amusement disappear from Ewan's eyes. So she said to him, "Do you know what Tess told me about marital consummation?"

He shook his head. "I trust it wasn't some foolishness about lying back and enduring."

"She told me that whatever my husband does to me, I should do to him," she said, making her voice as provocative as she could make it. And since Annabel had practiced the art of provocation for years, she was very, very good at that particular skill. "That means, oh, my almost-husband," she clarified, "that tonight . . ."

There wasn't a trace of laughter on his face now.

She let her smile turn from provocative to wicked. Then she reached out one finger and put it on the smooth skin of his chest. Delicately, delicately, she trailed that finger down . . . down . . .

"And what do they call the coney's kiss when it's not a coney being kissed?" she said, relishing the tightness of his jaw.

Her finger swept down to the rigid length of him. Ewan shuddered. He hadn't taken his eyes from hers, though. And he wasn't laughing.

She pursed her lips at him and then he was there, rolling over on her with a strength that she was powerless to resist, plunging into her mouth with a ferocity that made her shudder against him as if she weren't limp with pleasure but a moment before.

"Tonight," she whispered against his lips, once she regained her breath.

And he was the one who closed his eyes this time.

Twenty-five

Annabel woke some time later to a persistent banging noise. "What on earth?" she asked sleepily.

Ewan didn't seem to notice the noise. His strong arms came around her from behind, pulling her against him. Annabel's body melted. "No," she said uncertainly.

"Yes," he said into her hair.

Bang! went the shed door.

"The cow needs milking," Annabel said. If Ewan kept doing that even one more moment, she'd—she'd—

He groaned and rolled away.

Annabel sat up and then edged quickly to the side of the bed. The tablecloth appeared to be slightly soiled.

"I would give a sovereign for water to wash my face," Ewan muttered, pulling on his breeches. All the while the cow kept slamming its stable door.

A few moments later the noise stopped, and then

Annabel found that the chicken had very kindly laid an egg in the butter mold.

She felt less charitably inclined when she discovered that the bird had also soiled their only chair. Without water, she couldn't clean it, so she found her brush and started to work on her hair. But given the absence of a looking glass, she could only wind it into a graceless bun.

Ewan returned with a pail of milk in one hand and a pail of water in the other. His hair was wet.

"There's a stream down to the right, behind the woodshed," he said. "It's cold as the devil's behind. The only way to get clean is to jump in."

Annabel shivered. She would bathe without taking such drastic measures, even if she had to heat pans of water all morning. "Would you build up the fire, please?"

Ewan threw on two more logs, and then helped her swing a pot with the egg in it over the flames. "I've thought of a problem," he said.

Annabel had thought of about four hundred, but she was trying to keep them to himself.

"I don't expect Kettle has any tea or coffee."

"I doubt it," Annabel said. "We only had coffee on special occasions, and we were far better off than the Kettles."

Ewan didn't seem too happy.

"Did you see the other chickens?" Annabel asked, giving the white hen an oatcake.

Ewan shook his head. "Is there any bread left from the picnic basket?"

"No, but there's the egg," Annabel said, making a valiant effort to be cheerful.

Ewan grunted. At least she thought that's what that particular noise was known as. He did eat the egg, after some argument. But Annabel spent five minutes scraping that egg from the bottom of the pan, and she'd never yet eaten an egg the color of coal, so she won the squabble. It seemed to take a lot of chewing.

Finally he left, saying that he was going to try to root a large rock out of Kettle's field.

Annabel ate an oatcake and heated up four pans of water before she felt clean. Then she scrubbed the little house, shooing the chicken out the front door. The real problem was sheets. She couldn't possibly sleep on that stained tablecloth . . . she'd have to wash Peggy's sheet. She looked for a washbasin, and finally decided that Peggy did her laundry in the stream.

The ice-cold stream, according to Ewan. She shivered at the thought. But if she didn't wash the linens soon, they wouldn't dry. Who knows how long it took a sheet to dry? Probably at least an hour. She gathered them into a bundle and headed out the door.

The river frothed and gurgled on its way through the woods. It was surrounded by large stones. Anna found a flat one, knelt down and dropped the sheet into the water. It immediately turned an even darker gray color. She pulled it back out, splashing freezing water all over her skirts, and tried to rub soap over it. But the sheet seemed to weigh four times as much as it had previously, and it was so cold that her fingers ached just to touch it.

Annabel gritted her teeth. She wasn't going to be defeated by something as simple as laundry. She pushed the sheet back in the water, hanging on to a portion with her freezing hands. The sheet floated below her, looking as if it were getting dirtier by the moment. A surge of water dragged at it, and Annabel almost let it go. Her hands were wrinkled and aching from the cold; her skirts were pasted to her legs with water, and the sheet seemed to weigh fifteen stone.

But finally she wrestled it back out of the water. Clearly there was no way to return to the clearing without getting wet. So she took a deep breath and picked up the sheet. Icy water flowed down her neck, soaking her arms and skirts. Her teeth chattering, Annabel started running back to the house as quickly as she could. Once in the clearing, she did her best to wring out the water. Then she spread the sheet on top of a low bush.

Back in the house, she dragged her wet dress over her head, using her nightgown as a towel. Her arms ached, and her fingers were blue with cold. Then she looked in every nook and cranny of the cottage for tea. There was none. She sat on the step and drank a cup of steaming water. Surely the Kettles ate more than just boiled potatoes and an occasional egg? Peggy must have a larder somewhere.

Ewan emerged from the wood, looking as tired as she felt. "I can't move the bloody rock," he said without ceremony.

"I've washed the sheet!" Anna said with a flash of pride.

He looked at the huge puddle of water around the root of the bush. "Do you mind if I inquire what we are going to sleep on tonight?"

"It will dry in time," Annabel said, hoping she was right. She looked around, suddenly noticing that the clearing seemed ominously quiet. "Oh, Ewan, I think we lost the last chicken!"

"Look for a happy fox."

"Surely not! She was here a moment ago."

"Perhaps she's roosting in a tree," Ewan said, hoping he was right. He fully intended to eat that chicken for supper.

"I couldn't tell Peggy that I'd lost all three of her chickens. Her neighbors gave them as a wedding pres-

ent." Annabel walked toward the woods. "Last time I
saw her, she was over here. Oh, chicken! Chicken!"

Ewan grinned. Annabel looked as elegant as an
etching in *La Belle Assemblée*. She was wearing another
inappropriate traveling dress, not made of sturdy brown
to withstand dirt, but fashioned in deep ruby, with rows
and rows of white lace around her bosom.

"I must say, I like the current fashion in farmwife attire," he remarked.

"It's a promenade dress," Annabel said, poking
around the small trees at the edge of the clearing. "I
don't own anything sturdy. I know she's very close. She's
ignoring me, that's all." Without a look at Ewan, she
headed straight into the dusky woods.

"Annabel!" he called.

"Yes?" Her voice echoed back to him.

"Don't get lost!" He could hear her thrashing about.

He waited about four minutes and then shouted again.
"Are you lost yet?"

"Well, no . . . not exactly. I'm in a little clearing. Where
are you?"

"Just stay where you are," he said, and he headed toward the sound of her voice. He could hear her snapping
twigs. "Stay where you are! Otherwise we might both
get lost."

"There's an awful—" Suddenly there was a scream
and Ewan's heart jumped into his throat. He tore forward, catching Annabel in his arms as she dodged between two trees. "Ewan, Ewan! There's a lot of *bees*!"

In a ray of sunshine peaking between the tall firs,
Ewan saw exactly what she meant. Without a word, he
swung her to the far side of a large tree and pressed her
against his body, wrapping himself over her and tucking
her face securely against his shoulder. "Don't move," he
breathed.

They stayed frozen while the bees flew by, a whole swarm of them, from their angry hum.

"Oh, God," Annabel moaned a few moments later. "Ewan . . ."

"I think you found the honey tree," he said, lifting his head.

"Yes, it must be in that clearing," Annabel said, sounding a bit more cheerful. "Peggy will be happy to hear that, won't she? Even though she has no chickens left."

"A few of those bees found me," Ewan said glumly.

"Oh, no," she cried. "You've been stung!"

"Only twice." Then he added, "Perhaps three times."

"I'm very, very grateful that you rescued me," Annabel said. "Shall we return?" She started in the wrong direction.

"This way," Ewan said, tucking her under his arm.

"Where did they sting you?"

"In a most tender place." He was rewarded by her giggle. He thought fleetingly that he wouldn't mind a whole tribe of bees attacking his ass if he had that giggle as a reward. Annabel's giggle was just like herself: enchantingly feminine, with a husky undertone that showed both a wicked sense of humor and a sensual appetite.

"I could make some more potatoes," Annabel said, once they were back at the cabin. "Although the fire appears to have gone out again."

"It helps if you occasionally add a log," Ewan pointed out.

She shot him a look. "Why don't you sit down and rest while I heave a tree limb or two onto the fire?"

"I can't sit down," he said, giving her a rueful grin. "I'll put on a log."

"Does it hurt very much?" And, when he shook his

head, "I suppose it doesn't matter that we don't have a horse, because you wouldn't be comfortable riding it."

Ewan shuddered at the thought of sitting on a saddle. He was starting to feel like an idiot. He hadn't even thought about keeping a horse for their use. His Shake-spearean idea was seeming stupider by the moment. No wonder he didn't like the play when it was performed: clearly the whole idea was ludicrous.

"Let me guess," Annabel said in a voice that was ob-viously trying to be solicitous, "your stings are annoy-ing you."

Indeed, Ewan was starting to feel annoyed. Uncharac-teristically annoyed. Annabel looked so delectable that the only thing he wanted was to throw her onto the bed and make her happy in the best way possible. Except that his ass felt as if it had been burned by a red-hot poker, and it probably looked like the devil's pincush-ion. There went all his plans to seduce his almost-wife this afternoon. Plus his conscience was bothering him about that seduction in the first place. Why on earth had he lost his control and consummated a marriage that didn't exist? What was it about Annabel that had him throwing his principles to the winds?

He stomped outside, feeling thoroughly out of sorts. He had spent two hours trying to pry that damn rock out of Kettle's field, all for nothing. He scowled at the surrounding woods. According to Annabel, his life was overly comfortable, but at least he didn't break his back doing useless labor.

Then his eyes lightened. "Oh, Annabel!" he called. "My lovely wife!"

"I'm not your wife yet," she said, appearing in the doorway. His eyes slid over her and a familiar feeling of desire gripped him so hard he almost started shaking. It was embarrassing. He was out of control. He felt another surge of irritation, so he gave her his silkiest smile.

"I know that you will be enchanted to know that our lost chicken has returned home," he said, pointing.

Annabel's shriek startled the hen so much that she flew into the air with a squawk. "Get off my sheet!" she shouted. "You—you *idiot chicken*!"

Ewan threw back his head and laughed. "If only we'd trained her to use a chamber pot. That hen—"

She turned to him, fist clenched. "Don't you dare laugh at me! That sheet took two hours to wash! *Two hours!* And now—and now—she's ruined it! I'll have to go back to that awful stream and try again."

To Ewan's horror, tears welled in Annabel's eyes.

"I never cry!" she shouted at him.

"I know that," he said. "I mean, of course you don't."

"It's just that the water was so cold." She wiped the tears away. Ewan looked around the dusty clearing and felt like the dunce he was. Why did he bring a lady to live in a hovel? He prided himself on being thoughtful and kind to others. In his better moments, he would even have called himself intelligent.

"I'll wash the sheet," he said. "You make some potatoes."

An hour later Ewan was in a mood rivaled only by a man-eating tiger faced with an elephant stampede. The river water was frigid, and he was soaking wet. He couldn't get the spot made by the chicken to come off until he rubbed the sheet on a rock, and then the spot was replaced by a hole. Every time he bent over, the bee stings burned his ass. Water was dripping from his ears and trickling down inside his boots. He was starved, and he wanted a four-course meal, not another charred potato.

He walked into the house and realized that no potatoes, charred or otherwise, were forthcoming. The fire was out again, and Annabel was nowhere to be seen. He walked over and peered at the fireplace. It looked like she'd spilled water. Wonderful. They had freezing wet sheets, no fire and no food.

Was it too much to ask that she make a damned potato?

He stalked back out of the house to find Annabel emerging from the woodshed, a log clutched against her chest. The white lace that edged her bodice was specked with wood dust. She looked exhausted and dirty. The taste of guilt was like bitter metal in his mouth.

"What the hell are you doing?" he snarled, snatching the log.

She frowned at him. "The pan tipped again and I had to find a dry log."

"You could have waited for me and I would have fetched the wood."

Annabel put her hands on her hips. "*You* could have made sure that we had sufficient logs in the house!"

"I was busy washing that sheet," Ewan said, anger rising in his chest. "I'm damn well starving to death and I get back to find that you've doused the fire again, and there's not even a charred potato to eat!"

"How *dare* you say such a thing!" Annabel said furiously. "This is your foolish idea, and all because you have no imagination. I *told* you that it would be miserable to live here! But did you listen to me? No!"

Ewan could feel the shards of his composure dissolving like ice in the sun. "It would have been perfectly easy to stay here for a few days, if you showed a bit of competence," he growled.

"My father was unfortunate in his financial dealings, but he was never reduced to making his daughters into servants. I suppose I could apologize for being unable to cook, but, in fact, I am *not* sorry. I don't like cooking, and I didn't plan to spend my married life learning how."

Guilt and anger were roiling in Ewan's chest. "I apologize for asking you to do more than polish your smiles," he barked. "I'll buy you bales of silk when we reach my house. If I remember rightly, you judged silk the key to happiness."

"At least I've been honest with you. I told you that I hoped to marry a rich man, precisely so that I wouldn't have to agonize over the next meal. *You*, on the other hand, suggested that patience was your best virtue. In fact, if I remember correctly, you viewed marriage as some sort of a gift you would bestow on a poor, grief-stricken woman like my sister: the magnificent gift of your cheerful, patient self!"

"You make me sound like a damned boaster," Ewan snarled.

"I hope it doesn't upset your image of yourself if I point out that your use of curses indicates precisely how pious you truly are?"

"Oh, I believe in God," Ewan said bleakly. "That's got nothing to do with my lack of control around you."

"Don't blame me!" Annabel cried, her hands on her hips. "If you aren't peevish so *very* often, it's likely because everyone treats you like the king of the castle. More ordinary mortals learn from their mistakes."

Ewan's temper abruptly flared out of control again. "I hope you're not classing yourself with those ordinary mortals. Because most people I know can heat a pail of water without washing out the fireplace."

"Just how many people did you know who have ever heated a bucket of water?" Annabel demanded. "Or washed a sheet in a stream, for that matter? Your grandmother, the countess? Does she heat up huge pails of water over the fire for a spot of entertainment?"

Ewan scowled at her. "Nana could do so if she put her mind to it." In truth, he couldn't think of any of his intimates who had done such a thing. Why should they have? None of them had ever been stranded in a cabin in the woods. "I would judge my grandmother as able to conquer any situation," he stated.

"Well, there we differ," Annabel snapped. "I am not a farmwife with the skills to succeed in this sort of life."

"I can see that," Ewan returned. He was smouldering with anger.

"And this has nothing to do with your grandmother's supposed skills! The truth is that you've lived a life of such privilege that you couldn't imagine what it would be like to not have Mac to cater to your every wish. You thought it would be easy to be poor, and now you find out it's not so, you've turned disagreeable."

"I may not have grasped how difficult it would be to live in the Kettles' cottage with a wife who was incapable of heating a pan of water without spilling it—"

"I am *not* your wife," Annabel said icily.

"That gives me two things to be thankful for," Ewan snarled. "One that I'm not so poor that I have to live in a damned hovel, and second that—" He stopped.

Annabel was white with anger. "Too late! Never mind the scandal, after last night, you have to marry me. No matter how much we may both regret it."

Ewan took a deep breath and moved to the side of the little house. Deliberately he leaned against the wall, folding his arms over his chest. Silence fell on the courtyard.

Annabel could actually feel her heart breaking inside her chest. She'd always thought that a broken heart sounded rather romantic. But in truth it was physical. Her whole chest ached, as if she'd been struck with a knife. With all her witless calculations about how to make a man desire her, she'd never realized that the most important thing was to make him *like* her. Or even love her. What a fool she was.

"So you regret making love to me?" His voice was soft, casual almost. Normally Ewan had a lovely burr that sounded pleasurable and amused. But there was something dangerous in his voice now.

She cleared her throat. "I'm sure that we both regret something that leaves us with so few choices."

He straightened and took one step toward her. Annabel held her ground. The easygoing, amused expression that seemed Ewan's natural expression was gone. His eyes were a wild green, smoldering with anger. Suddenly she was afraid of what he was going to say. If he told her that he didn't like her—if he put it in words—she might not be able to bear it.

"Just because you're angry," she said hastily, "is no need to say something you might regret. We have no choice but marriage. We have to make the best of it."

"True," he said slowly, and his voice was still a growl. He took another step toward her.

There was no mistaking the look in his eyes. Pain wrenched her heart. All those skills she had developed so painstakingly as a girl were apparently going to destroy a dream that she'd never had the courage to hold. "I understand how you feel toward me," Annabel said carefully.

"Yes?" he said, breathing it. He was standing just before her, reaching out to pull her to him.

"Don't!" Annabel cried, stepping backward.

"Why not?"

She might as well say it. "It's only desire," she explained, watching his eyes. "Desire is an artificial thing, created by—by—"

He reached out and curled a hand around her neck. "By what?"

"By artificial things," Annabel said obstinately. "Smiles I *practiced*, Ewan." She stepped back from him again, and the warmth of his hand fell away. She raised her chin and stared at him, willing her tears back. "You don't understand how fabricated it all is. I wear corsets made in France: they make my breasts look twice as large, and no man can resist that. I let my hips sway when I walk, because men like it. *You* like it."

His eyebrow rose. "Your hips don't sway naturally?"

"No. Or perhaps they do by this point, but only because I consciously changed my walk when I was younger. But it's all just a facade, put on to inspire desire."

His eyes were inscrutable. "I've seen your breasts without a corset, Annabel, remember?"

"It's all for show," she said impatiently. "Nothing but show. Nothing but to create desire. It's been like a game, don't you see?"

"A game of desire?"

"No. A game to get what I wish from men." She swallowed back more tears and met his eyes. "I—I like you, Ewan. That's why you need to know just how good I am at this, and how artificial those feelings of desire you feel are. I'm no good at cooking. But I'm very, very good at making men do as I wish."

He reached out again and there was no mistaking the look in his eyes. "You're not listening—" she cried, jumping backward.

Inevitably, she tripped on her skirts. There was a ripping sound. He caught her in his arms, but he couldn't stop their tumble, only protect her from the ground. So she fell on top of him, and he rolled her over before she could protest and crushed his lips onto hers.

"Nothing but a game, is it?" he growled.

"You can't kiss me here," Annabel said, pushing against his shoulders. "Let me up! I'm lying on the ground!"

"I can't. I've lost my mind. Fallen victim to your feminine wiles. Besides, the sheet is sopping."

"Don't make fun of me!" He was pushing up her skirts, his fingers leaving a trail of fire on her legs. "Don't even think—Ewan, please!"

Flames danced over Annabel's body. "We're out-of-doors!" she said desperately.

But then his hand took her and she cried out, even though she was lying on the ground.

"A *game,*" he growled. She twisted against his hand, her breath burning in her chest. "I'm nothing more than a slave to your corset, if I understood you correctly."

Some small part of Annabel was resisting the strength of his fingers. But pleasure simmered in her legs, coursing in waves that followed every move of his fingers. Still, she gasped, "It's not so—"

His fingers stopped, leaving her on fire. "Don't move," he commanded.

She froze.

Then his thumb rubbed across her once, twice, deliberately slow. "You can move now," he said softly.

Fire surged through her bones, and she involuntarily shivered, gasping. His hands stilled again.

"Now, what were you trying to tell me?" he asked conversationally.

"Let go of me," she said. Every nerve in her body was connected and they were all dancing with fire. "This is intolerable. You must let me rise. Someone might ride down that road any moment."

One slow movement took her voice away. "I want you to tell me why our marriage won't work." He was kissing her jaw, his lips brushing against her skin.

"Because—because—" But she couldn't. She couldn't think, not when her whole body was pulsing around his hand, silently begging him to do things she could never say aloud.

"I'll use my male wiles on you," he said. His voice was sinful, and filled with a mad joy that was quite unlike his customary amusement.

Annabel shut her eyes and pretended she wasn't lying on the ground. Then his mouth came to hers again, ravenous, taking her with all the savagery of his anger and the pleasure of his possession.

Ewan almost groaned at the ragged sound of Annabel's breath, at the cries she couldn't stifle against his lips. His hand memorized her softness, the precise movements that made her moan with pleasure, clench around his fingers and finally—finally catch his hair in her fists and twist up against his chest with a cry that burst from her lungs, leaving her breathless with the pleasure of it.

A moment later he scooped her into his arms and carried her into the house. The need to take her, to possess her fully, was pounding through his blood. His only thought was to put her on the bed and—

How the hell had he forgotten that there were no sheets on the bed? Only the stained tablecloth was there. He couldn't put a lady on that. He stopped.

Annabel had her arms around his neck, but there were tears in her eyes. "What?" he asked, bending his head to kiss her. "Why tears?"

She shook her head and pressed her lips against his chin. He felt his body throb with need; he was coiled tighter than a spring, desperate for her body. So he rolled himself backward onto the cloth, stains and all. His ass burned from the bee stings, but her luxurious female curves hovered above him, making his vision blur.

Even though her eyes were still teary, she was smiling. After a hasty wrench at his breeches, he slid up, into her, completing her, completing him. She surged forward to meet him with a cry. And then he was thrusting into her with no apologies for his lack of finesse, just a joint madness and a shuddering pleasure that rocked between them.

Ewan threw back his head and tried to focus on the rough-hewn logs of the roof. He wouldn't go without her—he wouldn't—

His hips surged upward, demanding that she come deeper . . . his hands shaped her breasts until she fell forward, burying her face in his neck.

Harder and harder he pounded, his mind black, but the words kept beating in his head until finally he gasped them through the burning in his chest. "I don't have to marry you just because we slept together. Or due to that scandal in London."

She froze above him, her eyes wide.

"I *have* to marry you because you are mine." He stared at her, craving her even as he took her, with a desire that would never die. "You are mine. *Mine.*"

There were tears sliding down her cheeks now, but she was with him, her body shuddering with his every stroke, coming to meet him.

"God Almighty, Annabel," he finally said, his teeth clenched with his need to bring her with him. "I love you, don't you see that?"

But then he finally lost the battle with his hunger. The air exploded from his lungs and his vision went black, and the only thing he felt was the shuddering of her body against his. And dimly, dimly through the explosion of pleasure in his body, he felt gratitude for the way she sobbed his name as she clenched about him.

Twenty-six

"This has gone far enough," Imogen said, making her voice as clear and commanding as possible.

She and Mayne were alone in a sitting room in the Wood and Horn. They had traveled all day, and barely had time for baths and a change of clothing before a late supper. Directly thereafter, Griselda had taken Josie off to bed and left Imogen and Mayne together.

Yet that rather astonishing intimacy seemed to have gone unnoticed by Mayne. For the last hour, he had been seated before the fire wrapped in a fascinating book about halters and bridles he'd discovered in a corner. *She* had spent the time examining the room: one long-necked bottle of wine, one suit of armor minus an arm, one portrait of a Miss Jogg. She knew the name of the long-nosed young lady because she'd actually gone over to examine her tarnished name-plate.

That was how tedious the evening was.

"What has gone far enough?" he asked, not even looking up.

"Your indifference toward me."

She finally got his attention; Mayne blinked and looked up.

Imogen had meant to be seductive, once he stopped reading his musty book. She meant to dance across the floor and perch on the edge of his armchair and coax him into taking liberties with her, or flirting with her, or doing anything that would make her feel as if she were a beautiful, desired lady.

Instead she heard with horror her own voice crack as she said, "Surely you despise me."

Mayne put down his book. "Are you asking me to kiss you?"

The words were at her lips before she could stop them. "How *can* you spurn me when you've accepted every invitation offered in the past ten years?"

She was seated opposite him, her hair gleaming in the firelight, her low-necked gown a shade of rose that suited her dark coloring. With that wild light in her eyes she looked like a passionate gypsy, the kind who would steal a man's purse and his heart at once.

"I do not wish to go to bed with you." He saw her shoulders grow slightly rigid and felt a pang of guilt.

"Why not?"

"Put it down to my age."

"You're not so old. Don't you think—" She paused and he saw her throat work for a second. "Don't you think I'm beautiful?"

He stood up. She was right: he had always been catholic in his tastes, and she was both lovely and available. He brought her to her feet, but even as he did so, he knew . . . he just knew.

She met his eyes and now there was fury in hers. "I hate you!" she cried.

He dropped his hands instantly. "I expect you do."

"How dare you . . . how *dare* you. I saw you try to make yourself and then you—you—"

"Which has everything to do with my incapabilities and nothing to do with you."

She froze. "Are you incapable?"

For a second he toyed with the idea. Let her spread the word that he was a limp lily . . . but no. Instead he walked over to her and crushed his mouth onto hers. Her lips were plump and full and tasted of tears and anger. His body had never failed him, not even after two bottles of brandy, and it didn't now. He pulled away from her, took her hand and deliberately pressed it to the front of his trousers.

"There!" he said, voice bleak. "Am I incapable?"

A tiny, triumphant smile curled her lips. "No."

"But there's more to me than functioning equipment. I would guess that your husband was as bungling riding a woman as he was a horse."

She gave a small squeak but he didn't stop. "So now you're wanting to use me, like a square of gingerbread at the fair, to amuse yourself and make you forget your memories."

All that weariness he felt at the very idea of tending to another woman in bed, of making her dewy-eyed so that she'd coo and promise she'd never felt *that* before—all that weariness came into his voice. "You don't give a damn about me, Imogen. And to be brutally honest, I don't give much of a damn about you either. And that's where we are."

She stared at him, eyes wide, fist clenched to her mouth.

"People like us shouldn't be going to bed together. There's no bloody point in it. Don't you see that? You married for love, for God's sake!"

"But you said— you said Draven—"

"I'm sure he was crap in the sack," Mayne snarled. "But you loved him, didn't you? So even if he wasn't making you faint, he had something I've never had."

She whispered it. "What?"

"You loved him. Lucky bastard that he was." He said it deliberately, slowly. "Maitland didn't die unloved."

Then he swung about, on the point of leaving the room. "And he loved you too. So leave it be!" His voice echoed off the old walls. "The stupid sod loved you. He eloped with you. He said he loved you when he was dying, for God's sake. What right have *you* to discount his feelings?"

There were tears in her eyes, and he was in no mood for tears. But he waited.

"None," she said, and her voice broke. "I've no right at all."

He made to leave, but when she sank to her knees, he went over and picked her up.

But only because there was no one else around to do it.

Twenty-seven

Annabel sat on the bed and stared at the rough-hewn wall, but her view was blurred by hot, humiliated tears. She should be riotously happy. Ewan had said he loved her. A sob tore its way up her chest.

The truth of it was shockingly, brutally clear. She had spent her girlhood figuring out how to make a man desire her. She hadn't neglected a single item that might be helpful: she knew about kisses that fired a man's loins with their suggestiveness, about glances that promised private delight, about sleek movements of one's hips that could make a man's hands shake.

She was an expert at arousing desire.

No, the uglier word was more appropriate: *lust*.

The irony was that she had achieved precisely the marriage she hoped to gain from her practice: marriage to a rich man blinded by his lust for her. A man who was kindly and generous in his dealings with others, would never reproach her for having no dowry and would buy her all the gowns she wanted. Sobs were burning her throat.

Her life felt like one of those fairy tales that pretend to be enjoyable but finish up with an unpleasant moral. The richest man in Scotland was so riveted by lust that in the heat of the moment, he swore fidelity and even love.

It was unfortunate that she wasn't stupid enough to ignore the difference between lust and love.

If only she were ugly, or scarred, or even—she wiped away more tears—if she had a particularly nice personality, she might believe Ewan. But she'd never hidden truths from herself. Her only skill was figuring numbers, and yet she was lazy enough to never wish to do it. She was charming when it suited her, and a fishwife when it didn't, something her father would have attested to.

More tears slid down her face. If your own father doesn't love you, then it should be no surprise to find that other men aren't inclined to do so. Ewan had merely glimpsed what she was really like, and he had immediately blurted out his reluctance to marry—at least until lust got the better of him. But how long would lust last?

The pain of it was like a raw ache in her chest. She sat on the bed and shuddered with sobs, rubbing away the tears with her damp nightgown. It wasn't like her to succumb to tears in this fashion. She had rarely cried when her father was sharp with her, even in the worst moments of her childhood. Yet somehow the tears just started up again, for all her attempts to stop.

The door opened quietly. Ewan's hair was dripping wet again.

"How you can bear to enter that stream I don't know," she said, hastily blotting her face and pretending that her eyes weren't red.

"I'm used to cold water," he said. "My nurse used to say that I was fairly addicted to cleanliness. I often bathe in the river that runs behind the castle, and it's freezing in the depths of summer. Why are you crying, Annabel?"

She managed a weak smile. "Foolishness. I'm hungry, I think."

"I'll give you a glass of milk. And I'll put on potatoes," he said. "After that, I'm going to walk to the next village. I'll be back for you as soon as I can." His voice was grim. "I've been an idiotic bastard, Annabel. I can't even say how sorry I am."

"It's not so bad," she said, but her voice rasped, and he scowled. Then she realized what he was saying. "You can't walk to the next village! It's growing dark. How on earth will you find your way?"

Ewan put six potatoes into the pot. They should at least fill Annabel's stomach until he could return with a horse, a carriage and warm clothes of all kinds. "I'll find the way," he said curtly.

Then he came over to her and dropped a kiss on her head. "I've milked the cow. Expect me back before the morning."

"Ewan—"

But she spoke to empty space.

Four hours later, Ewan realized that he may have paid lip service to the idea of hell, but now he had a realistic idea of it. He had stumbled along for an hour or so, keeping to the path by luck rather than skill, until rain started to fall. By a half hour after that, he was wet to the skin. His boots—made of the finest leather and designed for a gentleman planning on an afternoon's drive—were taking in water like twin sieves. By his count, he'd fallen off the road three times, and once he had landed up to the knees in mud.

Moreover, there was no sign of a village. Finally Ewan

turned about. He couldn't leave Annabel alone with nothing but potatoes and a malevolent cow in need of milking.

For some reason, going back to her was easier than walking away. He managed to stay on the road, and walked into the house just as the rain began to slack off. Annabel was asleep, huddled under the Kettles' thin coverlet. Two gowns were draped on top of her for warmth, and the fire had burnt low again.

Ewan felt a searing stab of guilt. He'd taken an exquisite, laughing young woman away from the London ballrooms that were her natural milieu and reduced her to a tearful, freezing damsel in distress. What's more, he'd taken her virginity, and given her only potatoes to eat. And for what? Due to a quixotic idea that he would alleviate her fear of poverty?

No. Annabel had accused him of not being honest with himself. The truth of it was that he'd sent his carriages away out of pure, unadulterated lust, no matter how much he would like to dress it up in fancy ideas. He'd seen this cottage, and the idea of being alone with her sprang into his mind with the strength of any temptation.

The temptation of the devil, obviously.

He put a log on the fire as quietly as he could, grappling with a bout of self-dislike such as he'd never experienced before.

Annabel woke up with a little scream.

"Don't worry," he said, stripping off his shirt. One of the damnable things—in a long string of the same—was that he had no more clean shirts. He'd have to put on a shirt that was not entirely clean. Grimly he chose the least soiled and pulled it on.

"Did you bring a horse?" she asked groggily.

Somehow he managed to get the word out. "No."

"No?"

"I couldn't find my way to the village. I failed you, Annabel."

There was silence from the bed.

"I'll start out again the minute I've milked the cow."

"But Ewan, we can't just leave Peggy's house and the cow and the chicken. What would the animals eat?"

Ewan ground his teeth. He remembered this feeling. He'd had it before, when Rosy was brought to him after a week in the company of bandits. She had cowered and cried pitifully, when she wasn't staring into space. He knew then that all the money in the world couldn't solve some problems, but it seemed he must have needed to learn that lesson again.

"The fire feels so good," Annabel said sleepily. "Come lie down, Ewan." She rolled closer to the wall, a fragrant bundle of womanhood with no idea how she affected him.

Ewan had decided long ago that it was one thing to believe in God, and it was another to besiege Him with requests, like a peevish child asking for sweets. But he broke his own rule that night, and before he fell asleep— carefully leaving a space between himself and his not-quite-wife—he sent up a fervent prayer.

It wasn't very elegantly phrased, and Peggy might have been insulted had she heard it. But Peggy was in no mood to be listening to whispers on the wind. She was holding her tiny Annie (Annabel having been deemed too elegant). Annie's mop of bright red hair marked her Scots to the bone; her father couldn't stop grinning, and neither (when he had the news) could Mac.

Before Ewan even dropped off to sleep, the redoubtable Mac was already on his way to the cottage, prudently bringing with him a large basket of food and a change of clothes for his lordship. Mac had long been of the opinion that lords, like other men, are the better for a full belly and a change of clothing. Besides, he was itching with curiosity to see how the master survived without two hot baths and three square meals a day.

In the end, Mac had not time to form an opinion on this point: the carriage no sooner entered the square than the earl had popped his countess (or future countess) into the vehicle and ordered them to make haste.

Annabel's and Ewan's relief at being rescued was so acute that they didn't even speak once they were in the carriage. It wasn't until they were drawing to a halt in an inn yard that Annabel realized she did have one thing to say. "I'm afraid that I've taken a bit of a cold. So I'd like my own room, please."

A second ticked by, and then: "Of course. You'll be far more comfortable, and your maid can see to your comfort during the night. Annabel—I'm so *sorry*." There was something raw in Ewan's voice.

Annabel frowned at him. "You are hardly responsible for my cold."

"I took you to that awful place." His eyes were almost black and he really did have an anguished look in his eyes.

"You must think I'm wasting away from a romantic disease like consumption," Annabel said, forgetting that she was grief-stricken and almost giggling. "I only have a cold, Ewan. Probably my nose is bright red, but I assure you that I am not near death."

He didn't smile back at her. "Your nose is perfect," he said.

"Now you'll have to do penance for lying," she told him, moving toward the carriage door. But he stopped her, wrapping his arms around her and carrying her into the inn.

He didn't let her go until she was snug in a bedchamber with a tub of steaming water ready. The fact that Annabel dropped a few more tears into her bath was obviously due to her weakened condition.

Twenty-eight

It *was* a castle. A huge castle made of dark gray granite, with overhanging windows and little turrets and even what appeared to be a formal pond out front. They had been driving all morning, through woods so tall and dark that they seemed to stretch into infinity. They hadn't passed a house, or a village in hours. And then, all of a sudden . . .

They rounded a bend in the road, and it lay below them, shimmering in a pink mist left from a quick rainstorm. The trees on the surrounding hills looked black against the rain-drenched sky.

"That's Clashindarroch Forest," Ewan said. "The River Bogie runs down that way, behind the castle; we pipe it in through pipes my father installed. He was by all accounts a great innovator. I put in a plunge-bath off the kitchen because Uncle Pearce said he would have liked it."

"Is Pearce your father's brother, then?"

"My grandfather's brother, actually. He's a great-uncle."

"You have a plunge-bath?" she said, a little belatedly. "How wonderful!"

"Better than that. I had a proper heated bath put into the master bedchamber a few years ago."

"A welcome addition," she said.

But she didn't want to meet his eyes. For the last nights, after her cold lessened and they took to their journey again, she had kept to her own bedchamber. They hadn't spoken about the fact that the supposedly married Earl and Countess of Ardmore were occupying two bedchambers. In fact, they hadn't really spoken about anything since they left the Kettles' house. Ewan spent a great deal of each day on horseback, and since Annabel stayed up most of the night, staring at the ceiling, she had a continual nagging headache.

Now she kept thinking that she probably looked like a veritable hag in her dusty traveling clothing. Her nose was still faintly red. What would the staff think of her? Not to mention Ewan's family?

She looked back at the castle below. The outriders played a piping call on a trumpet.

" 'Tis customary," Ewan told her, leaning forward to look out the window. "I don't normally announce myself like a king, I promise you that."

The carriage seemed to pick up speed, rushing down the hill, and now Annabel could see that the great front doors were standing open and people were pouring out and lining themselves up in rows to the left and right. It was a far cry from her father's rotting shell of a house and the four servants he'd managed to keep on reduced wages.

Ewan was grinning down at the castle, his eyes sparkling. Then the coach drew up with a great rattle of gravel flying from the wheels. There was a cheer from the assembled servants.

The family stood in front. She knew at once who Gregory was. He was a skinny little shrimp of a boy, dressed all in black, with a serious expression.

Nana was more of a shock. She was a long way from the sweet, white-haired lady whom Annabel had imagined. Instead, she appeared to be wearing a straw-colored wig from the Elizabethan era. She had a beak of a nose and a slash of red lip rouge under it. All in all, she looked like a cross between a Roman emperor and Queen Elizabeth herself.

Ewan, naturally, was shouting hellos to all and sundry, and dragging her toward the group at a speed that didn't allow her to walk in a dignified manner. Nor smooth her hair. But Annabel straightened her back and told herself that she was a viscount's daughter.

He brought her to his grandmother first. The old woman looked from the tip of Annabel's hair to the tip of her toes. Her eyes slowly narrowed, and Annabel had the unnerving sensation that Ewan's grandmother knew precisely why they had to marry.

"Well!" the countess said after a long moment. "You look older than I expected. But then, Englishwomen do age at a faster rate." Her black eyes were bright with scorn.

Annabel straightened her back. This old woman would either conquer her or be conquered. "Whereas you don't look a day over eighty," she said, curtsying as if she stood before Queen Elizabeth herself.

"Eighty!" Nana roared. "I'll have you know, girl, that I'm not seventy-one."

Annabel smiled sweetly at her. "It must be those Scottish winds. They fairly howl, don't they? *Ruinous* for one's complexion."

Ewan turned around from giving Gregory a bear hug.
"Nana, Annabel is Scottish, so don't play off your tricks
on her. She's got the backbone of a Pict."

"You found a Scotswoman by going all the way to
London?" Nana snapped. "You could have had Miss
Mary from next door if that's what you wanted. These
yellow-haired types are flighty, you know that. She'll
likely go in childbirth."

A charming welcome, to Annabel's mind.

But Nana wasn't done. "Still, she's got good broad
hips," she said, eyeing Annabel's midsection.

Perfect. She was both sickly and plump.

"This is Gregory," Ewan said, leading her away. Gregory had white, white skin and hair as black as soot, with
eyelashes to match. He would break some woman's
heart one day, unless he disappeared into a monastery.
He looked at Annabel with a great deal of curiosity and
then bowed as elegantly as if *she* were Queen Elizabeth.

"It's a pleasure to meet you, Gregory," she said, taking his hand. "Ewan has told me quite a lot about you."

His cheeks turned red so fast that she didn't have time
to blink. "You told her I'm a miserable singer!" he cried,
turning to Ewan.

But Ewan just reached out and tousled his black curls.
"Told her that you caterwaul like a cat in heat," he said
cheerfully. "But mayhap Annabel has had voice training
and she can—"

She shook her head.

"Ach, then, we're stuck with your miserable voice,
lad," he said, giving Gregory another hug.

And just like that the red spots disappeared from his
cheeks and Gregory gave Annabel a sheepish grin from
within the circle of Ewan's arms. She wasn't the only one
who felt safe around the Earl of Ardmore.

Uncle Tobin and Uncle Pearce were like salt and sugar.

Uncle Tobin, the hunter, was lean and tall and keen-eyed. He bowed with great flair and twirled his mustache. "I knew Ewan would strike gold in London!" he said, giving her a very appreciative looking-over.

Annabel curtsied and gave him her very best flirting-with-old-men smile. He warmed up like a winter stove and told Ewan that he'd made a damn fine choice.

Uncle Pearce was as plump as Tobin was thin, and as irascible as Tobin was gallant. He had shiny black eyes that looked like river rocks, and a double chin. "Play speculation, do you?" he growled at her. "With any skill at all?"

"No," she said.

"We'll try your paces after supper," he said gloomily. "But I'll warn you, missy, I play for high stakes. I'll likely have your jointure by Friday next."

"No card games tonight," Ewan said. "I'm sure Annabel is exhausted from traveling all day, Uncle."

"Tomorrow, then," Pearce said, shrugging at the idea that exhaustion trumped cards. Annabel had a sinking feeling that the family sat around and played cards with Pearce every night.

A moment later she was holding the hand of Father Armailhac, and he was smiling at her in such a way that she forgot to give him one of her carefully selected expressions and actually smiled back.

He was the kind of monk who made you grin, no two ways about it. As she had with Nana, she'd built up a picture in her mind that was entirely mistaken. She thought of monks as dressed in black with cords tied around their straining middles. From what she'd heard, they crossed themselves every other moment, carried around any number of necklaces on which they counted out prayers and wore little black caps on the backs of their heads.

True, Father Armailhac was wearing a black cassock. But he didn't look serious, nor likely to pull out a string of beads and mumble a prayer over them. In fact, he looked like a llama Annabel had seen once at a fair. His hair was woolly, and his face narrow, like a llama's. He had the gentle eyes and thick eyelashes of those animals, along with an amiable curiosity that wasn't in the least cloying.

"My dear," he said, putting both his hands on hers. He had the rushing syllables of a Frenchman, but his English seemed impeccable. "This is a true pleasure. I had no idea when I sent Ewan to England that there were such lovely Scotswomen to be found there."

Annabel felt herself blushing.

He chuckled and turned to his right. "May I introduce my comrades? This is Brother Bodine, and Brother Dalmain." The two monks smiled at her. "Brother Dalmain," Armailhac continued, "is Scots by birth, and so 'tis he who persuaded us to come to this country and take care of Rosy. And here is Rosy. I'm sure that Ewan has told you of her."

He drew from behind him, rather like a mother cat pushing forward one of her kittens, one of the smallest, prettiest women Annabel had ever seen. She had her son's creamy skin, and his soft black curls, but without any of the angularity of a young boy. Instead she looked about fifteen, if not younger. And yet . . .

Obviously she was older. She held Father Armailhac's hand tightly, and now Annabel could see there were wrinkles at the corners of her eyes. She smiled obediently, and then curtsied. Her eyes showed no curiosity, and she said nothing. She curtsied again, and Annabel realized with a start that she would have kept curtsying if Father Armailhac had not quietly told her to stop.

The idea of anyone hurting this fairylike child of a

woman was agonizing. "Oh, dear," she breathed, turning to Ewan. He was standing behind her, waiting. Rosy's wandering eyes caught at his boots and a frown creased her face. Then slowly her eyes traveled up his breeches, and her fingers grew white on Father's arm.

"It's all right, Rosy," Armailhac said to her. "It's just Ewan, come back from England with his beautiful bride. Of course you know Ewan."

But she didn't stop frowning until her eyes reached Ewan's face, and then slowly the pinched frown smoothed out and she smiled at him, as cheerful as any child on Christmas morn. Only then did he step forward and kiss her cheek.

Annabel swallowed.

But Father Armailhac bent his head to the side, like a curious robin, and said to her, "There's no need to be sorry for Rosy, my dear."

"I think there is. Why, she—she—" Annabel waved her hand, and she meant it all, all the things that Rosy had lost: Ewan, and Gregory, and the castle . . .

"God's given her a wonderful gift in return," he said, and he didn't even sound preachy. "Joy."

Annabel looked back at Rosy, and sure enough, her face was lit with laughter. After a moment she went over to take Gregory by the hand and began pulling him away.

"Oh, Rosy," he groaned. "I don't want to play now."

But she reached up and touched his cheek and smiled at him, and with a sheepish nod of his head, he allowed himself to be pulled away.

"Doesn't she speak?" Annabel asked.

"Never. But I don't think she misses it."

"May I introduce you to your new home?" Ewan asked, holding out his arm.

"Of course," Annabel said weakly. She had wanted a knight in shining armor with a castle, hadn't she?

The castle had great doors hewn from oak that swung open to reveal a vast antechamber, large enough to receive a king and all his court. The ceiling arched far above them, the stone looking solid, ancient and dirty. The walls were hung with tapestries.

"The Battle of Flodden, 1513," Ewan remarked, bringing her to the left wall. "The first Earl of Ardmore had these tapestries woven in Brussels as a warning to all future Ardmores to avoid war. He lost two sons in the battle."

Annabel peered at the tapestries, which were positively littered with men and horses. The light was not the best.

"The ground is covered with dead young men," Ewan pointed out. "This tapestry and the warning in it saved our lands from being taken over by the Butcher in 1745."

A faint chill of ancient, raw stone hung in the air, and Annabel shivered. Living in a castle didn't seem quite as romantic as it did in fairy tales. But Ewan was leading her through a door to the right, and then they were in a warm, cheerful parlor, heated by a trim iron stove set in the enormous stone fireplace, but otherwise not looking very different from any of Rafe's best sitting rooms.

"My father ruthlessly modernized," Ewan explained. "He was fascinated by Count Rumford's inventions, and had several Rumford stoves installed, and a Rumford range placed in the kitchen that provides heated water. You can look at all this later. For now, why don't I show you to your chambers?"

Annabel murmured something.

The master bedchamber was dominated by an enormous bed. Over it hung a canopy of wildly entwined and colorful flowers, embroidered by a master.

"It's lovely," she said, awed.

"My parents brought it back from their wedding trip," Ewan said. "Shall we travel to celebrate our wedding? Perhaps up the Nile?"

"I will go nowhere in a coach for the foreseeable future," Annabel stated.

He laughed. "Then we're stuck here for the moment. I'm afraid that the coastline is some distance."

Annabel sighed and walked into the bathroom. She stopped still in surprise. The walls were tiled blue and white, with a frieze of laughing mermaids, and the bath itself was made of white marble. It was everything the Kettles' cottage was not: light, clean and exquisitely fashioned, designed to make a woman feel both serene and beautiful.

"Mac had the bathtub sent from Italy," Ewan said. "I do believe that it's large enough for two."

There was just a hint of laughter in his voice, but Annabel didn't meet his eyes, turning away instead. She was feeling about as sensual as a dishclout, and the last thing she wanted to do was share a bathtub.

Her maid, Elsie, bustled into the chamber, followed by footmen carrying Annabel's trunks on their shoulders.

"Perhaps we might sup in a half hour?" Ewan asked. There was nothing in his voice to indicate that Annabel had just snubbed his invitation . . . if that was an invitation.

"Miss Annabel must decide on a gown for the evening," Elsie said anxiously. "Then it must be sponged and pressed, and she needs to bathe, and her hair—"

"It's only six o'clock," Annabel said to Ewan, although to tell the truth, she felt like collapsing onto the bed and missing whatever there was for supper.

"We eat early in the Highlands," he said. "It grows dark quickly, even though summer is coming."

Annabel shivered.

As soon as he was gone, Elsie began clucking like a nervous chicken. "I'll run the bath," she said. "Although whether that great behemoth will actually fill with hot water is another thing. I've no doubt but what I'll have to call for buckets in the normal way of things."

"I could wear the plum-colored sarcenet tonight," Annabel said.

"The one with the falling lace in front?" Elsie said, thinking about it. "At least the sleeves are long, which will keep you warm. There's a powerful damp here, for all it's almost June. The sarcenet has a nice high bosom."

Annabel nodded. It seemed that future dress decisions were likely to be based on the chill in the air.

"It's at the bottom of one of the trunks, and will have been protected from the worst of the dust. We can sponge the lace thoroughly and it will dry in a twinkle." Elsie ran into the bathroom but trotted directly back into the bedroom. "I'd better find the gown first, and perhaps the housekeeper might have someone sponge it for me. Whether I'll be able to find Mrs. Warsop is another question. It's monstrously large, this place."

"The footmen can direct you."

"I never thought to work in a castle," Elsie told her. "Never!"

"I never thought to marry a man who lived in one either," Annabel said, a slight untruth given her girlhood dreams. "Now let's see if we can get this bath to work."

Of course it did. Hot water gushed from the taps into the smooth marble bath.

"The mermaids are a bit heathen to my mind," Elsie said with a sniff. "Not but what this is a most godly household, miss. Do you know that they have chapel on Sundays and the staff attends with the family, rather than going to the village?"

"You needn't join them if you don't wish to. I'll speak to Lord Ardmore."

"I wouldn't miss it," Elsie said earnestly. "The service is given by a monk, a real one. And though my mum never held with Catholics—thought them a terrible heathen lot, always kissing pictures and the like—the Father seems quite lovely, rather like my grandfather. Plus, I wouldn't want to miss the service, it might seem as if I were putting on airs, and that would never go over well with Mrs. Warsop."

Annabel cautiously put a toe into steaming water, and a second later she was leaning back in blissfully hot water.

"That's right, then," Elsie said. "If you don't mind, miss, I'll just take this dress down to Mrs. Warsop and ask her to have it sponged for me. I wouldn't like anyone to iron it whom I don't trust, but sponging is another matter."

"Don't hurry," Annabel said, wiggling her toes so that little ripples spread through the bath.

The door swung shut behind Elsie, and Annabel lay back and tried to think clearly. She would be marrying a man who was utterly her opposite. She prided herself on logical thinking, whereas Ewan seemed to embrace the idea of acting without forethought. How else could they have ended up at the Kettles'? She believed in the power of money; he believed in God. How long would it be before he wished that he had married someone who enjoyed endless prayer services?

Annabel regarded her pink toes. A better woman than she would send the earl into the sunset on his own, castle, money and all. A better woman would recognize that the holy part of him would never be matched in her. He would be happier married to a psalm singer like himself, a more virginal woman. And she would be happier without a broken heart.

Because she was in love with him. There wasn't any doubt in Annabel's mind about that: she was as crazed with love as ever Imogen was for Draven Maitland, and she'd always thought Imogen was fairly mad with the emotion.

Wasn't there the faintest possibility that Ewan might fall in love with her? Sometimes good things happened. Perhaps it was her turn. Annabel tried to imagine a white-haired old man looking at her from a cloud and deciding to toss a windfall in her direction, but she gave up after a moment. The whole idea of religion eluded her.

The truth was that Ewan was unlikely to fall in love with someone as greedy as herself, someone who had no understanding of his religion, and not a whiff of charitable doings about her either. The only thing they had between them was—was this *lust*. The thought made her cheeks hot.

Elsie came back, gasping and holding her sides. "These stairs, miss! To reach the housekeeper's chambers, I have to go down the back stairs, and then down another set on the left, and then up again, and then down once more!"

Annabel stepped out of the bath into a towel warmed before the fire.

"Your gown for this evening is ready. Mrs. Warsop offered to do it with her own hands, and a beautiful job she's done. Do you know, she and Mr. Warsop have been married these forty-three years? And he's been the butler here at the castle since he was a lad."

Elsie kept talking while Annabel's hair dried, and while she brushed it until it shone. Then Annabel put on her chemise and her corset, the French one. Her gown was a long sweep of plum-colored, figured sarcenet that hugged her curves and then widened into a small train. A lace fall emphasized her bodice.

Elsie tied Annabel's hair into a knot of curls and finally Annabel looked at herself in the glass. She thought she looked fit for a castle. For an earl. Even . . . perhaps . . . for a man such as Ewan. But she caught herself up trying to coax her face into a pious expression: the kind of look that Ewan's wife ought to wear. Marriage was one thing, and playacting quite another.

Twenty-nine

The dining room was cavernous, and dubiously heated by enormous fireplaces at either end.

"Once we're married, I suppose you'll have to sit down there," Ewan said, gesturing toward the far end of the huge table. "I remember my parents dining so, as if they were marooned on separate islands. But for tonight, I've asked Warsop to put us all at one end."

Beautiful old china was set for the family and the three monks, but even those ten places took only a fourth of the span. "But this table is surely meant for a whole clan," Annabel said. "Why on earth haven't you replaced it with a smaller one?"

"An excellent suggestion," Ewan said.

"Things should stay as they are," Lady Ardmore said, sweeping into a seat to Ewan's right. She had changed into a gown that had apparently been designed, if not made, in the days of Queen Elizabeth. Her petticoats alone must have weighed two stone, and a large, stiff ruff jutted from behind her neck. "There's no reason to turn everything topsy-turvy on account of a new bride in the castle. This castle's seen many a bride come and go, and maintaining the behavior contingent to an earl's dignity is more important than comfort."

Uncle Tobin sat to Lady Ardmore's right. "You're going to have to hand over the reins," he told her, clearly enjoying himself. "Everything will change when you're the dowager countess."

Lady Ardmore eyed Annabel. "If Miss Essex thinks she can run a household distinguished by such a large staff, I will be most content to relinquish control." She directed a smile at Annabel that would have felled a pirate.

But Annabel hadn't spend her youth skirmishing with unpaid tradesmen for nothing. She returned with a tolerant smile that indicated no wish to be unkind, while signaling its opposite. "You must be exhausted after all these years," she cooed. "It will be my pleasure to take some of the burden from your shoulders."

"You sound like a demmed missionary," Lady Ardmore said with revulsion. "You didn't find yourself a hymn singer to marry, did you?" she demanded of Ewan. "The castle's already overrun by them."

Father Armailhac smiled, unperturbed, and Gregory kept eating peacefully. "Absolutely not," Ewan told his grandmother. "I knew a bride with a churchgoing disposition would be upsetting for your digestion, Nana."

Lady Ardmore readjusted her wig and took a bite of her supper. "This house has gone to wrack and ruin since we moved the demmed Catholics in," she said loudly.

"Lady Ardmore, I promise you that I was merely experiencing a streak of luck last evening," Father Armailhac said. "I shall give you a chance to recoup your losses tonight."

She glared at Annabel, but there was a whiff of cama-
raderie in her glare. "Took all my money, he did. A gambling monk! I never thought I'd see the day. Perfectly
disgraceful."

"You're giving Miss Essex an erroneous impression of
us," Father Armailhac said, smiling. "We play for bawbees, Miss Essex."

"This family didn't gain its wealth by wasting its
coins, no matter if they are only worth a few pence," the
countess announced.

Annabel sipped her consommé. "This is delicious,"
she said to Ewan. "Did you have trouble finding a cook
so far up in the Highlands?"

"We're lucky enough to have a French chef," Ewan
replied. "Mac found him and lured him here for quite a
large salary—"

"Disgraceful!" his grandmother interjected.

"Monsieur Flambeau likely would have left us during
his first winter, except he fell in love with Mac's sister."

"Disgraceful!" from Lady Ardmore.

"Now they have two children and no plans to move
from Scotland, although I do have to raise his salary
every time the snow goes over five feet."

Ewan's grandmother opened her mouth, but Annabel
anticipated her. "Disgraceful?" she said, cocking an
eyebrow.

"French!" the countess snapped. "Of course, it re-
mains to be seen what you think of winter in the Highlands, Miss Essex."

Annabel wasn't sure whether the cook showed his
Frenchness by falling in love, or by disliking high snow.

Gregory was sitting quietly next to Uncle Tobin and
hadn't yet said a word. "Do you have a tutor, Gregory?"
Annabel asked him.

He looked up from his soup, seeming rather startled

to be addressed. "Not at the moment, Miss Essex. Last February my tutor decided to return to Cambridge, and since then Father Armailhac has been tutoring me in Latin and French."

"Do you enjoy the study of languages?" Annabel asked. Gregory seemed quite different from children whom she had known. He was remarkably self-possessed, with manners so exquisite as to be positively antique.

"Most certainly. But I do miss studying mathematics," he said, pushing back his hair from his forehead. "And archaeology."

"I thought it would do Gregory good to take a break from his studies," Ewan said. "I've asked him to join me in the fields this summer."

Lady Ardmore snorted. "The fields! Utterly unsuitable!"

Annabel raised an eyebrow. "The fields?"

"We raise all sorts of crops on my lands," Ewan explained. "I generally spend the greater part of the summer moving from one field to another." A look at Gregory's rather peaked, white face made Annabel think that Ewan's plan for sunshine and fresh air was a good one.

"Manual labor," Nana grumbled. "It's not befitting an earl. Your father would never have dirtied his hands in such a fashion."

"I'll be planting a number of experimental crops this year," Ewan said, ignoring his grandmother altogether.

When the meal was over Gregory and Father Armailhac left, talking of Socrates. Lady Ardmore walked out on Uncle Tobin's arm, swearing that she would take all of Father Armailhac's bawbees or die in the attempt. Ewan and Annabel were following until he waved the butler ahead of them and shut the door.

"By my count, I haven't kissed you in three days," he said, his voice casual.

Annabel's bones melted at the look in his eyes, but: "It's not proper," she said. "We should never—"

"Blame it on your corset," he said, snatching her into his arms.

It was some time before Annabel was free to finish her sentence, if she'd even remembered what it was. "I have to warn you of something," Ewan said. He was leaning against the wall and looking down at her, and the only thing she could think about was pulling his head down to hers again. "The news is spreading among the clans that we're about to marry."

"Will they come here?" Annabel asked, trying to focus on what he was saying.

"Certainly. I'm the earl, and we're a sociable lot of Scotsmen."

"How many people do you think will come to congratulate you?"

"Us," he said. "They'll come to congratulate us."

"Us, then," she said.

He had that lazy smile that seemed to come to him so easily—at least when he was adequately clothed and fed. "The last time I went to a Highland wedding, 'twas for the clan of McKiernie, and there were at least a hundred. But you're as Scots as I am. Haven't you been to a proper wedding before?"

Annabel's father didn't like to leave his stables, not for something as frivolous as a wedding. And they wouldn't have had proper clothes. "Not lately," she said. "Not since my mother died."

He raised an eyebrow. "Didn't your mother die when you were six?"

"Yes. So I've no idea what to expect," Annabel confessed.

"It means Clan Poley, but all the others as well. I should think we'll be seeing hundreds of Scots. Drunk, most of them, or they will be. Dancing, all of them. They'll be some fights, some crying, a lot of laughing, a few babies made, a few wives shrieking . . ." He reached out to open the door, and then hesitated. "We don't seem to be speaking to each other, Annabel."

She bit her lip and forced a smile. "Wedding nerves, I expect," she said lightly.

"But you're worried about something."

If he touched her, she would burst into the absurd tears that kept stealing up on her at odd moments. Of course, she couldn't admit that all of a sudden she'd developed an alarmingly romantic nature.

"Answer or I shall be forced to kiss you into speech," Ewan said with mock severity.

The words came so quickly she didn't realize she was going to speak before she did so. "Well, I do think that I shouldn't marry you," Annabel said. "At the heart I'm a terribly greedy person. I truly wished to marry a rich man. And I don't think I shall ever feel the way you do about the church. I'm just—I'm afraid that we shan't suit each other, in the long run."

He smiled at her and she felt a prickle of annoyance. She was starting to think that Ewan didn't listen to half the things she told him.

"I really did consider that adultery was a certain part of my future," she told him fiercely.

"If you had married someone else, God forbid," Ewan said, "and I met you after the fact, I expect I would be thinking about adultery as well."

"You are not listening to me," she told him. "I do *not* fear for my soul. I would have shot those robbers in London without blinking, if I'd had an appropriate weapon!"

"Man and wife do not have to be in agreement on all things," Ewan observed. He turned over her hand and brought her palm to his mouth. "Would you wish me to marry someone else?" he asked. "With honesty."

"No," she said, after a moment. "I'd kill the woman who tried to marry you, Ewan. With the first pistol that came to hand."

"I've married a bloodthirsty wench, that's for certain." But he wasn't laughing, and there was something burning in his eyes that made her heart thump in her chest. He held out his hand. "Would you like to retire, or may I tempt you into losing a bawbee or two?"

"You've already tempted me into losing something of greater value," Annabel said, before she thought. "What's a few bawbees?"

"Some things are priceless," Ewan said, his eyes utterly serious. "If I could take back my rash actions on our journey, Annabel, I would."

She forced another smile.

In the parlor, Uncle Pearce was fussily laying out the cards for speculation. Gregory was watching him like a hawk and the countess was complaining. Apparently no one other than Pearce ever won speculation.

"You put two on your own pile!" Gregory said, and then his face fell a little when Pearce counted out his cards, showing that he had the same number as everyone else.

"We're all fascinated by Pearce's cheating," Ewan whispered in Annabel's ear. "Gregory is particularly baffled by it, and yet he can't seem to catch Pearce at the practice."

Sure enough, by an hour later, not a one of them had any bawbees except Uncle Pearce. Gregory looked extremely disgusted and Lady Ardmore was positively gibbering with rage.

Annabel sat out the last two games, just watching the flow of cards. As they were preparing to retire, she put a hand on Gregory's arm. "Will you have tea with me to-morrow morning?" she asked.

"I would be most honored," he said with a quaint little bow. Annabel was touched to see that he had turned a bit pink.

"Perhaps you can teach me more about speculation," she said. "I'm afraid I'm woefully inept."

"No one ever wins at that game," he whispered to her. "Didn't you notice?"

Annabel grinned at him. "I have three sisters," she whispered back. "And the youngest likes to cheat."

Gregory's answering smile was huge.

She turned to find Father Armailhac offering her an arm. "I wonder if I might talk to you a moment about your marriage," he said.

Annabel felt herself blushing. Ewan was already halfway up the stairs, his grandmother leaning heavily on his arm. Gregory melted away, and Father Armailhac held out his arm, for all the world as if he were a French courtier. So she allowed herself to be drawn into the library.

"Do you wish to marry our Ewan?" he asked, when Annabel was seated in a velvet chair before the fire, sipping a tiny glass of something fiery that tasted like burnt oranges.

"I do," she said.

"And may I call you Annabel?"

"Please do." It was the first time she'd been on any sort of intimate terms with a clergy member. Annabel had a pulse of anxiety. She hoped he wouldn't ask her to say a prayer. She was sure to say it wrong.

"The most important thing," Father Armailhac said, turning his peaceful llama face toward her, "is whether you truly wish to marry Ewan. In your heart of hearts." And suddenly the monk looked almost as stern as any parish priest. "Because to make the sacrament of marriage without true feeling in your heart is wrongful."

"This is not a marriage for love," she said, her voice catching a little. "We are marrying because of scandal."

"Of course, I have no personal knowledge of the love between a man and a woman," the Father said, taking her hand in his large one. "But it seems to me very difficult to know precisely where love begins and ends."

"Oh, I—" Annabel said, and snatched back the rest of the sentence. She wasn't ready to tell near-strangers that she herself was in love, even if Ewan wasn't. "I understand," she said. She felt suddenly exhausted.

But there was one thing she did want to say. "Ewan has told me how very helpful you were in overcoming his grief over the death of his parents."

Father Armailhac was a great one for grinning. "He told you that, did he? And here I thought he never spoke of the flood at all. Nor of his parents either."

"It seems to me," Annabel said, "that he cannot remember his father well because you have become that father to him."

"When I came to Scotland, Ewan was already a man grown," the Father said. "In the beginning he was most reluctant to allow us to care about him; 'tis often so, I've found, with those who have no family. As I'm sure you've noticed, my dear, he guards his heart fiercely, though he's generous with his possessions. I am quite hopeful that you will change his life, as he, no doubt, will change yours."

Annabel smiled politely. If the Father thought she was going to traipse out onto the battlements in the rain singing prayers with Gregory, he was going to be disappointed. She didn't want to become a psalm-singing righteous type of woman. Father Armailhac said nothing more, merely took her arm and led her back to the stairs.

"Neither you nor Ewan are Catholic, so I shall perform a simple ritual of handfasting. Yet I would like to add what ceremony I may, and in France, marriages are generally performed on the Lord's day," he said tranquilly. "Since the two of you have waited almost a fortnight, I'm sure neither of you will mind waiting a few days. After all, as you said, it isn't a love match."

She glanced at him, but his face was bland and smiling.

"Just so," she said.

$\mathcal{T}$hirty

It was the following evening, and they were playing speculation. The game was being played by Lady Ardmore, Uncle Pearce, Ewan, Gregory and Annabel. But things were not going as usual.

Wonder of wonders, Gregory was winning hand after hand, and Annabel was holding her own as well. By another hand, Ewan and his grandmother dropped out, leaving a three-way battle.

"You play surprisingly well," the countess said as Annabel scooped up two of Uncle Pearce's bawbees. She managed to shade her compliment with enough doubt to turn it to an insult.

"I'd be happy to give you lessons, if you wish," Annabel said, giving her a consolatory smile.

To her surprise, Lady Ardmore gave a crack of laughter. "It looks to me as if you might already have given young Gregory lessons."

Gregory's eyes were shining and he was scoring trick

after trick. Pearce's black eyes were darting around the table. His cheeks had turned a port wine color as the pile of bawbees before him dwindled.

"How are you doing it?" Ewan breathed in Annabel's ear.

"It must be luck," she told him. "You know I can't play this game very well."

"I'm aware of that," he said to her severely. Then he leaned next to her ear and said, "But you cheat *very* well."

"Only when challenged by an expert," she told him, and put down her cards, handily winning the round.

"Times are changing!" Nana cackled. "I think you can't expect to win so effortlessly in the future, Pearce. I—" But she cocked her head and then they all heard the peal of trumpets from Ewan's sentries. "Visitors," she said. "I hope some of those reprobates in the clan haven't decided to anticipate your wedding. I don't approve of all those heathenish practices like blackening."

"What's blackening?" Annabel asked.

"A particularly repellent practice, traditional in Aberdeenshire," Nana told her. "I don't believe in it!" She thumped her stick.

"Were you blackened, Nana?" Gregory asked in some awe.

"It's so long ago I can't remember," she snapped. Then she said, "But there's naught to worry about. These are more civilized times, and no one would dare touch the earl's bride."

"I expect it's the Crogan boys," Ewan said resignedly. And, to Annabel, "They live down the road and once they've had something to drink, they grow rather excitable."

"Excitable? Debauched miscreants, that's what those Crogans are," Nana stated. "You tell them the wedding isn't until Sunday. They can take themselves straight back home. I shall go to my chambers. And Gregory, you come upstairs as well. Drunken Crogans are not fit for gentlemen's company." In the end, Uncle Pearce took himself to bed as well. His shining eyes darted from face to face, but he apparently couldn't bring himself to demand an explanation of precisely how he had managed to lose.

Yet when Warsop opened the door of the sitting room a short time later, it wasn't to introduce inebriated Scotsmen.

"My lord," Warsop said, standing back. "Lady Willoughby. Lady Maitland. Miss Josephine Essex. The Earl of Mayne."

For a moment Annabel froze with surprise, and then she jumped up with a happy cry. "Imogen! Josie!" Then Josie was hugging Annabel as if they'd been separated for months rather than weeks.

"But what are you doing here? This is such a lovely surprise," Annabel said.

"We've come to save you, of course!" Imogen said gaily.

"What?" Annabel asked, looking into her sister's face. Imogen's eyes, it seemed to her, were less grief-stricken. She pulled her into her arms. "How *are* you, truly?"

"I'm better," Imogen said simply. "Mayne has been a great comfort."

"Mayne!" Annabel exclaimed.

Sure enough, the Earl of Mayne turned from his conversation with Ewan. He bowed with all his usual finesse but somehow he seemed different. Rather than the exquisite, wind-swept kind of elegance he usually displayed, he looked . . . merely windswept. Rather than skin-tight trousers in the newest mode, he was wearing worn buckskin breeches. His shirt was clean but showed drove at night, even, to make sure we'd get here in time."

"Of course," Annabel said quickly. "What a terrible journey you must have had. I can't think how you managed to get here; why, we only arrived yesterday ourselves."

"I hope I *never* hear the word *carriage* again!" Griselda said. "Just look at me: I'm a shadow of my former self!" She looked down with horror at her figure. Sure enough, her luxuriant curves seemed slightly less generous.

"We just couldn't bear to think of how you cried, the night before you left for Scotland," Imogen said. "I know you planned to return to us after six months," she said, taking Annabel's hands in hers. "And we all know how common broken marriages are in London. But it's a terrible thing to endure a marriage of that sort. We all felt so. And then Lucius Felton announced that he'd discovered a way to quell the scandal."

Ewan was trying to rein in the temper that he would have sworn he didn't own—not until Annabel entered his life. "You did say six months?" he asked, as if he were merely trying to clarify a point of light conversation. Unfortunately, even he could hear the savage edge in his voice.

Imogen had the grace to look a little ashamed. "The plan was made in the heat of the moment," she told him. "But it's inconsequential now, because Felton found a Miss Alice Ellerby—a *Miss A.E.!*—who was desperate to escape her parents' grasp."

"A happy coincidence," Ewan said flatly. Annabel wasn't looking at him. Surely she couldn't believe he would ever allow her to return to London.

"Felton paid Miss Ellerby a large sum of money, and she published a truly scintillating account of her rela-

age. Even his jacket appeared to have been c
larger man.

"Please forgive me for appearing before you
dirt," he was saying, bringing her hand to his mou

"I am grateful to you for accompanying my sistei
your own to Scotland," she said. "May I introduc\
ther Armailhac?"

Mayne surprised Annabel by switching into flaw
French.

"Our mother is French," Griselda said, kissing h
cheek. "Please tell me that you haven't married Arc
more. Because if so, I'm liable to swoon to the floor."

"No, no, we're to marry on Sunday," Annabel said,
blinking at her.

Griselda smiled, and Imogen grinned as if Christmas
had come. "We have a wonderful surprise for you!" she
burst out.

And then Griselda said, "You needn't marry at all!
We've come to bring you back to England, and you can
choose your own husband, and needn't marry Ardmore."

"What?" Annabel said, shocked. "*What?*"

Suddenly the room seemed very quiet, and she was
aware of Ewan turning his head and looking at them.

"You needn't marry Ardmore," Imogen continued
happily. "The scandal is over. Isn't it wonderful?"

Wonderful, Annabel thought in bewilderment. Wonderful?

Ewan wasn't at all bewildered. The moment Annabel's
family entered the room he had a sickening sense about
what was coming. The worst of it was that he deserved
it. Merely on the grounds of egregious stupidity, he deserved to lose her. Not that he would allow it, whether
he was the village idiot or no.

As Annabel stared at her sister without speaking, Imogen's face fell a little. "You are happy, aren't you? We

tionship with you, Lord Ardmore, in *Bell's Weekly Messenger*."

"Her relationship with *me*?" Ewan repeated.

Imogen nodded. "Then she ran away to America with a groomsman, as I understand it. Thanks to Felton, she has a dowry."

"There will be a bit of palaver about the wedding that didn't happen," Griselda said, sounding utterly exhausted. "But since I had taken ill and didn't leave the house after you and Annabel left, we've put it about that Josie and I traveled with the two of you."

"Your reputation as a rake is blossoming," Imogen said, obviously trying to make up for spilling the news that Ewan's fiancée had intended to desert him promptly after the marriage ceremony. "What with my behavior on the dance floor and now the ardent Miss A.E., you're quite the man of the hour."

Ewan said nothing. Cursing before one's future wife's family was not considered good *ton*.

Imogen started talking faster. "There's nothing more heartbreaking than a loveless marriage," she said. "A marriage forced by circumstances is bound to be a tragedy."

"There are forced marriages and forced marriages," Ewan said. He swung around, knowing that Annabel would be able to read his face. "Don't you agree?"

She looked back at him, head high, her eyes inscrutable.

"I'd be grateful for a chamber in which to lay my head," Griselda said. "These Scottish roads are deplorable."

Ewan offered his arm. It was for the best that he leave the room before his temper got the best of him. That temper he didn't own . . . until a month ago.

"Josie, come with me!" Griselda called.

"This is a delightful surprise," Annabel said to Mayne, watching under her lashes as Ewan left the room. Clearly, he was ferociously angry. Annabel swallowed.

"It was a surprise for myself as well," Mayne said, looking annoyed. "I'm in grave need of a tailor. I was kidnapped by your sister."

Imogen laughed. "Poor Mayne has been complaining about the state of his dress all the way from London. He's had to wear Rafe's clothing, and a sad comedown it's been."

"You kidnapped Lord Mayne?" Annabel asked Imogen.

She waved her hands airily. "He is so dreadfully set in his ways, and truly, such an old-fashioned man. I knew he'd refuse to accompany us."

"Indeed," Annabel said, "why should he wish to make a fortnight's journey into Scotland?"

"In the middle of the racing season," Mayne put in.

"Because I asked him to," Imogen said stoutly.

"Except apparently you didn't *ask* him—"

"She did not," Mayne said. "She called at my house and naturally I entered her coach immediately, since I had not yet beat it into your sister's head that it is thoroughly indecorous to halt her carriage where all and sundry might see us. Next thing I knew, I was on my way to Scotland."

"Well, I'm very grateful to both of you," Annabel said, feeling queerly ungrateful. "It was very kind of you to come rescue me." It was so kind that she might break into tears at any moment.

"It was really Felton who took care of it, finding that Miss Ellerby and so on," Mayne said. "But I find myself wondering whether you are truly happy to greet us, Miss Essex."

"Of course she is!" Imogen said quickly. "How can you ask such a thing, Mayne?"

"I am always happy to see my sisters," Annabel said, meaning it. The very thought that they'd come all the way to Scotland to rescue her—even if she was ungrate-

ful enough to be unsure about her deliverance—was
likely to make those unruly tears appear. Imogen was
frowning, so Annabel added, "You must be exhausted.
Let me bring you to Ewan's housekeeper."

It was midnight by the time everyone was in a comfortable room, with a steaming bath and fresh night-
clothes. Imogen had demanded a room next to Mayne,
and he had insisted on a different floor. Josie hadn't
wanted to be in the schoolroom, as Griselda thought
proper, and then Griselda had discovered that her room
faced east, and she disliked an east-facing room due to
the possibility of morning sunlight.

Yet finally . . . finally, everyone seemed to be suitably
accommodated. She'd seen Ewan once, in passing. Their
eyes met, and then Annabel hurried past. What must he
think of her? She had planned adultery, but also deser-
tion. What man would want a wife with no scruples?
Pangs of regret and humiliation made her feel faintly
nauseated.

She just sat down on the edge of her bed when she
heard an awful shrilling noise. For a moment she didn't
even recognize it as a scream, it was so high and so
piercing.

Then she started running blindly in its direction,
chilled to the heart by the pure terror of it. The awful
screaming went on and on as Annabel flew down the
corridor, down to the stairs. Doors were opening up and
down the hallway, people's voices were calling out and
still she ran. It was the library, she thought.

And it was. She threw open the door, Ewan appearing
at her shoulder.

Rosy was screaming. She was standing in the middle
of the floor, shrilling. She looked up at them and
Annabel was shocked. The quiet, rather childlike Rosy
whom she'd met was replaced by a woman with a white,

enraged face, eyes snapping with fury. She wasn't
screaming in terror; she was screaming with rage. Ugly,
vicious rage.

And leaning against the wall, looking utterly limp,
was Mayne.

Ewan rushed across the room and shook Rosy. She
kept screaming. He shook her again, not roughly, but
firmly. "Stop it, Rosy. *Stop.*"

Mac appeared at the door and said, "I'll fetch Father
Armailhac," and rushed away.

Finally Rosy's voice faltered and stopped.

"God*damn,*" Mayne said into the silence that followed.

The hallway was full of people now, spilling in the
door. Ewan turned about. "No men in here!" he shouted.

He turned to Mayne, still leaning damply against the
wall. "If you wouldn't mind . . ." He nodded toward
the door.

"My pleasure," Mayne said. Then he stopped. "Just
so you know, I didn't touch her. I didn't—"

"We know that," Annabel said, taking his arm and
leading him back into the hallway. "Rosy is quite disturbed, that's all."

"Disturbed?" Mayne said, his voice rising now they
were in the hallway, surrounded by sympathetic faces.
"Disturbed? She's bloody mad, that's what she is. I wandered down there to see whether Ardmore took *Racing
News,* and there she was. So I said hello, and she started
looking at me from my toes up. Maybe she didn't like
my cravat. God knows I don't. The moment she caught
sight of it she started screaming, and she threw something at me as well. I felt as if I'd assaulted her."

Annabel caught the butler's eye. "Warsop, I think
Lord Mayne would be the better for a drink."

"Who is she?" Griselda asked from her position on
the stairs.

Annabel hesitated and Father Armailhac, who had just arrived, said, "She is Lord Ardmore's adopted sister, and quite harmless, I assure you."

Griselda looked unconvinced. "Well," she said acidly, "if the crisis is over for the night, I suggest we all return to bed."

"That settles it," Imogen said in a half whisper. She looked very shaken. "Oh, Annabel, I'm so glad we came. This castle literally has a madwoman—it's like a novel!"

"Not entirely," Josie added, peeping from behind Griselda's shoulder. "If this were all happening in a novel, that woman would be Ardmore's first wife, not his sister."

"I'm very sorry that you were disturbed," Annabel said firmly, heading off any discussion of Rosy's relationship with Ewan. "Rosy is easily unsettled and she finds strange men truly terrifying."

"I'm sure I can guess why without being told," Griselda said with a shudder. "Upstairs with you," she said to Josie.

Imogen gave Annabel a hug. "This is an awful house," she said. "Damp and cold, and it's miles from civilization. I'm so happy we got here in time. We shall leave as soon as possible. Those screams!" she shuddered. "You couldn't have survived six months. I'd have given you a month at the most before you would have returned to London."

Annabel raised her head and met Ewan's eyes. He was standing in the door of the library, just standing there, silent.

Slowly their guests filtered back upstairs, and then Annabel opened the door to the library again. Rosy and Ewan were seated on a couch before the fire, Rosy at one corner and Ewan at the other. But Ewan's arm was strung across the back of the sofa, and he was stroking

Rosy's hair. She had her customary, rather vacant expression again. She looked like someone who would never scream. In fact . . . she looked happy. Serene.

Ewan looked up at her. "I expect that took a year off Mayne's life."

"Ten, he would say. Is she all right?" She whispered it, for Rosy was humming a little tune and looking into the fire as if it depicted the most interesting of plays.

"She seems to be. Her nurse is supposed to prevent this sort of thing from happening. Whenever I have guests, she's to stay in her chambers."

"Oh, dear." They both looked at Rosy, who seemed oblivious to them.

"The problem is that she is used to freedom. You're the first visitor we've had in ages, and she accepted you. I forgot to be cautious."

"I gather it's men who pose a problem," Annabel said.

"She's getting worse," Ewan said flatly. "She attacked him, you know. Look." He nodded to the wall where Mayne had been leaning. The floor was littered with broken crockery. "She threw a vase at him that was half her size. If she'd hit him in the face, it could have done considerable damage."

Annabel couldn't think what to say.

"Gregory's getting older. She sometimes forgets who I am and attacks me. If she did that to Gregory . . ."

"He doesn't seem to think of her as his mother."

"But he knows the truth of it. And it would be damaging to have one's mother turn into a lunatic and attack. He didn't come downstairs, did you notice?"

Annabel shook her head.

"He can't stand seeing her like this."

Rosy got up and ambled away. Father Armailhac was waiting by the door. He gently took her arm and began to lead her upstairs.

Then Ewan stood up and Annabel saw something in his eyes change as he looked at her. "It appears our scandal has been papered over," he said.

"Yes," she managed, around the lump in her throat.

"I suppose that is better than a six-month marriage. Were you merely planning to leave me, or would you have started proceedings for divorce?" He was watching her so closely that Annabel felt as if she couldn't breath, couldn't say the things she might have said.

"I meant to just leave," she whispered.

"I should have known. A woman who plans her future adultery would never malinger in a castle in Scotland."

The truth of it burned in Annabel's chest.

"The only problem with Felton's solution"—and his voice didn't sound amused now—"is that I can't let you return to England when you might be carrying my child. I'm afraid that you'll have to marry me, whether you wish it or no."

Annabel opened her mouth, but he kept speaking. "But I would hope that you will choose to stay with me for better reasons. If there is no child and no scandal, you could certainly marry a rich Englishman. Yet in Peggy's terms, while my house is isolated, I do have a great number of cows." He hesitated. "I would ask you to stay, Annabel, because of the feeling between us."

He stood by the settee looking tall, proud and Scottish, so beautiful that her knees melted at the very sight of him, and yet she couldn't find the right words to say. She could never leave Ewan under her own volition: she loved him too much. And yet the knowledge that he didn't truly love her was breaking her heart.

"I would like you to marry me, cows or no," he said.

"I will marry you," Annabel whispered. And then she turned and walked from the room and up the stairs, quickly. Her hand was clenched so hard on the railing that she couldn't fall down, even though her knees were liquid. But she had to ask. So halfway up the stairs she turned and looked down at Ewan. He stood below her, and for a second she thought she caught a look of desolation in his eyes, but she must have been wrong.

"Don't you want me to—" She broke off. And started again. There had been so much honesty between them, and at the end it came down to one last question.

"Do you love me?"

Her question hung in the damp night air as if it were shouted. And yet she'd only whispered it, from the despair in her heart.

He stared up at her. "I told you the same, in the Kettles' cottage. I think we would make a strong marriage. You desire me, and I feel the same for you."

"You're confusing desire and love," she said, watching him. "They are not the same."

"I do love you. I feel near to murder at the idea of you marrying another man, and that's the truth of the matter."

Annabel said the first words that came to mind. "*Desire* is bloody, perjured, full of blame."

Ewan walked up the steps to her. "Is that poetry?" he asked, when he was next to her.

"Yes."

"I don't like the sound of it. There's something nasty about that poet."

"It's Shakespeare," Annabel said.

Ewan obviously dismissed Shakespeare as a lost cause. "We would be happy together," he said. "I will never be poor," he said. "That is important to you."

True, all true.

"We will have an excellent marriage."

Annabel forced a smile to her lips. She walked to the top of the stairs and turned left, going to the master bedchamber. She fell onto the bed without washing, in her chemise, without even summoning her maid.

The room was whirling around her. She'd known inside that she, Annabel Essex, was not the sort of woman with whom men fell in love. She was the sort with whom men fell into desire, and that's what Ewan felt for her: desire.

She should be happy. Freedom lay before her: freedom to return to London and find a rich Englishman, a sleek, practical man who would understand the limitations of their obligations to each other. Who wouldn't confuse her with talk of his soul or—worse—her soul.

Except she couldn't leave Ewan. She wanted his kisses, the way he kissed her as if he were starving, as if they hadn't already kissed so much that her lips were bruised. All those times when he had rocked against her gently, just a reminder. And she had melted against him and relished the rasp of his breathing, and the way he was about to pull his mouth away—because she knew before he did it.

Perhaps it would be enough . . . *he* thought it was enough.

But even though her heart beat quickly at the memories of his kisses, Annabel didn't agree with Ewan. All those years when she thought it would be enough to trade a man's desire for marriage, for security and for money . . .

Now she found it wasn't. Not at all.

She wanted something quite different.

She fell asleep in the middle of a sob.

Thirty-one

Annabel woke to the sound of her door handle turning. Her eyes felt as if they were glued to her eyelids, but she opened them to find that Josie was scrambling onto the bottom of the bed and chattering to Imogen, who had just slipped under the covers.

"When I get married," Josie was saying, "I want to marry a man just like Ardmore. I want a castle and a hundred servants." She turned to Annabel. "I know you don't like Scotland, Annabel, but I love it. I can't imagine wanting to stay in England. Do you think that perhaps Ardmore could wait to find a wife until next season, when I come out?"

"Don't be ridiculous," Annabel said, pushing up in the bed. Her head was pounding.

"You look awful," Josie said. "Didn't you sleep well? I was listening for footsteps outside my room all night long." She gave a delicious shiver.

"I told you that you've been reading too many novels," Imogen observed, propping herself up on the pillows next to Annabel.

"And I told you that there's a great deal of helpful guidance in them," Josie told her. "If this were a novel, Ardmore would turn out to be evil to the core. I know all the signs."

"And those are?" Imogen asked.

Annabel couldn't bring herself to even wish her sisters good morning. She just wished they'd leave. She had to talk to Ewan. She had to convince him of—

Of something important.

"Well, for one thing," Josie said, "villains all have black hair. And they stalk about, tossing their hair in the wind."

"Ardmore has reddish hair," Imogen put in. "But it's long enough to toss."

"If he were French, we would know for certain," Josie said.

"He's not perfidious!" Annabel couldn't help it; she snapped at Josie.

"That's what you're bound to think," Josie replied, "because you haven't married him. If Ardmore has a guilty secret, he'd talk about it only in his sleep. That's why heroines never find out what their husbands are like until it's too late. They wake up in the middle of the night and hear their husband talking like this." Josie put her hands up to her hair and rolled her eyes to the ceiling. "*Oooooo . . . Marguerite . . . I cannot forget her cries as she fell over the cliff . . . Oooooooo!*"

She put down her hands and turned to Annabel. "I don't suppose you know whether Ardmore talks in his sleep?"

"I have no idea," Annabel lied.

"You must admit that this castle has all the elements of a novel, complete with a mad wife in the attic."

"Making a joke of poor Rosy is a graceless thing to do, Josie."

"All right," Josie sighed. "I don't mean to be cruel. I would love to live here, and I wouldn't even mind Rosy, although her manners would certainly cut down on visitors."

"We should all take this as a lesson," Imogen said with a slightly pompous tone. "Just because a man has a title and a castle doesn't mean he's a tenable choice for matrimony."

Josie nudged Annabel's foot. "This is your cue to lecture us on appropriate reasons for marriage."

But Annabel was imagining Ewan marrying someone else and her heart was pounding miserably.

"You can't have forgotten all those lectures you gave us last year about marrying for practical reasons and not for love." Josie raised her voice to a hectoring level and said: "*The best marriages are those between levelheaded persons, entered into for levelheaded reasons and with a reasonable degree of confidence in compatibility.*"

"Yes, of course," Annabel said, twisting the sheet around her finger.

"You know," Imogen said, "we haven't even asked what your journey here was like, Annabel. How was it?"

"Fine. Quite—quite pleasant, really."

Annabel could feel Imogen staring at her.

"Annabel?"

"Yes?"

"Is something the matter? Look at me!"

Annabel turned her head and met Imogen's eyes.

"Oh, my God," Imogen said, flopping back on the pillows.

"What?" Josie asked. "What?"

"She's compromised," Imogen said hollowly.

"Compromised? We already knew that," Josie said.

"I'm not compromised!" Annabel said miserably. "That is, perhaps I am, but it doesn't matter."

"How can you say it doesn't matter?" Imogen half shrieked. "It—"

"It doesn't matter because I love him," Annabel said, tears spilling down her cheeks. "I love him, and he doesn't love me. And I want to marry him, and not for just six months either."

There was a moment of dead silence.

Then: "Oh, sweetheart," Imogen said, wrapping an arm around Annabel.

"You?" Josie asked incredulously. "Our logical, level-headed sister who was determined to marry for money?"

"I don't care . . . Even if Ewan were poor, I'd marry him."

"Goodness," Josie said, clearly shocked. "If you could contemplate poverty, then you are in love. Of course, Griselda is going to have strong convulsions when you tell her."

"But I can't marry him." Annabel stopped. "That is, I am going to marry him, but I don't want to." Tears were blocking her throat again.

"You're not making sense," Josie observed. "Imogen never made sense either, when she was in throes."

"He doesn't love me," Annabel said. "He—he likes me a great deal. He desires me. He thinks that's love, but it's not. I know that. Desire is very different."

"The important thing is . . ." Imogen hesitated, obviously picking her words carefully. "The important thing is not to marry a man who doesn't love you. You're right: it doesn't matter unless *you* love *him*. But it's terrible to be the only one in a marriage with that feeling." She stopped. Then she took a deep breath. "I thought my love for Draven would be enough for the two of us."

"But Draven did love you," Annabel protested. "He

told you so as he died. Don't diminish his love, now that he's not here to repeat it to you."

"I do not diminish his love for me," Imogen said. "I would never do that. I know precisely how much he loved me: as much as he was capable of loving any woman, probably. He loved me somewhat . . . after his stables, perhaps more than his mother."

"Oh, Imogen," Annabel said. "Why dwell on such a—"

"Grief is like that!" Imogen snapped. "You can only fool yourself so far. And now I've seen one of my sisters be truly loved. I saw it in Lucius Felton's face when we first met at the races, a few days after Tess married him."

"I do not agree that Draven did not love you," Annabel said firmly.

"He did love me! He just didn't love me very much. Tiny things each day tell you precisely how much you are valued by your husband. I have had nothing to do but think over the two weeks during which Draven and I were married. I know *precisely* how he valued me."

"Well, if you're right, you might as well stop weeping over him," Josie said with her customary brutal frankness. "Why grieve at all if he didn't treat you properly? And what did he do, anyway? How do you know he didn't love you? Did he say so?"

"That's none of your business!" Imogen snapped. "I'm not crying, am I?"

"Is that why you've taken up with Mayne?" Josie insisted.

"Mayne doesn't love me either."

"I feel as if violins should be wailing in the background," Josie said. "If you're looking for love, I think you're going about it the wrong way. Kidnapping Mayne is not going to make him love you."

"I don't give a damn if Mayne ever loves me!"

"You make it sound as if love is a quantifiable object," Josie pointed out. "As if you could positively identify men who love their wives, versus those who don't. If you ask me, it's a great deal more confusing than that."

"There's something to what you say," Imogen said slowly.

"There always is," Josie said with satisfaction.

"All I'm saying is that if you are truly in love with Ardmore," Imogen said, turning to Annabel, "you shouldn't marry him, not until he's in love with you too. It's too heartbreaking."

"But I expect Ardmore does love Annabel," Josie put in. "All men seem to. Remember when Papa had to have the curate sent to another parish because he was writing love letters to Annabel?"

"You're confusing desire and love," Annabel said, her voice breaking a little. "I asked Ewan, last night, if he loved me, and he said that he desired me." Her voice caught on a sob. "He doesn't even realize there's a difference! I'm tired of being a desirable woman."

"From what I've read of ancient poets," Josie said, "to most men, desire and love are the same thing. Perhaps you're being too meticulous in your reasoning."

"Truly, Annabel, I can't see any reason to despair," Imogen said, wrapping an arm around her shoulder. "If Ewan desires you, then he's well on the way to loving you. Josie, you should probably leave the room."

Josie's glare would have burnt a green tree, so Imogen shrugged. "All right. Tess and Felton weren't in love when they married. And yet he clearly fell in love with her directly after the wedding. I've thought and thought about why Draven didn't fall in love with me in the same way—" She swallowed.

"You don't have to tell us," Annabel said softly.

"I don't want your marriage to be like mine," Imogen

said fiercely. "So I do have to tell you. And the truth is that I don't think that Draven and I—well, that Draven was particularly happy in our bedchamber."

There was a moment's silence, and then Josie said, "I hope you haven't talked yourself into believing that he jumped on a horse and killed himself out of marital disappointment."

It was so blunt, and so Josie-like, that both Imogen and Annabel gave a little choke of laughter. And after that, things were easier.

"Tess let Felton kiss her right on the racetrack," Imogen said earnestly, "in the midst of a hundred people. And he kissed her in the open box where anyone might have seen them. And then they went off to his carriage, and when she came back, her hair was all mussed. I would never have allowed Draven such liberties. I just—just wouldn't have. But now, in retrospect, I wish I had."

"Well, Ewan has kissed me in public places," Annabel said, hoping her face wasn't turning pink at the very thought of some of those places.

"If all men needed to fall in love was desire," Josie objected, "there would be no unmarried night-walkers."

Imogen gasped. "Josie! You shouldn't know such a word, nor ever speak of those women either!"

"*Meretrix* in Latin," Josie said, without a semblance of repentance. "I know you won't like this, Annabel, but it seems to me that you simply want Ardmore to express himself more eloquently. Why don't you tell him you are going to leave with us? His heart will be riven, and he'll fall to his knees and plead with you to stay."

"I would never lie to him," Annabel said.

"I know!" Josie cried. "If you were in danger, Ardmore would suddenly realize that he might lose you forever. For example, if you fell off a bridge and were carried away in the white water, he would shriek your name." She grinned at the thought.

"But I would be dead," Annabel pointed out. "I don't want to fall from a bridge or a horse. I am taking Sweetpea out this morning, and I have no plans to plummet to the ground."

There was a gentle knock on the door. "That's Elsie," Annabel hissed, swinging her legs from the bed. "I don't want her to see I've been crying. Tell her that I'm taking a bath." And she dashed into the bathroom and closed the door.

Josie leaned forward and pinched Imogen's foot. "We have to do something!" she whispered as Elsie began fussing with Annabel's wardrobe. "I've never seen her so dreary. She really believes he doesn't love her."

"He's probably fairly tongue-tied on the subject," Imogen said. "Men tend to be."

"But you know how hardheaded Annabel is. She seems to have convinced herself that desire precludes love. At this rate, the poor man would have to play the role of an altered tomcat merely in order to convince her of love."

"What have you been doing in the schoolroom?" Imogen scolded. "Your conversion is entirely unsuitable for a young lady. In fact, for a lady of *any* age! It must be those books."

"I learned that phrase from you, not from a book! And I hate to tell you this, Imogen, but classical literature is a great deal more lurid than are the works of the Minerva Press. But don't distract me: I know Annabel. She's as stubborn as a mule, once she gets her mind to something. The only way to change this situation is to put her in danger . . . somehow."

"I hope you're wrong," Imogen said, getting up and going to the door.

"It worked for you," Josie reminded her. "You fell off

that horse and Draven promptly stole you away to Gretna Green."

"Annabel would never resort to such tactics," Imogen said, tacitly accepting responsibility for the fall. "She's ruthlessly honest, you know, and that would amount to lying to Ardmore. At any rate, I hope you're wrong. Ardmore looks like a man who could convince a woman of anything, if he put his mind to it."

But Josie found that she was very rarely wrong. Still, the solution didn't seem overly difficult: mild danger would certainly inspire indisputable signs of love in Ardmore, and convince Annabel of his feelings.

Josie smiled. She had an excellent idea of how to effect a spot of mild danger.

Thirty-two

Imogen opened the door into her bed-chamber and stopped in surprise. There, seated on an upright chair beside the dressing table, was a woman who appeared to be a reincarnation of an ancestral portrait. But she was clearly no ghost. "In the absence of others, I shall introduce myself," she announced, as if she were Her Majesty herself: "I am Lady Ardmore."

Imogen entered the room and dropped a low, formal curtsy. "What a great pleasure to meet you, Lady Ardmore. I am Lady Maitland, Miss Essex's sister." Ardmore's grandmother wore her hair curled and powdered, piled high on her head, and she was decked with two ropes of emeralds, which (according to Imogen's devout reading of *La Belle Assemblée*) was a blunder during the morning hours. Yet she was formidable. One could see the resemblance to her grandson. Ardmore's eyes were green, and hers were silvery and tired, but they had the same decided jaw and beautiful cheekbones.

Lady Ardmore waved a hand. "You may seat yourself."
Imogen promptly sat down.

"So you're the widow, are you?" Lady Ardmore said.
"I knew about Maitland's death, of course. Heard about
your elopement too. He was a bonny lad, your husband."

"Did you know him?" Imogen asked.

"I knew his mother, for all she was English. Lord Ardmore and I—that would be my husband, not my son—
went to London now and then. She wrote me a nice note
when Ardmore died, and then again when I lost my son
and his wife."

She was silent for a moment. Imogen bit her lip. She
couldn't imagine what it had been like, losing one's husband and then their only son. Not to mention her
daughter-in-law and the babies.

But before she could think what to say, Lady Ardmore
continued. "I was sorry to hear that Lady Clarice had
died—November, wasn't it?"

Imogen nodded. "She was never the same after Draven
died. She caught a chill and she simply didn't care to go
on."

" 'Twould have been easier, perhaps, if I could have
faded away in some sort of illness. There was many a
day when I would have wished it. But"—she looked at
Imogen, and her silvery eyes were sharp as ever, and
tearless—"there are those of us who cry, and those of
us who rage. 'Tis my guess that you're of the latter
kind."

Imogen managed a small smile. "Might I count myself
a member of both groups?"

"Oh, I cried," Lady Ardmore said. "When my James
and his wife died, and with them those bonny, bonny
children, I cried so hard I thought I'd drown myself, as
they had."

"I'm so sorry," Imogen said.

Lady Ardmore gave herself a little shake. "I can't imagine how we wandered into such maudlin territory," she said. "I'd like to know why you've come to Scotland, Lady Maitland. The castle's ripe with rumors. My maid tells me that Miss Essex will be wanting to return to London now, and not marry the earl."

"That is not correct," Imogen said, wondering how much to tell the countess.

"My grandson hasn't told me a smidgen." She fixed her bright eyes on Imogen. "Yet I can tell this is the marriage for him. He hadn't shown a scrap of interest in marriage, and though it galls me to admit it, Armailhac was right when he sent him off to London. Your sister's got backbone, and she's a Scot, and I can see as well as any that Ewan cares for her."

Imogen nodded.

"So what's the fly in the ointment, then?" Lady Ardmore barked. "Your sister looks a bit watery to me, and that's not her nature, any more than it's yours. So I'll ask you again, girl: What's the matter?"

"She doesn't believe that Lord Ardmore loves her," Imogen said obediently, helpless to resist the force of those silvery eyes.

"Loves her?" Lady Ardmore scoffed. "That's a piece of romantic foolery. Why, I was terrified of my husband. In the old days, that's the way it was supposed to be. The head of Clan Poley had agreed to marry me and my parents spent weeks impressing upon me that I was never to answer back, nor raise my voice, nor upset my husband in the slightest fashion."

"That must have been difficult," Imogen said.

"Ha!" Lady Ardmore said. She thought about it for a while. "It wasn't so difficult. I was doing my duty. 'Twas a great thing for my family when I married the head of the clan. And I stood by my side of the bargain."

"Did you ever raise your voice?" Imogen asked, unable to stop herself.

Lady Ardmore gave a little chuckle. "Now, what do you think, lass?" Then she stomped her stick again. "Not for at least a month. Mayhap even six months."

Imogen thought it had likely been about a week.

"Ardmore and I found a way to talk to each other, though he was none too fond of words. Ewan's like his grandfather; he waited until he found your sister, and now there'll be no other for him, not in this lifetime."

Imogen swallowed away the lump in her throat. "Annabel will come to know that," she said. "I'm afraid that our father was not always loving towards her, and she has little understanding of her worth."

Lady Ardmore snorted. "Then she's the first yellow-haired beauty I've found to be so."

"That's just it," Imogen said. "Her own beauty has made it hard for her to believe in Lord Ardmore."

"There's many a woman would like to share *that* problem!"

"Yes," Imogen admitted with a flash of disloyalty. "But she does feel it, all the same."

" 'Tis easy to solve," Lady Ardmore said, with a briskness that reminded Imogen, rather unnervingly, of Josie. "I shall do so myself."

"What?" Imogen asked, startled.

The countess stopped Imogen's question with a raised hand. "You'll have to trust me, young woman. Do you know, I only met my husband once before we were married."

"Really?" Imogen asked. Of course she knew that arranged marriages were common among the great families, but: "You had seen him, hadn't you?"

Lady Ardmore shook her head. "Young ladies were kept to themselves in those days. I was perhaps kept more closely than others, since I was destined to be a countess from the age of five."

"That's—" Imogen said, swallowing the word *awful*.

"The first time I saw Ardmore was two days before our wedding. His younger brothers were up to a lark. They thought to blacken me. Do you know what that is?"

Imogen shook her head.

" 'Tis akin to tarring and feathering but with treacle," Lady Ardmore said with a scowl. "Terrible custom, more observed in the breach than the observance, if you follow me."

Imogen didn't.

"That's a line from *Hamlet*," the countess said. "In other words, it's an ancient tradition in Aberdeenshire, but even back then, it wasn't practiced overmuch, and certainly not on future countesses. Well, these two young boys had got their dander up and determined to make a May's game of their brother's bride. Lord knows, they were wild enough for anything. One of them ran off to India and was never heard from again."

"Did they manage to do it?" Imogen asked, intrigued at the very notion of boys wild enough to lay a finger— or a feather—on this particular countess.

"No, no," Lady Ardmore said, waving her hand again. "My future husband saved me. Quite a thrilling scene it was." She nodded and looked to Imogen. "*Quite* exciting."

"No!" Imogen said.

"Yes," Lady Ardmore said with quiet satisfaction. "Yes, I think that will work nicely."

Thirty-three

When Josie found him, Mayne was sprawled in a chair in Ardmore's library. He was holding a copy of Weatherby's *General Stud Book*, but it looked to Josie as if he were just staring into the distance.

"What are you doing?" she asked him.

"Thinking about my mortality," Mayne said, raising his heavy-lidded eyes.

Josie felt herself turning slightly pink, which wasn't a normal reaction for her. But there was something so thrillingly wolfish about Mayne that it was impossible not to react to the man. How embarrassing. What sort of woman blushed at the sight of her own sister's lover, not to put too fine a point on it?

"Why do you bother thinking about mortality?" she asked, wandering around the study so that it didn't look as if she'd come looking specifically for him. "You're old, but not quite that old yet."

"God knows," he said. "Does Imogen have a request of me?"

She came over and sat on the arm of his chair. "I do. I need you to help me," she said. "Help me help Annabel."

"I'm tired of helping Annabel," he said, and the lines of weariness around his eyes deepened. He had beautiful eyes; Josie could certainly see why all those hundreds of women had made fools of themselves over him.

"You have no choice," Joise said firmly. "And don't fuss. You'll exhaust what little energy you have, and I need you to come with me."

"I have plenty of energy!" he said, looking a bit more alive.

"Good. Because I want to go to Ardmore's stables."

She saw a spark of interest in his eyes. "All right."

"We're going riding. With Annabel and Ardmore."

He was far too intelligent for his own good. "There's something here you're not telling me."

"What you don't know won't hurt you," Josie said. "Do you have riding clothes?"

"You know I don't!" Mayne snapped.

"Perhaps you can wear some of Ardmore's."

"The man's a bloody tree trunk. I've never seen muscles like those outside of bargemen."

"You *are* a bit willowy," Josie said consideringly. "Exercise will do you a world of good. Maybe Ardmore can give you some riding tips."

"That's enough insults from you," Mayne said, standing up. "I already said I'd come with you, for God's sake. Just give me a moment to wrestle some clothing from our host."

"And make him join us. I'll bring Annabel to the hallway in a half hour," Josie said.

She ran off to her room and fetched her satchel of

medicines. For a moment she was afraid that she'd forgotten to bring it—but no! She always loathed it when Papa asked for that particular salve, but she'd dutifully made it for him anyway. And carried a small pot of it all the way to England, and now back again to Scotland.

When Annabel walked down the stairs dressed in a habit a half hour later, she expected Josie, but she was mildly surprised to find Mayne there as well. Ewan came out of the breakfast room dressed in riding breeches.

"This is a true party!" Josie cried rather shrilly, herding them all out the door so quickly that Annabel didn't even exchange a greeting with Ewan.

Her own horse, Sweetpea, was waiting for her, all saddled and ready to go. He arched his great head, blowing into her hand, and Annabel thought with a pulse of shame that he had traveled all the way from Rafe's estate, and she hadn't even visited him to see whether he liked his new quarters.

"Annabel!" Josie called. She was standing beside a squat Welsh pony. It was one of the mysteries of their family that Josie, who fearlessly treated the most irritable injured animal, was terrified to ride on them. "Sweetpea looks as if she might have some saddle tenderness."

"Really?" Annabel ran a finger around the sidesaddle. Sweetpea didn't react.

"I saw it as he was first brought from the stables, although he seems fine now."

They started down a winding path that led down a great stretch of lawn to the back of the castle. The grass was still a tender pale green, a May green.

Josie tried hard not to think about how far it was from the broad back of her mount to the ground. Annabel's horse was twice the height of hers, and of a muscled, sleek type that filled her with terror. But it didn't matter how many times she compared her plump little pony to Annabel's great mount; she was still stiff with terror, and the pony knew it. He was expressing his disregard for her by bending his head and taking bites of grass, no matter how sharply she pulled on his reins.

Ewan and Mayne had reached the edge of the lawn, stopping at a path that wound down and around a river. "This is a lovely stretch for a race," Ewan called back.

Suddenly Josie realized this was a perfect opportunity. "Mayne!" she cried. He turned around.

"Yes?"

"Help me off this horse," she said. "Please."

Thankfully he didn't make any jokes about the pony being nearly her height, or anything of that nature, just jumped off his own horse and helped her to the ground. "I was right," Josie said to Annabel, walking over to her. "Do you see how Sweetpea is shifting his legs? He's a little saddle sore. But look"—she reached into her pocket—"I brought along the salve. Mayne, if you would help Annabel to the ground, I could—"

But Ardmore was there before Mayne could move, reaching up to Annabel. Josie didn't watch them. She just moved over to Sweetpea and loosened his straps.

Mayne came to her shoulder. "I thought you were afraid of horses," he said.

Sweetpea was trying to lip some of her hair, and Josie gave him an affectionate little push. "How could anyone be afraid of a horse?" she said absentmindedly. Now she was reaching up under the saddle and rubbing the wintery-smelling salve into Sweetpea's back, saying a little mental apology as she did so.

"Well, you're riding a pony," Mayne persisted. "What are you putting on Annabel's mount, may I ask? That is not saddle salve. It doesn't smell right."

Josie glanced over his shoulder, but Annabel and Ardmore weren't paying any attention to them. Annabel was looking at the ground, and Ardmore was looking at her.

"Hush," Josie said to Mayne.

"Do you know that before I met the Essex sisters, no one ever told me what to do?" he said. His voice was incredulous.

Josie tightened the saddle, and then Mayne's hands came over hers and pulled the saddle even tighter.

"Whatever you're doing," he muttered, "I'm sure it's not something of which I'd approve."

"Likely not," she said, giving him a wide smile. She almost ran back to her pony, but then she had to wait for Mayne to put her up on its back.

Ardmore lifted Annabel on her horse with a flattering show of attention. Of course he was in love. All the man needed was a bit of a shock to realize it.

Josie clapped her hands. "Let's have a race!" she cried. "It wouldn't be fair to put Ardmore against Mayne, since Ardmore rides his own mount, so it will have to be Lord Ardmore against you, Annabel."

"Me?" her sister said, settling herself in the sidesaddle again.

"Of course, Ardmore must have a handicap," Josie said. "You're riding sidesaddle, after all."

"But she's riding Sweetpea," Ardmore put in. "Sweetpea won the Parthenon Cup a few years ago, didn't he?"

Annabel nodded. "Papa only gave him to me once it became clear that his ankle would never be the same."

"Well, I'm sure Sweetpea could manage a small race," Ardmore said. "For a forfeit, perhaps?"

Josie wasn't sure why that question had such significance, but Annabel looked taken aback. Sweetpea was shifting uneasily, dancing on his long legs as if he were longing to run.

"All right," Annabel said finally.

"Annabel takes a start of fifty meters," Josie said, thinking that should be just about the right distance.

And it was. Sweetpea melted into a smooth gallop, only to rear straight in the air thirty feet ahead of them, his front shoes cutting curlicues in the air as if he thought to topple over backward.

Despite herself, Josie gasped. It was her idea of a nightmare. But Annabel was a consummate horsewoman, adjusting to Sweetpea's pawing, fidgeting leaps as if they were a normal occurrence.

"What the hell!" Mayne said, and then suddenly Josie remembered that she should be watching the Earl of Ardmore, not her sister.

Her heart sank. Ardmore didn't look in the least terrified. He hadn't galloped forward to catch Annabel's reins, nor did he show any signs of wishing to help her. Why, Annabel could have been thrown off and broken her neck, for all the effort the man was making. He was just sitting there on his horse, his eyes alight with appreciation—she could see that—but with no more alarm than if he were watching a circus performance.

"Oh, no!" Josie gasped. "My poor sister will be thrown to the ground. She might be killed!"

Ardmore gave her a rather sweet smile. "I know you're afraid of horses," he said kindly, "and so this must seem terrifying to you—"

Josie didn't see how it could be viewed in any other way. No sooner did Sweetpea touch his front hooves to the ground than he whinnied and spiraled back up on his back legs, and nothing Annabel was doing seemed to calm him.

"But as you can see," Ardmore continued, "your sister is a consummate horsewoman. She's in no danger whatsoever."

"Of course she is!" Josie said crossly.

But Ardmore just sat on his horse, smiling, until Josie couldn't take it any more and shouted at Mayne, "Do *you* go and save her, then!"

At which point Ardmore easily cantered forward. But just then Annabel managed to keep Sweetpea to the ground long enough to jump down from her mount. So when Ardmore arrived, she was holding Sweetpea's head down and scolding him.

Poor Sweetpea. He was obeying her, even though his ears were twitching madly.

A moment later Ardmore had the sidesaddle off and Sweetpea was rolling gratefully on the new grass.

Mayne cleared his throat. "I gather you made a mistake in the ointment you applied?"

"I must have done so," Josie said gloomily.

Thirty-four

An hour later they all walked their horses back across the green meadow. Great washes of noise were spilling from the courtyard on the far side of the castle. They rounded the corner and stopped. The courtyard was full of people, hailing each other, shrieking over other people's heads. The sound was matched by color, great swathes of bright red and orange plaid, with darker green patches here and there.

"Interesting," Ewan said, handing his horse to a groomsman. "My grandmother seems to have summoned the Crogans. The men are here; I assume the women are following in carriages."

"Who are they?" Josie asked.

"A neighboring clan, and a boisterous lot," he replied. Josie could have seen that for herself. The men milling around the courtyard looked drunk, to her eyes.

"Let's enter in the rear." The earl led them around to

the kitchen gardens. "I will go greet our guests. Please join us whenever you wish."

"Ewan wasn't in the least frightened by whatever you did to Sweetpea," Annabel said quietly to Josie as they climbed the back stairs. "You should be ashamed of yourself. Poor Sweetpea. I suppose that was Papa's miracle lotion?"

Josie nodded guiltily.

The moment Annabel pushed open the door of her room, her maid jumped to her feet like an excited terrier. Elsie was looking white and strained, even for someone who ran on her nerves as a matter of course. "Oh, miss, the castle is absolutely crammed with people; you can't imagine. Most of two counties are either here or on their way. And it's not just the nobility either; it's everyone. The servants' hall is fair run over already."

"They're here to celebrate the wedding," Annabel said, feeling light-headed at the thought.

"Some of them!" Elsie snapped. "The rest are here for a free meal, Mrs. Warsop says. She's clean out of butter and had to send to the village for everything she can find. But it's the whiskey that's really likely to run out. They're already drinking down there, and it's not noon yet. And the ladies too, though some of them aren't acting like ladies by my definition. Mrs. Warsop says that the countess summoned the Crogans this morning, and by all accounts, they drink their breakfast every morning."

Annabel couldn't think what to say to that, so she sat at her dressing room table and let Elsie brush out her hair. "Mrs. Warsop needs every hand she can, just to keep pace with the serving. It's not as if all these servants are willing to help. They act as if they've just come for the celebration, and we're to serve them as well as everyone else."

Elsie was brushing so briskly that Annabel's hair

crackled. "I just don't see why those servants have to be so monstrous rude. If it hadn't been for my respect for Mrs. Warsop, I'd have had more to tell them."

"The more you match words with those sorts, the less respect you gain."

Elsie scowled. "All but that maid of Lady McFiefer. If her mistress is half as bad as she is, you'll have a pretty time with her. Apparently Lady McFiefer's daughter thought to marry his lordship, though to hear them talk in the servants' hall, half the county thought the same of their daughters."

She put the brush down. "I'm putting out your primrose sarcenet with the gossamer net."

"That's far too grand," Annabel objected. "I can't go downstairs dressed in a ball gown, Elsie."

"You must," her maid said. "They're all speculating on why his lordship married you, instead of Lady McFeifer's daughter. I caught a glimpse of her. She's beautiful enough, but she's brassy. You can tell she's not meant to be a countess by the look of her. Whereas you look like a countess."

"But Elsie—"

"There's that gown you haven't worn yet, the French one." Elsie laid it gently on the bed.

Annabel bit her lip. The frock was of pale gold crepe, trimmed all about the bottom with pale French roses, with a ribbon of green intermixed. It was meant to be worn for a formal dinner, since its bosom was extremely low and it had a slight train. On the other hand, it was both exquisite and expensive, and in her opinion, those two qualities were needed to bolster her courage.

"You'll wear it with the double row of pearls from Mrs. Felton," Elsie said, scurrying about the room. "And more of those French roses in your hair." She had her jaw firmly set.

"All right," Annabel said. "I'll wear the gown, but I'll not wear the slippers."

Elsie scowled and Annabel wondered just how it happened that she ended up ruled by her maid instead of the other way around.

The moment she put her jeweled foot onto the stone steps leading down into the entranceway, the noise died. Some fifty heads swung upward. One hundred eyes stared at her. Only the footmen near the door looked up and away. Everyone else seemed transfixed.

Annabel paused for a moment, to let them satisfy their curiosity, and then smiled, a smile she knew quite well made her look delectable. The faces below her responded appropriately, and she walked the last steps to the entrance hall.

Lady Ardmore elbowed her way through the crowd. "Miss Essex," she called, coming to the bottom of the stairs. "In the absence of my son, I welcome you to Ardmore Castle."

There was a happy hum in the entrance.

"I am most pleased to be here," Annabel said, sinking into a deep curtsy. A moment later she was surrounded by cheerful faces. As fast as a pair of guests were whisked up the steps to find a chamber for the night, more seemed to flood in the front door. Footmen staggered in and out and, belying Elsie's doom-filled notions about lack of food, the footmen seemed to be laden down with hams and bottles of spirit. Around an hour later Annabel heard a raucous squeaking outside that came closer and closer.

Lady Ardmore hadn't been out of motion, whisking here and there, bawling at a friend of hers and dispatching more with footmen. Now she trotted up to Annabel. "That'll be the heart of the party arriving. The pipers are here. Where's Ewan?"

Annabel shook her head. "I haven't seen him."

"Ardmore!" his grandmother howled. She caught sight of Mac down on the front steps, supervising the arrival of what appeared to be an entire suckling pig, ready roasted. "Mac, find Ardmore! The pipers are coming!"

Mac cocked an ear and then dashed around the house and toward the stables. But before he could reappear, a flood of men swept down the road, led by bagpipes. Two men were prancing unsteadily before the pipers, leading the pack with their dance.

Lady Ardmore drew Annabel outdoors, to the top of the steps. The throng milling about the courtyard drew back as the revelers approached, allowing the two leaders to prance up the stairs followed by ten pipers.

"They're the head of the Crogan clan," Nana said, under cover of the pipers' squealing. "Using the wedding as an excuse to get cast away, not that they need such an excuse on a normal day."

"Your neighboring clan?" Annabel said, watching the two men half stagger, half dance up the stairs to them. They were an unsavory pair, with flaming red hair that stood straight from the domes of their heads. They wore kilts and their hairy stout legs looked unattractively chilled.

"The same. I wonder where Ewan is. He should—"

But whatever Ewan should have done was lost as the Crogans lurched up the last stair, smiling liquorish smiles and looking Annabel up and down as if she were a tailor's dummy. "Well, now, isn't this nice, Crogan?" said the short one.

"Sure is, sure is," said the taller one. "I'm thinking— do you know what I'm thinking, Crogan?"

Lady Ardmore interrupted. "There isn't a soul here that cares what you think, Crogan." She poked at one of them with her stick. "Nor yet you either, Crogan. Keep your manners." There was a shrill note in her voice that made the Crogans blink.

"Do you have the same name?" Annabel asked, trying to edge backward so as not to get caught by their breath again.

"She's very pretty," the shorter Crogan said to his brother, staring at Annabel's breasts.

She stepped backward again.

"Now, brother," the other Crogan said genially. "If-fen our little monk has decided to have himself a taste o' the best, we can't begrudge him that. But we can't forget the old ways either."

Before Annabel knew what was happening, a strong arm curled around her and she was pulled sharply to the left down the steps. The last she saw was the rest of the clan genially throwing Ewan's footmen to the ground, while she was literally carried away over the shoulder of the larger Crogan.

"What are you *doing*!" she shrieked at him, beating his meaty shoulder.

The man ran surprisingly fast for someone barely able to keep his balance the moment before. In a second they were into the trees and Crogan was thrashing along, his brother chugging behind him as if he knew precisely where he was heading.

"What are you doing?" Annabel shrieked again, and this time she got hold of some of his red hair and pulled it as hard as she could.

"Ouch!" he cried, and put her down, careful not to let go of her arm. "I thought you were a Scots. They said you were!"

"I am!" Annabel said, glaring at him.

"Well, stap my vitals, if you aren't a pretty thing!" he said, his eyes falling to her bosom again.

"Lord Ardmore will kill you if you lay a hand on me," Annabel said.

"We'd never do that," said the fat one. "But you're Scots, aren't you?"

"What has that got to do with it?" she screamed. "Let me go!"

"Our brothers have gone for Ardmore," the thin one said. "And we've you. Take out the feathers, Crogan."

"*What?*"

"You've to be blackened," he said, grinning like a fool. "You know what that is, surely, or aren't you from hereabouts?"

"I haven't the faintest idea what you're talking about," she said. The fat one was taking what looked like a bag of feathers from his rucksack.

"You must be blackened," he repeated. " 'Tis a pity that you have such a pretty dress on." He reached out to touch the lace around her bosom. "But we have our instructions. Perhaps—"

But Annabel saw his dirty hand coming out to her breast and her scream was instinctive.

The Crogan holding her arm jumped. "Hush, now!" he said. "We're not going to hurt you!"

But Annabel was just getting into her stride. He tried to get a beefy hand over her mouth, and she bit him and screamed again.

"Damnation, Crogan," he grunted. "Would you get over here with that treacle, then? I'm thinking this one's a tartar as will rival Ardmore's grandmother. I'm thinking—"

Annabel kicked him with her jeweled shoes as hard as she could.

"Ouch!" he said, and: "Ouch! I'm thinking we should put in some Hail Marys for poor Ardmore—"

The shorter Crogan had finished mixing up something

that was unmistakably a pot of black treacle. Annabel twisted as best she could, screaming at the top of her lungs.

There wasn't a sound in the woods other than her own screams and the panting complaints of the Crogan who was holding on to her. But suddenly she heard a clear, sharp voice cry, "Stop that!"

"Help me!" she screamed. She was about to steel herself to bite the Crogan again when there was an *oof!* and he dropped her arm and flew away to the side.

Since she was in the midst of trying to kick him, Annabel fell smack on the ground and it took her a moment to pull herself from the tangled roots and leaves. Her hair was all over her eyes, and she couldn't see a thing.

She could hear, though. She heard a smack and a cry, a howl of pain and another crack that sounded like a head. She brushed her hair out of her eyes and looked up.

Rosy was standing over the shorter Crogan with a big rock in her hand. He was out cold, his cheek nestled in a little puddle of black treacle. Rosy looked extremely pleased, and not in the least befuddled. "I hit him," she said cheerfully.

"So you did," Annabel said, blinking at her.

Then she heard another thunk, and spun about.

It was Ewan. He had the bigger Crogan on the ground, the one who had been holding her. He was beating him mercilessly. "If you ever dare to touch her again," he said—*thunk!*—"I'll kill you." *Crack!* The man's head snapped back. "I'll kill you as easily as I'd feed slop to a hog!" Ewan said. His voice was so savage that Annabel's mouth fell open.

"Do you hear me, Crogan?" he shouted.

"Yesth," the man said. "I wathn't—"

"You were touching her," Ewan said, lifting him up into the air like a sack of meal and letting him fall again.

"I wasthn't!" Crogan wailed. "Ah, God, I won't ever come near her again. 'Twasn't me!" he wailed. " 'Twas your gran—"

Ewan drew back his fist again and walloped Crogan on the chin. The man gave a groan and his eyes rolled back into his head. He was out cold.

"Ewan!" Annabel breathed, putting a hand on his arm as he started to pick up Crogan and shake him back into consciousness.

"I'll find Father Armailhac," Rosy said, her voice as clear as a bell. She ran away, and Annabel snapped her head back to Ewan.

Ewan had dropped Crogan back on the leaves.

He was breathing as if he'd run ten leagues, so he concentrated on rolling down his sleeves. He, Ewan Poley, Earl of Ardmore, had just lost control for the first time in his life. Well, perhaps not exactly for the first time.

He took a sideways glance and saw that she was all right. His Annabel. They'd frightened her, but they hadn't really touched her. The feathers lay spilled on the ground, and a pot of treacle was soaking into other Crogan's hair.

So that first horrible glance he'd had, that first stark terror when he heard her screams, was incorrect. They weren't ravishing her: the Crogans were merely up to their stupid, drunken pranks again.

Finally he had to meet her eyes, because she had her hand on his arm. He knew she would have that little pucker between her brows, so he looked.

And almost closed his eyes against the beauty of her, all rumpled hair the color of gold coins falling over his arm, and her eyes, with their seductive tilt, and the intelligence of her face, and the courage there too.

"Are you all right?" she whispered.

"He didn't touch me, the drunken fool," Ewan said.

"Drunken or not," Annabel shuddered, "I'm so grateful that you saved me, Ewan."

"I was going to kill him," he said slowly. "Kill him."

Annabel looked at him.

"Do you remember when I was foolish enough to say that I couldn't see myself losing my soul?" Ewan asked.

She nodded.

"There'll be nothing difficult about it at all. When I saw him touch you—"

He stopped.

"I would kill him again and again," and there was a savagery in his tone that went through Annabel like a piercing wind. "God, Annabel, it's not a question of how or whether I could damn my soul. How many times would I damn myself for you? Ask me that."

"How many?" she said faintly, her eyes searching his face. She stopped breathing to hear his answer.

"Till the gates of hell close," he said flatly.

"Oh, Ewan," she whispered, taking his face in her hands. "I can't—" There were tears welling up in her eyes.

"What's that to cry about?" he said. But there was something in her face that made his heart lighten. "Until I met you, I was never in the way of sin. But now I'm losing my temper right and left, changing myself—and on the verge of killing one of my neighbors."

She started to laugh, but the tears were still there too. And she was kissing him all over his face, loving him, loving the smell of him and the taste of him, until his arms came around her and he stopped all those butterfly kisses and just devoured her mouth . . . as if there were no one in the world but the two of them, and the quiet woods around them.

"Annabel?" Ewan whispered after a while. His voice was rough and husky. "Have you forgiven me for desiring you too much yet?"

She blinked at him and started to laugh.

"I love you," he said hoarsely. "But damn, Annabel, even if I try not to desire you, it's not going to work."

She laughed again. "You never understood, did you?"

"Likely I never shall. I don't know what's made you so happy about the fact I nearly slaughtered a neighbor."

She put her hands on his heart, loving his confusion . . . loving him. "You said you would damn yourself for me," she said.

"That's no badge of honor."

"For me it is," she said achingly. "No one's ever valued me so much before, Ewan."

"I'm not sure that I've ever cared much for anyone before you. Oh, I love Gregory and Annabel and Nana, but—" He stopped.

"Since your parents died," she finished for him. She smiled through her tears. "Do you remember how you told me that you didn't care about your money, so you kept collecting it?"

"But I care about losing you," he said, his voice suddenly raw. "I would die before I would let you go."

"If you—" She swallowed and then looked up at him. "I don't know how to say it."

There was something close to tears in his eyes as well. "Will you guard my soul for me, then, Annabel Essex?" he asked, and his Scottish burr was as strong as she'd ever heard it.

"Oh, yes," she whispered. "Yes, yes, I will, Ewan Poley. And will you guard mine for me?"

" 'Twould be my honor," he whispered. "My love."

Thirty-five

When the future Countess Ardmore appeared in the door of the great north ballroom that evening, everyone gasped. Miss Annabel Essex was utterly exquisite, like a French lady in *La Belle Assemblée,* from the tips of her jeweled slippers to the perfection of her glowing curls. Lady MacGuire turned away with a scowl, but her daughter Mary's mouth fell open.

"Just look at that gown, Ma," she said, clutching her parent's arm. "No wonder Ardmore didn't want me."

"It's French," her mother said with a snort. And then, reversing her opinion of the last three years: "Ardmore's no great catch, after all. Not with all those monks and that crazed young woman in the house." She nodded toward a plump, rather short young lord, bobbing around on his tiptoes trying to get a glimpse of the future countess. "The young Buckston would be a good match for you."

Miss Mary pouted. "Buckston doesn't have a castle

and he's fat. Besides . . ." She watched Lord Ardmore walk across the room to greet his betrothed. He looked at Miss Essex as if he'd never seen a woman before. "Buckston will never look at me like that. Maybe he'd greet a roast turkey with such enthusiasm, but never a wife."

So Lady MacGuire looked across the room too. After a moment she nodded slowly, as if she were remembering something from a far distant past. "The cream of Scottish nobility is here tonight, Mary. You look about this room and find someone who will look at you in just that way. You're a beautiful young lady, and don't you forget it!"

But Mary was watching the way Ardmore and Miss Essex were dancing together and the way she was laughing up at him. "Ma!" she squealed. "Look at *that*!"

Her mother looked. "Such manners!" she snorted. "I've never seen the like!"

"He kissed her right in front of all of us," Mary said, awed.

On the other side of the ballroom, Imogen pulled her little sister close and gave her a hug. "Did you see that?" she whispered. "Did you *see that*?"

"Of course I did," Josie said. "I suppose this means that your plan worked and mine didn't." She sounded a little grumpy.

"I didn't have a plan," Imogen said happily. Ewan was turning Annabel in circle after circle while everyone watched. He was the picture of a man in love. "Lady Ardmore did."

"Really? It must have been an excellent stratagem. I must ask her for the details," Josie said. "For my study of men in love."

It was hours before Ewan managed to get Annabel alone. It seemed she had to dance with every drunken

Scotsman in the whole of the country. He kept losing sight of her, and then having to find her to make sure that she wasn't being pawed by an overenthusiastic clansman. At some point Father Armailhac found him leaning against the wall and watching Annabel dance.

"You seem to be counting your blessings," he said, with his gentle smile.

"There are many to count," Ewan said. "Has Rosy said much more?"

"No. I doubt she will ever be talkative. But she is content to use her few words, and I think, unfortunate though it was for the younger Crogan, that encounter in the woods was a wonderful thing for her. She defended herself (or so she thinks of it), and in the process she found her voice again. A blessing indeed."

Ewan was watching Annabel again.

Father Armailhac smiled. " 'Tis a fearsome thing to love someone, after losing as much as you lost," he said.

Ewan turned his head and blinked at him. "That's—that's what Annabel said."

Armailhac's smile became a grin. "Am I not the wisest man in Scotland, to have sent you to London, then?"

Ewan suddenly pulled the little monk into a rough hug. "You are," he said. "You certainly are."

Finally . . . finally, Ewan managed to whisk Annabel away to his private study and get her snug on a couch before the fire.

Of course, he kissed her first. And she closed her eyes, and fell into his arms with that boneless enthusiasm that he loved. Now it was obvious to him. He'd fallen in love the moment that he saw Annabel surveying those great statues of an Egyptian god, looking puzzled, intelligent and altogether delectable.

So he tipped up her chin and skimmed her mouth with his. "Open your eyes, Annabel."

She opened them, drowsy with exhaustion and desire and the love for him that he could read so clearly now.

"I love you," he said, his voice coming out rough with the emotion of it.

She smiled at him, and all of a sudden her eyes were brilliant with tears. "Oh, Ewan, I never understood, all the time I was worrying about money and planning to find a husband who desired me—"

He opened his mouth, but she shook her head. "That's what it amounted to. I thought I would feel safe if I could just wear silk every day."

She dropped a kiss on his cheek. "I had no idea that the only currency that mattered was love. You haven't kissed me in hours," she said, her voice an aching whisper. "I haven't felt safe."

Slowly, slowly he bent his head to hers and their lips touched. It was like all their kisses: the sweetness was there, but the wildness too, the sense that they had only just stopped kissing and now they were continuing the same kiss they'd first shared in April. Two seconds later, he was devouring her, pouring his soul and his love into the kiss. And she was kissing him back . . . she was, she was.

Ewan came back to himself to find he was babbling of love, worse than any poet.

"You're becoming a romantic!" Annabel teased, but he could hear the joy in her voice.

"And you're not?" he said. "You love me, Annabel," he said. "You promised me that you did, and I'm going to hold you to that promise for another seventy years. You're in love with me." He kissed her eyes. "You're deliriously in love," he said, kissing her nose. "You're beside yourself in love," and he'd reached her mouth.

"Yes," she said, winding her arms around his neck. "Oh, yes, Ewan. Yes."

"I'm even more in love with you," he whispered.

Sometime later the fire was tumbling in on itself, sending just a wavering spark now and then into the darkening chimney. The great huge castle was quiet, even with Scotsmen tucked into every bedroom and cranny of the place.

Ewan was thinking about taking Annabel upstairs. After all, they had a perfectly comfortable bed waiting for them, and although this couch was very nice, it wasn't quite long enough. Of course, they weren't *quite* married yet, but first thing in the morning—

"Ewan," she said. She was pulling off his cravat, which really meant that he should pick up his betrothed and make their way upstairs before they were discovered and caused a scandal that would put the English one to shame. "Do you remember the coney's kiss?" she whispered into his neck. Her hands were making their way under his shirt now.

"And you the one of us with a decent memory. I suppose I'll have to give you a demonstration."

"Do you remember when I asked you what its mate might be?" Her eyes were sparkling in the last glow of the fire.

"Its mate?" he asked, but her hands were at his waistline. "No!"

"What's sauce for the goose is fit for the gander," she said severely, and started to kiss a line down his chest.

Ewan looked down at her curls and made one last attempt at gentlemanly behavior. "You needn't," he gasped.

"Of course I needn't," she said, looking up at him for a moment. "I want to." She smiled. "I locked the door behind us."

"But—"

"Wouldn't you like me to?"

He blinked at her. No decent gentlewoman— He couldn't think how to phrase it.

"Ewan," she said. "An honest answer. Wouldn't you like me to?"

There was no way to answer that but with honesty. They'd hewed that between them, with all their question games on their trip here. Anytime one of them mentioned honesty in the same breath with a question . . .

"Aye," he said at last, "I'd love nothing better."

She smiled at him brilliantly. "In that case . . ."

Thirty-six

Some months later

"How was practice today?" Annabel asked.

"It's the most annoying thing," Josie said, with the readiness of a sixteen-year-old to discuss herself at any moment. "I simply can't dance. I don't understand it!" She looked stunned.

Annabel laughed. "What do you mean, you can't dance? I thought you were just having trouble counting the beats in your head."

"I'm terrible," Josie pronounced. "Monsieur Jaumont despairs of me. And here's the worst of it—Gregory is flawless!"

"That *is* a cruel twist of fate," Annabel said, grinning. Josie had decided to winter with them in Scotland. She and Gregory were just apart enough in age so that she wished to govern him in everything, and he wished for the same of her.

"He glides about the floor as if he knew instinctively what to do next," Josie said, her mouth turning down at the corners. "Whereas I try to think about what's coming next, and I get twisted up, and then I panic—and then it's all over and Monsieur Jaumont is shrieking again." She sighed. "I'd better go back to the schoolroom. Miss Flecknoe is all fidgety because of the snow, and it puts her in a terrible temper. We were supposed to go see Rosy and all the babies, but there's too much snow."

Rosy was living happily in an orphanage just an hour's drive down the road. Ewan had built a little house for her on the grounds, and she and her nurse spent their days playing with the babies. The children never minded that Rosy said only a word or two; and since men rarely ventured onto the premises, she was quite happy.

But of course winter was settling into the Highlands now, and they wouldn't be able to visit Rosy as much as they had in the fall. It was midway through October and they were having an early snowstorm. Annabel lay on the chaise longue in her bedchamber, lazily looking out the window. At first the snow had danced from the sky, but now it was starting to hurtle down, darkening the window and weighing down the vines that climbed around her window.

Perhaps it was time for a nap . . . She curled on her side, her hand caressing her stomach. The baby was moving inside her, quickening into life, as they called it. At the moment she felt as if it were dancing with the snowflakes. Smiling, Annabel pulled a light cover over herself and drifted off to sleep.

It had been a long fortnight since Ewan last saw his wife. He'd gone to Glasgow on business, but an agree-

ment that was supposed to be quickly settled had
stretched into a long and tedious affair, made all the
more so because he chafed so much at being away.

He turned the doorknob and opened the door.
Annabel was lying on her side, facing him, her cheek
resting peacefully on her hand. Her hair was bundled in
a shining heap of curls on top of her head. He woke her
with a kiss.

Even half asleep her arms went around his neck and
his lips came down hard on hers.

"I taste you, and I am hopelessly drunk," he whispered finally, kissing her closed eyes.

Annabel smiled but she had that little frown again.
"What is it, sweetheart?" he whispered, kissing her eyebrows.

"Are you sure you desire me?"

Surprised, he pulled back and looked at her. His wife
had a face like a delicate triangle, delicate eyebrows, tip-
tilted blue eyes, lips that looked kissable even when she
was scowling at him. She was the most desirable, beautiful woman in the world. "Of course I do," he said, tilt-
ing her face so that his lips could touch hers. "How can
you doubt it?"

Annabel hesitated, but she had to say it. "I'm so fat!
I'm not desirable at *all* anymore!"

He grinned at that. "You've gone blind, darling."

"But what if you stopped desiring me because I grew
too ungainly? And I want an honest answer," she added.
"What if I had to keep to my bed for months? Or I came
out all in spots? Or my ankles start looking like twin
mountains? Nana said that sometimes women don't
wish to have relations until the baby is born, and well after that."

"I missed making love to you while I was gone," he
said softly. "But what I missed had little to do with our

bodies joining. What made me wake, aching, in the middle of the night was my *heart*, not any other part of my body."

"Are you quite sure?" she whispered.

He just shook his head at her, laughter in his eyes. "As sure I am of life itself."

Then she pulled down her covers and put his hand on her great, hard tummy.

He almost fell back. "Lord Almighty, the babe grew in this fortnight!" Ewan said, spreading his large hands over the child.

"Father Armailhac would not like to hear you use the Lord's name in vain," Annabel laughed. And: "The doctor was here two days ago. I think we created this child on our very first night together, Ewan."

A slow smile spread across his face. "In the Kettles' cottage? 'Twas a beautiful night."

She put her hands on top of his. "As Father would say, it's a precious gift we've been given."

His eyes were unashamedly brilliant with tears. "*You* are that to me." He kissed her. "My wife. My heart. My beloved."

He kissed her tears away. "You're so beautiful," he breathed. "Look at your breasts, Annabel." His hands hovered, uncertain. "I think they grew as well!"

"I won't break," she giggled, joy welling up inside her like a flood.

A moment later her head had fallen against the back of the couch. Her heart was beating in her ears; his hands were shaping her into fire. She opened her eyes and saw that his eyes had gone pitch-black. "Who knew that women became so beautiful during this time?" he said hoarsely. "We're going to have to sleep in different rooms, Annabel, if you don't want me to touch you."

He rubbed a thumb across her nipple and she moaned, her hips involuntarily flexing. He pulled his hands away and actually stumbled as he rose. " 'Twill be a trial," he said, dragging his hair back from his forehead.

Annabel stretched. She hadn't felt so good in months. Nor so—so beautiful. Nor certainly so desirable. "It will be like our first journey to Scotland together," she suggested. "Perhaps we could play the kissing game again."

"*No,*" he said. His face looked agonized. "No. No kisses."

She rose to her feet and stretched again. He wrenched his eyes away. "Aye, a trial," he muttered to himself.

Annabel grinned. She had never felt more provocative, more potent, more—more loved in her life. She strolled over to the bed and sat down, stretching her arms behind her so that her breasts showed to their best advantage.

"Lass, you're going to have to help me," her husband said earnestly. "No looking at me in such a way."

She hid her smile and her joy, and pouted. "But I need help. And you are here to aid me."

"Anything," he said. "I'll do anything you wish, Annabel."

"In that case," she said gently, "I'd like you to take this gown off."

He stayed utterly still in the middle of the room.

"And then," she said, her voice drugged with desire, "I'd like you to kiss me *here.*" She touched her breast. "And *here.*" She touched her great stomach. "And then . . ."

But he was there, next to her on the bed, gathering her into his arms in a movement so quick that she didn't see it happen. "I love you, Annabel," he said to her, his voice deep with the promise, the honesty and the truth.

"Ask me how much I love you," she said, cupping his face in her hands. "I promise you an honest answer."

"How much do you love me?" he whispered.

"Too much," she whispered back. " 'Twill go past death, there's so much of it. And now you owe me a kiss." A moment later, they were on the bed, nothing between them but the growing child.

And as it happened, Samuel Raphael Poley, future Earl of Ardmore, was fast asleep.

A Note About Shrews, Coneys and Reading to Six-Year-Olds

I am writing this note after reviewing the copyedited manuscript of *Kiss Me, Annabel*, which means that it's been six months since I saw it last. In the interim, I finished reading aloud the entire series of Laura Ingalls Wilder's *Little House* books to my daughter, and moved on to *Pippi Longstocking*. I'd forgotten that in the midst of a Wilder binge I made Tess churn butter and Ewan milk a cow . . . put it up to literary influence!

The larger structure of this book is very loosely based on Shakespeare's *Taming of the Shrew*. Obviously, Annabel is no shrew. But the part of my novel that isolates Annabel and Ewan in a house in the country, during which they are tested by hunger and frustration, stems from Shakespeare's play. I dislike his project of taming the shrew and would never want my Annabel to respond to adversity by becoming docile. So I reversed the circumstances by having Ewan discover that when he's cold, wet and hungry, he becomes rather cranky . . . tamed, naturally, by Annabel.

Undoubtedly I will receive letters asking about the coney's kiss. The truth is that I made it up. There are many Renaissance jokes about coneys, or rabbits. The word was associated with women, particularly with their sexual parts, and young men in plays tend to boast of their coney-catching ways. I've never read a joke about a coney's kiss: One has to hope that that doesn't reflect a lack of imagination of the part of sixteenth-century men.